THE RACE

T. D. Walters

authorHOUSE®

AuthorHouse™
1663 Liberty Drive, Suite 200
Bloomington, IN 47403
www.authorhouse.com
Phone: 1-800-839-8640

First published by AuthorHouse 10/15/2007

ISBN: 978-1-4343-3586-9 (sc)
ISBN: 978-1-4343-3593-7 (hc)

Printed in the United States of America
Bloomington, Indiana

This book is printed on acid-free paper.

ACKNOWLEDGEMENTS

Only a fool would try to write a book and produce a documentary film at the same time, so, say hello to that fool. The truth is we only go around once, and both were my dreams. That said, imagine my support structure to make it all happen. There are so many people to thank and so few pages. There are, however, those people who made this book possible, and I cannot ignore their contributions. Jan Neuharth, my fellow author and friend, walked me through the thorny process of self-publishing, plot thickening and general all-around 'shoulder crying'. I know she read past the typo's, and cringed each time, but held her tongue to see the emerging story. Pete Hakel may not know it, but it is his love of history that led me to the historical facts that give the book its teeth. Few have studied Civil War History more than Pete, and only Pete dared look beyond what historians wanted us to know, to uncover the truth. To my mini-me Taylor, who inhales books, your judgement stands without question. I look forward to reading your first novel! Mackie, my characters spring from your endless imagination. To Mom and Dad, thanks for all your kind words of support. And last but certainly not least, Robin. In her I see perfection, she corrects the typo's, and is honest enough to correct me when I need correcting, praise me when I need praise, and honor me when I need honor. She is my rock and my foundation and fortunately for me, she is also my best friend and wife. To God be the glory! To everyone else, enjoy!

APRIL 12TH, 1980

Monrovia Liberia, West Africa

THE little boy about to pull the trigger was not yet old enough to shave, let alone shoot a rifle that stood almost as tall as he. Still, there he was, his barely blemished caramel skin, wearing the oversized boots of a real soldier he had already killed and the tattered tee shirt that bestowed upon him the right to "Just do it!" The instructions were so simple...killing became fun. It was just one of many games he played where killing was all that mattered. He was the captain in the "Kwi-ir-u" or, children of the departed ghosts, and thus proudly wore the cap, that came with the boots. and the tee shirt, that provided rank and importance, to an otherwise unimportant life.

One day the captain would be called assassin.

"Today it is a priest you will kill…one day perhaps a president!" The words echoed in his mind. He had been chosen for greatness.

Caught on the other side, in the crosshairs of a world gone mad, was a man, a priest, who said a silent prayer for the *child* he once knew. Father Grebo Barclay, headed the Baptist Mission in Liberia, where most of the boys were taught when they were still children. Now, one by one, they returned the favor in blood. First the nuns, then the western volunteers, and finally father Barclay himself. Stripped of his vestments but not his dignity, Father Barclay chose no to beg, but to pray for the boy who would soon be his assassin. He knew a child of God could not commit murder, even though the boy behind the barrel would surely take his life.

"Father forgive him for he knows not what he has done"...As he prayed, a trickle of sweat made its way down his brow, betraying his desire to show no sign of fear, no signs of weakness. Still, it was better than a tear. He had seen others soil themselves under such circumstances and took comfort in his last measure of resolve. Strength, Father. "*That is all that I ask. Strength and soon I will be home.* "

Maurice Lacroix on the other hand, paid little attention to the heat, his own sweat, or his target, instead focusing on the chamber of his Russian made Kalisnikov assault rifle.

"Point...Breathe.....kill.." he said to himself, knowing soon the shiny brass shell casings would one by one catapult from the rifle and dance atop the mystical cloud of smoke the gun created. It was another one of his games, the one he enjoyed the most.

He was too young and too drugged to understand the gravity of his actions. At least that's what Father Barclay had told them, before he and his fellow students became soldiers. The little boy in Maurice Lacroix discovered, that when he closed his eyes ever so tightly...allowing only the slightest hint of sunshine to creep in...the shell casings looked like tiny metal soldiers leaping into the sky. Each would leap from the chamber...conduct a mesmerizing piroet...and fall slowly onto the sandy soil that had already begun to cover his boots with the bloodied clumps from someone who had died earlier. Perhaps it was somebody he killed. Perhaps not. It was becoming hard to tell.

"Point...Breathe...kill..." he said drawing in a deep breath before letting out an unexpected cough.

"Look at Lacroix! He can't...." one of the other boys cackled before falling silent when the rifle turned his way. The stare that followed made it clear Lacroix meant business, no matter the target.

Lacroix could tell the air was already filled with the smell of the previous days battle. At first the smell burned his nostrils. Now he was a seasoned soldier who had earned his reputation as the leader of the "Kwi-ir-u" and the leader of the "Kwi-ir-u" was not supposed to cough, or for that matter, flinch in the face of danger. He was a killing machine and machines don't feel. At least that is what he was told.

"*"Point...Breathe...kill...*" That was the way they were taught, and always the mantra worked. After he had repeated it several times, the smell went away and instead became as intoxicating as it always was. It was the smell of death.

"*Father forgive them, for they know not what they have done,*" Father Barclay continued to pray. "*He is a little boy. It is the others you should punish. He will pull the trigger, Holy Father, but it is they who provide the guns.*" He then allowed his head to rotate ever so slightly to the towering figure looking down from the massive window of the American Embassy. *"He is the one who must be punished Dear Lord. The white devil who sits in the tower!"* It was only a passing glance, but, in a lifetime that was about to end, it was long enough. *"Point...Breathe... kill..."*

At ten, maybe eleven, Maurice Lacroix had only two concerns that day. He hated the fact his rifle sometimes dragged along the ground as he walked At first, like most children, he thought it was funny. He would walk across the sand leaving trails to show where the gun had been. Now Lacroix was shamed by the fact the gun was almost as tall as he was, and vowed one day to find a smaller one, "*perhaps an Uzi.*"

He quickly learned the other end of the rifle was just as deadly. A sharp blow to the face followed by the words,"*The rifle is meant to kill.*

It is not a toy," he was told over and over again. *"You will use it to punish your enemies. It is your new best friend. With it you are a man. Without it you are the boy who is of no use to us."*

Still the boy who was the soldier wanted to grow taller. Perhaps as tall as his father. He struggled each day to remember his mother. The first thing to disappear was her name. "Lucy, that was her name. Or was it Linda, or Lorraine. The next thing to fade was her face. Finally her smell. His father's name and face faded long ago, along with his real age. Like most parents, they were charged with keeping track of time. Birthdays, Christmas, and the assortment of holidays. Now they too were dead, killed by other children with guns..just like his...or was it him.

Counting was now his job. The student was now a soldier and it was his job to count the bodies of the dead. Sometimes he got the numbers wrong and the other kids would tease him. Today the counting would be easy, there weren't that many bodies tied to the polls.

Lacroix also knew *he* was being watched. He too could see the man in the window out of the corner of his eye. Lacroix couldn't tell if he were white or black. He assumed he was white. All of the men who worked inside *that building* were white. He had seen them before in the camps. They always had money. They always had guns. They always brought death. Today seemed no different. The reason for the killings was.

"Point...Breathe...kill..."

As he focused on the target in front of him, he longed for the days when the little boy behind all of the killing was still a child. He wanted one more shot at recess. One more chance to play kickball with his friends. He was good, and once kicked the ball so hard it cleared the walls of their small school yard. He especially liked the scars the ball left on the white walls of the compound that he and his fellow students were forced to whitewash each summer before classes.

He also missed his tree. It was a massive Cassava tree, with wide branches, and, his teachers said, deep roots that spread across the soil of the compound. His teachers compared it to his ancestors who were watching his each and every move. There he would sit for hours and talk to the man he believed to be God. Like his mother and father, the school, and its shade tree were all gone. God, he feared, would not be able to find him now, and wouldn't care if he did.

"Point...Breathe...kill..."

Lacroix pushed the cap he seized from the man tied to the poll in front of him, and focused on the job at hand. Even though it was too big, it suited him well. After all he was the leader of "the Kwi-ir-u."

"Point...Breathe...kill..." he kept repeating over and over again.

Then he closed his eyes, once more, allowing only the slightest bit of sunshine to creep in, and pulled the trigger.

"Point...Breathe...kill..."

He looked down a the sand beneath is feet as it turned a bright crimson red. Thirteen toy soldiers had danced their dance of death and were now marching off to the sea. They had sapped the life from the thirteen bodies who tied to the polls. Thirteen men, one priest. The leader of the "Kwi-ir-u" had won.

He could have sworn, the man in the window was smiling.

CHAPTER ONE

THE massive V8 engine, under the hood of the armor plated limousine, showed no signs of strain as it made its way south down I-95 toward Washington DC, and in truth seemed to relish the fact the accelerator was once again asking for more. The custom made Cadillac Coupe de Ville was outfitted with five inch thick armor, strong enough to protect the man sitting inside from a direct attack with rocket propelled grenades. Under the armor, a sheath of Kevlar protected those inside from roof to carriage, all of which added to its bulk, and yet the car was still able to travel with the speed and agility of a formula one race car. If speed failed, there were gun ports and tear gas cannons, and the air supply was self-contained, in the event of a chemical or biological attack. It was all needed, as the passenger inside was considered the number one target of choice among terrorists, domestic, foreign and political and the occasional spurned lover.

The Cadillac was followed by a complement of five black Chevy Suburbans, each carrying five Secret Service Agents, and a virtual arsenal of weapons. A sixth Suburban trailed closely behind, loaded with a larger cache of weapons, and enough ammunition to fight a small war. Everyone, whoever stuffed a wad of tobacco inside their cheek, wanted the man inside dead, but he was oblivious to it all, even though in the last week alone, the Secret Service investigated some 200 threats to his life.

As the motorcade continued, trouble lay ahead. Fifteen minutes earlier, a mini-van, headed southbound on I-95 for North Carolina, suddenly spun out of control and burst into flames, killing all five passengers on board. Radio reported that the beltway was closed in both directions and would be for hours. To most it was a terrible accident, but to those tasked with protecting 'the package' it had all the makings of a set up, a trap. As a result, the motorcade would have to make a detour on to the Baltimore/Washington Parkway, an alternative route that had not yet been secured.

"*Jesus Christ, not again*," the sniper, who was identified only as Bravo, muttered to himself.

On a moments notice, each sniper, who had been positioned along the chosen route, seized their weapons and loaded into separate war wagons, to take up positions on the new route.

Now there were eight different Suburbans racing toward Washington, flanked by a cadre of local police and sheriff's deputies, their lights and sirens blaring. The man inside was still being kept in the dark, concerning any threat the detour posed.

The entrance to Washington DC from the BW Parkway was used by millions each year, and yet with the exception of the National Arboretum, where some of the most beautiful and exotic plants in the world were grown, few of the sites that lined the thoroughfare ever made it to the covers of the brochures that welcomed visitors to Washington. The Parkway fed into New York Avenue, which fed into blight.

A popular motel along New York Avenue, had been converted into a homeless shelter, and now was once again a motel, where homeless families stayed, subsidized by the government. Vendors, representing melting pot America, lined the Avenue selling everything from imitation Persian rugs to bootleg videos. Fast-food restaurants morphed into Korean soul food joints. Each represented the changing demographics of the neighborhood. The man inside the limousine saw none of it. He was on the phone talking to his father.

"Are you sure this will be safe?" He asked, speaking into the specially secured phone.

"Are you kidding," the man on the other end of the phone call replied. "You're probably safer now than you were on the interstate. No one would ever think of trying to take you out in any of those neighborhoods, they'd be outgunned!"

The Secret Service Agent in the front of the limousine seemed to be less certain.

"Update security…" he shouted into a tiny microphone in the sleeve of his jacket… "Is *Moor One* secure?" There was no response.

The detour took the procession past neighborhoods that were not used to seeing the Presidential motorcade. Young children ran to chain link fences that showed signs of rust and breach, to catch a glimpse of history. They wanted to see *him*.

He paid no attention to the children, but instead, seemed more concerned with an array of the latest polls and the roughness of the road. "Potholes!" Why don't they fix these damned things? It's not like this city doesn't have the highest taxes in the region." The roads caused the glass of sparkling water on the console to his right to tremble. "Damn it, hand me a towel," he shouted to the little blond aide sitting across from him. She scurried quickly to follow his orders.

"Do you think that's him?" a little boy with his face pressed against the fence, asked another, who was also straining to get a better view of the motorcade as it roared by. By now the motorcade was doing sixty in a forty five mile an hour zone.

"One...two...three...four..." the other little boy was counting the cars in the motorcade, when he was quickly interrupted by the other.

"You missed one!"

"Did not..."

"Did so..." and the battle of words, known as *the dozens,* was on.

"Too much construction on New York," the Secret Agent speaking into his sleeve announced to an anonymous Agent on the other end. "Are the snipers in place on Florida?"

A slight bit of static caused the radio to crackle...before the answer came back, "Florida Avenue is secure."

Florida Avenue snaked past a series of Brownstones that had been taken over by so-called urban pioneers; white couples who were willing to risk the crack addicts, prostitutes and nightly drive-by shootings, if it meant the promise of a view of the Capitol Building and the ever escalating property values. The black families, who once lived in the houses, left at the first sign of appreciation, moving to the suburbs of Maryland. The crime went with them. The man in the limousine was still on the phone.

"I don't feel comfortable getting out *there*," he said, dining on an assortment of fruits and crudités that were always on hand inside the limo. It was, as they say in Washington, protocol.

"You *have* to get out there," the man on the other end responded. "It's the perfect photo op. The press is less than five minutes behind, by then you'll be surrounded by a sea of the people who are going to put you in office. Remember Reagan and Connecticut Avenue with Gorbachev?" He was at the top of every nightly news program. And one other thing,"

A troubled expression crossed the face of the young man on the other end of the phone call inside the limo. "What?"

"Don't use a knife and fork. Eat the damn things with your hands."

The man inside the limo was, as always, impeccably dressed, and bothered by the fact carpet lint blemished an otherwise opulent shoe shine. His gray pants were cuffed at the bottom, and pleated at the waist. His handmade white French cuffed shirt sported his monogram on the sleeve..."B.J."

Just up the road, at the intersection of Thirteenth and U streets, the Secret Service Agents, were wrestling with a street vendor who complained, what *they* were doing, was what was wrong with American society. It was an argument he quickly lost. They were removing all of the vendors from their spots, securing trash cans, and welding any manhole covers shut.

The motorcade was about to turn onto "U Street" which used to be known as the Black Hollywood. Top flight entertainers like as Lionel Hampton, Duke Ellington, and Lena Horne, played venues such as the Historic Lincoln Theater. It was a Mecca for all things black and successful. Jazz clubs and juke joints stayed open all night. Afterwards, patrons spilled into the numerous restaurants that lined the block. Black couples wearing fancy clothes and driving fancier cars gave proof that black America was about to become part of the melting pot. There were doctors and lawyers, Congressmen and statesmen. Then came the sixties.

Riots burned out of control for days, fueled, in part, by racist attitudes and firefighters afraid to enter burning inner cities. *Those* neighborhoods were not safe. It would remain that way for years. The fires that burned out of control, led to out of control crime, fueled by an epidemic of crack cocaine. Needles and shell casings lined the alleys leading to and around U Street. Used condoms were also common, left behind by heroin whores and their suburban customers who wanted a cheap thrill.

When the shooting stopped, only one restaurant survived. The Chili Bowl, became an urban Mecca for every political 'wanna-be' who wanted to get elected. An explosion of condos and the white yuppies who bought them, transformed The Chili Bowl into Washington's newest monument. It was the place to see and to be seen. Only the staff resembled the Washington that once was. They were black. The customers were white. Now it was about to be invaded once more.

The first wave of Secret Service Agents arrived at "The Chili Bowl," in swarms. A sniper took up a position on the roof of the Old Masonic Temple, less than a block away. Another chased away a few lovers out of nearby Malcolm X Park.

"*Moor One* is less than five minutes away," an Agent said speaking into the microphone in his sleeve. "The area is secure. I repeat…the area is secure. Will *the Moor* be on the move?"

On the move, was the agencies worst nightmare. The unscripted departure from a Presidential limousine by then President Ronald Reagan, caused panic to spread through the Secret Service and a new set of protocol to be written. Every appearance now carried with it a set of contingency plans, just in case The President wanted to leave the limousine. But this time, the man inside the limousine wasn't the President, even though it was hard to tell from the enormous security. The man inside the limo was *a presidential candidate* who was poised to make history if the agency could keep him alive! Baron James was poised to become the first black President of The United States!

The hulking limousine pulled up in front of The Chili bowl, causing the staff that was hard at work behind the grills to strain for a look at what was causing the commotion. Even though his arrival was not planned, a massive crowd had gathered anyway. The crowd was a cornucopia of society. Black workers, Asian tourists, white "yuppies," and others, swelled to numbers that caused the Secret Service to be more than a little concerned.

"It is my opinion *Moor One* should be kept under wraps. Location is no longer secure; repeat...location is no longer secure!"

The heavy door of the limousine started to open. As it did, the sniper poised on top of the Masonic Temple locked his sights on a target. Ever so slightly, squeezing the trigger, enough to fire quickly if necessary and recover to fire another round, but not enough to cause the gun to discharge at that point in time.

As the door opened, a complement of Secret Service Agents suddenly appeared as if out of nowhere, surrounding the car. Each wore the standard issue black rain coat, white shirt and black tie. The dark sunglasses kept the glare out and allowed them to continuously scan the crowd for any not so well wishers. That's when they spotted ***him.***

A man, who appeared to have been a homeless person, was making his way through the crowd, pushing all others aside. Somehow, he had managed to elude the first perimeter of the presidential gauntlet, and was now less than fifty feet from *Moor One*.

"Take him down...I repeat take him down..."

It was too late. Baron James was now fully outside the limousine, and *the man* was less than two feet away. James didn't see his approach, but felt the man's heavy hand on his shoulder, causing him to spin around with a look of panic on his face.

Members of the press corps, who were racing to the scene, clicked off hundreds of photos in mere seconds as they continued their pursuit. Television cameramen elbowed any obstacles out of their way. The Secret Service formed a circle, separating James from the rest of the crowd, but not before the threat managed to get in and he now appeared unstoppable.

The Special Agent in Charge, known only as Alpha, felt his pulse quicken, and his throat grow dry. He was living in the brief moment, between action and panic. It was less than a second, but enough time to change history forever. He had seen it over and over again during his training and knew what must be done.

"Baron James..." The man shouted, in a voice that was deeper than his body indicated it should be. The hand that landed on James's shoulder, was heavy and left no doubt that the arm behind it, had spent a great deal of time working out in someone's gym. "I spent some time in the joint...you know prison. I'm innocent you know, but I gotta say..."

The Secret Service Agents were frozen in place. In a fraction of a second, they had to decide whether to forcibly remove the man, or let the episode play out. It happened thousands of times along the campaign trail, and each time the decision caused more than a little anxiety. This man was no different. He fit every profile they had feared. He was black, apparently unemployed, and he spent time behind bars. The sniper on the rooftop spoke into his sleeve, his hand still poised on the trigger; "Do I have a green-light?"

The homeless man knew nothing of the danger he faced. As he spoke, a network microphone was thrust into his face, from an extension pole that kept the sound technician at a safe distance. "I just want you to know...how proud...we...I mean...those of us, like myself, are of you man!"

The sniper on the roof of the Masonic Temple tightened his grip on the trigger of his Heckler and Koch Sniper-rifle, even though he had not been given the green light. A millimeter more, and the weapon would send its fifty caliber projectile racing toward the temple of the man, causing his to drop instantly and rendering him helpless.

"Baron James, you son-of-a-bitch!" The unidentified man wrapped two massive arms around the candidate in a warm embrace, with the army of photographers capturing each and every minute. "I love you man." He then planted a wet kiss on James' cheek, leaving a trail of saliva behind it. The stark white shirt was no match for the urban grime the man carried with him. It was a photo-op made in heaven.

Baron James, the man poised to become the nation's first black president… had arrived!

CHAPTER TWO

106 Healy Hall… on the campus of Georgetown University, Washington, D.C.

VANESSA Sullivan mused as she looked at the words plastered on the blackboard of room 106 Healy Hall on the campus of Georgetown University. "Can we possibly get through a history class without hearing a lecture about…The First Black President!" To underscore the importance of the class, the white chalk was reinforced by a yellow chalk boarder. It was as if the words written were the most important words of the English Language, on par with those of Shakespeare, and Socrates. She hated the words, the history, and the fact she was about to be intellectually insulted and emotionally assaulted once more. Sensing the worst, she slumped down in her desk chair and quietly mouthed the words…"Here we go again." It had become her mantra even though it happened to be her favorite class and he was her favorite teacher, Father Michael Haynes.

Father Haynes taught history but Vanessa was haunted by it. She was tormented by humble beginnings and, *a birth curse* that only a trailer park could deliver. It was the type of curse that predetermined her lot in life, long before she would ever utter her first words.

He believed in the founding fathers, white men who wrote in lofty speeches that *all men were created equal.*

She, on the other hand, lived the horrors of the politicians, preachers, and philanderers who'd come calling at night, seeking her mother's comforts. Her friends were their bastard children and she wondered where history buried its bodies.

His was an ivory tower, ruled by men with letters.

Hers…tin roofs and tobacco stains, and a life defined by the asterisk, the exception, and countless other unknown comments in the columns of her checkered past.

He knew his lineage, she feared hers.

They were perfect for each other.

"Please open your textbooks to page 101," Father Haynes began.

Those, however, were not the words heard by Vanessa Sullivan.

"Okay idiots, here comes the past, as told by the liars, adulterers and bigots of history!" Vanessa smiled at her own inside joke, knowing not a word had been uttered save those of Father Haynes.

Even though Father Haynes was teaching from the text he wanted his students at Georgetown University to read between the lines. He feared they had become programmable, willing to accept whatever was thrown their way so long as it came in the form of a hard bound book.

"The truth, my dear students, can be found between the layers of lies we historians die trying to correct! You…must determine truth from fiction...in politics...in religion...and in life."

Father Haynes had a habit of pushing the frames of his wire rimmed glasses forward each and every time he wanted to make a point. This was one of those classes.

"If George Washington was the father of our country, to the British, he was a traitor. To the slaves, Jefferson was the man who came creeping into their bedrooms at night." The wire rimmed glasses were now pushed fully forward. "And do any of you still believe that Abraham Lincoln, a politician, was really honest? Not even the slightest of fibs?" Father Haynes paused for a moment to let the thoughts seep in. "This brings us to today's elections. What do we *really* think of Baron James? And perhaps even more importantly, what do we know about him at all?" He glanced over and noticed most of his students were lost in thought, or simply lost. There was one however, who disturbed him the most. His prized student Vanessa, seemed more lost than the rest

"Vanessa!"

"Sorry Father, I guess I was just daydreaming."

"Dreaming is for when you sleep! Your parents, the state, or the taxpayers, pay dearly for this time...*my time*....I suggest you use it wisely."

Like the rest of Washington, Father Michael Haynes believed his every word was gospel. And like the rest of Washington, he was hard at work extolling the virtues of the fact that history was about to be made on his watch. It was to be monumental history because America was on the verge of electing it's first African American President, and he was to be both judge and jury.

Ethnic pride was sweeping the country and everyone was once again examining their roots. For most the topic was a source of pride. For Vanessa Sullivan, it was a source of pain. Another reminder that people like her weren't meant to inherit the American dream...but only to watch it from afar.

Father Haynes, on the other hand, left little doubt as to *his* ethnicity. He looked as if he leapt from the pages of *The Potato Farmer*. His gaunt face, dandruff filled mop hairstyle and angular gait, made him appear drunk when he walked. He smelled of cheap cologne that covered the badly needed shower that was always a day too late. His voice possessed the melodic qualities of an Irish baritone and he used it frequently to make a point in his class. Today, he relished the fact, history was about to be made, and it was about to be made on his watch. As he glanced around the room, he realized there was one student who couldn't have cared less. He was troubled because she was his favorite student.

Like Father Haynes, Vanessa Sullivan deeply loved the subject of history, but on this day she found herself transfixed with *where* it was being taught, and that was all that mattered. Father Haynes always said Healy Hall, Room 106, was a mystery wrapped inside an enigma. It was the first thing he said when his students entered the classroom on the first day. For Vanessa, it was a room that reminded her of her own past. She hated Healy Hall on the campus of Georgetown University, and had begun referring to it as Hypocrite Hall. Father Healy, for whom the hall was named, should have been a source of pride. Like Vanessa, he was born of mixed parents. His mother, it read on a small plaque outside of the entrance to the building, was a former slave, his father was not. Healy's father was an educated Irishman who fell in love with a slave. Theirs was a loving union that, in the end, escaped the shackles of prejudice, or so the plaque implied. The truth was the family moved to Canada out of fear that they would be discovered. The Jesuits raised Father Healy, prior to his return to Washington. The problem was, unlike Vanessa, Father Healy chose to hide the fact that he was black, and did so for years. The truth wasn't discovered until long after his death. As her eyes roamed the classroom, she discovered why she hated Room 106 even more. This time, however, she was beginning to smile.

"Ms. Sullivan!" Father Haynes said in a demanding tone... "daydreaming again?"

"Not really," she answered. "Let's just say I'm about to unlock the mystery you placed before us on day one."

With that statement, Vanessa captured the attention of the entire class, and Father Haynes. If she had indeed unraveled the mystery of Healy Hall Room 106, she would be the first in generations. For years students turned over desks, removed wall paper, and in one case, even the floorboards, wondering what the great mystery of the hall might be. Father Haynes could tell by the look on Vanessa's face, if she had not guessed it, she was close.

Vanessa was not only brilliant, she was also one of the most beautiful women on the Georgetown campus, and one of the most opinionated. Few knew anything about *her* history, except for the fact, whoever was responsible for her birth, spit out a beauty. Her olive complexion and flowing black hair framed the face of an angel. Most of her professors only wished her temperament matched her looks.

Vanessa fidgeted in her seat with her hands under her thighs as if to restrain her movements. It didn't work. "The truth is," she began, "this room stands as an offense to anyone who considers himself a serious historian."

"And what do you take offense with *this* time?" Father Haynes quizzed. Haynes' advanced class on U.S. History, had students waiting semesters just to get in. Few ever questioned his wisdom; none even came close to deciphering the mystery of the room. Looking out, over his pair of glasses he used more for effect and his always tossed hair, he was staring at the one student who not only questioned his wisdom, but did so, on a continual basis.

"Let's just say, this room has quite the story to tell, one that raises questions about our past and our present." Vanessa Sullivan had a dual major; Political Science and an advanced course in the Human genome. Science she believed, unlocked the mysteries of race, but few knew of her true motivations. Her real motivations lay deep beneath the skin, where the soul meets the subconscious, the true meaning of race. It was one of those mysteries that caused her growing discontent.

The hands were no longer tucked under the corners of her skirt, and Vanessa was about to rise from her seat. She knew what was next, as did her fellow students. They had seen it before when she debated Father Haynes on topics such as the ethnicity of Christ, and whether The Crown Jewels were actually a stolen treasure. Always their exchanges were welcomed with great anticipation.

"Ooh oh, here we go again," a girl toward the rear of the room, whispered to a young man wearing a varsity letter jacket, who had awakened long enough to witness the upcoming confrontation. "This is going to be good!"

"Do you think she's figured it out?" another questioned.

"It's impossible. There is no real mystery," a girl in a bright yellow sweater that revealed more of her personality and body than was needed replied. "I supposed next you'll want to go 'tripe hunting'."

"Father Haynes," Vanessa began, drawing in a long breath, as if one would be needed for the upcoming explanation. "Any historian worth his, or should I say her salt, should be offended by *this*!" Vanessa was pointing to a painting on the left side of the room.

Father Haynes removed his glasses to show his surprise and fired back, "I suppose you take issue with the founding fathers?" Inwardly he was smiling, knowing that for the first time in decades, a student had taken the first step.

"Not the founding fathers, although I'll have much more on that to come. I'm upset with this painting. If my research is correct, it should be sold in a yard sale as a fraud!"

"A fraud?"

"Yes, take your pick; fraud, forgery, plagiarism. Let's start with this painting. I believe it is a copy of the famous *Christy painting* that hangs in the Capitol Rotunda. I believe you put it here on purpose!"

"On purpose you say?"

"Yes, you always tell us to read between the lines and look for the layers of lies…But what about that which sits right in front of us?"

Father Haynes could barely contain his enthusiasm. Had his students looked closely, they would have noticed his cheeks were now flush with a redness he had not experienced in years. All teachers lived for such a moment, and this was one. He knew she had unraveled the first mystery, and was about to tell all.

"First of all, we should state clearly for the record, there was no photographic equipment present at the time this painting was made. No digitals, or for your generation Father Haynes, no Polaroid. That means all of these paintings represent someone's recollections of what really happened. Sadly, in the case of the *Christy painting*, they are a recollection, of a recollection."

Father Haynes removed his glasses, and placed the tip in his mouth. A student, who was asleep, was now wide awake. This was the type of history that wasn't found in the books. It was the type of history that Vanessa Sullivan wanted to learn and sought to change.

"If I might continue..."

"As if you could be stopped," Father Haynes said to the amusement of the students assembled.

"As I was saying, the *Christy painting* gives a portrait of a happy assembly. For instance, there's Hamilton whispering something in

Franklin's ear. The truth is, they rarely spoke, and *never*, in public. It is one of those truths living in the layers of lies, as you put it. There is evidence that Franklin even had a subordinate speak to Hamilton on his behalf…not to mention that the painting wasn't completed until 1940. 1940! That means, unless there is evidence to the contrary, not even *you,* Father Haynes, would take exception to the fact that we are looking at one man's interpretation of history."

Father Haynes smiled. His prized student had come through. He knew there was something special about her the first day she entered his class. The past debates laid the foundation. Today she was about to prove her historical superiority. He also knew the other students were soaking up every minute of it. He could also see that Vanessa had returned to her seat to fetch her purse. There was more to come. Something he didn't expect.

Vanessa returned to the front of the class, holding a crisp green two dollar bill she kept in her purse as a source of her continuing devotion to the truth. Holding it above her head for all to see she began again.

"As I was researching the *Christy painting*, I saw this on the Internet last night. Ever wonder where the phrase, *as phony as a two dollar bill*, comes from?"

The look of bewilderment on the faces of those assembled was reason enough for Vanessa to continue. Her pacing back and forth made a creaking sound on the wooden floor below, and the students, sitting on the benches that lined the classroom, were straining for a closer look.

"I'll explain, as you look," she said, passing the bill around for all to get a closer look.

"The *Trumbell painting* which is depicted on the back of the two dollar bill is no less controversial than the paintings in this room. Some historians criticize it, because it depicts a scene that never took place. You see, *Trumbell* was painting a picture---his version of a scene that took place on June 28th, days before the Declaration of Independence was signed. Historians also point out the *Trumbell painting* contains portraits of men who might not have even been there."

The students who had already viewed the bill were smiling, but none was more proud than Father Haynes, who by now, had surrendered his classroom completely.

Vanessa continued to walk up and down the center of the room, in much the same manner as a courtroom lawyer, as he presented his closing arguments to the jury.

"Many of the faces you see on the painting before you," she said looking closely into the eyes of her fellow students, "were actually *copies of portraits* he had painted years earlier...or years after the initial event. And there is one major fact both paintings fail to illustrate."

Father Haynes, glancing at his watch, decided to assume control of his classroom, albeit it briefly. "I assume you can complete your summations in time for the closing bell? And one other thing, what does this have to do with Baron James?"

Vanessa smiled. She liked Father Haynes, not only because he tolerated her curiosity but was a student of history just like her. She knew he allowed her to continue because he respected her tenacity. She suspected he knew why.

"Yes, Father I believe I can." Vanessa turned away from the professor in much the same manner a lawyer would to a judge, before turning his attention to the jury once more. "The truth is, our founding fathers were exactly that, in more ways than one." Now she hurriedly made her way back to the front of the room once more, pointing to the faces of the paintings as she spoke.

"Take Benjamin Franklin, for instance. He was rumored to have had affairs with many a slave, and yet, that fact has simply disappeared from history. *Hidden in the layer of lies!* We know about Thomas Jefferson and Sally Hemings, and yet to this day, historians try to gloss over their relationship, as well, focusing only on his positive writings and not the ones that are racist, like his *Letters to Virginia.* Which is why..."Vanessa was still pacing and about to enter into high gear, "we should all hold the United States Mint, especially, in contempt. Each one of these men become memorialized each and every time we part with our precious money."

"Lincoln's face is the most photographed in the world. Because he is on the front and back of the penny and five dollar bill, his face has been copied at least three billion times. Three billion coins and dollars bear his face, most of which wind up sitting next to the cash register at the 7-Eleven." Her latest remark prompted applause. "Don't their descendants deserve some semblance of the real truth? Aren't they heirs to the so called *historical throne*?"

"Vanessa, whoooo cares?" In every classroom there is one, and on this day it was William Christopher (Chip) Newport, who chose to interrupt Vanessa in the middle of her summation. Chip was the poster child of high society and low tolerance, especially when it came to issues of money. His parents were rich, and for him school was an intermediate step to a corporate boardroom. He wore shirts with horses, jeans with names, and glasses with labels on the side. "This is ancient history."

"Let me see if I can make this work for all of you *trust account turtles*." Vanessa used the phrase to describe all of those who simply went to school to party. "Say for instance, Mummy and Daddums set aside money for you in the form of a trust, which in your case, I am assuming they did."

A couple of the students in the rear of the class chuckled upon hearing that. "Now, lets suppose, Daddums had an active libido and wandering penis and you have someone new to share your inheritance with. Can you say...duh half?

Chip Newport was silent. Vanessa's words had struck a nerve. He knew his father had strayed, which was why he and his mother lived apart. He never considered the fact that there might be other Newports. He assumed....

"That's why *this* is so important," Vanessa continued this time uninterrupted. There are people out there, still living, who are entitled to their share of history and its spoils, not to mention the truth. A simple strand of Jefferson's hair, or one of Washington's teeth, or Ben Franklin's saliva would more than settle the score genetically. DNA provides the truth that years of rumors have sought to hide. There are people out there directly related to each and every one of these men who don't know it. Some historians would like to keep it that way."

Several of the students were nodding their heads in agreement. The counselor was making her mark on the jury. One student had even begun to take notes. Vanessa chose the moment to focus on her, before continuing, as if to point out, that what she was about to say was too important, even for note taking.

"What about Patrick Henry's black child? Yes, our dear Patrick Henry. It seems the founding fathers couldn't keep it in their pants." Sporadic laughter broke out. "There is one other thing for you to ponder. Consider it homework. Get your own two dollar bill and ask yourself, *who is that black man on the back, in the powdered wig?* Here's a hint, some believe ***he*** was our nation's first president."

The room was now in a state of uproar. Vanessa proved her point and yet she was far from finished. She had won over the jury of her peers, but still had to complete her closing.

"*How long?*" she pleaded before pausing once more, for effect. "*How long*, must we as a society, continue to live their lies. *Black people* have been a part of the fabric of this nation's history for as long as there has been anything remotely resembling America. We, too, are the founding fathers, and sons and daughters. It is our job as students of history to make sure that what is taught to future generations represent the facts as we know them, *not as we would like them to be.*" Vanessa placed the chalk inside the grooves of the metal strip that encased the blackboard and glanced upwards toward something that had been in the room for as long as anyone could remember, and yet few had noticed. She then looked toward Father Haynes. It was in that glance that he realized she had unraveled the other part of the mystery of the room.

"Isaiah, 51:1 Look until the rock whence ye are hewn! I know what its means to me, but what does it mean to you? History is more than just what we read. Our rock is science. In the case of our generation, it's DNA. With each generation, science adds new possibilities to retell old stories, even better. It affords us the opportunity to get it right!"

"Ah, but Vanessa, as I mentioned before, what does all of this have to do with Baron James?" Father Haynes asserted from a now sitting position.

"I'm glad you asked. All we know of Baron James is from the pictures we see on the TV. Like the Christy and Trumbell paintings, they were one mans interpretation of the facts. If politics has taught us anything, it is that the truth about most politicians is hidden in layers of well crafted lies, spin machines, and image consultants. I would suggest we know as much about Baron James, as we do about those paintings that have mystified your students for years. Is he the real deal, or..." She now held the two dollar bill above her head, "is he as phony as this?"

Vanessa returned to her seat to thunderous applause, just as the bell was ringing signaling the end of class. As she did, Vanessa found herself surrounded by those who had other questions, including the girl who was taking the notes.

"Where does your *passion* come from," she said, trying to gather her books and begin preparations for the next class, at the same time. "I mean, when you talk, history seems to come *alive!*"

Vanessa reached over and placed her hand on the girl's shoulder to provide comfort. "We should all be troubled by the lies we have been taught. It really is true, if we don't know our past, we are doomed to repeat our mistakes. What if...what if Thomas Jefferson actually had *feelings* for Sally Hemings and *second thoughts* about his mistreatment of black women? What if George Washington felt remorse because he owned slaves, or Patrick Henry tried to secretly honor his child, by providing some type of child support? None of these questions are out of the realm of possibility and would have a tremendous affect on one of the most important phrases of our time. **All men are created equal.** We spend so much time talking about reparations. What if the founding fathers truly believed slavery was not only immoral, but illegal? What if they were bound by the politics of *their time?* Were they being manipulated by the powers that be much like modern day politicians?"

The girl, with the books, was smiling and making her way toward the door. It was Father Haynes turn to speak. He softly touched Vanessa's shoulder in much the same way she had touched the woman who just left.

"Vanessa," he said softly, "your passion cannot be overlooked. I sense you are driven by something much deeper than a mere appreciation of history. Perhaps sometime you would like to talk about it."

"Perhaps...Vanessa began, as if she were about to accept the invitation, but caution took hold. "Perhaps, someday, but not today. It would make me late for work."

Father Haynes watched Vanessa walk out the door as the others made their way, in, for his next class. He knew she would interrupt his proceedings again, and knew, deep down, he welcomed her every question. His mystery had been unraveled and tomorrow he would begin creating a new one. Students, who thought, were rare. Students, who questioned authority, were rarer, still. The truth was, he also knew, despite his vows, students of history with such stunning beauty, were even harder to come by.

A cool breeze welcomed Vanessa as she made her way across campus. Still she found herself haunted by the memories of her past, and angered by the events of her present. Each day it was a different battle, but always for the same reasons. She wondered what the kids back home would think of her now...a college coed wowing her professors. She remembered each and every one of their words that were her true motivation to achieve. She had been called *"half breed"* and *"nigger,"* by those too ignorant to know, she couldn't possibly be *both*. That was why she was at Georgetown...to use science to eliminate the divisions of race, both in history and in everyday life...first history, then the present, after work.

The campus coffee shop was just a few blocks off the main road. It was too far to walk, but did allow a commute just long enough to unwind. Inside the confines of her car, the radio was usually her only solace. Lately, it too had betrayed her and for that, she had Baron James to thank.

Another man, who's skin was just as bright as hers, was about to make history. It was all over the radio. Campaign spots, touting the virtues of Baron James, aired repeatedly. Each was followed by one analyst or another pointing out the historical significance of the man who would be the nation's first black President. There were so many commercials and analysts that Vanessa soon found herself arguing with the radio, in much the same way she had interrupted Father Haynes's class.

"Is it history...*if all he is black?"* she shouted at the announcer on the radio. "Baron James has done *nothing* for black people except to be black," she continued. "He hasn't taken a position on social programs, and in fact, seems to distance himself from any mention of the word, race."

It seemed Vanessa's line of thought had permeated the airwaves. As she switched the dial to the republican diatribe that continued nonstop on the AM frequency, analysts were asking just that. Powers Murdock, who was by far the most popular of the hosts, made it a point to ask daily what James had done for blacks. The problem was, Murdock had a, not so hidden, agenda. It mattered little to Murdock that James was black. Murdock was only interested in the fact that James was a democrat. This time, however, he had an unlikely ally on the other side of the political aisle.

"*Prove me wrong, Baron*" she said, turning into the parking space not far from the coffee shop. "*Prove me wrong*."

CHAPTER THREE

"SENATOR, your ten o'clock is here," the pleasant sounding woman on the other end of the intercom announced.

"Please send him in, but give me five minutes," he replied curtly. The voice belonged to Senator Maximillian Webb. To the friends and voters who sent him to Washington so long ago, he was Max, but most of those constituents weren't even born when he took his first oath of office.

Max Webb was the "**Lion of the Legislature**," a powerful voice on all things constitutional. A man who had been a part of Washington so long, they referred to him as an institution. He often remarked at how close 'institution' was to 'institutional', which is why he preferred his other nickname. Part of that nickname came from the thick mane of silver hair that topped his towering six foot plus frame. There was another reason, he told his closest associates, but he chose to keep that reason secret. It was part of the mystery of a man that Washington claimed to know well, but really knew nothing about. That was the way Max Webb liked it. The public knew only what Webb allowed them to see, and he made sure there was nothing to disapprove of there, as well. He was incredibly physically fit for a man his age, tan to perfection, and the choice of the Republican Party to become the next President of the United States.

A steady stream of visitors made their way to his office on a daily basis…a corner spot reserved for senior senators. It had the location closest to the elevator for crucial votes and a view to die for. The massive window, directly behind a mammoth oak desk, provided the perfect backdrop. There, in the foreground, the monument dedicated to the first President of the United States, and behind that, the one reserved for Lincoln, the one President that Webb admired most. He liked it when the Republicans called themselves "*The Party of Lincoln.*" Webb posed for photos, with visiting constituents, in front of the window, a task he deplored. The *voters* kept him in Washington, but the ones who came with their *checkbooks* in hand and their demands in tow, *kept* him in power.

Their donations were directly proportional to the size and status of *their corporations.* The larger corporations and special interest groups preferred to work beneath the surface, pumping in hundreds of thousands of dollars from constituents, many of whom never really existed, except on paper. New associates, to growing law firms, were instructed 'who' to vote for and 'who' to back with their year end bonuses. It was so Washington.

The smaller contributions poured in from campaign stops along the trail and were just what they appeared, small contributions from people who thought small and dreamed big. He would shake their hands, kiss their babies and then reappear at the next campaign spot and do it all over again. It was the part of the politics he hated most. He knew with each handshake, he sold a piece of his soul, making promises he would never keep, because of the other contributors…the ones with the big bucks and bigger demands. Sadly, both groups were about to be disappointed. There was less than a month to go before the presidential election of 2008, and the man they wanted to win was trailing in the polls, and trailing badly.

There was also a third group of contributors...the special interest groups. As the senior senator on the Foreign Relations Committee, Max Webb commanded a worldwide audience with global contributors. He was the darling of the conservatives and its right wing fringe. Gun groups held rallies in the woods of states like Michigan and Arkansas, where the militia movements were in full gear. Arms suppliers needed *a hawk* in the senate, as it was equally good for business.

Then there were the **"God Squads,"** Christian conservative groups, hoping a Webb administration would finally put an end to legalized abortion. Technological advances made it possible to reserve a spot at an abortion clinic, online. That, coupled with the growing number of Hispanics being added to the Democratic voter rolls, meant the Republican Party was no longer in the majority. A Democratic victory in November would all but end any chance of stopping 'abortion on demand'.

Max could also count on votes from groups as extreme as the Ku Klux Klan and Christians at the Cross. The Klan actually held bake sales in one small southern town. The Christians were the kind that fed their opponents to the lions. Today it was Prescott Marshall who'd come calling, and Webb wasn't sure if he were friend or foe.

"Good to see you again, old friend," Marshall proclaimed, thrusting his right hand forward as if it he were in the beginning stages of launching an attack.

"And you, as well," the Senator responded, refusing to give any ground to the advancing threat. "What brings you here?'

"Polls, my dear friend, polls. We've been conducting our own research and I must admit, our polls do not look promising."

"By 'we,' I am assuming you mean...?"

"Yes, *that* 'we'....as you know, 'we,' myself and the others, have a vested interest in the outcome of this election."

"Don't they all," Webb responded, wanting not to be heard, but not caring if he was.

"Don't they all." With that, he walked across the room to the bar, a holdover from when politics demanded more than a handshake. "Can I pour you a drink?"

"No time for cordials," Marshall responded. In fact I suggest we get right down to business. What do you propose we should do about this problem we seem to have, or more specifically, *that problem*." Marshall was pointing to the television located in the corner of the room opposite the desk. The TV was airing one of the many commercials touting his Democratic opponent, Senator Baron James, the rising star of the Democratic Party.

Webb said nothing, as if, out of courtesy, allowing the commercial to end. When he spoke, he made his contempt clear. *The problem*, as you put it, happens to be riding a wave of history loving liberals to the White House," the Senator shot back. "How do you fight a man who stands for nothing?" Even though Webb asked a question, it was clear he wasn't seeking any answers. "He hasn't been a Senator long enough to have a record, and when controversial votes surface, he's always on the road, saving the world. He's handsome, intelligent..."

"And no problem at all, I guarantee you," Marshall said, as he began to smile. "He is simply, a man, nothing more, nothing less. And all men have problems, if you know what I mean." Marshall then paused, allowing the weight of what he had just said, to sink in. Prescott Marshall was known as a man who could get things done. It appeared he was about to do so, once more. "He has a *penis* doesn't he?" Not allowing Max Webb to question his motives, Marshall continued, "Yes, I guarantee you, he *does* have a penis."

Max swallowed hard on the drink he had just prepared. He hated Prescott Marshall's smugness. He hated the fact Marshall always seemed to be in control. He knew Marshall was up to something even before he entered the room. Marshall's plans always involved something most politicians didn't want to know about. Usually someone disappeared.

"It's not like you can just *get rid of him*," Webb began. "He has the popular vote, and unless our technical friends can come through on *the computer solution*, we will sink like a rock, at the ballot boxes, in almost every state, including my own."

"I can assure you, the popular vote poses no problem. Still, since the last election, every investigative reporter and journalist with a blog site is watching the situation closely. They won't find anything, but some of those computer types are good and have a future in this sort of thing, if you catch my drift?"

'But you can't rig..."

"Rig what? A general election?, of course we can, we have and we will again. We've been doing it for almost a decade now. Remember when America went to bed believing it had a new president and awoke learning the real truth about politics? Surely you don't believe it had anything to do with actual votes? Why do you think our friends at the court intervened? Remember, you always have to have a safety valve. We have *Friends* everywhere. *E-V-E-R-Y-W-H-E-R-E!"*

"So *do you have a plan*?" Webb inquired, slowly turning his back to Webb as a magician might before pulling a rabbit from his hat.

"Call it more of an *Achilles heel.* And quite *an attractive one*, I might add."

Prescott reached into his briefcase producing a manila envelope that contained a series of photographs inside. Each of the photos was grainy in appearance, and at first, were hard to make out. But a closer glance left no doubt as to what was going on. They were *those* types of photos. The photos every beauty queen and politician dreads. Photos from that one instance in a person's past that everyone prayed had long since been destroyed. Clearly in the case of Baron James, they were not. His life was about to be ruined and the photos were the weapon of choice. Save one. It was the fifth photo that caused Max Webb to pause. One he had not expected to see.

"Who is the girl?" Webb inquired trying not to sound too curious.

"A coed at Georgetown University. Quite attractive, don't you think? I was struck by her beauty, as well, when I first saw the photos." Marshall's next words caused Webb's heart to race. "It's a pity she will have to be taken care of, too. Consider it, a genetic curse, if you will. We all pay for the sins of our father's, don' t we."

Max studied the photos closely, spending more time in the photo of the girl than the others. "A pity," he said, trying to maintain his composure. "She looks so innocent."

CHAPTER FOUR

"HOW is *this* possible!," the voice in the opposite room cried out loud enough to be heard through the paper thin walls of the campaign headquarters. My opponent once belonged to the *Klan* and you're telling me that that isn't hurting his numbers?" Baron James survived the Chili Bowl and was once again comfortably ensconced inside his office for another day's drama. Once again he was panicking at the slightest hint of a problem.

"Welcome to the politics of polarization," the other man in the room chimed in. "He's not perfect, but then again he's not *black*. And that dear boy...loosely translated, means *he's* not you…which, according to our research, is the only thing that he has going for him, and the only thing you have going against you." The other man was his father, Mercer James, and the only man Baron James trusted, although their relationship was strained for reasons Baron never fully understood, and Mercer never revealed.

The truth was, Mercer James knew his son was as gray as the suit he was wearing. Not black, not white, not really well defined. It was a character flaw that would haunt him for the rest of his life. Multiple generations of mixed-race marriages left his son void of any features that would either offend or define. His son looked Hispanic, and black, and white, and somewhere in his genetic makeup, he knew he probably was. Mercer, sarcastically, referred to his son as '*Gamaliel-ian' Gray.* It was a vague reference to the fact that Baron bore a striking resemblance to the 29th President of the United States, Warren G. Harding. Few knew the G. actually stood for *Gamaliel*, although it was easy to see why he chose his first name, Warren.

Physically, Mercer knew early on that Baron was the perfect amalgamation of melting pot America. He looked like what America wanted its President to look like, and acted Presidential, as well. Personally, however, Mercer hated the fact that his son stood for nothing and no one. Any compassion he had for his constituents disappeared along with his pigment.

The man the public knew was the man who appeared almost endlessly on TV. The talk shows, the round tables, the Sunday morning talk shows. Always, the message was the same 24/7.

Baron James was Perfect for America…

The real Baron James was born in rural North Carolina. As a young man, he kept his head of wavy black hair closely cropped, not wanting to appear white. But later in life, he let it grow out. Glasses once accented hazel green eyes, but consultants told him they made him appear frail, weak, and white. The glasses were replaced by contacts that colored his eyes brown. The mustache and sideburns of his youth were gone, as well. His face was now clean shaven and chiseled.

Baron James was Perfect for America....

Baron James, the candidate, had an approval rating of seventy percent, a fifteen point lead in the latest polls, and was poised to become the first black president of the United States. He shook hands, kissed babies, and once even traveled to Africa in search of his "roots"… something he never found, but the press never felt the need to follow up.

Baron James was Perfect for America…

Few realized Mercer James considered his own son a "*damned disgrace*," so pathetic, his very sight made him sick to the stomach… even though it was Mercer James who molded Baron's mediocrity, and had no one else to blame but himself, for shaping a son in an image the exact opposite of his own.

Baron James was Perfect for America…

Mercer James *was the exact opposite of his son.* He *kept* his mustache, wore the glasses, and proclaimed his ethnicity. His skin was darker, his hair, salt and pepper gray, and coarse. He was every bit as ethnic as his son was not. He was black *and* proud.

The sad fact was they had only two things in common, their size, both were well over six feet, and a desire to make history. Mercer James dreamed of greatness in his youth, but saw no room for opportunity. Instead he embraced the civil rights to achieve what his skin color prohibited. As a result, obstacles became hurdles and Mercer became an Olympian. He knew his time had come and gone, and because of that, he and a well paid group of consultants and television producers, made sure Baron's had just arrived.

The TV commercials ran nonstop, **"Baron James, raised in poverty on North Carolina's tobacco road; a high school stand out, who went on to excel on and off the field of athletics, in college; a business leader who then turned his attention to the Senate; Baron James is America, and Baron James will be America's next President."** The commercial ended with a shot of the perfect candidate standing next to the perfect family. A wife and two kids. They, too, appeared perfect, almost too perfect, and beyond the campaign ads, were seldom seen.

Each time the commercial would play, Mercer couldn't help but to stop and watch. It was like a sculptor admiring his work. "Pretty impressive, if I may say so, myself,"

"And yes dad, you *must* say so, and you do!" Baron sensed his father was more impressed with his creation than his son, and he was growing weary of the ads *and* his father, and frequently let it be known. "That ad's been running for months now and you've had the same thing to say *every* time."

Mercer James didn't respond, but instead, continued the pacing that had increased as the Election Day grew closer. He knew only the *unexpected* could derail his son's chances, and that's the one thing they chose not to discuss…at least, not in public, or even in private spaces that had not been swept for bugs. It was those things you place in the back of your mind, hoping to one day confuse it with something you might have dreamt. It happened so long ago. Or did it?

CHAPTER FIVE

THE student parking lot emptied out onto Canal Road. Maneuvering the busy intersection was something Vanessa usually did without incident. Today, however, she was focused on the radio.

"Baron James is perfect for America!" The announcer blared nonstop.

"I can't take this anymore," she said reaching down to switch the station. That's when it happened.

She should have heard the sirens announcing a nonstop motorcade of the dozen or more cars. At the very least, the lights should have been a distraction, but the radio was the only thing she could focus on and its continuous coronation of Baron James. He may have been perfect for America, but today he almost cost a cop his life

Vanessa slammed on the brake causing the cup of coffee that was sitting in the cup holder to her right, to spill into her lap.

"Shi..." but it was too late. When she looked up, she saw the motorcycle spinning out of control across the pavement. The officer appeared to move in slow motion as his bike slid out from under him, leaving behind a shower of sparks and making a horrible sound as it crashed into a nearby lamp post. It is what *didn't* happen that caused Vanessa's heart to stop.

First, the officer did not move, and then the motorcade proceeded on without him. As he rose from the ground still moving as if he were part of a dream she was having, his image was obscured by an endless stream of Limos and police cruisers intent on making it to their journey unobstructed, even if it meant the death or injury of a fellow officer.

"Jesus Christ, they didn't even stop!" That's when Vanessa saw the face. The face of the man who, unknowingly, caused it all...that unmistakable face. The one she had seen in countless TV commercials and on posters and billboards at every turn. There, staring out from the back of the third limousine in the procession, oblivious to it all, was Baron James. The next face she saw was that of a very angry motorcycle cop, who in the confusion had gathered himself and was making his way toward Vanessa's car.

"Drivers license and registration, ma'am."

"Are you okay?" Vanessa inquired out of sheer concern.

The officer was stunned. At first, even in his anger, he was struck by her beauty. Then, the fact that his safety was her first concern, caused him to pause, if only briefly. "Didn't you see the motorcade?"

"To be honest with you officer, I was distracted by the radio!"

That statement was enough to bring the boil back to the officer's face. "Hip hop, I can only assume!"

"Actually I was listening to talk radio!" Vanessa shot back. "And that damned Baron James!"

"Ma'am, he was in the limo and couldn't possibly have caused this accident."

"No sir" Vanessa replied sheepishly, realizing how ridiculous she must have sounded. "It wasn't the motorcade, but the endless stream of commercials on the radio. When I heard another one I just snapped. I stopped to change the channel and when I looked up you were right in front of me. I'm sorry officer, I was in such a hurry to get to work

I didn't see you." Vanessa could see the officer softening before her eyes. She could also see she struck a cord when she mentioned her annoyance with Baron James.

"So I take it you're not a James supporter?"

"The truth is, officer, I don't know anything about him. I suppose being black is enough to make a difference for some, but I still believe a man has to prove himself presidential." Vanessa could see a smile start to appear on the officer's face. He looked up the street at his bike and could see it suffered only superficial wounds, much worse than his bruised ego. "Truth is ma'am, Mrs. ..."

"Ms. Sullivan. I'm a student here at Georgetown," she said smiling.

"Ms. Sullivan, I can tell you that the man inside that limousine, who just sped by, is an arrogant prick! I have worked for candidates who would have demanded the motorcade stop, even though they're not supposed to. He didn't. In fact, I doubt that he even knew me and my bike almost took a dip in he Potomac. But I assure you, he did notice you!"

Vanessa then noticed the officer was putting away his citation book.

"I gotta tell ya...I was ready to write you up. But I got a soft spot in my heart for young kids who think. Everyone is buying this James crap hook, line, and sinker. So I'll make you a deal...."

Vanessa's heart began to pound. She feared the officer was about to make an unwelcome advance. She began preparing to demand a ticket, instead, when he stopped her before she could utter any protest. "Officer...."

"Patrick, Ms. Sullivan. Let's just say I won't write you a ticket if you keep our little conversation private. Bike's okay. I'll take a ribbing from the other guys back at the station, but other than that, no harm no foul. I gotta daughter you age. I can only hope she acts as savvy as you do." With that, he closed the book, walked back to his bike, and road off to either catch up with the others, or head back to the station.

As for the man on the radio, another commercial had just begun.

"Baron James is perfect for America!"

Fortunately the rest of the drive to the Bolivian Coffee Shop was without incident. No motorcades or cops spinning out of control… just the continuous blabber about Baron James. As for Vanessa, she had returned to the routine that is the real danger that confronts all students. Because of it, she had no idea, that on this day, she was being watched.

Once inside the coffee shop, Vanessa cleaned up the coffee that left a pleasant aroma on her clothes and abandoned the attitude of an opinionated student along with it. She, instead, donned the subservient uniform of a waitress. She tucked her long black hair under a net, and put on the apron that showcased the name of the coffee shop across her breasts. Advertisement was advertisement, and this, was the cheapest of all.

As she wiped off the tables in her station, she found herself thinking more and more about Father Haynes and the freedom she felt inside his classroom. She felt free because her classmates respected her, for her mind, and not her looks. She wondered what the kids back home would say if they could see her now. Theirs were voices that haunted her. Today they were difficult to drown out.

"*Vanessa? Vanessa Sullivan! Are you going to work or spend the rest of your life daydreaming?*"

The little girl, from tobacco road, was a young woman now, and her job demanded she do what all college coeds do; work to pay the bills. Still, she found it difficult to concentrate when so much seemed to be going on elsewhere. The election electrified Washington. Everyone was talking politics and Vanessa was no different.

"*Vanessa!" There are tables to be bused.*"

The Bolivian didn't pay much, but the tips were good. The shop had an eclectic mix of patrons; rich, poor, young and old, one of whom was a man at the table in front of her who was waiting to be served. Truth be known, he mysteriously showed up right at the beginning of Vanessa's shift.

. "This **"Val'** girl must be pretty special for you to wear her name on your sleeve," Vanessa asked, by way of polite conversation, noticing the man's initials on the cuffs of his shirt.

As always, Vanessa looked for ways to make her customers feel more like friends. It was also a good way to improve tips.

"It's actually *Vai*," the man offered up.

"I'm sorry, I thought it said Val."

"Most do, at first glance," the mystery man replied. "It's the name of a *trib*e in Africa. A strong tribe, where the men do *whatever is necessary* to survive. They're not initials, but instead, a name. It just looks that way on the cuff of a shirt. You are not the first to make the mistake."

"That sounds fascinating," Vanessa replied, with only the slightest hint of sarcasm in her voice, moving closer with a warm pot of coffee at the same time. "What happens to the women?"

"They are worshipped from afar."

Vanessa suddenly found herself blushing. There was something about the old man. Something powerful. He seemed more than confident and in control of the situation. Vanessa was used to controlling things, and for the first time in a long time, found herself off balance.

"Can I offer you a warm up?"

"Thank you, a warm up would be great," the man responded.

Vanessa poured the cup, and then awkwardly turned her attention to the others who had gathered at her station. It was a group of coeds that she was certain would drink and dash. That was the name given to students who drank coffee all evening and then ducked out on the check. She would eye them carefully. Her attention, however, was never far from the mystery man who seemed oblivious to her every movement. At least so she thought.

'The Bolivian coffee shop played home to older men, usually lawyers, and the occasional freshman members of congress, who would stop in for a quick cup and an even quicker opportunity to glance at any impressionable young college students. Students like Vanessa proved especially vulnerable. Val, it appeared, was one of those men, and he, was trying to get her attention. This time he was smiling.

As she walked back toward his table, she could have sworn the old codger was flirting. She noticed the last time she walked away; he seemed to be following her every move. She was both flattered and somewhat unnerved. The hairs on the back of her neck signaled caution. All of the students knew to be on alert, and Vanessa was no different. In Washington, power brought with it the *abuse of power.* The news reports were legend. Coed meets congressman; wife becomes angry; coed disappears… forever…wife gets rich.

Val, it seemed had no such plans and only wanted her attention so that she could pick up his tip, before the drink-and-dash coeds moved in. Rising from his table, he placed his coat over his shoulder, motioned to a spot on the table and simply walked away. So much for the mystery man. Instead, it seemed he was only interested in a simple cup of coffee.

"I'll be damned, he's gone." That's when she noticed the business card tucked inside a sizable tip. *"Twenty bucks for a cup of coffee."* The card read, Prescott Marshall, President/CEO Vai-Gene Inc.

"President and CEO." Picking it up, Vanessa mused for a moment, trying to put the mystery back in the man who had just left. . She thought about what life might be like for girls her age, who took up residence with older men. "*Mrs. Vanessa Marshall…hmmm… it does have a ring.*"

She discretely placed the tip in her pocket, glancing over her shoulder, making sure the others were not watching. It was a common practice at The Bolivian for all tips to be shared. It was also common knowledge that the larger tips never made it to the tip jar. She was being so discreet that the sound of another voice startled her.

"Kinda slow today, Vanessa, if you want to check out a little early." Standing just over her shoulder, was Tracey Stafford, a transfer student from the University of Texas.

"Tracey, this is from the old codger who sat at table one." Vanessa said as she produced the twenty dollar bill from her apron. Tracey was the one person at The Bolivian that Vanessa thought she could trust. They hid nothing from each other, not even tips…50/50, right down the middle.

At first, Tracey's eyes expressed her disbelief in the *size* of the tip. "Damn."

"Damn what?"

"Damn...just damn." Tracey spotted the man the moment he entered the coffee shop, and secretly wished he would sit at her station. "Damn, if you don't sleep with that man tonight, I will!"

Vanessa chuckled softly. "I don't think either of us will do any sleeping around, tonight, or any other night. Besides, don't you think there was something *creep*y about him?"

"Let's see; an old man, probably rich enough to drown us both in diamonds, hangs out at a local college coffee shop. *Creepy?* No. Normal? Yes."

The two exchanged polite chuckles before realizing that during their discussion, the "drink and dash" group did just that and The Bolivian was almost empty.

"Look Vanessa, with your newfound wealth and our lack of customers, I see no need for you to stick around tonight. Why don't you take off early?"

"Thanks Tracey, I do have a lot of homework to do. Still, there was something about that guy that gives me the willies. Would you watch me as I walk to my car?"

"You got it girl," Tracey responded. "Besides, girls like us can never be too careful, can we? Who knows when someone might try and rape us, forcing us to kick their ass. And what will that look like for future old men trying to get in our pants?"

The two girls shared their mutual amusement before Vanessa turned and walked away. Her hard shoes made a pronounced sound on the cobblestone streets of Georgetown and Vanessa liked it that way. There was both purpose and grace in her stride. Vanessa always left the appearance that she was a girl headed somewhere. She was determined to go anywhere that would take her away from her past.

"Who are you Mr. Marshall?" she said, examining the card as she walked. *"And just what is Vai-gene?"*

As she made her way past the BMWs and Mercedes that lined "M" Street, the chirping sound of her car announced she had arrived at her chosen destination. There, sitting wedged in between the wealth was a 1979 Chevrolet Monte Carlo, with an after-market alarm system. The body was silver, accented by an aging vinyl opera roof that matched the years of rust, in color. It was her graduation gift from her family.

It was old then and even older now, but it reminded her of where she was from.

"*Hopefully you come with a set of jumper cables, just in case,*" she said once again placing the card inside the pocket of her apron. The mystery man was gone, the mystery over. it was time to turn her attention to her nightly prayer. The student's prayer was that their car would start. Placing the key inside the ignition she was pleased to discover, that on this night, her prayer had been answered.

"One day," she said softly to herself. *"One day there will be no more Bolivian duties. One day someone will be gazing at my card."*

Vanessa failed to notice that as soon as her car left its spot, another, just down the street, pulled out at exactly the same time. A dark colored Lincoln Town Car, with the type of windows you couldn't see through. The car was common in Washington. It was the type of car that ushered senators and congressmen to and from Capitol Hill. Tonight, it wasn't taking anyone anywhere. Tonight it was following someone. It was following Vanessa Sullivan.

CHAPTER SIX

VOTE Baron James for the next president of the United States, and remember, a vote for James, is a vote for history!" The television, in the bar, was blaring nonstop. The football game, sharing the airtime, seemed to be splattered between the campaign commercials.

"Jesus Christ! Not again!" one of the patrons exclaimed. A debate on the subject of politics quickly ensued.

As always, Smitty's Bar was filled with the powerful, those who wanted to be, and those who once were. The man expressing his disgust at the commercial, sitting at the end of the bar, was the exception to both rules. He was handsome, but not like a fashion model…flawed enough to make him attractive to the rich and to the poor. Sitting, it appeared as if he might be a little taller than your average height. He sat slumped over and appeared to be badly in need of a shave. His face was a familiar fixture on the evening news.

"Set me up again Smitty and keep a cork on the conversation." Matt Walker had just graduated from coke to scotch and faced a night of hell once he got home. He knew his wife would be angry at him, and the sofa would be his bed, but he found comfort in *the bottle.* Over the last few months it had become his friend. Walker held the glass gingerly, like a wino coveting his precious flask. His old friend had returned. This time the friend was less than welcomed.

"One day, this shit's gonna' kill me, but not tonight...not tonight!" With that he took another swig.

As a journalist Matt Walker was on the short end of a long losing streak. Investigative reporters were supposed to break news, not follow it. Lately, the only thing Matt Walker had broken was the globe on one of his aging Emmys that lined the shelves inside his office. If the story wasn't about the upcoming election, it wasn't news. Matt Walker hated politics and he hated the politicians, in *this* election, even worse.

As Walker drowned his sorrows, the television played an endless string of commercials heralding the change that was sweeping the nation, and with each commercial, Walker drank even more. Baron James, the commercials announced, was so far ahead in the polls, his election seemed all but a *fait accompli*. James' approval ratings were so high, his ascension to the presidency was all but a formality.

"The man's a fraud. Can't you people see it?" Matt Walker knew that a story lay behind the movement and the man, but few journalists were bold enough to try and chip away at the veneer that the James machine had so carefully constructed. Not to mention the fact that all journalists now found themselves taking on the rich and powerful, and their own station's ownership as well. *"Name one position he's taken?"*

A constant series of media mergers resulted in a medium that was mediocre, at best. Local TV believed pursuing stories like Baron James was the duty of the networks. The networks relied on newspapers, and newspapers were bleeding circulation. Most newspapers relied on their local television stations to keep their finances afloat. The cycle was now complete. No one covered anything except the agendas handed out by the candidates, and they were taken as *gospel*. To reporters like Matt

Walker, Baron James was not just about to be *elected*, he was marching toward his *coronation*.

"Hey Walker," Smitty bellowed. "Have you checked this out yet?" Walking with the swagger of a man whose uniform included a towel slung over his shoulder, he tossed the morning's newspaper Matt's way.

The newspaper landed with an unusual thud, but the impact on Matt was even more pronounced. It was exactly what had been torturing him in recent weeks.

"Who writes this shit?" Walker said to himself, before reaching, once more, for the glass in front of him.

"Lincoln's tomb robbed by microscopic burglars."

Walker knew the editors of the paper had stooped beneath the tabloids lately, but this stole the cake. The article then went on to describe how a man's body was found near the tomb of the nation's sixteenth President, Abraham Lincoln, several years ago, and covered up by the FBI. He had been shot once, though the head, with what was believed to have been an antique pistol. Some speculated that it was the type of Derringer Booth used to shoot Lincoln at Fords Theater. The word 'Exclusive' was splashed across the front, as if that would make it all true. . The article pointed out there were no signs of any vandalism, save a small eighth inch hole that bore through the numerous layers of concrete, steel, and lead that encased the crypt. The author quoted experts who said only a specialized drill could accomplish such a feat. A drill that would cost hundreds of thousands of dollars to make, which lead officials to believe whoever was behind the break in, was *hi tech*.

"They were stealing his DNA," Smitty said confidently.

"Smitty," Matt began with resignation in his voice, "who would want Lincoln's DNA?" "You tell me?" Smitty shot back. "You're the hotshot investigative reporter."

"Or at least I was," Matt said softly, out of earshot. "Another," he demanded to the bartender, nowhere near surrendering. "So do you think he was shot with the actual gun that killed Lincoln?"

"Smitty, questions have surrounded that gun since it was first stolen back in 1960. Most serious collectors believe the one in the museum is a fraud and the real one is in the hands of a collector." Matt then took another look at the article, and examined it more closely, well past the point where he knew most readers had already moved on to the next screaming headline.

Lincoln's tomb is the most secure in U.S. history. His body has been moved 17 times and is now incased in two feet of concrete, ten feet beneath the surface. The stainless steel vault contains a lead sarcophagus, and inside that, a simple casket. The rock for the monument was quarried in Rome from the tomb of Service Tillus, the man who freed Rome's slaves. It was a gift to the United States from Rome that sat in the basement of the U.S. Capitol until an embarrassed White House demanded it be placed above Lincoln's crypt in Springfield, Illinois....

"Why would Lincoln be buried in what has to be the most secure tomb in U.S. history?"

Matt wasn't long with his thoughts before his concentration was interrupted by the latest Baron James ad.

"Baron James is perfect for America. Baron James *is* America."

"Whatdaya' think about that?" Smitty continued, proving America's attention span was indeed as short as the research showed. He failed to notice his switch of topics only added to the sour expression on Matt Walker's face. An expression that telegraphed his answer long in advance. "Oh God, here we go again."

"You black people must be proud!" Smitty proclaimed, as if erasing two hundred years of racism, in one sentence, was enough to break the ice.

"Just keep 'em comin', I ain't in the mood for history, past or present, right now, Smitty." Matt, then, took the remaining sip of a glass that was about to be refilled. *"Besides, he's only black on the outside and barely, at that."* Matt had heard enough from Smitty and everyone else. He just wanted to get drunk, and leave.

"I heard that! " Smitty yelled, not willing to let go. "So *now* who's racist?" There was certain sarcasm in his voice, as if 'I told you so' would be next. It wasn't. Instead, Smitty continued with his Irish wisdom which was the only wisdom an eighth grade education could summon. "I thought you guys would be proud of a guy like Baron James? Look at him, he's handsome! Hell, even my old lady thinks he'd be worth a roll in the hay. So what *you* got against him?"

"First of all, Smitty, *'you guys'* is insulting. Remember '*We are the world?"* Matt added, trying to make sure each of the syllables leaving his lips could be distinguished. "Name one thing...tell me one thing that makes him different from all the others, and that's your answer. I hate politicians that are manufactured and slickly packaged. This guys a fraud."

By now, several of the bar's patrons had noticed that the man talking was a fixture on the evening news. They could also see he wasn't finished.

"Besides, Smitty, I thought you'd be a Webb man."

Smitty feigned as if he had been insulted with the insinuation that all white men vote white. "The man's a former Klansman. As I see it, once a klucker, always a klucker. You know, Matt, not *all* of us whites are bigots. Talk about your insults. Besides, remember, **a vote for James is a vote for history!** And me and the misses plan on making **history**", Smitty countered. "The only thing black about Baron James is his skin and hell, it ain't all that," Walker shot back. "Besides, *just being black* ain't good enough. The man forgot who he was long ago, as if he ever really knew in the first place. He forgot about being *black* when they put the Heisman in his hands," Walker added, in a vain effort to remind his bartender friend that the man about to become president was once a football player. "Once that Heisman touched his hands, he was as white as they came…smiling at the right times, and making sure he was black when needed."

"Oh and I suppose you also think *O.J., did it,*" Smitty fired back, offering up his own dose of sarcasm, snapping the towel back over his shoulder.

"Face it Smitty, *the man* is always writing the checks, and guys like Baron are always there, in the front of the line, waiting for them to get cashed." Matt Walker was on drunken roll, but to the small audience that gathered around him, he was making sense. "Baron James is no more *for* black America than Max Webb is *for* whites. They're politicians, bought, sold, and packaged for production." He continued his diatribe with no need to rise from his drink and make eye contact with Smitty. The truth is, he wasn't talking to Smitty anyway. He was trying to convince himself his instincts hadn't disappeared in a bottle. In addition, Smitty was now a moving target, pouring drinks for the other customers and servicing their needs at the same time.

"Sounds like you need another," Smitty replied. "This one's on me."

With that, Smitty slid another scotch down the bar, where it met the hands of Matt Walker. Walker was clearly ready for its contents. The glass left a liquid trail behind it that was soon swiped by a rag Smitty kept neatly tucked inside his belt. As for Matt, he had a different problem. He had not yet figured out how he would explain to his wife and family, the smell of alcohol on his breath. He also knew he was drunk.

On this night, Matt Walker was in no form for fighting. He was more inclined to go someplace and sleep it off, inventing a lie about an assignment that caused him to work late. "It was better to check in for the night, than to risk driving home, as tired as I was." He had rehearsed the lines over and over again. He had told the lie so many times that even he had started to believe it. But the truth was, she knew. She knew he had started drinking again, and she knew why.

Cecilia Walker knew success haunted Matt Walker more than failure. Matthias A. Walker, which was his given name, was born into poverty, but rose with the pride, that only working class families could provide. His father had been active in the civil rights movement and made sure when certain schools allowed integration, his children were on the front lines. His father was a strict disciplinarian. Ted Walker made sure his children knew C's were unacceptable. He believed education was the only way to escape poverty and Matthias was his oldest son. He also believed in hard work.

Matthias worked hard as a young man, holding down small jobs, while most of his classmates went on spring break. The end result was a work ethic that followed him to this day. A lucky break landed him a job in television. Inner cities across America were burning, white reporters were afraid to enter predominantly black neighborhoods, and newsrooms were looking for minorities to cover what then, *the story.*

Matthias A. Walker then became Matt Walker, reporter at large. Cecilia married Matthias.

"Another one, and then I'm hittin' the road," Matt promised.

"Only in America," Smitty remarked, as he delivered what both men knew to be the last round. "Only in America," he added looking at yet another commercial for Baron James. "Here you go, Mr. Walker, God bless her and drink up. This one's on me."

By the time the drink arrived, Matt Walker was already standing, with one arm inside his coat and the other, groping for the sleeve. The arm that was resting comfortably, reached over and grabbed the last one for the evening. The drink was consumed without hesitation, and the glass slammed to the bar. Walker was leaving, coat on or not. He had had enough of booze, Smitty and Baron James. He really wanted to go home, but he knew better.

Walker snatched up his keys and was headed out the door, banging into several bar stools and chairs that cluttered his path. Little did the patrons inside realize Matt Walker wouldn't get far.

As for Smitty, he was still standing there, taking it all in, looking proud.

CHAPTER SEVEN

"MY my, you are quite the beauty." Prescott Marshall found the face of the girl he had just met in the coffee shop hard to get off his mind. He knew she was beautiful, but even he had to admit, *her picture* did no justice to her beauty, in person. He also was struck by how much she resembled her mother. Even though the photos were grainy, the type taken by cheap investigators from hidden locations, up close, the girl was striking!

"I believe you'll find my pictures interesting!"

As he made his way west bound on the GW Parkway out of Washington, his thoughts turned away from the meeting he had just had, and returned to one he had just days earlier. Fate was always the best messenger in Washington. It seemed, a jealous boyfriend had come to possess some unseemly photos. As always, the boyfriend wanted revenge, but when one of the faces on the photos captured national headlines, revenge quickly turned to greed.

Greed quickly turned to fear when the man realized the gravity of the photos he was holding, and that fear led him to the police, and the police to the Secret Service. No one knew; the Secret Service made sure copies of the photos also went to Prescott Marshall. The head of the Secret Service knew *he* would know what to do. He did.

Marshall's black Mercedes roadster had become his trademark, well known, especially, to the park police, who, on more than one occasion, lay in wait. He especially enjoyed nights like this one, where the weather was just right for putting the top down. The cool fresh air, combined with the car's more efficient heater, took the bite off the chillier temperatures that were fast approaching. It took an hour to get to his Potomac home, and less, if the park police had already abandoned their perch, just before the entrance to the CIA. .

No one questioned Marshall's lavish lifestyle. He lived in a Potomac home that more closely resembled a mansion, and owned a fleet of fancy cars that filled each stall of a six car garage. The Mercedes was his favorite. Most people believed Prescott Marshall lived alone, invested wisely, and shared his wealth with those less fortunate. On top of it all, he was drawing a government pension and working as a paid consultant to some of the nation's largest defense contractors. He was also a man who had his finger on the pulse of just about everything and everyone in Washington, including Vanessa Sullivan.

A pity. She truly is beautiful, just like her mother!

"Max Webb," he said into the speaker phone mounted on the dash. With that, the sound of a phone dialing interrupted the sound of the compact disc that had been playing. Soon the voice of Webb's Senate Secretary was on the line.

"Two visits in one day, what makes us so special?" the voice on the other end of the line inquired politely.

"I need not remind you how close the election is," Marshall began, "so could I bother the Senator one last time?"

"Certainly, I'll fetch him from his meeting, he'll be glad to get out of this one," she said, before leaving Prescott to the soothing sounds of elevator music, blaring in the background.

"I thought we had settled all of our business," Max Webb began, cutting quickly to the chase.

"We have," Marshall began, "we have."

"Then why the phone call?"

"I think I may have come up with the solution to your problem at the polls," Marshall continued, before there was a longer than usual pause on the other the end of the phone.

Webb could feel his pulse beginning to quicken. "What *type* of solution are we talking about?"

"*We* aren't talking about anything. *I* will handle everything, *You* just be *Presidential.*"

Max Webb was left staring at the phone. The call ended almost as quickly as it began. Betty, however, was right. He was happy to be out of his last meeting of the day and ready to go home.

Prescott had already arrived at his locations. He turned the black Mercedes Roadster into the long sweeping driveway that led to his house. The lights came on immediately, and the special security cameras, he had installed, *whirled* to attention.

Once inside, Marshall turned off the home's extensive security system. The system was elaborate, and required both voice and iris ID. It was much more elaborate than any signs located outside the home, suggested. Prescott liked it that way.

Prescott tossed his suit coat to a man waiting in the wings and proceeded to climb the elegant marble staircase that led to his study. The walls, lining the hallways, contained an extensive collection of hand painted masterpieces and sculptures. Each was hand picked by the man who was now opening the massive oak doors to the room he considered to be his *war room.*

A massive oak desk in the center of the room commanded as much attention as the man who would soon sit behind it. It was made of the finest timber from Africa, where Marshall once worked inside the American Embassy in Liberia. The desk was littered with small reminders from his stay in that country, and oddly, the shell casing from a Russian Assault Rifle.

The usual complement of bills and correspondence from a variety of sources, were all stacked into neat piles by the staff who knew, well in advance, never to be seen or heard while *The Principal* was inside the residence. To the right of that pile, Marshall found the one package he had been expecting. It was a weighty envelope that bore no postal markings, indicating it had been delivered by hand. The outside of the envelope read:

UNITED STATES DISTRICT COURT
KANSAS CITY, MISSOURI

Like a child at Christmas, Marshall opened the envelope revealing the massive lawsuit inside. He could feel his heart quicken and temperature rise, as he shuffled through its contents. Visibly, his face grew sterner, with each page he turned. He stared at the document for what appeared to be an eternity.

This one was intercepted, but what about the others?

The silence was suddenly interrupted by the copier, sitting on a table on the opposite side of the room. The printer was old, with a flywheel, that scanned the paper, leaving behind the message that had been sent. Marshall made his way to the copier, where he watched as one by one, a series of twenty seven random names were being printed out in an antique computer font. As he watched the names being rendered, he smiled when two of the names seemed more than familiar. In fact he was grinning ear to ear.

If you can't eliminate the lawsuit, eliminate the evidence.

Seated behind his massive desk once more, Marshall reached down to pick up the phone that sat off to the right, opposite several books he collected. The others would have to be notified, but first he had a *special call to make.*

CHAPTER EIGHT

"YOU know what must be done!" The man on the other end of the phone never offered anything in the way of identification. Always, the call was anonymous to the phone he provided. No other calls were to be made on *that phone.* The bill was always paid, well in advance. Always, the call meant someone was going to die.

"Have the arrangements been made?"

"The money is already in your account. You'll find your travel documents there and your instructions."

Maurice Lacroix placed the phone on the night stand beside his bed and stared at the ceiling for what seemed to be an eternity. He needed the time to collect his thoughts. He awakened as always, without the use of any alarms. He was a light sleeper and had been that way since the war. Besides, it was hot this time of year, making resting difficult. The small oscillating fan worked only to keep the mosquitoes away, and then only when it swung toward his body.

Another mission, hopefully this will be the last.

As he maneuvered his legs allowing his feet to touch the floor, the rough tile surface reminded him of so much that was wrong with his country. The house once belonged to a wealthy settler, but now it was his. When he found it, there was no roof, no electricity, and no running water. A generator served to provide the latter two and the roof was put in place by hand, using labor from the nearby displacement camp.

"Maurice is that you?" the voice called out, softly, from the darkness.

"Yes, mama, but you should go back to sleep. You need your rest, as you are older now."

The truth was, the woman in the other room was not his mother, but she had been the closest thing to one he had ever known. He found her among the thousands, displaced after the war, in the same camp where many of his laborers came from. She was eighty-seven years old and frail, but possessing a sense of nobility that showed even through the worst of times. And that is how he found her.

The others in the camp took care of the woman they called "Grandma." What little rations of rice they had, a portion went to her. In return, she departed wisdom and learning. In her former life, she was a school teacher. Now her wrinkled hands, still turned the pages, but more slowly than before. Her students were also getting older.

They called him "*Le Vashti, the gray ghost*" in part, because of the way he looked, and the way he killed. It was common, during the war, for child soldiers to hide behind masks. Lacroix abandoned his captain's hat as the leader of the Kwi-ir-u and took on a more frightening visage. "*Le Vashti'* hid behind a coating of palm ash that gave his skin a grayish tint. A leaf from cassava trees, that became known as "*war face,*" was used to make the eyes, blood red. The combination created the effect of a ghost, and in the case of Maurice Lacroix, *a gray ghost.*

He hated the name because it made him seem less than human, but he knew, as the war dragged on, he had grown to fit the name. He had committed atrocities he could never atone for. Some, well documented, but one that would haunt him for the rest of his days. *That* was the reason that he took the old woman in.

One room, inside the house, would be used for study. No one ever asked where Lacroix got the money; they just knew he had it. Money that paid for meals better than the ones served by the relief agencies; and books, real books, with titles and pages that went on without interruption. The room where the old women slept was as comfortable as any around. She had a small dresser with a mirror attached. It sat in the middle of the room with her simple queen sized bed, sitting opposite, on the other wall. There was, on top of the dresser, another oscillating fan much larger than the one in Lacroix's room. It worked well to keep her cool.

The woman never questioned his past, but he suspected she knew more than she let on. She was his salvation, the one thing he could point to that never failed him. He would do whatever it took to make her happy. She was well worth dying for, and if need be, *killing* for. He had done so, for so many before, but her cause was noble.

"Will you be coming back?"

"Soon, ma soon," although he knew this time the chances were he would not.

As he exited the room and made his way toward the front of the house, he was now fully clothed. He had learned during the war how to dress quickly, a habit that also served him well in peacetime. He walked quietly through what was once a living room, making sure to avoid the one board that would signal his exit. He knew she was not asleep, and he knew she would wait for him to leave. He did not want to see her. Instead, he chose to remember her face.

She had the face of a kindly old woman, caramel in complexion, wrinkled in all the right places, around the eyes and mouth, revealing wisdom. Course gray hair, placed gently in a French braid. In his mind she would always be smiling, because he never saw her frown.

In the back of the house, a towering bread tree captured the sun as it set over the St. Paul River to the West. The tree had been there since the first settlers arrived in the late 1800s. It was there that *he hid it.*

The digging began beneath the tree. The sound of the shovel seemed so loud in the still night air. He wondered how the old woman could sleep. The truth was, he made little or no sound at all.

There was less than a foot of dirt to remove. Red, rich soil that once produced the crops, would now, once again, give way to the hate that welled up inside *the gray ghost*. The shovel announced its arrival with a dull thud that seemed to shatter the stillness he sought to preserve.

He had found it!

Lacroix paused one last time to look upon the land he now called home. The moon was setting quickly over the banks of the river. He reflected back over the many fish it had produced. He could smell the charcoal that burned constantly in the refugee camp near by. It felt strange, as this was now his home, and he knew deep in his heart, *he would be leaving it forever.*

As he stopped to pry the box loose from its grave, a small bead of sweat fell onto its surface, providing the only hint as to its contents.

"U.S. Govt..."

Inside was the one thing that would shatter the peace he had constructed for himself since the days of the war. But he knew this time his reason for opening the box was different. This time he was thinking of the old woman and the children. He would do it for them, he whispered to himself. "*I will do it for them.*"

Carefully wrapping its contents in a single leather pouch, he quickly placed the soil back beneath the base of the tree, so not as to disturb what had been there before him and what would be there long after his death. His destiny was now sitting in the driveway.

By now, the late model Toyota Land Cruiser was parked in the front of his house. The engine had long since been killed, as per his instructions. Because the house sat on an angle, they would roll down the hill, just out of earshot, before starting the engine. That way, he could leave without being detected. He knew the old woman would want to talk as she always did, but not this time. He couldn't face her anymore. Each time he left, she argued he stayed away too long. *The children needed him...she needed him.* She was his conscience, but on this night, he did not want a conscience.

"Ishmael, my friend, I see you have been waiting,"

"As you instructed Mr. Lacroix; I arrived shortly after midnight, when the sounds from the village were still loud, and have been sitting here, silently, ever since."

"You have been a good friend, Ishmael, and for that I shall reward you. But first, you must do what I have told you."

"I understand."

Ishmael, sensing they were far enough away, started the engine, and the truck roared to life.

Lacroix would enjoy the ride. He always did. The roads were dark and had been since the war. Because it was late, few souls ventured out. Except for the moonlight, there was nothing to expose the evils that would emerge when daylight came. And this is how he wanted to remember it. He liked the night. He savored this night more than others.

Suddenly Ishmael slammed on the brakes, causing Lacroix to lurch forward so hard his head almost struck the dashboard.

"What the hell..."

"Look," Ishmael responded, and that's when Lacroix saw it.

It had become a game in Liberia, for children to dart in and out of traffic, wearing dark clothes. In a land torn apart by war, it had become a street game, similar to others he had heard about in the states, where children would tempt fate, for fun. But this was no laughing matter. Hundreds of children died...their bodies dragged alongside the road and dumped in ditches, to become unofficial casualties of war.

"Assholes."

"*Children,*" Lacroix responded.

The rest of the ride went without incident. There were no animals to avoid as they scattered during the war, or were consumed in its aftermath. Now the window in the Land Cruiser was down and Lacroix was enjoying the breeze. It was hot, but the humid night air felt good. It always did.

As the Land Cruiser turned off the road to the right, entering the long gravel driveway that led to **Robert's International Airport**, Lacroix found himself gazing at another graphic reminder of Liberia's brutal past. The Airport, once a proud symbol of what Liberia did right, was now just a shell. The large windows that allowed Liberians to welcome outsiders to their world were gone. Mortar fire from Nigerian soldiers, reduced it to rubble. The newer structure was no longer in use. Instead visitors entered and exited the country via the older airport, which once served only commuter flights.

Even there, electricity was scarce, provided only by generators. To the left of the entrance, a white tank with the bold letters, '**UN**', sat outside. Manning it were troops of the Philippines who really didn't care for the Liberians, but instead saw *The UN* work as a source of steady income. Many came from villages where conditions were no better than those of the people they guarded. And they would stay in similar villages, choosing to send the bulk of their income home to loved ones.

The tanks guarded a white concrete structure, where it was obvious that the bullet holes, from the war, had been painted over.

There was one entrance in, and one out; the door to each, so small, even the most insignificant of flights, could cause congestion. Window and ceiling fans provided the only comforts. The metal detectors screened passengers who failed to pay the necessary bribes. There was no set fee.

"We are here."

Lacroix turned to face his friend for the last time, amazed at how dignified the men of Liberia were during times of peace. Their perfect use of the language betrayed the fact that most had either lost a loved one, or claimed a life during the war. Ishmael, he knew was no different. It was just an understated fact of life. The war had touched everyone. Ishmael was no exception.

"Thank you," Lacroix responded, "*Please don't forget.*"

"I will fulfill your wishes as you instructed."

"The old lady..."

"She will be taken care of."

Lacroix turned to embrace his friend, but Ishmael was already at work, removing his belongings from the trunk of the Land Cruiser. He carefully placed the leather pouch inside the diplomatic container that had been provided. There, it would remain until being claimed at its final destination. The markings, on the outside, left little doubt as to where it was going.

EMBASSY OF THE UNITED STATES OF AMERICA.

Ishmael, then, produced a smaller pouch, with the same stenciling on the outside. Lacroix placed inside it, a small container of palm ash, and a grouping of war leaves. There was another item wrapped in leather was well. Ishmael could barely see the contents, but it looked as if it might be a knife. Because of the elaborate markings on the handle, it was, possibly a ceremonial knife. Ishmael didn't see Lacroix place it in the pouch, but he had no doubt it was equally important to his mission.

Ishmael watched as his friend made his way through the metal detectors and across the runway to the small plane, awaiting it's only passenger. It would take off without ever being recorded as having landed. Like the man on board and the two pouches that were its only cargo, its mission was to remain secret.

The gray ghost was now airborne and on his way to the United States of America.

CHAPTER NINE

THE driver of the car followed the instructions to the letter, making sure no one saw him following the young coed as she left the coffee shop…a task made easier because of the unusual make and model of the car he was pursuing. There weren't many Chevy Monte Carlos in Georgetown, Sylvio Ramirez was certain that the one he was following may have, in fact, been the *only* one.

Vanessa Sullivan followed her normal route, turning right onto Wisconsin, then another right onto "M" street.

"Christmas already," she uttered as if someone were sitting next to her. "Next thing you know, it'll be July. Whatever happened to Halloween?" In fact, there was only one store on "M" street, that night, that seemed to be catering to the Halloween crowd, and it was a costume store. Halloween in Georgetown was always a festive event. The police would block off the major streets but still allow for a curious mix of coeds, drunks, and older men looking to score. Now, most of the stores had already signaled that Halloween was over, as it was time for the Christmas shopping season to begin.

Vanessa Sullivan was so preoccupied with the notion of Christmas decorations,]that she failed to notice that the late model Lincoln Town Car was the same one parked up the street, as when she left the coffee shop. Because of the shortness of each block, Sylvio was forced to abandon any pretext of not being seen, and was now positioned directly behind Vanessa Sullivan's car. It wasn't until they reached the George Washington Parkway, a few blocks later, that he could put some distance between him and his prey.

"Such a pity. A beautiful lady like you should never be alone. Too many strangers...too many things that go bump in the night."

By now, Vanessa Sullivan was on the Parkway, about to take the first exit where she would be less than two blocks away from her small, but comfortable townhouse. Crystal City, where she lived, used to be known for its pawnshops. It was located near the Pentagon, where each year, hundreds of soldiers were forced to sell everything they owned to pay debts, settle scores, or make restitution to lovers who had come and gone. Then, someone realized it was the one place in Washington where the view of the monuments was unobstructed. College coeds were the first to case it, followed by developers, seeking to build high rises on every inch of real estate they could get their hands on. That's what made Vanessa Sullivan's apartment so attractive. She leased it from Mrs. Avery, a widow and former government worker, who remembered when Washington was a sleepy southern town, located on a swamp.

"This used to be nothing, nothing but swamp," she was fond of saying. But now, Mrs.

Avery was in her eighties, lived alone, and welcomed Vanessa Sullivan's companionship as much as Vanessa valued the low rent. It was a match made in heaven. There was another thing about Mrs. Avery Vanessa liked; in a very real sense, she made the townhouse seem more like home. Mrs. Avery was more of a mother than her own mother. She worried when Vanessa stayed out too late, and woke her when she overslept. If there was an aggressive boyfriend, it was Mrs. Avery who summoned the police. Aside from Mrs. Avery, Vanessa Sullivan lived alone, except for Sebastian.

Sebastian was a pure white and obnoxiously obese cat. Not pedigreed, by any stretch of the imagination, but just a cat. A former stray, who mysteriously wound up on Vanessa's doorstep, looking for food one day, and never left. Sometimes it was hard for Vanessa to determine who did the most doting, Sebastian or Mrs. Avery. Both were always waiting at the door.

Vanessa pulled into the driveway, behind the town home's only garage, never bothering to check to see if she was alone, and as a matter of fact, she was not. Just down the block, Sylvio Ramirez had pulled to a stop, as instructed, but remained far enough away not to be noticed by any passersby, and yet close enough to move in quickly.

As Vanessa climbed the single flight of stairs to the front door and inserted her keys, Sylvio Ramirez began to make his move. First, putting on the pair of black leather driving gloves, he kept his distance, as instructed. Then, he reached over to open the glove box to remove the envelope he had been given just hours earlier. The sound of the keys knocking against the brass plate was always enough to awaken Mrs. Avery and summon Sebastian. Like most students, Vanessa kept enough keys on her key ring to look like a maintenance worker, but *this* key ring also included a small canister of mace. She had never needed to use it, but kept it just in case. Stories about murders in Washington were common on the evening news, as were stories about coeds disappearing.

Sylvio was not used to this line of work. The money seemed good at first, but faded quickly with each footstep. If he was to make his move, he would have to do so quickly. Soon the door would be open, and Vanessa Sullivan would be safely inside. He was told to work quickly and not make a scene. He knew about Mrs. Avery and her penchant for the police.

As Vanessa reached for the knob to open the door, she felt a heavy hand on her shoulder. Startled at first, she grabbed for the keys and the mace, but lost control of them as they tumbled to the ground. As she reeled around, she saw him for the first time. A man she had never seen before, obviously Hispanic, with a ruddy complexion which made it all the more disturbing because of the time of night. Her heart raced as her mind filled with the images she had seen, over and over again, on the evening news. There was one other thought. One that also came from the news. She had seen stories on what women were to do when being attacked. And yet for that brief instance, she was frozen with fear.

Sylvio Ramirez could see it on her face. He knew things were not going as planned. And yet, he went ahead with his mission as if nothing had changed. With his right hand on her shoulder, he reached into his jacket pocket with his left.

"Who the hell are you!?" Vanessa shouted, remembering the news report and all of its details. She made sure, as the reporter had instructed, to say it loudly, as if signaling to some unknown person that they were not alone. Then she proceeded to do what the reporter suggested that all women in similar situations should do next.

Sylvio Ramirez quickly removed his hand from her shoulder to block her advance but it was too late. Vanessa Sullivan's fingernails were soon implanted in his face and making their way downward. Ramirez recoiled, as if he had been struck by a prize fighter, backed up two steps and then blurted the words that caused Vanessa to realize she had made a terrible mistake.

"To hell with this," he said, "you crazy bitch."

It was then that Vanessa realized that her attacker was not really an attacker at all, but instead a messenger, and a poor one, at that.

"What makes you think you can just sneak up on someone like you did?" Vanessa shouted.

"I wasn't sneaking," I was told to give you this envelope tonight and to make sure no one saw me do it. For that I got a lousy hundred dollars and this!" He said pointing to a scratch that had already started to show signs the wound was deep enough to bleed. Who did you think I was, the slasher or something? Take it, I'm getting the hell out of here." With that Ramirez delivered the envelope and it's contents, beating a hasty retreat backwards, down the stairs from Vanessa's town home, but not before a startled Mrs. Avery had made her way to the doorway and to the side of Vanessa..

"Who sent you?" Vanessa screamed out, but by then it was already too late. Sylvio Ramirez was already down the street and getting further away with each footstep. She strained to catch a glimpse of any license plate on the car, but it was parked too far away.

"Are you all right dear?" Mrs. Avery inquired. "Should I call the police?"

"I'm not sure," Vanessa responded. "I don't think he was here to hurt me, and in fact he may have bitten off more than he could chew if he was. Judging from his face and my fingernails, the police might be more inclined to charge me."

That statement brought a chuckle to both of the women, enough to break the ice of an awkwardly tense movement. Vanessa could even feel the familiar softness of Sebastian as he made his way through her legs and into the townhouse where he would instinctively park himself in front of his feeding bowl.

"He gave me this."

"What's in it?" Mrs. Avery inquired.

"Not sure," Vanessa responded.

"Then open it dear girl, you know I'm not getting any younger, and even us old girls like a little suspense."

The envelope bore no markings. No return address or letterhead. The outside was no different than the stationary on the inside...Gray in appearance and definitely unusual, as if it had come from an expensive stationary store. It was a cross between parchment and gray construction paper, with a message that left more questions than it answered.

"VAL wishes to dine with you!"

Her polite chuckle soon turned to all out laughter. The old man in the coffee shop...The monogram on his shirt...VAI...Her mistaking it for VAL.

She turned, explaining the evening's events to Mrs. Avery. She told her about the man and the monogram on the cuffs of his shirt. She explained the true meaning behind the VAI. She never noticed the change in the expression on the face of Mrs. Avery...one that changed from curiosity to concern.

"Why, the letter?" She mused. He could have delivered it in person less than an hour earlier. She knew there was only one way to find out. She had his card and his phone number. She would make the call, but not now. This night had already been filled with too much drama. "First things first," she said, looking down at Sebastian. I believe we have a date.

Sebastian looked up as if he understood. Mrs. Avery, however, was not as quick to dismiss this sudden turn of events.

"VAI," she said softly. "Vanessa my dear, I've heard that name before, somewhere. Somewhere." Returning to her room, Mrs. Avery stopped and opened the top drawer of her night stand. Beneath a pile of medicines, most of which seem to cancel out the others, was an address book, that clearly had seen better days. Looking inside, she turned the pages until she came to the name she was looking for. It was there, wedged between two of her closest friends. "I wonder if you are still alive."

CHAPTER TEN

MATT Walker had barely made it past the doorway of "Smitty's Bar," when it happened. There was no time to prepare or for that matter defend himself. The first crushing blow came from out of nowhere.

"Consider yourself warned, you cocky bastard!"

The warm salty taste of his own blood filled his mouth, mixed in with small bone fragments from several teeth that were damaged by the impact of the blow. He started to turn around in a vain effort to identify his attacker, but his legs gave way. Everything was spinning, going black.

The men then began to savagely kick Walker, taunting him with each blow. Walker assumed the fetal position but found it difficult to decide which needed protecting more. When he covered his head, the blows came to his mid section. Reflexes caused him to curl up even tighter, but the onslaught continued.

There were *two attackers,* he surmised. One of the men was striking him from in front, the other from behind. One had a burley voice.

"You're not so bad without your cameras, are you Walker?" The man with the burley voice said.

He had been recognized. But how? By whom?

The other man, he assumed to be smaller, because his blows were not as severe and did little, if any, talking. Instead, what he lacked in severity, he made up for in frequency. He could sense, from the piercing pain that accompanied each blow, the man had been some type of fighter.

The blows are coming too fast....passing out....

CHAPTER ELEVEN

"WHAT mysteries await us today?"

Unlike most students, Vanessa found comfort in the University's library. History, she found, was always hidden in plain sight. Nothing was secret in America. Instead she found most students were just too lazy to solve its many mysteries. In many cases, there were countless volumes written about the same subjects, such as the civil war. Scholars knew it was those volumes, contrary to the *established* truth, that told the real story. Vanessa believed that the real mysteries of history that couldn't be solved with a textbook or be found in a library, could be solved with science.

"The Da Vinci Code!"

Vanessa spotted a young woman reading the popular novel. The book appeared as if it had been passed back and forth several times. She marveled at how one book caused millions, worldwide, to question the *established* way of thinking. As she watched the coed devour the contents of the book, she remembered how she, too, couldn't put it down. So many of the symbols in book had been overlooked, even though they were well established for centuries.. She hoped her own graduate thesis would do the same.

"Excuse me ma'am." The young woman standing before her had a short-cropped afro, wore blue jeans and spoke in soft tones. Vanessa spotted her when she entered the library. That's when she was seated behind the main desk, clearly performing some type of work study job.

"Yes?," Vanessa answered in equally hushed tones.

"Is your name Vanessa Sullivan?" the woman whispered.

"Yes, why?"

"This was left at the desk for you. The man who bought it said you'd be here and I gotta tell you, he left a pretty good description." The work study student handed Vanessa a small slip of paper that had been folded over once.

Vanessa opened it with the young woman looking on. She did so slowly, out of habit, as if it hid some deep dark secret. Instead it was a simple note, with an even simpler message.

> Vanessa:
>
> Please see me immediately. It has to do with Father Haynes, and your studies.
>
> Father Charles Chiniquy

The woman could tell by the expression on Vanessa face, she had no idea who sent it, and Vanessa could tell by her expression, the girl had read the note long before delivering it. Vanessa studied the contents, once more, before realizing the girl was still standing there.

"May I help you?" Vanessa asked innocently, slightly increasing the volume of her voice but not loud enough to attract too much attention.

"Sorry," the young woman began. "Just thought you might like to know...there is no Father Chiniquy at Georgetown University. I already checked."

CHAPTER TWELVE

"WHAT the hell..."

The envelope was there when Baron James arrived at his Senate office. It was sitting in the center of an antique wood and marble desk that had been given to him by his father. The envelope contained few markings or anything else that would betray its contents. Instead, he, at first, mistook it for his morning briefing papers. He was prepared for anything, but not this. Not now.

"Shit..."

From a full standing position, James collapsed into the thick leather chair just behind his desk, causing it to roll backwards almost to the window. His eyes darted wildly, left, then right, searching for witnesses. His reactions were similar to those of a little boy caught reading his first girlie magazine. He wanted to look away, to imagine the man in the photos was someone else, but it was not. Younger and exposed for all the world to see, *it was him*! The other face was unmistakable as well. He had seen it over and over again, in dreams, that turned into nightmares and recently questionable memories. The face, staring back from the naked man atop her, belonged to Susan Sullivan. The next set of photos left no doubt as to who the man was. *It was him!*

"Jesus..." But there were no other words to follow. For the first time, in as long as anyone could remember, Baron James was speechless. As he stared at the photos, his entire world flashed before him. He was nauseous and could feel the entire contents of his stomach, as if it had suddenly been set on fire. He wanted to vomit. All thoughts of becoming president took a back seat to the obvious. *Who took the photos? Who delivered them, and were there more?*

Perhaps, more importantly, for a man who had grown accustomed to people wanting something for nothing, *what did they want? Was it blackmail? Was there a note attached?*

It may have been minutes or even hours, since time mattered little at this point. He just sat there, staring. Staring...surrounded by silence. There were no sounds in the room, save the painful ringing of the phone. It was his private line.

"What the hell do you want?" he said before realizing how he must have sounded to the person on the other end. He then glanced at the caller ID and didn't care.

"Senator James, aren't we a bit testy these days."

"Yes, but how did you get this number?"

"The same way I managed to get those photos into your office without being noticed."

"What photo..." James answered, desperately hoping the caller had somehow been bluffing.

"Not photo, you arrogant asshole, photos, and I assure you, there are plenty more where those came from. I must admit however, they do you little justice. Especially from the angle I am looking at."

"I'll have you know that what you are attempting to do is against the law!" Baron shouted into the receiver at the person on the other end of the line. "Extortion is a federal offense!"

"It seems, Senator, you are way ahead of yourself. I was simply delivering some photos I thought might have belonged to you. I was calling to let you know how you could get possession of the others. But.... *if* you would like me to turn them over the proper authorities...."

"Don't be an idiot; you know what that would do to my career..."

"You, should have thought of that, a long time ago my friend. Now, listen carefully, and I will instruct you on what to do next. I assure you, any attempt to contact law enforcement will not been seen as welcome news." The man on the other end then proceeded to issue a carefully thought out series of instructions for Baron James to follow, with the entire process lasting less than five minutes. "Remember Senator, this will always be *our* little secret, so long as you do as you are told."

When the call went dead, it may as well have taken Baron James with it. All he could do was to sit there, staring at the photos on his desk. The sudden urge to vomit, returned. This time, his body succeeded.

A day that was to include several scheduled campaign appearances with nothing out of the routine, now had become anything but that. He was being *blackmailed*, and the person on the other end of the call regarding the photos, couldn't have been clearer. Senator James meant nothing to him, President James did. All Baron had to do was to win the election. That is, if he trusted the man to keep his word. He had been a politician too long to trust anyone. Anyone, save one man.

"Sandra," he said recovering enough composure to summon his secretary and placing the photos in the top drawer of his desk at the same time, "get my father on the line."

CHAPTER THIRTEEN

Healy Hall/Room 106

VANESSA waited for the other students to clear out, before rising from her seat and making her way to the front of the room. Father Haynes had just finished lecturing a young woman about what *she* had to do to *get her grades up,* when he turned and spotted Vanessa standing directly behind him.

"Vanessa, you startled me!" he said.

"Sorry Father, I was wondering if you had a moment." she said rather sheepishly.

Father Haynes smiled, as if he were a father making time for his favorite child. "I always have time for the curious. Are you here to talk, or would you like to teach my next class?" He expected a rise but quickly realized she was in no mood for cordiality's.

Vanessa reached inside her backpack, producing the note and placing it face down on the desk in front of her. *"Who is Father Chiniquy?"*

"Father Chiniquy...the famous Father Chiniquy has surfaced again," Father Haynes held the tiny sliver of paper as if he had known the man all his life. There was also a troubled expression on his face that did not escape Vanessa's attention.

"Where did you get this?"

"That's the problem. It was waiting for me at the library. Even more troubling, I searched the campus directory, and there is no mention of a Father Chiniquy," she answered.

Father Haynes smiled. "Perhaps it has something to do with the fact that Father Chiniquy has been *dead* for more than a century now and, I should add, there are a lot of powerful people who would want him to stay dead!"

Vanessa now had a puzzled look on her face. "Then how could he…"

"Obviously *he* didn't send you *this* note, but *someone* did. The question is who, and why?" Father Haynes responded.

Suddenly, Vanessa found herself even more confused and more concerned about the note than she was at the library. She could tell by the look on Father Haynes' face that he knew who Father Chiniquy was, and that he was worried as well. But, why?

"So who is...or should I say…*was* this Father Chiniquy?" Vanessa asked.

Father Haynes turned and looked at the blackboard over his shoulder. "Even in the ivy towers of academia, as I have told you before, the truth lies hidden within the layers of lies. This city, like this University has many mysteries. *The story of Father Chiniquy and his writings, represent perhaps the greatest conspiracy theory ever...the one history never told!*"

"I don't understand."

"It is, my dear Vanessa, a story of life, death, and an international plot to kill the President of the United States. Countless lives were destroyed, and yet it was all covered up by the very historians who say they are the guardians of the truth!"

Vanessa was even more befuddled than she was when she entered the room. "Since when has history tried to cover up a plot to assassinate a President? What you're saying doesn't make sense. Every Presidential assassination attempt has been well documented...over and over and over again. "

"Not the plot to kill the most controversial President ever."

"Bush?"

"No my dear, there were others who have been unpopular in their time. None, however, more so than the sixteenth President Abraham Lincoln!"

"Lincoln?"

"Exactly! During Lincoln's presidency, the nation was at war with itself. North versus South. Brother against brother. There is also something else that troubles me about this message, which is why I believe there is more to it than meets the eye." Father Haynes added emphatically.

"What do you mean?' she questioned moving in, even closer.

"Like you," Father Haynes began, peering over his wire rimmed glasses, "Father Chiniquy had an insatiable sense of curiosity, and an *even more unfortunate* sense of timing. He was a former Catholic Priest who decided to take on the Vatican," Father Haynes continued, pointing at the blackboard. "Father Chiniquy," he said, "Is the man many believe to be *behind this! This is the one mystery not even you have unlocked."*

Vanessa looked at the blackboard, and aside from the paintings she had already studied over and over again, she saw nothing new and nothing that bore signs pointing to anyone named Chiniquy. "I don't get it......"

"And you would not be alone..." Father Haynes continued. "Father Chiniquy was *quite controversial in his time*. Depending on who you believe, he was either Lincoln's confidante, a man who fingered the *real men* behind Lincoln's assassination....or a *fraud!*"

"What does that have to do with any of the paintings behind you? Correct me if I'm wrong, but Abraham Lincoln wasn't anywhere near the signing of the Constitution."

Father Haynes continued. "No he wasn't, because like the historians who come and go, you see only what you wish to see. You are looking at the picture. Perhaps you should focus on the quotation above it." "*Look to the stone from whence you are sewn,*" Vanessa said reading it out loud as if by just reading the quote a vault of information would burst forth. It did not.

"The quotation is the first verse of the fifty first chapter of Isaiah, as it says beneath the quotation. In Isaiah, the writer was referring to *Abraham*...and his wife...*Sarah*. Those who read the verse often failed to read the following verses, and therefore walked away not knowing the *whole* story. In fact, the Bible says that *Abraham is the rock*. It is, if you will, *Biblical code*! It is the last mystery of the classroom. What does it mean?"

Vanessa smiled, in part due to the enthusiasm Father Haynes evoked, and in part due to her own fortune. She and she alone had been chosen to learn the last mystery. She was both enthralled and flattered. Father Haynes could tell.

"I knew you would like that! Like you, Father Chiniquy looked beyond the obvious and was never satisfied with the answers he was given. Unfortunately for him, he locked horns with the most powerful legislative body on earth at that time...The Vatican! You see...Father Chiniquy went so far as to finger *The Pope as the man responsible for Lincoln's assassination!*"

The puzzled look on Vanessa's face returned. "You lost me. I thought Lincoln's assassination had been solved? You know...John Wilkes Booth and all? "

"Look between the lines, Vanessa. Look between the lines. Where did Booth get his money? How did he get out of Washington so quickly? Where did he hide? Think about it Vanessa. We are talking about a man who had just assassinated the President of the United States, and yet one of his co-conspirators just disappeared and wound up Italy...at the Vatican!"

"The Vatican?!"

"Yes Vanessa, the Vatican! Chiniquy believed *The Vatican* was responsible for the *murder of Abraham Lincoln.* He challenged the traditional thought that Lincoln was killed by the crazed southerner John Wilkes Booth and looked at the larger picture. You see, he asked why? Why would Booth kill Lincoln knowing he would be caught and hung? Chiniquy believed there was more to the story. He was, if you will, a civil war conspiracy theorist."

"So what is the big mystery about Lincoln's assassination? John Wilkes Booth assassinated Lincoln in front of a packed theater. They had the man and the murder weapon, a small Derringer Pistol that is still on display inside Fords Theater."

"Is it?" Father Haynes questioned. "If you would check your history books, you might find that the FBI investigated the theft of the pistol in the late 1990s after it was stolen some three decades earlier. They *believe* they have the right gun now, but they're not really sure!"

"So why would someone steal the gun Lincoln was assassinated with?"

"That gun, my dear Vanessa would be priceless in the hands of a collector. It is also the most important piece of evidence in one of the biggest murder mysteries in our history, and yet when it disappeared, few blinked an eye!"

Vanessa rose from her seat and resumed her trademark pacing. "Gun or no gun, the only mystery, I can see, has to do with what Lincoln really accomplished while in office. I think that was the crime! Historians write that Lincoln freed the slaves, but did he? Vanessa questioned. "I think he was a cop out."

"And that, if I might be so bold, is part of *your problem*," Father Haynes answered. "You see everything in black and white, but ignore the shades of gray. You, like all historians, view history through your eyes. You think Lincoln should have done more and most people who only glance at history, do. The problem is, history never happens in a vacuum and always looks better in hindsight. Political campaigns, then, were no different then they are now.

We talk about Baron James being the first African American who might be elected President, but what do we really know about the man or the people who are trying the put him in office?" Father Haynes adjusted his glasses. "People back then, as is the case now, had agendas. Those people backed the candidate who they thought backed their cause. Lincoln was a man of honor, but he was also a *politician. That meant, contrary to history, he told lies.* Father Chiniquy was a priest, but if he had the ear of the President, he was *dangerous.* It's difficult for me to explain here. Let's go to my office. There are some things you need to see."

CHAPTER FOURTEEN

"THAT was a *close one*." Shaun Hinton was Captain Shaun Hinton, from the Metropolitan Police Department, and one of Matt's closest friends on the force. To his right, Cecilia, his wife who had been by his side since he had arrived at the hospital. "They got your wallet and seemed to want to take your life with it, as well. From the looks of those bruises on your hands, looks like you tried to fight back, but from the looks of the rest of you, looks like you lost. Somewhere out there is a person with a 'Matt Walker right' tattooed on his face, but I gotta tell you, this time *they* won."

"No, this time, you're *lucky*," Cecilia began. "What were you doing out so late anyway? I got worried waiting for you and called Shaun. That's when the call came in that they had found you in the alley, on the city's south side."

"But that's...."

"Right," Hinton chimed in, "a long way from Smitty's. Right after Cecilia called, I called Smitty, who then told me you left hours earlier." He continued as if for emphasis," the guys who did this to you were serious. Deadly serious! And you're lucky you're not dead."

Cecilia Walker began to sob softly. She knew the last few years had been difficult for her husband, but until that moment in time she had no idea how dangerous his life truly was. She knew he had never stopped looking for the next big scoop, and feared it would kill him in the process. Her husband was proud. Too proud, she believed, at times. He was also determined, willing to go to great lengths to get the next scoop and save his reputation.

"When can I get out of here?" Matt said, by way of interrupting his own funeral.

"The doctors say, with the exception of a few bruises and a nasty cut over your eye, you'll be fine," Hinton told him." Although I gotta tell ya...you look like shit."

"Battle scars, they'll love this on camera." Matt replied, trying to muster the cocky swagger that endeared him to police, but his sarcasm fell on deaf ears. As he continued trying to catch a glimpse of the scar in the mirror adjacent to his hospital bed, he could see Cecilia's face looking back at him. She was not happy.

"*That'll have to wait,*" Cecilia began. "I can't *believe* you are even thinking about going into the office. You belong to me and the kids, who you *also* scared to death! That damn station can have you later. For now, you're coming with me, and I don't want to hear any argument."

"Perhaps the noon show..."

"File...they have plenty of file tape on you," Cecilia insisted. Besides, the *drama* will do you good. The longer they wait, the more people will think you barely escaped death. But I'll warn you mister, if you even think about going to work, I'll kill you, myself!"

Matt loved that about his wife. Cecilia Walker was certainly much tougher than she let on. The truth was, she had been with him through his ups and downs, and today was no different. Every time he believed she wouldn't be there for him, she was. She, too, came from an environment that wanted her to fail, and quitting was no more a part of her vocabulary than it was, his. She would patch him up, pat him on his butt, and send him back out to conquer the world once more, but she would do it her way and in her own time.

"*Does she*?" Matt whispered to Captain Hinton, noticing that Cecilia was now carefully unpacking the fresh clothes she brought for him to change into, and preparing to throw away the clothes he had on the night before… bloodied and torn.

"Does she know you were drunk?" Hinton responded in a hush tone, as well. He then moved in closer with a stern gaze that let Matt know he meant business. "No, and I won't tell her, but you might want to lay off the sauce. You know there are lot of people out there that don't like your sorry ass as much as we do. What the..." Captain Hinton noticed Cecilia, hard at work, destroying the evidence of her husband's assault. "I'll take that Cecilia," he said interrupting her chores. "I believe we call that 'evidence'."

Talk of it being a crime caused the tears to form in Cecilia's eyes once again. "Of course," she said softly, "I'm just eager to get him out of here. You understand Shaun…don't you?"

"You know I do Cecilia. I know this must be hard on you."

Matt noticed his wife's hands were trembling. It was the sight of *his* blood on *his* shirt that brought home the narrowness of the call. He had seen it before. The victims of crimes were sometimes the lucky ones. They were often rendered unconscious, shortly after the attacks, and spared the agony of the pain, until recovery. The brain, he learned, had its own defense mechanism. Instead, it was the spouses who were often impacted the most. They were victims of their own imaginations with mental images of what the attacks must have been like. Sometimes they would awaken in the middle of the night crying. For others the images would lie suppressed for years, before returning with a vengeance.

"I'll be fine," Matt offered up, trying to comfort Cecilia. "Look at me." A forced smile led to an unpleasant grimace. Experience told him only time would heal both his wounds and hers. He didn't expect his body to betray him. "I just want to get home, and if you don't mind, back to work."

'You're 'FINE', all right," Cecilia quipped. "Need I remind you that to ME, **FINE** means **F**reaked-out, **I**nsecure, **N**eurotic, and **E**motional!" Cecilia seized the opportunity to clear the air about what she also believed was behind her husband's peculiar behavior. He had been distant in recent weeks…treating her and the children as if they were strangers. Sometimes he would stare for hours without saying anything. Always, he was staring at the TV. It's this damned election and that damned **Baron James!**

"There's something about him, Matt responded somewhat defensively. He knew he had been caught and as always, instinctively fought back. "Everyone thinks he's the second coming. I think he's a crook. I can just feel it."

"Well, he'll have to wait, too. Baron James…the station. They all can kiss my ass until you get better."

"Cecilia...I'm surprised at your tone…"

"Don't be. All of this has me quite pissed off!," she said with defiance in her voice.

Sadly, not even Cecilia believed Matt would wait. She had seen that look in her husbands' eyes before. She knew it wouldn't be long before he would heal and be back out there again, looking for something that would make him believe his instincts were correct. It wasn't about the story, she knew. It was about getting old and being right. Her husband needed to be 'right' to believe he wasn't getting old.

CHAPTER FIFTEEN

"VANESSA?" Father Haynes began. "History is filled with those gray areas. Think, Vanessa, think. Some believe Lincoln has reached out from the grave to influence history. When Martin Luther King delivered his famous "*I have a dream*" speech at the Lincoln Memorial, he, himself, admitted to dropping his prepared text and launching into a speech he had delivered days earlier"

"Dodododododo..." Vanessa said humming the tune to "The Twilight Zone."

"Be serious, if you would, for a moment," Father Haynes shot back. "The end result was one of the most important speeches of our time, and yet few ever question what caused him to alter his plans. History, it has been written, is one continuous lie told long enough to become the truth. It also pays little attention to what those of us in the world of faith would call...the spiritual side of history. Great men in history have always turned toward men of faith, sometimes to survive."

"And ministers pray before their sermons..."

"Exactly, Vanessa. That's exactly what I am saying. Father Chiniquy was a priest, a man of God who had the ear of the most important person of his time. That made him a double threat."

Vanessa found herself taking two steps to each of Father Haynes steps, just to keep up. She was amazed at how quickly he moved...and how short of breath she had become. "Again I ask, what does this have to do with my note from a person parading as Father Chiniquy?"

Father Haynes hesitated before answering, and then gestured toward his office, which was only a few feet further. "Patience, Vanessa, patience. In a moment you will see it has everything to do with Father Chiniquy...and the others just like him."

Like most graduate students, Vanessa knew Father Haynes had an office, but she had never ventured inside. There she saw walls lined with books, some young, but most of them old, in binders color coded like the colors of fall. There, on the shelves of Father Haynes office, she spotted the books that revealed he not only knew who Father Chiniquy was…He seemed to be obsessed with the man.

"Father Haynes slung his overcoat over a chair behind his desk, walked over to a set of aging books on his shelves and pulled out a dusty, yellowed volume entitled "*Fifty Years in the Church of Rome.*" He then handed the book to Vanessa. The book, like the one the girl was reading in the library, seemed well worn. Many of the pages were dog eared, and marked with paper clips. Many of the quotes, on the corresponding pages, were *highlighted.*

"Father Chiniquy was not only interested in Lincoln's life, he was *obsessed* with who wanted him dead. He wanted to know who killed our 16th President... *who killed Lincoln.* Like the most seasoned of investigative reporters, he followed the money and the money led...*to Rome.*"

Vanessa could see where Father Haynes was headed, but she had her own opinions. "*John Wilkes Booth killed Lincoln.* I read reports that Rome had something to do with it, but those reports have been downplayed by just about every historian since, much like the Kennedy assassination, I suspect. I'm sure that for every man who writes that there was some grand conspiracy, there is another scholar to disagree."

Father Haynes enjoyed the challenge. He liked to see his students think. "The truth is Vanessa, Father Chiniquy and Lincoln had a history that was grounded in fact. When Lincoln was a youthful lawyer, he defended Father Chiniquy in a court case. *Chiniquy was the defendant, Rome filed the charges.* The trial took place in Urbana, Illinois. In fact, a statue commemorating the event exists even today." Father Haynes, then, refocused his attention on the book." The book you are holding is one of the most controversial books of those times. Consider it a *"Da Vinci Code"* for the new republic. Chiniquy blamed the Catholic Church…and more specifically, the Pope, at that time...for Lincoln's assassination. *The Society of Jesus .had just been reinstated.* You know them as *The Jesuits*. Chiniquy believed Booth was just a pawn of a Papal conspiracy engineered by those very same people… *The Jesuits!"*

Vanessa interrupted, "But that's absurd, why would the Catholic Church want to assassinate Abraham Lincoln? It would seem that if anyone championed the cause of freeing the slaves, it would be a religious institution. I would think they would be on the same page in this controversy."

"Oh Vanessa, there is so much about our history we don't know that historians like to omit. Let's start with the facts. The Catholic Church...*owned slaves*…and backed *The Confederacy* during the war. This schools' colors, gray and blue, represent a conciliatory gesture on the part of this institution."

"I never thought about Georgetown during the Civil War."

"You see, Vanessa, history never happens in a vacuum. This was a Southern school at first, founded by the Catholic Church, and Rome made no secret of the fact that it backed the South. There are actually letters from the Pope to Jefferson Davis, the President of the

Confederacy, cheering them on...if you will. It made good economic sense." Father Haynes could see Vanessa needed more in the way of explanation. The doors of her curiosity had been opened and she was standing in the door. "Slavery, you see was quite profitable for many of the countries that were loyal to the church. *Those countries* had sizable investments in the South. The Catholic Church got caught with its *hands in the cookie jar.* If history is clear on any one subject...it is that Rome can never really *wash* its hands of past controversies."

"...Like the Jews following World War Two," Vanessa offered up.

"Exactly. Jews made the same argument about Rome in hiding the Nazis. If you look at American history during Lincoln's time, you will see for instance, why Father Healy kept his *true ethnic identity* hidden."

Vanessa seemed intrigued at what she was hearing, but she had long since stopped being surprised. "So are you saying that the Catholics had *a motive*?"

Father Haynes continued. "That is exactly what Chiniquy argued; they had two of the oldest motives in the book. He maintained, because there was *money and power* at stake, Lincoln's life was in jeopardy. The other issue was ego. The Pope believed *he* was *the ultimate authority.* He and others across Europe hated the Protestant movement in the States. It was like the other holy wars we have witnessed in recent years. Also, keep in mind those *rebellious Colonies* had just declared their independence."

"It sounds as if you're describing the American Civil War as if it were some sort of holy war?"

"It was; the split from Europe and the Protestant movement left a lot of Europeans angry...and even more importantly, broke. Chiniquy wrote in his book that he had no doubt the Pope had targeted Lincoln for death."

Vanessa picked opened the pages of Chiniquy's book and read a passage out loud:

"My dear Mr. President, I must repeat to you here what I said when at Urbana in 1856. My fear is that you will fall under the blows of a Jesuit assassin if you do not pay more attention than you have done, now, to protect yourself...My blood chills in my veins when I contemplate the day which may come, sooner or later, when Rome will add to all her other iniquities the Murder of Abraham Lincoln."

"There is something else, even more troubling," Father Haynes continued.

"And what could that possibly be?" Vanessa asked.

"Chiniquy writes that Lincoln underwent some sort of *spiritual transformation.* Lincoln, he writes, told him that freeing the slaves was an *act of God.* If you continue you will see the passages indicating just that."

"Here it is," Vanessa said, "*I made a solemn vow, before God, that if General Lee was driven back from Pennsylvania, I would crown the result by the declaration of the freedom of the slaves."*

Father Haynes shifted momentarily in his seat. "There is another factor historians like to ignore. Chiniquy was not alone."

"There were others?" Vanessa asked.

"One of the most famous anti-Catholics of the time was a man by the name of Samuel Morse, the man who invented the telegraph. Morse hated the Catholics, even though he favored slavery. He was part of a group that became known as the '*Know Nothings*'."

"Know Nothings," surely they had a better name."

" *The Know Nothings had quite the history.* First of all, they hijacked the *Pope's Stone!*"

"The *Pope's Stone?!*"

"Yes. As you know, or perhaps may not know, the Vatican sent a stone to Washington to be added to the Washington Monument. It became known as *The Pope's Stone*. The *Know Nothings* stole the stone, and are believed to have tossed it into the Anacostia River. It has not been seen since."

"Serves the Vatican right," Vanessa added by way of sarcasm.

"They also hijacked the construction of the Washington Monument!" Father Haynes continued. "When questioned about their activities, their first response was to always deny any knowledge of what they *actually knew*. They *knew nothing*. Some believe Morse and Chiniquy went one step further. Some historians believe they left behind clues as to who they really believed was behind Lincoln's death."

Vanessa was now searching Father Haynes eyes. She could tell he believed in what he was saying, and that her next question would be unwelcomed, but needed to be asked anyway. "Are you saying *you believe all this?*"

"I am a history teacher. I believe that which can be proven. History has shown that there are numerous secrets that have been left behind for future generations to unravel."

"Secrets?"

"Yes secrets, Vanessa. I have spent a lifetime studying many of the clues that some say were left behind, and I am more than just a little intrigued." Father Haynes added. "I know that Chiniquy was punished dearly for his writings, and continues to be, to this day, by those who say his writings are the works of a madman."

"So why should anyone care?" Vanessa asked.

"Because the truth...in this case...demands that we continue to ask questions. Take John Surratt, for instance. Mary Surratt, his mother, was hanged for her role in Lincoln's death, but John escaped to Canada and was spirited away to Europe."

"Let me guess," Vanessa interjected. "The conspirator you referenced who wound up in Rome."

"Yes, once there, he spent time as one of the *Papal Guards, a Zouave* , before finally being arrested in Egypt and returned to the United States. At the time of his return, America no longer had the stomach for the continuing the gut wrenching ordeal it had just gone through. Surratt walked away a free man."

Vanessa, then, remembered one of Father Haynes earlier homework assignments. Does this have anything to do with *"The Secret Treaty of Verona that we studied?"*

"I see you *were* paying attention," Father Haynes continued. "Following Lincoln's assassination, it was learned that a group referred to as the "*Holy Alliance,*" The Vatican, Prussia and others, drafted what became known as the *'The Secret Treaty of Verona.'* Remember, a government for the people and by the people meant no Kings or Popes. Some believe the "*The Secret Treaty of Verona,"* was a document giving the green light to assassinate those who stood in the way of such well established European traditions. The document proved to be so inflammatory, in 1916, it was actually entered into the Congressional Record, and the policy you know as the " *The Monroe Doctrine,*" was introduced.

"In fact," Vanessa added, "I read in our homework assignment that it was read in its entirety when it was placed into the Congressional Record.

"*The Monroe Doctrine,*" Father Haynes added, "made it an act of war if any European Nation sought colonial expansion in the Western Hemisphere."

"So it appears that Chiniquy may have had cause to be concerned about Lincoln's safety," Vanessa answered. "But what about Lincoln? Did he know, any of this?"

"Of course he did. Lincoln was a *brilliant man* who, many believed, was trapped by his circumstances. He was tasked with trying to keep the union together, free the slaves, and placate Europe at the same time. He had also survived assassination plots, one just down the road in Baltimore."

"Baltimore?"

"They tried to kidnap him. Chiniquy wrote Lincoln once and told him he knew he was going to die. I argue that some of Lincoln's most famous works were not meant to be taken literally, but instead were written in some sort of code."

Vanessa perked up. "You mentioned that once before. What type of codes?"

"The Emancipation Proclamation, for instance. It is no secret this document did little to actually free the slaves. Some historians believe it was intended to be more of an Emancipation Prophecy. Ironically, it was the 13th amendment that actually freed the slaves, but there was already a 13th amendment...one that made it unconstitutional for any type of nobility to be recognized. As for the "Gettysburg Address," is there a secret to the first four numbers, signaling an event that is yet to come? *Numerologists believe something is going to happen, and now is the time!*"

"Father Haynes! Clearly you don't believe there was some grand plan to hide clues for future generations?!" Vanessa was intrigued by what she was hearing, but not enough to believe that for some reason, the note she had just received was anything more than a coed prank.

Father Haynes could see the change in Vanessa's expression. At first, he was embarrassed, but realized, it was *she* who brought it up.

Someone wanted her to know who Father Chiniquy was. That someone had a reason. "You need to understand, when it comes to these matters there is little to laugh about. Father Chiniquy's life was ruined!" The disappointment in his voice was measurable. "Of all people, Vanessa, I expected you to be more understanding when it comes to history's omissions."

Vanessa wasn't ready to bite. "Aren't conspiracy theories, just that...theories?"

"Vanessa...do you remember your little demonstration with that two dollar bill? He was a real man. His name was John Hansen, he was black and a confidant of George Washington. Do you believe his image was added by mistake? "

Vanessa nodded in agreement.

"Have you ever looked into the many mysteries of its single digit predecessor, the one dollar bill?" Father Haynes stood again, and walked over the numerous books on his shelves. He pulled down several copies of newer books.

"Volumes, Vanessa, have been written on *The Great Seal* on the back of The One Dollar Bill, especially the number thirteen. If you have a dollar, follow with me."

Vanessa fumbled through her purse. There she found a crumpled up one dollar bill that was left as a tip from the night before.

"The most widely believed bed of knowledge, suggests that the number 13 had something to do with the thirteen colonies, but a closer examination of the bill reveals there are 13 letters in E Pluribus Unum and 13 Levels of stones in the pyramid shown. Take a look at the word Annuit Coeptis, it has 13 letters. Count the number of stars in the constellation above the eagle…the horizontal lines on the band on the top of the shield...olive leaves...berries...vertical strips...arrows held by the eagle and the list goes on and on. Notice the Roman numeral at the bottom, added up it comes to 26, two times the number 13. *Coincidence?* Let's talk DNA."

"DNA? They didn't have DNA back then," Vanessa added incredulously.

Father Haynes reached over and grabbed the dollar from Vanessa's hand. No, but they did have math. In a book entitled *The Secret Geometry of the Dollar,* a man by the name of Ken McGrath writes that the measurements of the dollar represent what *The Da Vinci Code describes as De Divinia Proportiona*. . . or the golden ratio. The same ratio is found in art, nature, including the number of spiral patterns in pine cones and seashells, and DNA."

"Okay, you've proven your point when it comes to money, but what does this have to do with Father Chiniquy and Lincoln and I hate to say it even more importantly, me?' Vanessa asked.

"I don't know," Father Haynes added, but I wouldn't take these matters lightly.

"You act as if this is something serious." Vanessa countered.

"It is...it is..." Father Haynes continued. "It seems both Lincoln and Chiniquy left a trail of bodies behind them. Lincoln's were so numerous, some called it the Lincoln curse."

Vanessa shuffled in her chair, uneasily, "and Chiniquy?'

Once again the expression on Father Haynes face was grim. "He had an associate who traveled to Africa, but he died not long after his arrival in the country, from disease. There was said to be another, a priest, who lived to a ripe old age. The priest established a school in a remote region of the country that was said to have taught hundreds, but in the end, he died as well."

"Disease?" Vanessa asked.

"No," Father Haynes began, "his fate was man made...*murder*. When rebels seized the capital of the country in a bloody coup,

Chiniquy's associate was *executed by firing squad.* There was no trial, or for that matter, any indication why the students he taught, suddenly turned on him. Our own government was suspected. To add insult to injury, they *burned the school complex to the ground!"*

CHAPTER SIXTEEN

MAX Webb spent several moments staring at the phone that sat on the desk in his office. He knew Prescott Marshall all too well. He knew it would only be a matter of time before the people in the photos, the girl, and the others were dead. His mind raced, trying to figure out how Prescott Marshall would go about killing a man who was about to be elected President. He, then, thought about himself.

Webb knew better than most that photos had a way of backfiring. He thought about the polls. Had they been manipulated? Was he being set up for a possible suicide that followed an even longer bout of depression? Was Prescott behind the photos that almost derailed *his* campaign just weeks earlier? Those photos taken at a Klan rally in the fifties had somehow been enhanced to reveal his presence. He had always believed it was Baron James who leaked the photos, but why? James was already ahead in the polls and the photos actually had the reverse effect on his campaign. Southern conservatives relished the fact that their candidate might have belonged to the Klan. Instead of alienating voters, it solidified his base.

Moderates in the media called the episode a dirty trick, not fit for modern politics. Things couldn't have gone better had he planned it himself. His darkest political moment had turned into one of his greatest political triumphs. That is when a warm rush of blood began flowing to his head. Now it was a different set of photos. This time the photos were of Baron James. Clearly, everyone would believe he leaked them.

"That bastard, that lousy bastard!" The thought caused Webb to leave his desk and beat a quick path to the cabinet of liquor he kept on the other side of the room. There he filled a small crystal glass with a healthy dose of scotch, followed by two ice cubes that made an awkward clanking sound as if they knew in advance the order had been broken. "Of course...that's it! I'll be blamed for the photos…and the girls death. I'll be blamed for blackmailing Baron James, in retaliation for, what most believed, he did to me. He's done it. Prescott has cut a deal with the James campaign to deliver my head on a platter."

"You are not the only one who knows how to play this game, Mr. Marshall. I assure you, I am better at it than you think."

Scotch in hand, Max Webb soon placed the glass beside the phone, and pressed the last button to the right. The one that summoned his secretary.

"Betty?"

"Yes, Senator."

"I need you to make a phone call for me."

"Sure Senator, who should I place the call to."

"Please place it to Matt Walker."

"Should I try to contact him at home?" the response came back.

"No, just reach him at his office," the Senator replied.

"Senator, you really need to watch the news more often. The poor devil was almost beaten to death last night. All reports say he is recuperating at home and will return to work sometime next week."

"Next week will be too late," Max thought to himself. "You'd better try to reach him at home," he instructed his secretary.

"I'll bet you your last dollar, you're the last person he'll want to hear from," Betty responded.

"Just dial the number Betty, please, just dial the number."

CHAPTER SEVENTEEN

CECILIA Walker had been taking calls all day. It was both uplifting and exhausting. Uplifting, because neither she nor her husband, realized how many friends they had. Exhausting, because the phone never stopped ringing. As she reached down to take it off the hook, it rang, again.

"This is the last call," she said picking up the handset once more.

"Please hold for Senator Max Webb," the caller on the other side began.

"I don't think my husband is up for any more calls today," Cecilia answered before being interrupted.

"Cecilia...this is Betty..."

"Oh hi Betty..."

Betty could tell from the chilly response on the other end, the call was not welcomed. "I told the Senator he would be the last person your husband would want to talk to today..."

"I am certain you informed your boss correctly," Cecilia said protectively. "The last time he trusted your boss, it almost cost him his career, and I'm still not sure how much it damaged his ego."

"There is more to that story than you know," Betty countered.

"There always is," Cecilia replied," there always is."

"The senator insisted he speak to your husband, Cecilia. And to be perfectly honest, I've never seen him acting so strangely."

"Perhaps it has to do with the fact he is trailing, miserably, in the polls?"

"No, honestly, I don't believe that bothers him as much as people think. It's almost as if he knows the outcome of the election before the votes are counted."

"That would be typical for the Republican Party these days, now wouldn't it?"

"Touché, Cecilia, touché..."

"Hold on Betty, I'll get Matt, if he'll take the call." With that, there was only silence and the sound of footsteps making their way to the other side of the room where Matt was comfortably reclining, in front of the TV, watching reports about his own demise.

"Matt Walker."

"Matt," the voice on the other end responded.

Matt knew instantly who it was. "I can't be that hurt that a Presidential candidate stops campaigning to wish me well, so what is it?"

"No, it's not that at all, but I should say I was horrified at the reports of your injuries. You're a lucky man, Matt Walker, a very lucky man."

"You mean lucky to be gainfully employed, don't you?" Matt said cutting through any layers of formalities that still had not yet been carved away. "Let's just cut to the chase. You want something or you wouldn't be calling. And need I remind you the last time..."

"Let me explain, Matt. By not publishing those photographs, you saved my career. A man of your stature would have ruined me."

Matt interrupted the senator in mid sentence, "But the simple fact is, the photos *were* published. Not by me, but by my competition, leaving me with a lot of egg on my face and a lot of explaining to do to my editors."

"Matt, I need your help!"

There was a change in the Senator's tone. Almost as if he had resigned himself to some awful truth. Matt knew powerful men never asked for help. When things were bad, they let others do battle for them. Max Webb was one of those men.

"You make it sound as if this is a matter of life and death," Matt responded.

"I assure you, *it is,*" he answered. He wanted to explain, in detail, how many lives were on the line, but he knew that would only open the door to further questions. Questions he was not prepared to answer.

Matt had heard it all before. Politicians always needed something and never offered anything in return. "So why not call the police?"

This time there was a condescending tone in Max Webb's voice, "Matt, you know the police are blind to problems of power. I would not have called you if I didn't think you and only you could help...but obviously I thought wrong...."

Matt interrupted the Senator in mid-sentence, "Wait a minute Max," he continued dropping any pretense of formalities, "whatever it is, it must be serious or you wouldn't have called me at home. I can hear it in your voice."

"Perhaps I can explain." Max then proceeded to tell Matt as little as possible, but just enough to keep him curious. "Soon, you will receive a list of names. You won't know where it came from and you won't recognize most of the names. All I am asking is for you to take a look at the list and do what you do best. That's all. Just look at it."

"There's no harm in looking," Matt replied. "If it's as serious as you think, perhaps this list is worth just a quick glance!"

Max knew the hook sat well within the jaw of his journalistic friend. "I assure you," he began, drawing out each word as if to magnify the significance, "this may very well be the one story, not even *you,* will be able to walk away from."

"Seeing is believing," Matt said, as he calmly placed the phone on the receiver, "seeing is believing."

The call on the other end of the line was now dead. Max Webb knew it had fallen on deaf ears. Undeterred, he reached down and grabbed the envelope he had so carefully prepared and placed Matt Walker's name on it.

"Betty, please have this delivered, by hand, and make sure the messenger sees to it that Matt Walker receives it." Lifting his finger off the intercom, he waited patiently for Betty to enter the office. He admired her loyalty, and knew she also chose to see the best in him.

Cecilia walked across the room and, once again, saw her husband sitting on the sofa, the phone back on the receiver. "What did the Senator have to say?"

Matt had that 'seen it all before look on his face'. "Global conspiracy theories, changing the course of history, death and destruction, you know the same old stuff. I also think the Senator was quite tanked!"

"So what are you going to do?"

"Sleep, I need some sleep!"

CHAPTER EIGHTEEN

THE young associate was told to wear blue jeans and look no different than a teenager roaming the local mall. Inside his backpack, he carried one of the most important documents of the twentieth century. He was told to look for *people who looked suspicious.* He was told to anticipate problems. Glancing at his watch, he knew the time was nearing. Soon he would walk through those doors and change history. He chose to take a seat on a park bench located directly across from the building that left no secret as to why it was there.

FEDERAL COURTHOUSE
U.S. DISTRICT COURT
WHEELING, WEST VIRGINIA

Wait until almost five o'clock. Then wait until the woman with the red coat leaves through the front doors. He was told that the others inside the massive building would wait until she left, before leaving themselves for the weekend. Then he was told he would have a total of five minutes, tops, to file the papers. *Others will be watching.* He heard the words over and over again. He was not told about the contents of the envelope, and wouldn't have understood the wording anyway.

He only knew the papers were important, and he was being paid a substantial amount of money to walk through that lobby.

Marcell Peterson walked through the doorway of the courthouse at exactly 4:55 PM. There were guards in the entrance who watched him closely. One stood to the right of a metal detector. The other was on the left hand side, holding a tray. He knew the drill.

"Any keys or other metal objects?" the armed guard inquired. He was wearing a dark blue shirt with a white patch on the outside and fancy gold stitching that read, "U.S. MARSHALLS SERVICE."

You mean, hand over your gun, Peterson thought, causing the slightest of smiles to pierce his usually stoic face.

"Then walk through the metal detector. Those jeans could be a problem."

Do you mean they might set off the metal detector, or that they are hanging too low beneath my waist? Truth be known, yours ain't hanging to high. He stopped his thoughts from wandering to watch, as his backpack, with the massive envelope inside, made its way through the metal detector, on top of the conveyor belt. The other officer, examining its contents, paused the belt, as if something was wrong.

Peterson glanced at his watch. 4:58pm. *The papers **have** to be filed today. They **must** be filed by close of business!*

The guard on the other side of the machine was now summoning his partner. "Larry, take a look this!"

Marcell knew the drill. They would act like they saw something and he was supposed to act like he was hiding something. They did it in his school all the time. *These guys act like the drop out boys.* The drop out boys were former cops who believed all young black men, like him, were guilty of some type of crime. They would throw students up against the wall and then act like something dropped out of their pants when they were being frisked. Perfectly innocent young men, then, found themselves in the cross hairs of a judicial system that viewed anything young and black as trouble...and guilty. Brilliant students suddenly wound up on the other end of the law.

Larry and the other guard waited for what seemed like an eternity before realizing Marcell wasn't biting. They, too, had learned not to push too far. Preppy students at the private schools were getting off by dressing like the *street thugs.* Some of those preppy students had fathers who were lawyers.

4:59pm. The clock was ticking.

Marcell's heart was starting to race. He knew that if he didn't act soon, all would be lost. The men told him the only way he was going to be paid was if the papers made it to their destination on time. Marcell had to do something and he had to do something fast.

Think! Damn it...think. Eyeing another young man, in a shirt and tie, walking down the hallway, he acted as if he knew the young man, raising his hand in a friendly wave. The other man, not wanting to appear rude, raised his hand and waved back, passing with a blank expression on his face as if to say *do I know you?*

Satisfied that the man before them was not a terrorist, or for that matter, a street thug, the guard handed Peterson his knapsack and permitted him to pass.

"Clerks office?" Marcell asked.

The man named Larry appeared to do all of the speaking. "Just down the hall to the right, but you'd better hurry! Oh, too bad," the guard added sarcastically. "It looks like we're closed!" "Not quite closed yet!" A gray haired man wearing a worn sweater, that looked like he wore it everyday, interrupted, the street cop celebration. "Not quite!" he said looking at Marcell and searching his face carefully. "Follow me young man. I'll take you where you need to go."

Marcell hastily slung the knapsack over his shoulder and followed the man down a long narrow hallway. The faces of past and present judges lined both sides of the hallway. He noticed most of the faces were white, and then as if overnight, the faces changed. The hue of the black skinned faces darkened with each footstep. At first the city was under colonial rule and all of the faces of the appointed officials were white. They looked like overseers on a government plantation. With "Home Rule," the faces changed. "Home Rule," allowed the District's blacks to govern themselves.

"Those men play us for fools," The man in the sweater remarked. "I watched you from the landing. Knew they'd give you grief. "

Marcell had been told to expect problems, but no one told him there might be a friendly face inside the building. This man represented the unexpected.

"One of the things you have to understand about the Federal system, is there are two systems. One for *them* and one for *us,"* the man in the sweater continued. "I've been clerking here since those faces were white." He noticed Marcell's attention had shifted once again to the faces on the wall. "First time in a federal courthouse?"

First and hopefully last, Marcell thought to himself. "Yes sir," was the answer that came from his mouth.

"These places can seem quite intimidating," the man in the sweater said. "Like any other business, there are *rules* and there are *rules. Rules for us and rules for them."*

Marcell knew what was happening. He had seen it before in the supermarkets when he was a little boy. His mother would pay for a pound of beef, but two pounds would come back. Or sometimes, he would notice as the man behind the counter reached into his pocket to pull out the money needed for the balance of the bill. They would look at each other, nod, and then she would be on her way. He wondered whether this was one of those times.

The man, in the sweater, reached inside his right pants pocket, and produced a set of keys. There appeared to be twenty two keys on the ring, but only one with a piece of tape attached to it holding a small white piece of paper in place. He inserted the key into the lock, and opened the door to a room that appeared to be vacant. The sign, in black letters, on the glass paneled door, simply stated, 'CLERKS OFFICE'.

Once through the door, the man in the sweater turned on the lights and walked behind a counter where he turned and faced Marcell, and asked politely, "Was there something you needed to file?"

Marcell glanced at the clock on the wall. It was now 5:05pm. *It was too late. He was not going to be paid!*

Noticing the panic on his young face, the man in the sweater reached down and opened the top of a small machine located to the right of the counter. He then reached up, as if to scratch his head, and produced a small government issued pen. Using the tip of the pen, he manipulated the numbers on the inside of the machine, to read: 4:59. "I can make it sooner, if you would like."

Marcell smiled and handed the man the large envelope. He could see the man's eyes follow his hand as he pulled it from inside the backpack. It was almost too heavy to hold with one hand, but he managed to do so.

"I suppose you typed this by yourself?" the man in the sweater asked. He then placed the first two pages of the document into the machine he had just been fumbling with. A loud stamp sound followed, and the man did the same thing to the last two pages. A second loud stamp sound followed. He then scribbled something on a piece of paper, affixed his signature and handed the paper to Marcell.

"The people who sent you here will want this. By the way, tell your grandmother, I said hi."

Marcell, reached out and took the paper from the man's hand, and for the first time realized where he had seen him before. He sat in the pews on the right side of the church. They sat on the left. He has seen his grandmother talk to him before and after services. He still had no idea *what was inside the envelope he had just delivered.* All he knew was that he was going to be *paid!*

CHAPTER NINETEEN

"WASHINGTON will be on line, in five...four...three...two...one..."

The massive television screen was split into fifteen different sections and cast an eerie bluish glow on the ancient mahogany paneled walls. No sound came from the TV, as each panel displayed the same word. Each set was on MUTE. Above the room, frescos, that were painted by the masters, adorned the ceiling in the bright colors of the Renaissance. The parquet floor announced any visitors long before they reached the desk of Cardinal Louis Boucher. Boucher was the Vatican's *"Black Pope,"* because his vestments matched his title and temperament. He was the head of the *Secret Society of Jesus,* better known by the modern day moniker, *The Jesuits.* Boucher watched intently, as one by one, each dark quadrant of the TV monitor came to life. Two feeds were from Washington, one from England, three from France, and the others represented the private members of *The Consortium.*

"Good evening, Prescott."

"And good evening..." Prescott answered, before checking his watch and realizing the time difference, "I mean...afternoon to you, *Your Excellency.* Are the other members present?"

One by one, the others on line responded in the affirmative.

"I didn't hear Max."

"I assure you, I am listening, Prescott, although there is a vote that demands my attention on the floor of the Senate, so I am keeping both eyes on the TV."

"It can wait. We have more pressing matters to attend to."

Boucher, speaking with a thick French accent, agreed. "I believe…whatever...your... legislation might be, it pales in comparison to matters we will discuss."

"The fax is being transmitted," Prescott offered up.

Down the hall in Room 142, the priest, huddled over a printer, was there to receive it. "*Jesus Christ*! Could this printer possibly be any slower?" Father Giovani Antonelli cursed the machine and then cursed himself for his latest sin. "Forgive me Father, but one would think The Vatican could afford a decent copier," Antonelli was looking *upwards* and praying God was looking *elsewhere*.

Father Antonelli came from a long line of priests who made the forty mile commute to the Vatican each day, from the tiny Italian city of Velleteri. His brothers were priests, as was his father, and father's, father. Velleteri, itself, had no distinguishing characteristics, save one. Velleteri was the city that once played host to the American, John Surratt.

Surratt stood accused of being the mastermind behind the assassination of President Abraham Lincoln, and joined the *Papal Zouave*, or guard, in Velleteri, upon his escape from the United States. Like most youth, Father Antonelli marveled at how history forgot those things he found most fascinating. He studied, endlessly, the Vatican's role in hiding Surratt, and wondered why American historians glossed over that chapter in their history.

"He was a Papal Guard! The man believed to have been the mastermind behind the assassination of an American President, hiding out in the Vatican, and no one questioned why?" "Three hundred, twenty

three pages so far, that means there are still twenty three more to go. The Cardinal will have my head on a platter!"

Antonelli mused at the saga of how Washington expressed its anger at the Vatican during the construction of the Washington Monument. "*The Pope's Stone was stolen*. The...what is the word... *The Know Nothings*...They threw it in the river. They knew how Rome viewed your country. And *The Rome Stone* faired no better. He even found himself laughing, as the copies came in, at the irony of the stone being shipped overseas on a boat piloted by a *Captain Lincoln.* Antonelli burst out laughing, and then contained himself, when he thought of what happened to the Pope who was in Rome when Lincoln was assassinated. "*They threw the body of Pope Pius, IX, into the Tiber River.*"

Privately, Antonelli admired The Colonies, that, many, inside the Vatican, still referred to as the United States. He spent hours studying the American books on the Civil War. Rome, he discovered in his readings, aligned itself with the South during the war, because it had invested millions in their war effort. But they did not know his *Uncle Giuseppe*.

Giuseppe Garibaldi, one of the greatest patriots in all of Italy, had been considered by Lincoln to lead the Union troops, but instead, he selected General Ulysses S. Grant. Five years after the end of the Civil War, and Lincoln's death, *Garibaldi returned to free the Papal States from Rome*. Fewer still knew that *Giuseppe Garibaldi* was Antonelli's great, great uncle, and his greatest source of pride. It was his Italian connection to The Colonies.

The copier chugged on at a speed that betrayed, even, *its* aging software.

Antonelli had been instructed, never to read anything that came into the Vatican. The documents were *not for his eyes*, he was told time and time again, and yet he found it impossible not to examine their contents. At twenty three, he was one of the few in the Vatican who knew the inner workings of the Internet and would often plug in different bits of information on the pages of bloggers. He knew that the pages, that were clearing the copier, would be welcome news to *conspiracy buffs.*

325...326...327...one by one the pages printed out, line by line, each of which was being scanned by Father Antonelli. The more he read, the more disturbed he became.

"History does repeat itself. These men are planning murder," he mumbled as the pages continued to fall off the printer. "*Oh, but we are sinister men, indeed.*"

344...345...346... *"Finally."*

As he read the last page silently to himself, he was too stunned to continue. A vow of silence was his oath to God, but these men were planning something very sinister, indeed. He would have to do something. He did not know what.

The sound of Father Antonelli's thick black soles, combined with the rustling sound of his vestments, echoed through the hollow halls of the Vatican. Each footstep seemed to be louder than the last. The soft light, that lined the hallways, caused his shadow to appear gigantic against the ancient plastered walls. There was history in this building, and Antonelli knew that once the documents were delivered, history would be made once more. It was *not* the type of history he enjoyed reading. He could tell from the pages he read, someone would die because of what had been copied. *The list of names that comprised the last two pages solidified his views.*

"Do you have the copy?"

"Yes, *Your Excellency,* I do." Antonelli's Italian was as thick as his waistline, although his command of the English language was without question. He spoke five tongues, each without the slightest bit of his native Italian seeping through.

"Was the communiqué secure?"

"It was... *Your Excellency*. No eyes fell upon these documents from the time they were transmitted, to the time they reached your hands, not even my own."

"Merci... Father, You *have served me well*, you are free to leave."

Antonelli's footsteps could be heard, once again, as he left the Cardinal's chambers. He could not help but look at the frescoes that were painted above and marvel at the handcrafted wood paneling.

"The outside world must be told of what I have learned tonight. This information cannot remain hidden!" Father Antonelli tightened the belt to his vestments, and closed the giant door behind him. The door closed with a tremendous **thud** that drowned out all other sounds, including those of his heavy feet.

Sitting behind his desk, Cardinal Boucher examined the document, as the others watched from their secure lines and offices. After a few brief moments, he spoke.

"Que ce que? Ce n'est pas possible!" It was clear, from the tone of his voice, Boucher was troubled by something he saw.

"Oh I assure you, *it is very possible*, Your Excellency. I sense you see why I summoned this meeting..." Prescott answered. One by one, he could see the faces of the others nod in agreement, on the massive display inside his offices on Connecticut Avenue. A smaller screen sat on the desk of Senator Max Webb. Each had been faxed the same copy Cardinal Boucher was looking at. One by one, their expressions revealed they, too, realized the gravity of the situation.

Meanwhile, Father Antonelli was scanning his copy of the documents as he hurried down the hallway. He stopped at page one hundred fifty three. *They are quoting from Humani Generis Unitas, all men are created equal. They are quoting from the encyclical of Pope Pius XI, before he died. He wrote the document to protest Germany's treatment of the Jews. Wasn't he poisoned?"*

"These, *noms*...er...names," Cardinal Boucher continued. "They are...who?"

Prescott pressed the key to the intercom once more. "They are the people we must take care of."

"And by take care of, I assume you mean to..."

"Yes, Cardinal, they will be dealt with *in the appropriate manner.*"

"Good!" A third party entered the conversation. Baron Schneider was one of the wealthiest men in Europe. At first his family made a fortune in the slave trade. They then became merchants of death. The top arms salesmen in all of Europe. The call was originating from his castle in Scotland. "My firm, alone, stands to lose billions, if this case makes its way through the courts. I thought we were done with this *ordeal* long ago!"

Cardinal Boucher replied. "*L'histoire*, history, does have a way of rearing its ugly head, now and again. Who, among us, could have conceived such a science as...how do you say it, Prescott?...*genetics?"*

"I believe the operative word here, *Your Excellency*, is DNA. It is DNA that gives this lawsuit its *gravitas*. If you will, *Your Excellency*, you killed the head, but it is *the body of the snake* that has come back to bite us all."

Max Webb listened intently to the conversation. He knew the direction it was taking and did not like what he was hearing. He also knew, that to disagree with the members of *The Consortium*, meant something he was also not prepared for. Those who disagreed with *The Consortium* usually wound up dead.

Cardinal Boucher rose to address the others on the feed; "*Nous sommes d'accord* on *dis* matter." His eyes scanned the video feeds. He saw everyone present was nodding in agreement. No words would be spoken. Words always made things messy. He knew there would be no dissent. There rarely was. One by one, the bluish video screens went dead, until Cardinal Boucher was standing alone in his dimly lit chambers. *"I like that...the snake...has come back to bite the head. We shall see...Mr. Marshall...we shall see."*

Outside the gates of the Vatican, Father Antonelli looked into his rear view mirror to see if he was being followed. Spotting no one, he reached into a dingy leather bag he kept with him at all times, and thumbed through the other pages of the document he had just copied. *"They can't be allowed to get away with murder again. They must be stopped, and I, just like my uncle, will come to the rescue of the Americans."* He gunned the engine of the tiny Fiat and the car lurched forward. Glancing back into his rearview mirror, he noticed that the pair of headlights that were with him when he had left the Vatican was getting larger. The tiny Fiat navigated the narrow streets in and around The Vatican, as if the man behind the wheel had a different Italian name. Mario Andretti. The headlights, in the mirror, were getting bigger and bigger, and the car coming closer and closer.

The man in the car, however, was not trying to run Father Antonelli off the road; he just wanted to get close. A small piece of plastic explosive had been placed under the gas tank of Father Antonelli's car. Once in range, the detonator would be triggered. The explosive, combined with the tank, conveniently topped off, would more than do the trick. The trigger was a small transmitter on the back of Father Antonelli's watch. It was a gift from Cardinal Boucher. It was too small to be triggered from a distance. It would not survive the explosion.

Cardinal Boucher, saw the explosion from the room of his chambers. "A pity, Father. These walls have eyes. *The snake...although we prefer the serpent...is still very much alive."*

CHAPTER TWENTY

MAURICE Lacroix cleared customs in New York as Grebo Barclay, a career diplomat, based out of the U. S Embassy in Liberia, who, according to his passport, was no stranger to travel or to the U.S.

"Business or pleasure, Mr. Grebo?" The customs officer questioned.

"Grebo…as if you were saying a gray bow," he responded, as if he had said it a thousand times, when in fact he had actually rehearsed it over and over again in the tiny room of the house on the outskirts of Monrovia. "A little of both," he added. For once he was being honest. He enjoyed the travel, but hated the job ahead. Killing was never easy, but the fact he never knew the mark made it all worthwhile. Besides, it was the only way he could protect "her."

"Your bags will be waiting for you on the other side."

"Thank you Mrs..."

"Ms. Smith, or Cindy," she said politely with a smile. "It's my pleasure. Do you mind if I ask a question?"

"No, shoot."

"What is Liberia like? I mean, all we ever hear about is the war."

"The scars are there," he began, "the city has no lights or running water, but the land is as beautiful as it was when the first freed slaves settled there more than a century ago. Besides, for some of us, it is still home."

"And that is where the heart is."

"It is, indeed." It was amazing how quickly he left Maurice Lacroix behind and became Grebo Barclay. Grebo Barclay was his alter ego. He was educated and sophisticated. He spoke with a slight accent that added an air of sophistication. Soon, however, it would be time for Grebo Barclay to leave and the Gray Ghost to reappear. He had but one more connection to make. Global flight 267 to Raleigh, North Carolina.

The flight to Raleigh took less than three hours. Enough time to catch up on some badly needed rest, and enough time to map out a strategy. Prescott told him *the mark* was in a remote location. He warned that the woman would put up a fight, but said there would be no one to hear the struggle. Exiting the site would be easy, as long as no one saw him enter. He was told to arrive late, and leave between the shifts of the local sheriffs' deputies, who had a tendency to drop by, unannounced.

The rental car was at the airport in the name of Grebo Barclay, who was in town to meet with local representatives interested in economic issues. No such meetings were planned. Instead, he would follow the mapped out instructions located inside the dash, taking the highway out of town, past Carey, and into what, for years, had been called T*obacco Road.*

He followed the directions to the letter…Taking Avent Ferry Road, out of Raleigh, to where civilization ended. It didn't take long. The endless parade of pine trees made the ride monotonous and yet, pleasant. He enjoyed escaping civilization for the country. It reminded him of home.

Forty minutes later, he was looking for county road 212, where he would turn right onto a dirt road. The trailer would be the last on the end, down the road, less than quarter of a mile. He steered the car down the road that separated the newer trailers from what could only be described as the trash. It quickly became clear *Shady Acres* was anything but that. As was usually the case, there was little, in the way of shade, during the normally sweltering North Carolina summers. He could hear the flow of water, and was certain that when daybreak came, he would spot a stream flowing behind it. Trailer parks were always located on or near flood plains. Tornadoes found them naturally. *It was God's curse on the poor.*

The light outside was amber, in tone, the type used to keep away mosquitoes. There, Susan Sullivan would be inside, awaiting her next customer.

Susan Sullivan made a living on her back. She had a steady stream of clients ,and a few would venture out, for their first time, from the local colleges and universities. She was strategically located close to the University of North Carolina, Duke University and North Carolina State. Her best time of year was when the local fraternities pledged. Often times she would cut them a discount. She was used to unexpected knocks at her door. She was not ready for what happened next.

The response to his knock on the door went as scripted, as well.

"Come in," she said in a voice that left little doubt why so many men found her instantly attractive.

"Mrs. Sullivan?" Lacroix inquired.

"I've been waiting for you," she said softly, fluffing the pillows on the bed as if she were the black widow she had been accused of being. The look of horror on her face revealed that the man standing in the doorway was no ordinary customer.

Lacroix knew the line had been well rehearsed, as she couldn't have known who was waiting on the other side of the door. He knew she could not have expected what was to come next.

There she stood, her body silhouetted by the light of a lamp in the other room. Even in the dim light in that trailer, he could see she was different. He could see the outline of a woman men would lust after. He could see her skin. At first glance, it seemed flawless.

Her skin had an olive appearance to it, as if she vacationed, daily, in the Caribbean sun. It was perfectly tanned, but not burned. Her long dark hair perfectly framed a face that was almost haunting in appearance. Her body betrayed her age. It showed no traces of fat or cellulite. He had never seen such a woman. It was a pity he had been sent there to kill her.

"Please come in so I can see you, don't be *shy*." It was now obvious to Lacroix she considered him to be just another of her many customers. Lacroix turned and bolted the door behind him, and then revealed the contents of the pouch that had made its way across an ocean. The ceremonial knife was clearly visible, even in the low lights of the trailer.

"If it's money you want, I'll give you everything I have." It was clear the knife had been spotted. It was also clear she had no idea why he was there. This was a woman who had many enemies. She would spend the last moments of her life trying to determine which one killed her.

Lacroix said nothing. Instead, he began moving, ever so slowly, toward his prey. They moved like dancers, both knowing the end result. She was looking for an exit, and he was looking for the quickest way to finish the task.

"Please don't hurt me," Sullivan uttered as she made her way toward the corner of the room. There, edging along the way, she found what she was looking for. It was never far from her reach and had been used before. It was a Louisville slugger that had been used to ward off more than one stranger. It was about to be used again. But as she raised it, she felt the warm flow of blood enter the recesses of her mouth. Her blood had an unmistakable salty taste, and yet she was at a loss to explain how anyone could move so fast. She barely had time to raise the bat when the knife entered her midsection. But she was not about to go down without a fight.

"*If you don't struggle, I can make this almost painless.*"

"Who sent you?" She inquired, barely able to stay on her feet. "Why?"

There was no mistaking the second entry point of the knife. It was located just beneath her sternum, and he was not letting go. That is when Susan Sullivan lashed out with what was left of her strength. Sharp fingernails found their mark inside Lacroix face, causing him to recoil, but all the while keeping the knife intact.

"*I told you not to struggle.*" He said angrily pushing the knife deeper into the woman's chest cavity. It was as if he was gutting a deer, but in this case the prey was a woman. A woman, who just hours earlier had been entertaining frat boys, would soon be dead. "I was told to give you a message, but to wait until *the moment before your death.*"

Lacroix pulled the knife out of the wound and watched the woman collapse to the ground, writhing in pain. He walked over to the side of the room and located a light switch, where he turned on the room's only source of normal illumination. There, standing in the soft light of a forty watt bulb, in a broken lamp, was the last face Susan Sullivan would ever see. The horrible visage of a man whose skin was colored completely gray and eyes as red as any coals produced by the hottest of fires. Maurice Lacroix was the gray ghost once more. *The Vashti* had accomplished his task.

A gurgling sound signaled the end for Susan Sullivan was near. She had fallen next to the Louisville slugger that never found its mark. The light revealed the contents of the room that would serve as her grave...a soiled carpet and sofa that had seen better days...a night stand that originated in a discount furniture outlet, and the bed that had entertained so many. In a strange sense, death almost appeared to be welcomed. After all, it would deliver her from the hellish life she had come to accept as norm, the life of a common whore.

"*There is one other thing*," Lacroix said as he turned to make his way toward the door. Making sure her eyes were opened, at just the right moment, he uttered the words that would haunt her last few moments of life. He uttered the words that would signal why he was there, why this was no ordinary robbery. He uttered the words that left no doubt as to why he was sent. *"Vanessa is next."*

Susan Sullivan then made a blood curdling sound no words could ever describe. It was the sound of a mother mourning her own death, and that, of her daughter at the same time. She believed it to be so loud, everyone, for miles, would hear it. But in truth, there was little or no sound at all, just the pathetic sight of a pathetic woman, dying alone.

Stooping to wipe the blood from the blade of his knife, Lacroix then did as he was told. First he positioned the woman's hands as he was instructed to do.

"I had to break them to get it done. The sound was horrible. I vow, this day, to never talk about the rest of what I have done here... this day!"

Walking calmly to the car, he retrieved the gas can from the trunk, and emptied its contents inside the trailer. A single match caused the trailer to burst into flames, consuming the sofa, the rug and Susan Sullivan along with it. Calmly walking back to the rental car, he turned the key that had never the left the ignition, reached inside the glove box, took out the wipes that would remove any vestiges of *The Vashti*, and then placed the knife back inside it's pouch.

An hour later, Grebo Barclay would be resting comfortably in bed, at the Red Coat Hotel, room 342. As far as anyone was concerned, he was holding meetings.

In the morning he would board American Airlines flight 87, bound for Washington, DC. Grebo Barclay would once again, yield to Maurice Lacroix. There was one more mission for the *Gray Ghost* to accomplish.

CHAPTER TWENTY-ONE

VANESSA Sullivan was excited. In fact, she was down right giddy at the prospect of her dinner date. The days between the invitation and the actual dinner date had flown by, and with each passing hour she found herself growing more and more apprehensive.

"What do you think, Sebastian?; the black Gucci or something a little more conservative?"

It was obvious from his expression that Sebastian could care less about the dinner date or what she was wearing. Instead, he just maintained his position, atop the ottoman, at the foot of the bed, and slowly lowered his head until his eyes were completely closed. He had now, officially, rendered himself oblivious to all that was going on. "A fine friend you turned out to be. Men, can't live with'em, can't live without'em."

"*I* think the little Gucci will have him eating out of your hands." While Sebastian was fast asleep, Mrs. Avery was not. She entered the room, as always, with little notice. It was a practice Vanessa found comforting, at times, and disturbing, at others.

"You don't think I might look a little too aggressive by wearing the black one?"

"Nonsense girl, after all, who pursued whom?" Mrs. Avery reminded her.

Vanessa always admired that quality in Mrs. Avery. She was at times a mother, and at times a best friend, but always the consummate feminist. She didn't believe in women waiting for the right man to make life seem perfect. Mrs. Avery had seen the world, albeit, most of it alone, and was comfortable with living out the remainder of her years the same way with all her memories intact.

"Was there ever a man?" Vanessa inquired, knowing, in advance, the can of worms she had just opened.

"…One in every port, my dear, one in every port."

"And how many broken hearts?" Vanessa inquired sheepishly.

'How many ports?" Mrs. Avery responded, prompting both women to burst into simultaneous laughter.

Laughter was just what Vanessa Sullivan needed. She was looking forward to dinner, but if she were being perfectly honest with herself, she'd realize that there was something about Prescott Marshall she found to be a little unsettling. Every woman liked a little mystery, but not too much. *That* is what prompted Vanessa to log onto the nearest Lexus Nexus machine in the school's library. She needed to do some homework on her mystery date.

Prescott Marshall was clearly a man of means. A self-made millionaire the old fashioned way. He made his money as the result of blind luck. Marshall, it seems, invested his life savings in DNA technology. Vai-genetics or Vai-gene for short, marketed DNA test kits in the early eighties.

A generation of African Americans, weaned on "Roots," seemed eager to reconnect with their ancestors. What two hundred years of slavery made impossible, genetics would make probable, down to the nearest village. Or at least that's what Vai-gene promised. For a modest fee, participants would submit two swabs, taken from inside their cheek. The contents of the kit would be mailed to Vai-gene for further testing.

The newspaper article showed a picture of the Congressional Black Caucus and some Liberal white allies lining up to allow Vai-gene to sample DNA. The article went on to describe a PR nightmare. DNA, it seemed, had an unanticipated darker side. A famous Dixiecrat found he had some *black* in him; a cabinet secretary found Jewish genetics in her background, and reporters had a field day.

Subsequent articles linked Vai-gene's DNA database to insurance companies, the military, and even major universities seeking federal funding to determine whether blacks contained a gene thought to render them predisposed to crime. Vai-gene weathered the storms, and Marshall emerged to be one of the most powerful men in Washington.

"There's a man here," Mrs. Avery shouted, loud enough to wake Sebastian from his slumber. "And he looks like he is driving a magic pumpkin."

Vanessa glanced down at her watch. Her daydreaming had caused the remaining hour to fly. Any thoughts of the VAI and Prescott Marshall would have to wait. There was a little Gucci dress to be put on. Sebastian had now left his perch and was headed downstairs. Nothing got by him.

The limo driver proved to be quite the gentleman, acting as if he didn't notice the awkwardness at which Vanessa entered the car. The little Gucci dress was much smaller on Vanessa than it was on the hanger, making for a rather uncomfortable entrance. As they made their way across the Key Bridge into Georgetown, he opened the moon roof, allowing a welcome rush of fresh air to enter the rear cabin. He even offered up bits of trivia. Limo drivers, in Washington, were like that…Part limo driver, part tour guide.

"Did you know those were the steps where the priest took a tumble in the Exorcist movie?" he said expecting an answer of utter amazement.

"No, is that so," Vanessa responded, not wanting the driver to know it was probably the hundredth time she had heard the story. In fact, when she first moved to Washington, she took her mother to that very spot. Susan Sullivan would be proud of her daughter, right now. Prescott Marshall was quite the catch, even if he was old enough to be her father.

"That's your restaurant right there," the driver said pointing to a restaurant with a large green awning in front. "The Palm Coast. That's where the movers and shakers eat. The boss has his own table. You gotta be somebody for something like that."

"I hear your boss is one of those '*somebody's*,'" Vanessa inquired, conducting her own fishing expedition, but getting no where.

"He is, but I gotta tell you, I been with him two years now and couldn't even tell you his favorite color. The truth is, I rarely ever get to drive him. I shine this car everyday and sometimes at night, out of boredom. But Mr. M. likes to drive himself most of the time. That might have something to do with the way he drives. More than one cop is hot on his tail when he comes home at night, but most never catch him. Mr. M. don't like cops."

"That so," Vanessa said, keeping the conversation going. "Why not?"

"You'll have to ask him that yourself. My job is to deliver the lady to The Palm Coast and here we are. And might I add, the pleasure has been all mine."

Vanessa could see the man was blushing behind his smile. She could also tell he was a man who had a story to tell. One who would make some woman a perfect husband. Tonight, however, there was another man of mystery. One, she hoped, would be waiting inside.

"Good evening, Ma'am." The man speaking was Georgie Antonio, the Maitre'd at The Palm. Georgie knew everybody and everybody knew Georgie. He also made it *his* business to know *everybody's* business, as well, because that was what The Palm was about...Business, personal or otherwise, it didn't matter. In Washington, information was as good as gold and Georgie had lots of information to dish out. "You must be Mrs. Sullivan," Georgie began by way of introduction.

"*Ms.*" came the response.

"Excuse me, that makes this conversation all the better." With that, Georgie reached out his right hand and when Vanessa placed hers inside it, he used it to pull her closer in one sweeping motion. Then beside her right cheek, he planted a sizable Italian kiss that the regulars were used to. "Welcome to the Palm Coast or PC for short. You'll be sitting at Mr. Marshall's table, *Ms.* Sullivan."

As he escorted her through the room, he made sure everyone knew who she was, and where she was headed. Georgie wanted everyone to know, there was someone new being added to Prescott's mix. *New information.*

"Sorry I'm late; I'll take it from here, Georgie."

Vanessa spun around to see Prescott Marshall standing directly behind her. For the first time, she noticed just how striking he was. Gone was the elderly man, drinking a cup of coffee at her station. Instead, the man standing before her was the perfect physical specimen. He was wearing a gray flannel suit, accented by a burgundy tie and pocket square. One glance around the room, and Vanessa could see she was not the only one noticing Prescott Marshall and he was not the only one being noticed.

Once seated, Prescott wasted no time in taking control, ordering a bottle of wine that cost more than Vanessa made in a year. She was impressed by the way he pronounced everything on the menu correctly. She marveled at how he seemed to work the room with his eyes. He knew he was being watched and quickly disarmed anyone daring to cast a glimpse in his direction. A simple nod was all that was needed. Those gazing wildly would then look away, sometimes out of embarrassment and sometimes because they could think of nothing else to do.

"You are indeed a man of mystery," Vanessa began by way of breaking the ice between them.

"Mystery?"

"Why, a note? Why not just a simple phone call? You could have asked me in the coffee shop."

Marshall countered, "I should apologize, again, for the delivery of my invitation. I assure you the messenger has been dealt with."

"He's okay isn't he?'

"You make it sound as if I had him assassinated," Prescott replied.

"Well there *are* those rumors!" As always Vanessa was fishing, but unlike Father Haynes, Prescott was no easy mark.

"My word, young lady, you have quite the imagination!" Prescott responded politely.

"I just like to know who I am dining with." she answered innocently.

Prescott, unfazed, wanted his younger charge to know that in her case, he kept no secrets." Let us begin with the truth. You ask the question and I will answer it."

"Let's start with the Vai-gene; what is it exactly?" Vanessa inquired.

"It is what you have read," Prescott responded. "I spent some time in Africa in the late seventies and early eighties. Tragic, what has happened to those people. When I returned, I came into some wealth and made it my life's mission to use science to undo that which centuries of slavery produced. Others shared my vision and the company grew to what it is today. I am quite proud of what we have accomplished. Through DNA, blacks can learn where they are from, and even more importantly, their *roots.* We have benefactors around the world who share my dream and contribute dearly toward the cause. Nothing more. Nothing less."

"Sounds great, but there have been controversies," Vanessa continued.

"Yes," Prescott replied. "The sword of science can cut both ways. I am, of course referring to...."

Vanessa quickly seized the opportunity to impress Prescott with her own credentials. "The double Helix of DNA... Some have described it as Watson's sword; *Watson and Crick*, being the two scientists who discovered DNA back in the fifties."

"You are quite well versed on this subject, I see," Prescott said admiringly; although there was a trace of curiosity in his voice.

Vanessa found herself drawn in closer. "It is my major," she said proudly. She knew she was talking to a man who could offer her the world in more than one way. She knew, well, about Vai-genes capabilities and on more than one occasion, considered the possibility of approaching the massive company for a grant to complete her thesis. Now here *she* was sitting opposite the one man who could write *the check.* "

Careful girl, go slowly!

Vanessa Sullivan, however, was never one to proceed with caution. When it came to information, she was like a bull in a China shop, and tonight was no different. "And *The Consortium?*"

For the first time, Prescott appeared as if he had been caught slightly off guard. He had grown accustomed to answering questions about Vai-gene, but few knew anything of his association with "*The Consortium*."

"A *think tank*, like so many others in this city," he answered.

Vanessa was once again on the attack. "A *think tank* with some pretty deep pockets, and a lot of political pull."

Any hint that he was perturbed, was gone. Prescott Marshall was impressed with the line of questioning being offered up. He hated women who simply rolled over. This girl had fight and he lived for the battle. "We back candidates, but beyond that, we're no different than any other organization, with interests worldwide. Let's examine the way democracies *really* work," Prescott continued. "Governments, my dear, run on money. People invest in governments, and with all investments, they tend to favor the people they trust. Take America, for instance, the French invested heavily in our government during the revolutionary war. *The Consortium* backs the candidates we think best represent us!"

"So," Vanessa said, searching Prescott's eyes for the *real* truth, "Are you a James man, or will you vote for Webb?"

"I can tell from your line of questioning that you have done your homework. That means you already know Max sits on our board." Marshall paused. "That said, like all Americans, my vote is a private matter. I will cast my ballot for the best qualified candidate."

Vanessa's response had an edge of sarcasm attached to it, "or *the wealthiest*."

Marshall wasn't taking the bait. "You make it seem like wealth is a vice. Our founding fathers set up a government designed to protect their wealth. We have a House and a Senate. It is no secret money plays a roll. Name one Senator who is not a millionaire!"

"Baron James," Vanessa blurted out.

"Baron James, interesting choice indeed," Prescott quipped. "But I ask you, how poor is he? He made millions on the football field, as an athlete, and then parlayed that money into a career in business, followed by politics. The only people who believe he is from the working class are those who buy into his campaign spots. That's his table over there. You'll notice it is empty. It is kept that way by Georgie, at Baron's request. Georgie is paid handsomely for his efforts."

It was clear Prescott was now starting to tire of the line of questions being offered up, and obviously, his answers were producing the desired effect on his young guest. It was also clear that the black Gucci dress was having its effect on Prescott Marshall, as well.

"All of this talk has distracted me from the matters at hand. It reminds me of work, and you remind me of why all work and no play..."

..."Makes Vanessa a dull date."

"I have been dying to tell you that you look simply marvelous in that dress," Prescott flirted.

"Oh, this?" Vanessa was now beginning to blush. "It's just something I picked out of the closet."

"Ms. Sullivan, I am no stranger to women, or to the clothes they wear. Simply take these words as a compliment. You do me great honor by being my guest tonight. I assure you, what you are wearing required great thought and with that being said, I am flattered."

Vanessa was suitably swept off her feet. Any line of defense that presented itself earlier in the evening, evaporated with each glass of wine. She was being seduced by wealth and power, and welcomed every minute of it. Mrs. Avery taught her well. When in over your head, drown happily, and tonight Vanessa intended to do just that.

The wine traveled quickly to her head, but even faster to her bladder. She excused herself and proceeded toward the rest room. As she rose to make her exit, Marshall stood to pull out her seat. As soon as she was out of sight, he carefully removed his perfectly folded pocket square from his jacket pocket, wrapped it around her wine glass and deposited it inside his jacket.

Much can be learned from something as simple as a lipstick stain.

Vanessa quickly noticed her dinner date seemed giddy, if not boyish. “You seem to be awfully happy,” she remarked.

“Just the present company. You are quite beautiful, young lady, any man would be proud to have you on his arm.”

CHAPTER TWENTY-TWO

THE headline on the front page of the *Raleigh News Standard* screamed, **"Murder in Mayberry."** Inner city killings were commonplace but this story "had legs." The double box on the front page told the story in graphic detail, with the photos leading the way. The left hand section of the paper had a picture of Susan Sullivan in her prime, probably from a high school year book. The crime scene photos were located to the right. Those photos left little doubt that Susan Sullivan met a grisly death.

The headline in the competing tabloid was far less kind. "Madame Murdered," was the language used. It *screamed sensationalism*, and the story that accompanied the litany of crime scene photos, was no better.

"I never seen nothing like it, the most grisly thing I ever seen," was the quote from the first deputy to arrive on the scene. "She was a beautiful woman, if you know what I mean, and someone musta' been awful mad to do that to her."

The article then went onto describe, in graphic detail, how she appeared to have been gutted like a fish in the gruesome moments before her death. What made the death even more bizarre was that the woman was cut in two. The upper half of her body found in one portion of the trailer; the torso and legs, found twenty eight feet away. Official cause of death was the fire that consumed just about everything in sight, but the coroner made it clear, she was dying as the fire was being set. There were unsubstantiated rumors in the article quoting anonymous sources as saying the woman had welcomed all manner of *strangers* into her house.

"That woman was *a freak*," a neighbor was quoted as saying. Judging from *her* accompanying photo, jealousy appeared to be *her* motivation for talking. Any beauty she may have once possessed had long since left her body. She was fat and wore a 'moo moo' with flowers on it. Her hair was in curlers, and her glasses were in vogue when flat tops and saddle oxfords were the style of the day.

Others described a modern day brothel where all manner of mankind was serviced. They reported unconfirmed rumors that suitors were photographed against their will, and blackmailed. Despite the rumors, none of the photos were ever found, and the rumors were more for gossip than for widespread dissemination. Once the people, quoted, had their fifteen minutes of small town fame, even the most curious of deputies moved on, to other more pressing cases.

The last article written about the murder was an exclusive. The local paper reported that investigators discovered an unknown substance at the scene. One investigator, who had served in the Peace Corps, said that what appeared to be Cassava Leaves were found at the scene. A man, who called himself the paper's investigative reporter, traced them back to the killing fields of Liberia, West Africa, and hinted that Susan Sullivan's death may have been part of *a larger conspiracy.* Soon, even those rumors faded. The pieces of the puzzle didn't fit, and as time dragged, fewer seemed to care.

Officially, the case was investigated and dozens of suitors interviewed, but no one would ever learn of what really happened.

This was not *CSI.* There was no real crime scene investigation where the type of knife would be studied against any and all possible knife wounds No DNA was taken, or carpet fibers, or semen samples. No, this woman was *trailer trash*, and like trailer trash, her death would, *forever*, remain a mystery.

Even in death, poverty robbed its victims of any dignity.

An incinerator finished the job the fire had started. Her ashes were buried in a field near where she and Gary Wayne Sullivan played as kids. Life on tobacco row was cruel. Death was crueler still. The truth was, her ashes were mixed in with the ashes of at least a dozen others who had died in the months and weeks proceeding and following her death. The funeral director simply scooped up a handful of ashes and placed them in an urn. The urn was picked up by her closest of kin.

Vanessa Sullivan was no where to be seen.

CHAPTER TWENTY-THREE

"SIX forty five, in the Nation's Capitol, and if you have a flight to catch, sleep in." The voice on the all news radio station was unmistakable, and so was the message. Washington's rush was about to be a nightmare for anyone who ventured out. The forecaster who followed called it, "a thermal inversion."

"We've already got a nasty tie up on the outer loop, and rubber neckers are causing the same situation on the other side. Stay home, if you can."

Because of the "thermal inversion," the fog hung low over the monuments that make up what is known as the National Mall. The cloud ceiling was so low, only the top of the Washington Monument could be seen rising above the surface, like the Egyptian Pyramid it was modeled after. All other monuments were obscured by the cloud bank that ground all flights out of nearby Washington National Airport. It was unusual weather for November, a combination of mild temperatures and high humidity.

Two men made their way through the fog as if they were agents in some bizarre World War II movie, to meet at the steps of the Lincoln Memorial. This site, that had seen so many historic moments, was about to witness another, but this one would never make it to the history books even though history was about to be made. It was the type of history, Washington preferred to keep secret.

"Prescott Marshall! I'd like to say I'm glad to see you but the truth is the world would be better off if you were to be found dead."

"Mercer...Mercer James? Is that any way to treat an old friend?" Marshall said returning the sarcasm.

Mercer James angled to get a better view, and climbed up a step at the foot of the monument to gain the advantage of size. The two resembled prize fighters feeling each other out before landing the first blow. A much more violent reunion would take place later...but not now. This was the time for both men to see what the other was made of. They had heard of each other in Washington social circles, and read about each other in the press. Now they were standing face to face.

"Might I suggest we get down to business?" Mercer said.

Always sarcastic, Prescott answered, "What? No time for pleasantries, after all your son is about to become the next president of the United States if the polls have anything to say."

"There are some however, who would do anything to derail that campaign." Mercers voice reflected the anger he was trying hard to control, "which brings us to the matter at hand. *The photos*."

"Ah yes, *the photos*, I almost forgot," Marshall said, now starting his move to gain the advantage of size. "There is the matter of *those photos*. Seems this campaign is full of photos at the wrong time. First there were the photos of Max Webb in that hideous Klan outfit. One has to wonder where men come up with such *historic photos*? It seems, at times, that people with nasty things to say or show come out of the woodwork around this time of the year, but then again that is politics isn't it?" Marshall was smiling the type of smile that involved only half of his face, making it seem more like a sneer. The truth was, he relished moments liked this. Prescott Marshall lived for the battle and there was no better opponent than Mercer James. He knew the man standing before him had been reduced to a pathetic object of pity. After all, he had spent a lifetime shaping a son to be President of the United States, only to watch his son fall victim to that which had claimed so many before him, a woman!

"Let's just get this damn thing over. If it is about money, name your price." Mercer began by way of opening any negotiations.

Prescott laughed a hollow laugh, "What, Mercer, do *I* need with money? This isn't about money, don't be so melodramatic. We both know when it all boils down to it, nothing in Washington is about money. People come here rich, and raise hundreds of millions of dollars to live in a house smaller than the one they came from, and for considerably less money. No my dear Mercer, this is about power, pure and simple. Your son will have it...we only wish to make sure he uses it wisely."

"I supposed you already have something in mind?"

"My my, aren't we perceptive. Seems there is the matter of a *certain lawsuit* that has some of my associates rather concerned. They simply wish to know what position your son will take after he becomes President, assuming he *does* become President."

"What lawsuit?"

"Don't be coy with me Mercer; you know damned well *what lawsuit!* The people behind it have pinned their success on your son. It's also possible he will get the chance to name three people to the court before his administration ends. That would be *catastrophic* for the people I represent. They simply want your word, in writing, I might suggest, to eliminate any misunderstandings. When Baron raises his hand to take the oath, *the lawsuit goes away*."

"That's blackmail." Mercer snapped.

"Curious choice of words from a man who's son looks nothing like the man his campaign ads describe. No, my dear Mercer, this is something that is as American as cherry pie. After all, it was the cherry tree he chopped down, wasn't it? "

"Baron James is America."

Prescott was mocking Mercer, with biting sarcasm in every word. Your son is a *disgrace*. If you thought he would find a sympathetic ear, you would have taken this to the police. No...you can see the damage these photos represent...a so called *black man* in bed with a *white woman.* Now how will that play in Peoria, or for that matter the Southwest Washington? By the way, who took them in the first place? They're a bit on the *grainy side* but that seems to add to the *ambiance*, don't you think?"

Rage was welling up inside Mercer James. As a young man growing up in a tough environment he knew exactly how to handle men like Prescott Marshall. He would bash his head in, leaving the body behind for police to add to a growing list of unsolved black crimes...but not this time. Mercer knew any move would have to be calculated. He knew Prescott Marshall had the upper hand, and hated having to listen to his taunts. Still, like any prize fighter he would wait for an opening, and then strike. He didn't have to wait long.

"I am prepared to make these photos go away, or should I say, disappear unless needed. When Baron becomes President, he will simply take the same course of action as every President who preceded him. He will pronounce the lawsuit frivolous and scuttle any attempts at revising any *Legislation* as well. As you know, one of your associates slyly introduced a rather peculiar bill, just before the last legislative session ended. How convenient it would have been, sitting there waiting for Baron to sign. Pity it will never see the light of day. "

Mercer countered with his own dose of sarcasm. "For a moment there I thought you would be more interested in *extortion*. Fortunately, you don't want *anything*, you want *everything*."

"Now, now, my dear Mercer, can't you see, I already *have* everything. I have everything I need to *destroy your son* and everything the two of you have spent so many years working toward. I could have called the press long ago. I know a certain reporter who desperately is looking for a second chance at some photos. Surely you remember *those* photos...after all you leaked them to his competition, didn't you?"

Touché

"How do I know you will keep your word?"

"You don't."

Marshall reached down to recover a brief case that had been sitting on the steps less than a foot out of reach. Unsnapping the buckles, he reached inside, making sure not to take his eyes off of Mercer and then produced a copy of a newspaper article. He handed the article to Mercer, who then realized the gravity of the situation has suddenly grown worse.

The article detailed how a woman in Raleigh met a grizzly death. He recognized the name of the woman immediately, and panicked at the suggestion that her death could somehow be linked to his son.

Does he know about the payments?

In that instance Mercer realized, Prescott Marshall was not only in possession of the photos, but in all likelihood, evidence of murder. This meeting went well beyond *extortion*! Glancing down again at the article, he realized they were in the fight for their lives.

"I'll have to clear this with Baron...."

"You'll do *nothing* of the sort. You know and I know, Baron is your *lapdog*. If you tell him how grave the situation is, he'll follow your every word." Marshall knew he was in complete control. He also knew that Mercer knew it, as well.

"We'll play by your rules, but how do we know?" Mercer stammered.

"That I won't double cross you? You don't. That's the beauty of it all, isn't it? Speaking of beauty, she was quite the looker in her day, wasn't she?" Mercer was holding the photos up to the light as if he were a photographer examining a set of negatives. Mercer glanced around nervously looking to see if others were watching as well. They were still alone, and Prescott was still in charge. I'm curious, how did your son get hooked up with such a tragic figure anyway?

Mercer realized Prescott knew enough to destroy the James campaign. There was one thing however, that didn't seem to make sense. He was determined to find out why.

"I thought *The Consortium* backed Max Webb," James offered up.

Prescott was impressed. Even in defeat, his opponent was angling for some sort of opening. "We do, but in the world of politics, one can't be too careful. It wasn't so long ago, that *The Consortium* had backed the right man, then came the photos and the dip in the polls, all but assuring your son would win. America doesn't like it when politics get too dirty, and it appears we have reached that threshold. In short, we are prepared to let the electorate decide the winner. We are also making sure *we win,* no matter who the voters pick."

As the morning sun began to make its appearance over the Capitol Building located just over his shoulder, Mercer knew it wouldn't be long before the mall would be alive with activity. If any deals were to be made, they would be made now. There were worse compromises made by politicians, although at this precise time he couldn't think of any. Prescott would be dealt with, but this round was already over.

Extending his right hand, awkwardly at first and then in a more expressive manner, he waited for Marshall to return the gesture.

He would still be waiting, but Marshall had already stooped down to retrieve his brief case and the article from the Raleigh Newspaper. A handshake to Prescott Marshall was nothing more than a formality, and he hated formalities. He knew he had won, long before setting foot on the steps of the Lincoln Memorial. He simply came for the satisfaction of seeing one of the most powerful men in Washington, *grovel* at his feet.

As the sun began to burn off the fog on the monument ground, Marshall, now seated in the cockpit of his Mercedes Roadster, reached over to crank up the heat and drop the top. It was a perfect Washington morning!

CHAPTER TWENTY-FOUR

"I'M off to see the world and everything that is perfect about it!" Vanessa awoke the next day, exuding an aura that Mrs. Avery had not seen in recent years. The bouquet of two dozen red roses sitting on the dining room table left no doubt her evening with Prescott was a success. Although, Vanessa found the enclosed card puzzling, at best.

CURIOSITY....

"That must have been quite a dinner," Mrs. Avery said, smiling from ear to ear sharing Vanessa's exuberance.

Vanessa was almost blushing. "I must say, he is quite the romantic. What girl doesn't like being wined and dined, but the card...well that's a different story."

Mrs. Avery picked up the card, studied it, and then as always acted as Vanessa's inner voice of reason. "Caution, Vanessa, caution. Keep in mind that we know very little about your mystery man, and this *is* Washington.""

Vanessa knew that Mrs. Avery was right, and would return to her senses soon, but not too soon. "Mrs. Avery, I think I'm going to take a day off from classes." She studied Mrs. Avery's expression and seeing no visible objection, continued. "I'm behind on my graduate thesis. It's time to do some studying in the field."

It took Vanessa less than fifteen minutes to throw on her favorite pair of blue jeans and a worn work shirt. Still, despite the hurried look of her ensemble, she looked better than most women who spent hours in front of the mirror. A short time later, she was standing on the curb in front of her town home, frantically waving her arm in the air.

"Taxi!"

Rather than fight for a parking space, Vanessa decided to take a cab downtown. Fieldwork for Vanessa involved walking "The Mall." The mall, was to Washington, what "Times Square" was to New Yorkers, frequently traveled and seldom studied. She marveled at the many mysteries Washington had to offer, that lay beneath the surface. They were the questions that shaped her thesis.

As the cab crossed over The Memorial Bridge, she realized generations had passed since the funeral of President John F. Kennedy. Everyone in America, who saw that funeral, remembered the horse drawn caisson, as it made its way across to Arlington National Cemetery. Those people, she realized, were now in their forties and fifties and beyond. The others, who vacationed with their families, studied it and Vietnam, in history classes.

"*Two chapters*," she mused, "*and then it was on to the Emperors of Rome*."

"Right here!" She told the cabby, slipping him a ten dollar bill, as they rounded the bend just behind the Memorial. She knew she had traveled less than *one zone*, the antiquated cab system in Washington, but was feeling rather liberated after the sizable tip she received from Prescott and her subsequent night out on the town. The cab stopped on the North side of Independence Avenue, just down the street from the White House and across the street from the Lincoln Memorial.

It was cool outside, but not so cold that a brisk walk wouldn't remove the chill. Vanessa's conversations with Father Haynes about Chinquy made this trip to the mall extra special. She was curious about something she heard, and had to *see* for herself. As she started up the steps toward the statue sitting in the middle, several obvious peculiarities leaped out.

"There are clues hidden in the monuments," she recalled Father Haynes as saying. He was right. The Lincoln Memorial was one of the most famous landmarks in Washington, and yet few ever questioned the obvious. Lincoln was facing east, not toward the rest of the country, he said, was freed from slavery, but toward the true home of those slaves, towards *Africa.* She had read the various accounts questioning his ethnicity, and found it *curious.* She remembered Father Haynes reading an account from Lincoln's autobiography. The wording seemed so strange for a man credited with freeing the slaves. They almost begged for more explanation. *"I am dark skinned with coarse black hair."*

She, then, took a stroll around the back of the monument and was so engrossed in thought she almost knocked over her favorite Park Ranger.

Thornton Ellis was a fixture around the monument. He was there when Dr. Martin Luther King delivered his famous "I have a dream" speech, and for every anti-war protest from Vietnam to Iraq, but like Vanessa, his fascination was with Lincoln.

"So what brings you out today?" he said collecting the items that spilled from his cart in the collision.

"History, Thornton, History."

"Have you found the answers to my questions in your ivory tower?" Thornton took great pleasure in pointing out the oddities of Washington's monuments, and Vanessa loved every minute of it. Many of his questions became the foundation for her arguments in Father Haynes's history class. It was their little secret.

"I have found those answers and more," she replied.

"Then try these on for size." He crossed his arms and placed them above the head of the rake in his cart as if he were about to take a long needed and deserved break. "Why is Illinois, the "Land of Lincoln" listed on the back of the monument?" He could see from the expression on Vanessa's face, it was something, even she, had not noticed. "Why would Lincoln turn his back on his homeland?"

Not to be outdone, Vanessa responded with her own instant hypothesis. "Perhaps, because they wanted Lincoln to face the Capitol building."

"Vanessa, if anyone, surely you must realize nothing here is accidental. Great planning goes into the placement of these monuments. I assure you, it wasn't a simple oversight. I suspect it has more to do with the Custis Estate." Thornton pointed at the towering colonial mansion that overlooked the mall in all its expanse from neighboring Arlington. The yellow facade and stately columns made it hard to miss. "Custis, you know, was the maiden name of Martha Washington. The Washingtons had slaves, and even though he freed them on his death bed, I wondered how a man like Lincoln would have regarded *the founding fathers.*

Making her way back to the front of the monument, with Thornton in tow, and climbing the steps, she walked past a group of Asian tourists snapping the same photos as every tourist before her, and walked to the center of the monument where the large statue of Lincoln sitting was located.

"Lenn-colin!" One of the tourists remarked, as if she had won a prize in a trivia contest.

"He freed all of America's slaves!"

Thornton smiled. "This time it's your turn."

"*If only they knew!*" Vanessa thought, as she listened more closely to the conversation unfolding before her. *Lincoln was a flawed man. He suffered from bouts of deep depression, that, he himself described in his writings.* She knew, historians long determined his elongated hands and fingers were the result of Marfans syndrome, and yet they refused to allow any of his DNA to be tested. That was the subject of her thesis. *"Could modern science rewrite history? What would Lincoln's DNA reveal? What would a sample of that coarse black hair produce?"*

DNA, the scientific marvel of the twentieth century could be used to eliminate race all together. Vanessa believed that history's true mysteries were hidden behind its code. Father Haynes was right, it was *the proportiona divina. It* was perfect.

Vanessa remembered how fascinated she was, when she learned that the entire genetic history of a person would fit inside an ice cube, and yet unraveled, would stretch from the earth to the sun and back, some four hundred times. Why not let science determine why Lincoln acted in the manner he chose? His opponents referred to him as the *"Negro President."* Was freeing the slaves an act of heroism, or was he a sell out?

Washington was full of irony and she wondered why history glossed over the things most people would find fascinating about their leaders. She watched Washington at work through the eyes of a student. Policy decisions that made rich men richer were called economic stimulus packages. Welfare was the way handouts for the poor were described. Perhaps Father Haynes was right. "The truth can be found beneath the layers of lies history chooses to ignore."

By now she had reached her destination…a tiny gift shop, located in a small space behind the massive statue. She made it her business to check it frequently to see what new information was available on her favorite topic. By now, Thornton and the tourists were far from her thoughts.

"That'll be five dollars and ninety five cents with tax," the woman in the gift shop said smiling. "I think you'll find that one, one of the most interesting books we sell."

Vanessa purchased a copy of a grade school text on Lincoln trivia and was instantly amazed at what was inside. *None of this was taught in any classes I attended.* The book revealed, like the leaders, the monuments were flawed, as well, and hid clues as to the identities of those who designed them. Lincoln's hands on his statue were formed to sign the letters "A" and "L." Daniel Chester French, the designer of the sculpture, was said to do so for his deaf daughter. In the first column of Lincoln's second inaugural address the word *"FUTURE"* was misspelled and instead read *"EUTURE."*

How could such a mistake go undetected she wondered?, as she continued reading the book. The book revealed that one of the most popular myths was that there was an outline of the face of Robert E. Lee on the back of Lincoln's head, but like the others before her, she saw no evidence to support such an absurd theory. Instead, the thought about Jules Guerin's fresco showing an angel, and wondered what it meant. The angel, the book said, represented *truth*, and was shown freeing a slave. What was the *truth* Guerin was pointing to?

"Excuse me young lady, but where did you get that book?" A young woman with two children in tow, noticed Vanessa's fascination with her gift shop treasure and wanted one of her own.

"At the gift shop and it is recommended reading," Vanessa politely answered back.

The woman smiled and then hurried off, pushing the strollers as if she was on some sort of treasure hunt for a reality television game show.

As Vanessa continued to walk around the massive granite site, she also wondered why historians never made much mention of what she called the '*curiosities*'. For instance, what was the battle like when Lincoln appointed Samuel Chase to be his Chief Justice of the Supreme Court? Chase was well known for defending freed slaves. Did Lincoln avoid controversy or welcome it? She thought about the contentious hearings concerning new Supreme Court nominees. Were things then, as they are now?

Another tourist, another snapshot. Vanessa decided it was time to mix in some interviews. "Excuse me ma'am, what do you know about Warren G. Harding?"

The woman was wearing a large sweatshirt boasting that she was from Nebraska. She didn't do the state proud. "Warren, who?"

"*Precisely!*"

Warren G. Harding dedicated the memorial she was standing in front of, and yet the woman knew nothing about him. Harding was also accused, at the time, of being from mixed descent. She thought of modern day politics and wondered if there was there more to Lincoln's assassination than historians knew.

John Wilkes Booth?

Vanessa found herself thinking back to her conversation with Father Haynes concerning Father Chiniquy. The more she studied the monument, the more she was convinced that history reported only what it wanted the American public to read. Were there layers of lies, just like Father Haynes had mentioned?

Lincoln freed the slaves! How's that for controversy?! Was Chinquy right?

Historians have long studied the true motivations behind John Wilkes Booth's assassination of Lincoln at Fords Theater, but the true motives behind his crimes were never made known. He was sympathetic to the Southern cause, but conspiracies require money and planning. Booth may have been an assassin, but he was no dummy. Suddenly, the thought of a Vatican conspiracy didn't seem so far fetched.

Was Racism then, like it is now?

Vanessa made her way down the steps and began looking upwards toward the landmark. Her thoughts shifted to something else both, Thornton Ellis and Father Haynes, had said. Both almost made it seem as if history's ghosts influenced the present. 250,000 African Americans marched on Washington, for equal rights and to hear the address of Dr. Martin Luther King. Both men believed the monument was only a symbol of something deeper beneath the surface that calls us all.

As a middle school student, she remembered reading about the crowd counts at The Million Man March. Crowd organizers placed the number at one million. The U.S. Park Police said it was considerably less, more in the neighborhood of 250 thousand. Studies showed the organizers were right, and the Park Police announced they were no longer in the business of predicting crowd size.

Is the city one big mystery itself? Was the truth hidden somewhere within the layers of lies?

Another tourist...another question. "Sir, do you have any idea who Benjamin Bannaker was?"

This time the man, with children in tow, answered proudly, "He spent twenty eight years in a South African prison before being released and ending Apartheid!"

Precisely! She thought, placing another check in the box marked, "did not know" on the survey for her research thesis.

"Sir, Benjamin Bannaker was in all the black history books as the man who designed the city, but it is L'Enfant who received the glory. Bannaker was also one of the best known mathematicians of his time, and believed deeply in astrology!"

"Astrology," the man said in amazement. "I didn't know that. I have, however, heard that the Mason's hid clues all over Washington. Is that true?"

"Yes it is," Vanessa answered. "The question I think historians need to ask is did Bannaker leave behind additional clues, or, based on his ethnicity, 'inside jokes' that only blacks knew about? We know that the city, itself, is laid out to resemble a Masonic Symbol."

"You mean one of those secret societies?"

"Yes Sir."

The man walked away, glancing back with utter amazement at the young woman he had just met.

Vanessa knew knowledge was power, but the real reason for her fascination with Lincoln and Bannaker was the foundation for her thesis. She knew from her classes with Father Haynes, that Bannaker's story was also never fully explored. His father was black, but his mother was white. Bannaker, Booker T. Washington, and others, including Frederick Douglass, were all noted figures in black history. The truth was that they were all of mixed blood. All three were the intellectual giants of their time, and yet history writes off the fact that they moved with relative ease, but instead writing as if all blacks were ignorant slaves.

These men were not the type of men who would hide their opinions!

In fact, Washington frequented the White House, dined with millionaires, and did battle with Frederick Douglass and other great statesmen associated with black history, and a mixed background.

Another group of tourists!

A woman from Idaho pointed proudly to the fact that she knew, more than most, about Lincoln. The others near her were listening intently. "The Gettysburg address is one of the shortest speeches on record,' she said.

"Excuse me ma'am," Vanessa said, seizing the moment, this time noticing that Thornton had reappeared to listen to his protégé. "Did you know that the day after the speech is was considered a flop? Very little mention was made of it in the local press."

"You seem to know a lot about history," the woman began. "Where do you get your information?"

"I read. Sometimes my professors say too much, but I read. And there are others," she said shooting an appreciative glance toward Thornton. It was their secret. He would teach, and she would tell the world. He would remain anonymous.

"Then you should continue reading. I like the way you think."

Turning around, Vanessa focused on the other subject her thesis covered, Washington's other famous monument. Most tourists knew the change in color on the Washington Monument was because of a gap in construction, but few knew why. Making her way up the mall, she noticed another set of tourists trying to put the monument in perspective as they took their pictures. Most chose to stand near the Lincoln Memorial, to capture its true size. She knew few had ever heard the story of '*The Pope's Stone*'.

That's when it dawned on her that perhaps Chiniquy was right that history did choose to ignore the facts, and the *"Pope's Stone"* as it was called, was proof. She knew from her past research that the stone never made it to the monument, but was, instead, stolen by a group who called themselves the '*Know Nothings*'. There *were* men back then who were upset with the policies of the Vatican, and feared undue influence on the part of Catholics. Most historians believed that the *Pope's Stone* sits at the bottom of the Tidal Basin. Despite its historic significance, there was never a concerted effort to find it.

As always, her journey to the mall, ultimately, led her to reexamine her own painful past. What happened to those whose lives were written off inside the womb? Was there any place in history of the child of a *whore,* who was raised by an uncle, who was a *member of the Klan, or would history simply rewrite the truth to fit the times?*

The sound of her cell phone quickly ended the absurd daydream. Clearly there was no grand conspiracy to uncover, just a random set of circumstances, that added together, would one day make for good reading.

Nothing else.

"This is Vanessa..."

The voice on the other end caused Vanessa to drop her phone and race across the mall, knocking several tourists to the ground. A woman who was about to ask a question, thought she noticed Vanessa crying. As she made her way across the mall, there would be no apologies. There was no time.

TWENTY-FIVE

"YOU'RE not ready yet," Cecilia was in protective mode. She had *that look* on her face. The one that meant, *she* was in charge, and *he* wasn't going anywhere.

"There's something about that phone call last night that bugs me," Matt intoned.

"You mean something more than the ramblings of an old fool?"

"It wasn't *what* he said Cecilia; it was *how* he said it. I've known Max Webb for a long time. I've been around him when he was drunk, and he has always had a reputation for being one of the tightest lipped son-of-a-bitch in Washington. There was *fear* in his voice, Cecilia. *Genuine fear.*"

Cecilia wasn't yielding any ground, "Then perhaps, *you* should hear the fear in *my voice.* I fear that if my husband doesn't let go of his quest for the holy grail of broadcasting, he'll kill himself. Let it go, Matt, you have enough Emmys."

Matt was listening, all the while putting his coat on. He trusted his instincts and his instincts had never let him down. Max Webb wouldn't call out of the blue for no reason at all, and he wouldn't humble himself. Max had a reason to call, and that reason was real.

"I have to go, Cecilia. You, more than anyone should understand." Matt's tone was almost pleading for his wife's understanding.

"I understand that you take it for granted that I'll be here when you come home. I've had enough Matt, I've had it. I almost *lost* you when those thugs attacked. You should have seen how you looked. They left you for dead. You were pathetic and ranting like a madman when I got to the hospital. Captain Hinton said you were lucky to be alive. He also said you'd been drinking!"

"*That son-of-a-bitch*!"

Tears were welling in Cecilia's eyes. She hated it when she became emotional. It made her look so weak. This time, however, she was being honest. She was afraid for her husband, and more afraid, she too, had reached the end of her rope.

Matt said nothing, but let the look on his face explain his feelings. He took a heavy breath, as if he were starting to explain his position verbally, and then stopped. He knew they would go back and forth forever. He also knew he had to get to the bottom of Max Webb's phone calls, or it would destroy him.

Perhaps she is right. Perhaps it is the holy grail he was looking for, but it is My "holy grail." It was what kept him alive!

He closed the door behind him without looking back. He realized the extent of the attack when he attempted to turn the key in the ignition. His fingers ached as if, one by one, they had been taken off his hands, beaten and then put back in place. Every muscle on his body followed hurt as well. The attack had taken a toll on him physically and mentally. He felt as if his entire body was betraying him.

The road ahead only served to make matters worse. In his rush to escape Cecilia, he violated the number one rule of Washington traffic, the clock. Rush hour was in full swing. The toll road was bumper to bumper, and everyone seemed 'pissed off'. Struggling to escape the pain, he reached down and turned on his right blinker to escape the HOV lane. That's when he realized there was someone in traffic more 'pissed off' than him.

"Hey asshole, where'd ya git your drivers license, Sears?" Matt had been in traffic jams so long, he could actually read the man's lips. He found it amazing that people could become so animated, when everyone reached their destinations within seconds of the people they just cut off. First, the attack, then Cecilia, Max, and now this asshole. It was going to be one hell of a day.

The rest of the commute was predictable. When he arrived at the station, his space was taken by his producer, who obviously believed it was hers until he healed. He wound up circling the parking lot for what seemed to be an eternity, before finally finding a spot.

"Welcome back Matt. Sweetie, you look like shit." Mrs. Green, the receptionist, was always there with a welcome smile and usually unwelcomed wit. It was obvious she was oblivious to everything that happened around her. She had been at the station for years, and laughed when she was told she would have to retire. She impolitely informed the owners, she was there when the station signed on, and would be there when it signed off.

Matt tried to avoid the well wishers as he made his way across the newsroom. He could see it on their faces. There were those who truly wished him well, and others who had already measured his office, to see if *their* things would fit. He endured the human gauntlet of hypocrisy, and was ready to enter his office, when it dawned on him his parking space wasn't the only thing that had already been taken.

"Oh I'm sorry Mr. Walker. I didn't think..."

"That's okay Julie." Matt's smiled signaling that all was okay. Julie was the semester intern. She was bright and articulate and had been an asset to the office. He knew she enjoyed the perks of his office and because he didn't pay her, it all seemed to work out. "I'll just set my things down here."

Julie however, realized she had already overstayed her welcome. She promptly told her boyfriend good-bye and returned to her rightful spot down the hall. Matt was alone for the first time in days.

He liked his office. It reminded him of better times. Closing the door behind him, he looked forward to opening the day's mail, snail, and otherwise. He looked forward to getting back to the chaos of his normal life.

Once again he felt the pain shooting through his fingers, as he painfully typed in the password to open his mailbox. There was an endless stream of emails. Most were from well wishers concerned about his encounter. There were the typical collect calls from inmates, declaring they were the *only* people who had ever been jailed unjustly, and only *he* could solve their alleged frame-ups. There were also the conspiracy theories, which, in Washington, were never ending. Matt listened to those calls closely, because he had learned long ago, the only difference between a source and a kook in Washington was their level of *clearance.*

You have one more voice message.

"Mr. Walker, this is Vanessa Sullivan." The sound of the voice immediately caught Matt's attention. It was soft and pleasant. He could almost picture the woman on the other end. In his mind, she seemed attractive. "It seems I have a rather interesting story you might be interested in." The caller went onto describe a man named Chiniquy, and, a conspiracy to kill a president that involved the Vatican.

"Viola," he said, writing the woman's name on a pad he kept next to the phone. It was exactly the type of story he liked. He knew from experience in Washington, history had a tendency to gloss over anything school kids would find boring. The city was in too much of a hurry. It worked well for those wanting to cover things up.

"*You have no more voice messages.*"

Matt reached down and pressed the hands-free button, causing the endless string of old messages to cease. He then turned his attention to the endless stack of letters that had spread across the top of his desk. There were bills and computer generated checks from banks hoping he would be foolish enough to open an account. And, there were the *letters* from the same inmates who vainly tried to reach him by phone. His favorites were the photographs of properties that slumlords left behind. Then, there was the one letter he had hoped to see. It was there in a plain gray envelope, marked HAND DELIVERED. In the upper left hand corner, the return address said, Senator Max Webb, United States Capitol.

"What the hell!"

The envelope contained a list of names and addresses, none of whom made any sense, at first. Only one seemed even vaguely familiar; the name of a well known Hollywood actor, who was notoriously media shy. The other names on the list could have been plucked from the phone book. They were random and offered no clue of the vast global conspiracy that Max Webb described over the phone. At the bottom of the list was what appeared to be some sort of computer code, or bar code sequence; 1.31.60/05.

"Perhaps Cecilia is right," he said, somewhat resigned. "Perhaps it is time for me to call it quits."

Matt looked at the list, one more time, and headed for the door. His trip to the office had been a waste of time. Cecilia was right, he was searching for straws. Max Webb was drunk and there was nothing more to it. Suddenly, a newspaper article that Julie had been reading,caught his attention.

The name. I've seen that name before.

The newspaper article described the grizzly death of a woman in North Carolina. It was no different than all the others, except for the name.

I know I have seen that name before. Susan Sullivan; the list!

Matt dropped his jacket and searched through the stack of papers on his desk, fumbling, as if he were an old man looking for a lost set of keys when he found it. He used his finger to scan down the list of names before arriving at the name 'Susan Sullivan'; below it, the name he was looking for.

Vanessa Sullivan; what are the odds?

Her name was written in pencil on the pad next to his phone. She was the woman who had just called...the one with the voice.

CHAPTER TWENTY-SIX

WHEN Mercer James arrived at the Capitol Hill townhouse of his son Baron, Baron was waiting in the living room. The security detail maintained a safe distance outside the doors, far enough from earshot, but never too far for quick action. Mercer wasted no time updating his son on his meeting with Prescott. Even though it was early, Baron was already fully dressed and being prepped for the upcoming Presidential Debates.

"Well?"

That single word caused Mercer James to hate his son, even more. Sure he was about to become President, but he was so weak. How could he let things get so out of control? He had always warned him about, women and in particular, *white women*. Now he was left to clean up after his son, once more. This time, he had no good news to deliver.

"He holds *all of the cards*, I'm afraid."

"Who?"

"Who, else?"

"Prescott!"

"Precisely, we met at the monument this morning, shortly after sunrise. No one saw us, but he had a copy of the pictures, and made it clear he was prepared to use them to his advantage," Mercer, removed his top coat and slung it over a winged back chair that was located, just inside the doorway, to the right of the room.

"So, I can assume we can look forward to seeing them on the evening news, any day now." Baron was nervously pacing back and forth across the room.

"I don't…think…so, at least not anytime soon. It appears, Prescott, relishes his new found power over you, and our campaign. He didn't say *what* he plans to do with the photos, and I suspect *that* is his strategy, to keep us guessing. He wants to keep us, *you*, off balance."

"Or living under the constant threat of exposure."

"You brought this on yourself. I told you the woman was bad news."

"How long are you going to hold this over my head?" Baron fired back. "I made a *mistake.* All men make mistakes. You..."

"Yes, I have made mistakes, but I spent a lifetime making sure you didn't make those same mistakes...."

"You make it sound as if you and mother..."

"Forget the past; we have more pressing matters at hand. Prescott will use those photos to *control you,* should you win, and ruin you, if you lose. There is one other thing you should know about."

"More embarrassing than the photos?"

"More embarrassing, and potentially criminal."

Baron slumped in the chair he had been pacing around, just moments before. It was hard to imagine any news worse than photos. He had gone over the possible scenarios over and over again in his mind, and imagined himself in the position of other politicians who had succumbed to similar fates. Proud men, forced to apologize on prime time TV, while a symphony of photographers snapped every grimace and frown. The evening news was only the beginning. The twenty four hour news cycle was next, shifting into a high octane feeding frenzy, and scandal was the fuel. Each paper would, somehow, select the same pictures, one that would not be sympathetic to his cause. Then, a week later, the magazines would hit the newsstands, followed by the tabloids, and the debate would start all over again. The magazines would uncover some sleazy fact he thought he'd hidden from history, and that is how his legacy would be written. A legacy that was about to get worse.

"Susan Sullivan is dead."

"What?"

"You heard me, the woman is dead. Your whore was murdered!"

"How?" The expression on Baron's face left no doubt he had feelings for the woman. She was part of his past and now she was dead. He didn't want his father to know, but at that moment in time, a part of him died, as well.

"Someone broke into her trailer, roughed her up pretty badly, and then set the whole place on fire. Nothing survived, not even Susan."

Baron James knew, but for one moments' indiscretion, that she would still be alive. She would have forever remained a childhood memory. He hated what happened, but not the woman. He would never tell his father the real truth, because his father would not hear of it. He prayed for a happier ending, but deep down inside he knew that could never be. Their paths crossed somewhere on the way to the White House, and she would be the ghost that haunted him forever. "The issue must be dealt with," Mercer continued. "I have been thinking about what to do, ever since Prescott walked away. If we do nothing, you will be a puppet of Prescott, and whoever else he associates with, for the rest of your life. We have only one course of action."

"The woman is dead, father, and he has the pictures. What else *can* be done?"

"The *mother* is gone, if the *daughter* goes away, there will be no concrete evidence linking you to this woman."

"But what about the photos?"

"You leave the girl and the photos to me. The less you know about this, the better for you and *your presidency*. Without DNA, there is no proof that the child is yours. The pictures become just that...tawdry photos that will prove embarrassing, but not *fatal*, because they are part of your past." Mercer could see the relief in his son's eyes. Once again, he was forced to do the dirty work for his failure of a son. Once again, he was prepared to shoulder the blame for all of his son's transgressions, even if it meant going to prison. Even if it meant committing murder. He had to come up with a plan.

"*You* have a debate to prepare, don't you?"

Baron was on his feet once more, "Yes, but I am well prepared."

"Don't be so cocky. Max Webb didn't get the nickname, "The Lion of the Legislature," by taking such things lightly. Remember, the voters favor the underdog, *even if he is Max Webb.*"

CHAPTER TWENTY-SEVEN

MAX Webb knew the next days would spell the difference between saving his presidential possibilities, and saving the life of the young woman in the photos. He wanted to help, but felt powerless to do so. She seemed too fragile to be caught up in such matters. He was used to the rough and tumble of politics, but she… she was so young. He also knew Prescott Marshall. The man was ruthless, and preyed on such innocence. Men like him had to be stopped, but how?

"Everyone has an Achilles heel, but what is his?"

Max was secluded inside his Capitol Hill office. His aids believed he was prepping for the upcoming debates, but the truth was, he was a veteran of such matters. Thirty years, in Congress, schooled him on the ins and outs of political life. He had sparred with the best, and defeated them all, young and old, alike. Baron James was no different. Deep down, Max Webb knew America voted selfishly. He knew voters would elect the man who would make them rich, no matter how unseemly they seemed to be. It was a political reality; America was deeply divided along lines of race. Some voters would never vote black, no matter how unsavory the white candidate appeared. Those were the voters he needed to impress during the debates.

Welcome to America, land of the free, home of the bigot.

Max unlocked his desk and reached inside the envelope he had been given, days earlier, by Prescott Marshall. The envelope contained his copy of the photos. He could use them to his advantage and let the chips fall where they may. After all, it was Baron who was caught in such an unfortunate position, not he. The girl, like so many others, would simply become collateral damage.

"Hell," he thought, *"She'll probably wind up on the talk shows, land a seven digit book deal, and retire rich!"* Scandal, he thought, while painful, might *ultimately* be the *best* thing for her. It was the politicians who lost all, the women went on to head think tanks, design clothes and lead alternate lives. Sadly, this girl was different. He knew *she* would be ruined.

Placing the photos, once more, inside the envelope from which they came, Webb knew the best defense was always a good offense, and what better place to start than with Prescott Marshall. He reached over to pick up the phone and punched the number that connected him, immediately, to his receptionist.

"Betty?"

"Yes, Senator?"

"Get me Prescott Marshall on the line."

"Certainly sir. Just a moment please."

Sometimes, it seemed as if Prescott spent his entire life waiting by the phone. Today was no different. In less time than it took Max to cross the room and retrieve the stack of morning news papers, Prescott Marshall was on the line.

"Aren't you prepping for the debates?" Prescott began, skipping any semblance of greetings altogether.

"Debates are old school. I called to see what our next plan of attack might be concerning our opponent. I half expected to open the morning's papers and see him spread eagle, if you'll excuse the pun, above the fold."

"Excuse me, but the last time we were together, I sensed a hesitance on your part to use such draconian measures."

Max liked what he was hearing. He knew the phone call was the last thing Prescott was expecting. "I think it is time we strike. That gives us two weeks until Election Day. By my calculations, Baron will never survive the next news cycle, and if he does, there is scarcely enough time to recover. In fact, I've already started to write my acceptance speech."

"Not so fast my friend. I assure you, the James campaign is far from finished. "

"It sounds like *you* are playing both sides. You wouldn't have gone behind my back, did you old friend?"

"Not at all Max, it has always been you and me. It's just that my experience dictates these matters be handled, delicately, that's all. Things, of such a *grave nature,* have a way of backfiring on a candidate. They could *backfire on you.*"

Max never let on he knew any more than he did. Prescott had taken the bait. Any further conversation would damage his strategy to protect the girl. There was a place for the photos and a chance to salvage his last shot at the presidency, but to do so, required a fool proof strategy. This conversation was over.

"I assume, as always, you will do what is best."

"I always do," Prescott added, hanging up his end of the receiver first, as was his custom. "I always do."

Max Webb was on the line again, to his secretary.

"Betty, get me Matt Walker."

CHAPTER TWENTY-EIGHT

"GOOD night doctor, should I lock up?" The nurse asked.

Dr. Felix Mays was, as always, pouring over the charts of his patients. One by one he held their X- rays up to see what mischief they had gotten into between visits. He enjoyed his work and knew his patients were among the most important in the world. As a result, he expected the best from his staff, and his favorite was his nurse of some twenty years, Peggy White.

White always checked in on Dr. Mays, to see if there was anything that should be done. She knew he always toiled late. It was a work ethic that he had developed, as a result of growing up poor in Appalachia. She admired that trait in him. She also knew his office, less than a block from the White House, represented the end to a dream. The offices once belonged to Dr. G.S. Wolf, who once served as the dentist to President Abraham Lincoln. There *was history* in the office and by claiming it, Dr. Mays believed he held title to that history.

Dr. Mays continued to examine his X-rays, long after Peggy White had left. Had he been listening, he would have realized the familiar sound of the office door closing, had not happened. Shortly after Peggy White said good-bye to Dr. Mays, the world said good-bye to Peggy White. Her body was dragged into a recess in the hallway, between his office and the doors of the elevator. Her heels made tracks in the carpet, in much the same way footprints disturb newly fallen snow.

Slowly the assassin made his way through the lobby of the office, making his way silently past an assembly of multi colored files, each one containing the misery of each and every individual patient Dr. Mays had treated. Peggy White took great pride in the files, making sure nothing was out of place. Today, however, she was gone and there was a stranger in their midst.

Dr. Mays left his precious x rays behind long enough to place a CD on the console behind him. The office was usually filled with the sounds of soothing music, but in his quiet time, Dr. Mays chose noise. Country music filled the room of a graying doctor who wore thick glasses, and battled the same bulge of everyone his age.

As the assassin made his way past the files, he spotted Dr. Mays, hard at work with chart still in hand. He appeared almost comical…a man of science, with the tools of his trade, stomping his feet to a song that offered little in the way of rhythm. Moments later, he began to sing.

Realizing the sound of his voice bore little in common to the sounds on the CD, Dr. Mays rose, once more, before learning he was not alone. He looked up to see the face of a man whose may, as well, have been a ghost. Had he been called to testify, he would have described the visage of a man who's face appeared almost totally white, with the exception of a pair of blazing red eyes. He would have sworn he was looking into the face of the devil.

"Take what you want," Dr. Mays offered up, realizing most of the time these men were looking for either money or drugs. The truth was, this assassin was looking for neither. Instead he pulled out a long sharp knife that almost looked as if it were cast from surgical steel. He knew this evening would not end peacefully.

"Please, I have a wife and kids," Dr. Mays pleaded, all the while backing to the rear of the room. As he stumbled backwards, the country music told of a man whose wife had left him. The assassin made no sudden moves. It was as if he knew where the doctor was headed before he got there. With no place left to back up, Dr. Mays began what would be the fight of his life.

Lunging over the top of the chair, that hours earlier, saw a string of patients, Dr. Mays looked no different than the others in his position. Men of science, suddenly forced to confront the very nature of man...survival. He knew if he was to survive, he would have to use raw strength to do so. The office was not a fortress and had no tools. There were hypodermics, but unlike the movies, they contained no sedatives that would render an assassin lifeless. Instead, they were but empty needles.

The assassin sidestepped the doctor's move, causing him to fall motionless to the ground, after he struck his head on the stark white counter that housed the dental tools of his trade. As he fell to the ground, the assassin plunged the knife squarely in the nap of his neck causing the vertebrae to shatter with an ugly sound... ugly enough to pierce the shrills of the country music singer who continued on. Dr. Mays rose, only slightly, off the ground before collapsing in a pool of bright red blood that offered a sharp contrast to the stark whiteness of his office.

The doctor in him caused the dentist to realize the wound would soon claim his life. His legs were already numb, and he could feel the coldness creeping into his arms and fingers, as well. In the moments before his death, he knew his eyes would witness his killer, and his mind would record it all. There was no one to document his death, hear his screams, or save his life.

Realizing the job was finished, the assassin turned his attention to the knife he had used moments ago, removed it from the neck of its victim, and wiped it off with one of the blue cloths dentists use to catch the saliva of their patients. He then focused on the task at hand. First, he stopped to look for any prints, or tell tale signs of evidence that may have been left behind. His hands were covered with gloves, but that didn't mean there weren't prints. He would dispose of the common pair of tennis shoes he wore, in the next day's trash. Because the doctor had fallen *away* from him, there wouldn't be any blood splatters on his clothes to worry about.

As the music played, the assassin turned over tables and emptied drawers to make it look as if the room had been vandalized. Had anyone been listening below, they would have thought the office was being wrecked, but the assassin made sure that no one else was inside the building. He had sat patiently inside his rental car, waiting for the last regular to depart. Peggy White was an unwelcomed surprise.

He smashed open the doors of the medical cabinet as that of a junkie looking for drugs. He proceeded to the front office and rifled the drawers that Mrs. White, and the rest of her staff, spent hours organizing. He knew there was little in the way of money, but took any spare change he could find. Twenty three dollars and thirty two cents was all the office managed to offer, but it would be enough.

He knew from experience, investigators would conclude it was random violence in a city that had seen too much. He also knew the bodies of Dr. Mays and Peggy White would sit in a morgue overwhelmed with hundreds of others, waiting months for an autopsy to be performed. Hurried detectives would reach hasty conclusions and settle on the obvious. In reality, the only robbery that took place happened while Dr. Mays looked on in his last moments of life.

After he was finished trashing the office and making it look like a burglary, he searched the pockets of his victim and retrieved a single set of keys. He marveled at how much he could tell about a man, just from a key chain and the number of keys on it. Each key ring also offered up a clue as to the person who possessed it. Dr. Mays kept, on his key ring, the only thing he really prized. It came with the office, and upped the asking price. In 1862, the building's most famous occupant, entered for dental surgery. The patient had a healthy fear of dentists and came to have a tooth pulled. The tooth was pulled, as was part of his jaw. The most prized possession of Dr. Mays was a single tooth he kept in a vial, attached to his key chain *He kept it with him at all times.*

There was one thing left to do. Frantically searching the drawers for the proper surgical instrument, the assassin reached down, and using a pair of surgical pliers, removed the exact same tooth from the mouth of Dr. Mays.

CHAPTER TWENTY-NINE

"WHO in the hell is that calling at this hour. Excuse me Father."

Father Haynes looked at the clock, and realized the lateness of the hour. He was used to students calling, especially on weekends as pranks. Whoever was calling, was calling later than the latest student, and he didn't like it.

"Father Haynes, do you still take confessions?"

"All priests do, but don't you think it's a little late. Unless you've just murdered the President, can't this wait?"

"You are closer to the truth that you might think, and no, this can't wait."

"If this is some type of prank, I assure you, this is in no way funny."

"It is no prank, and no one on this end of the conversation is laughing. It involves a murder, and the safety of my daughter. I need to confess my sins."

"Okay I've heard enough, unless you have something more to say, I'm hanging up."

"You know my daughter. Her name is Vanessa."

Father Haynes was no longer asleep but was staring at the stark contents of the room as if he had been awake for hours. The man on the phone was talking about Vanessa...Vanessa Sullivan.

"How do you know Vanessa?"

"I told you, she is my daughter?"

"Is she in any danger?"

"I believe so. In fact, I believe the threat to her life to be very real."

"Then why not call the police?"

The caller on the other end paused, drew back a deep breath that Father Haynes could hear on the other end, and replied. "The police are part of the problem. Only I can protect her, but you must protect my secret. I need to confess my sins.

"Can you come to the grotto, tomorrow morning?"

"No...by then it may be too late. I need to come now.!"

"Okay...okay...I'll get dressed. Meet me at the grotto in a half an hour. Who, should I be looking for?"

"I believe the person you are looking for, goes by the name, *Father Chiniquy*."

"So you are the one..."

"Yes...I am *that Father Chiniquy*. I will meet you at the grotto in a half hour, but you must give me your solemn vow to never speak of this conversation, or the one that lies ahead."

"You have my word."

"Your word is not good enough; I must have *your solemn vow.*"

CHAPTER THIRTY

Nashville Tennessee:

THE name on the tombstone read, Rachel Donelson Jackson. According to the marker, she died on Christmas Eve in March of 1828, but none of this mattered to the three young men who were about to disturb her slumber.

"I can't believe someone would pay *this* type of money to rob a grave. *This is Bitchin'*."

Jake O' Donnel stood less than six feet tall, wore sloppy blue jeans, and had pale white skin that glowed in the Tennessee moonlight, as if he were a ghost. The only thing not reflecting the moon's glow was the massive tattoo that covered most of his back and arms. It was warm that night, so he and his partner took off their shirts.

"I don't care nothin' bout the money; this is creepy!" His partner, Elliot Denny, was the type who feared everything, and cemeteries were clearly no exception.

"What if she wakes up?"

Jake seemed annoyed, and could only think of what the money would buy. Still he stopped his shoveling long enough to answer. "She ain't wakin' up; she's as dead as that wino we rolled last week, so stop your yappin' and keep diggin'."

The sound of the shovels carried much further than anyone might expect, but the truth was, no one, alive, was listening, save the dead, and one other person. He was very much alive. There, perched behind a hedge at the cemeteries gates, was a man who was told to let the men finish their task, and then give them what they deserved.

"What ya gonna do with the money?" Elliot asked, never being one to stop asking questions, or for that matter stop talking.

"I been looking at a bike down at the wharf. It's got a flamin' skull on the gas tank and the owner said he'd pay to have my initials put on it, if I take it off his hands...some mid-life dude. Seems he bought it, and then his old lady cursed him out. Said it was either the bike or her, so he said he ditched it. Truth is, he kept the bike and he was afraid to tell the old lady about it." Jake was now in a full sweat, working harder with each thought of his dream bike.

Elliot, on the other hand, was still asking questions. "Why didn't he whack her?"

Jake, growing even more annoyed, stopped once again, this time with a hint of frustration in his voice. "Don't you get it you asshole? Rich folk don't whack no one, they pay others to whack people *for them.*"

Both shovels struck what they were looking for, almost in unison. Beneath the dirt, at the legal depth, was a cement crypt. The sight caused the two, to work even faster. The sound of the shovels, removing the last vestiges of dirt, produced even more noise, than before. So much noise, neither man heard the footsteps of the man who had been watching their every move. It wasn't until Elliot started his next question that their intruder was spotted.

"Holly shi......" Elliot began, before Jake chimed in.

"Who in the hell are you?" Jake seemed angry for two reasons. First he knew the man was trouble. He also knew a third party meant less money and he wasn't about to have any. That's when the moonlight offered both men a glimpse of the man's face.

"Damn, Jake, he looks like that gas tank you was talkin' about," Elliot said.

Seeing the face of the man before him, Jake sensed trouble was not far away. He always kept *a shank* inside the upper portion of his biker boots, and only needed an excuse to get it.

"Come on man," he said. "If you're here for the money, then you have to do some of the work."

The man said nothing, and just stood there staring, for what seemed to be an eternity. The sweat on Jake's back was beginning to flow from the tension. Droplets were now starting to form on his brow, as well, and he could taste them as they made their way to his mouth. Elliot was also sweating, but saying nothing, for once, leaving all the talking to Jake.

Jake acted as if he dropped his shovel and then stooped down toward the top of the casket. Both men were well inside the hole and Jake knew he would have to retrieve the knife and exit the hole in one quick movement. He didn't like the situation, but welcomed the possibility of a good fight, no matter how bizarre his attacker looked. Jake would quickly discover, his attacker, believed only in quick battles.

It took less than an instance. The man was on Jake almost as quickly as it took Jake to remove the knife from his boot. He had no chance to use it. As soon as the knife was raised, a second, sharper, knife, was implanted in his gut. The man used a jerking movement, raising the knife higher and higher until blood began to spurt from Jakes mouth. The depth of the wound was deep enough to pierce part of Jake's spine, causing *his shank* to drop to the ground, producing a metallic sound as it struck the top of the crypt.

Elliot pissed his pants, and was once again in question mode, only this time his voice was whinier. "What ya' want?" He had just seen his best friend gutted like a deer, and knew he faced a similar fate soon, if that's what the man desired.

"Dig!" The man with the ghastly face ordered.

"But the casket's already been exposed." Elliot responded.

"Not that one, but the one next to it," the man ordered. He then climbed out of the hole and sat next to the mound of dirt that had already accumulated beside it and took a seat. The moon was now ducking in and out of the clouds making the night warmer and cooler with each pass. None of this mattered to Elliot who knew, the hole he was digging would soon be his grave, as well.

The shovel hit the second crypt with a thud, eerily reminiscent of the first. Elliot was both relieved and saddened. He knew as long as he kept digging he would be alive. He also realized once the task was finished, he faced the same fate as his friend, who was now halfway covered with the dirt that had fallen from Elliot's shovel.

The man with the ghastly face was standing. The moon had just emerged from a bank of clouds allowing Elliot to see the face of the last man he would see alive. He wasn't sure whether it was a man or a ghost. He would not live long enough to learn the truth.

"Use the shovel to pry the cover off the crypt," the man ordered.

Elliot did as he was ordered. At first, the cover of the crypt refused to budge. Then it gave a little, followed by a loud "Snap." The handle on Elliot's shovel had broken in two.

"Use his," the man with the ghostly face ordered.

Elliot wasted no time, and with just a little more coaxing, he removed the lid of the crypt to reveal the contents of an elaborate casket. The copper fixtures had turned green with age. Dirt covered what appeared to be some type of symbol on top. Clearly, the man inside had status. The torn remnants of an American flag had fallen off to the sides of the casket. Oddly, the flag had only a few stars, an indication of the man's age.

"Open it," the man ordered.

Elliot's fear of the dead quickly gave way to his own common sense. Like a mouse, cornered by a cat, about to face certain death, Elliot offered up his last piece of resistance. Few would be surprised that Elliot chose to fight back with his mouth.

"Fuck you," he said in a defiant tone that would be his last.

The man, with the ghostly face, struck Elliot over the head with the half of the shovel that had broken in two just moments ago. The sound of the blade coming in contact with his skull, made a sound similar to that made when the two shovels came in contact with the crypt. This sound, however, was different. The cemetery was home to the dead, and they recognized the sounds of death.

Elliot landed face down, next to the dead man inside the casket. The blood, from a gash on his head, flowed freely into the silken remains of what once was a glorious good-bye. His exit from the living was not so honorable. The man with the ghostly face used the other side of the shovel to impale Elliot face down in the casket. The sight of the two men made for an unusual sight in the pale moonlight. Looking up was the face of a man who had died centuries earlier. Face down, beside him, a man who spent his entire living in fear, and therefore had died years to early.

"Good-bye!" With that, the man with the ghostly face, reached down, grabbing the head of the corpse and pulling the knife he had just used to kill Jake, cut off a swath of the man's long graying head of hair.

"I doubt you'll be missing this," he said sarcastically," "Besides looks like you could use a hair cut."

The ghostly man left the cemetery, leaving only the dead behind, to bear witness to the gruesome events that unfolded. The mornings headlines would claim 'grave robbers met a grisly death…Foolish young men in search of a piece of history who got what they deserved'. Because nothing appeared to be stolen, the bodies were reentered, and those responsible for guarding the cemetery fired. Police kept their investigation open but seemed to be in no hurry to solve the crime.

The FBI was called in.

"Jesus Christ, not again!" Special Agent in Charge Robert Helms arrived on an overnight flight from headquarters. Not even he could believe it would happen again. "Can't they just let the poor bastards lie?'

"Who?" A young agent asked.

"Suffice to say, in his prime, this guy would have been your boss," Helms replied. "And suffice to say, this is the second time this type of shit has happened on my watch, and if I have anything to do with it, it's gonna' be the last!"

CHAPTER THIRTY-ONE

FATHER Haynes arrived first, and waited patiently behind the screen of the confessional located near the grotto. Few knew the grotto even existed. It was located between the cemetery on the back of the campus, and a dirt service road, that had long been turned into a lover's lane. He hurriedly dressed, and rushed to the location following the startling phone call. He was amazed to see that even at this late hour, there were still other priests milling around the Monastery. He feared what he was about to hear.

The first thing he heard was the sound of tires on gravel, as the vehicle approached. Two headlights grew larger as the car drew near, until he was blinded by their light. He could barely make out the large man who exited the driver's side of the car and walked around to open the door for the other man. He could tell from the sound of the engine, the car was large, and knew from experience it closely resembled the type reserved for dignitaries. When the door closed, he knew it was heavy; heavier than anything he could remember.

Still silhouetted by the car's headlights, a man walked toward the confessional, opened the door on the side opposite of Father Haynes and stepped inside. Father Haynes was now comfortably seated on the opposite side of the curtain.

"I trust you told no one about our meeting?"

"And I assume you are the same Father Chiniquy who's been sending the notes?"

"Yes I am. As I indicated by phone, there is not much time. I believe the life of the young lady is in serious jeopardy."

"You also indicated you believe she is your daughter."

Silence suddenly filled the room. Only the sound of the engine that idled close by could be heard. Father Haynes knew he had hit a nerve, but he also knew it was the only way to get to the truth. This was a confession, but based on their prior conversation, he wasn't about to hear it until he knew more.

"Yes…Vanessa…is my daughter. But she must never learn the truth. It would put her life, and quite frankly yours, in great danger."

"You make it sound like there is some great conspiracy out there."

"There is…I believe you know them as the Holy Alliance."

This time the silence came from Father Haynes's side of the confessional. He knew the Holy Alliance, but only from the history classes he taught. The Holy Alliance was the brain trust behind the Secret Treaty of Verona. European Royalty and the Vatican elite, who wanted nothing to do with the United States, or for that matter, their idea of religious freedom. According the history of the time, the Holy Alliance paid more than twenty thousand dollars to overthrow the ruling elite of Spain, before setting their sights on other nations.

"The Holy Alliance is history…"

The man on the other side of the confessional spoke as if he already knew what Father Haynes response would be. "Yes, but 'The Consortium' is not. They are as real as you and me, and so is the threat to Vanessa."

Father Haynes was puzzled. "If we are to believe Chiniquy, The Alliance killed Lincoln because he was about to free the slaves. What does that have to do with now, and even more importantly, what does it have to do with Vanessa?

"Imagine, if you will Father, that Lincoln was not only prepared to free the slaves, but write them a check as well. The implications would have been staggering. African Americans would have been *made whole*. Imagine an America where the civil rights movement occurred decades earlier. The economic wealth blacks would have. Now fast forward to present times. Imagine the threat from a President who really was prepared to do the right thing. Do you know how large that check would be?"

"You make it sound as if you are the President..."

"Not yet father, but soon."

"So Vanessa *is* your daughter?"

"Perhaps, now you see why her life is in danger. Once again, 'The Holy Alliance', or as you know them, 'The Consortium', has set their sights on assassinating a President."

"How much of this does she know?"

"None of it, not even the fact, she is my daughter, and for her safety it must always remain that way."

"But…"

"Why? The Consortium will stop at nothing to protect their interests. If that means eliminating the President and his offspring, they will only consider it the cost of doing business. Nothing more, nothing less."

"You make it sound as if you know you are about to die."

The man on the other side of the screen paused for a moment. Father Haynes could hear as he took a deep breath.

"Few realize that Lincoln dreamed his death long before John Wilkes Booth made it possible. He walked down the stairs one night, hearing cries. As he walked closer to the sounds he heard, he noticed they were gathered around a man lying on the table. That man was him. Lincoln was prepared to die, and in fact according to Chiniquy, made peace. Like Chiniquy, I am at peace, but I do not wish to see my daughter sacrificed. That is why I came to you."

"You are asking me to be your Chiniquy, aren't you?"

Father Haynes's last words fell on deaf ears. The man on the other side of the confessional left before his next question could be queried. The only sound he heard was the sound of a car door closing, and the sound of flying gravel hitting against the grotto's stone walls, as it sped off.

CHAPTER THIRTY-TWO

Lagos, Nigeria

THE massive structure, known as Vai International towered above the skyline of Lagos, Nigeria. Located in the newly developed region that included the Abuja International Tower and Hotel, the structure represented all that was good and bad with Africa. It represented a marriage of U.S. and African industry. The problem was, no one knew anything about the Vai, or for that matter, where the money to build such a massive structure came from. The common denominators were oil, blood diamonds, and illegal gun running, none of which endeared the conglomerate to the people of Nigeria. The locals suspected the Vai represented all of the above. The first floor was a massive shopping center that brought to that section of Nigeria, every store known to the western world. The next ten floors housed various businesses and corporations. International law firms also sought out the prestigious address. The last nineteen floors were used by Nigeria's newly emerging oil elite…Nineteen floors of luxurious living facilities that offered tenants an unobstructed view of the Lagos skyline. Lagos was the second largest city in Africa, behind Cairo. It wanted to be number one.

Ten stories below the surface of the thirty story building, the massive super computer, known as *MDA 3213,* started to awaken. The computer was located in a secure section of the building, accessible only by a special key that unlocked a panel where an optical scanner read the iris of the person seeking entrance. Only after the correct iris was scanned would the massive rear doors of the elevator open. There, a palm print was required before the visitor was finally able to gain entrance. Today, however, there were no visitors. Instead the red lights on the control panel signaled it was being activated, by a remote source. Within a few seconds, the lights on the panel indicated *Mandela* was fully functional and awaiting further instruction. It didn't take long for those instructions to arrive.

IMPUT DNA SEQUENCE 41280, SEARCH FOR MATCH.

Few, inside the complex, knew of *Mandela's* existence. The super computer arrived by way of The Congo, and rebel leaders were grateful to include it in a shipment of guns that were provided in exchange for diamonds and timber. The guns arrived via a U.S. transport plane, evacuating Americans from Liberia. The evacuees occupied the upper reaches of the plane, and the guns and other supplies were located beneath, in crates, stamped **"Humanitarian Aid."**

It is hard to imagine what type of humanitarian aid came, with enough ammo, to outfit a small army, but that's how *Mandela* made its way across Africa. Officially, the super computer was seized by hostiles, during the fall of Liberia. The U.S. believed it self-destructed, when the *abort code* was entered from a small room inside the NSA complex, in suburban Maryland. The truth is, no one knew that Mandela's travel plans were made long before any civilians left Liberia. No one knew, the man in charge of the Embassy at the time, Prescott Marshall, reprogrammed the abort code, rendering any instructions from Maryland, useless.

"Not nooww..." Marshall screamed, doubled over in pain, in obvious agony. He could barely focus on the computer screen in front of him, as the digital display faded in and out. The sharp shooting pains began in his abdomen and ripped upwards through his stomach. It was the type of pain normally reserved for childbirth, or kidney stones. It was not the first time he had experienced such pain, and as the tears welled in his eyes he knew it would not be the last. This was the curse *Africa left in him*, and with it, the gut wrenching realization that *his* life had been changed forever by those who tried to save it. "God...." he screamed before realizing, God was not on his side, and never would be. He swallowed hard, consuming with it any anger or belief that some higher power would come to his rescue. Pain had become his friend over the years, and his unpleasant reminder, of why he hated any and all things black.

In less time than it took a stop watch to click five seconds, Mandela was finished with its task. It would take longer for the information to make its way back across the Atlantic, to the offices of the man who controlled it. There, a flashing light on a laptop sitting atop an oak desk, instructed the owner of that laptop, to press the enter key, allowing the computer on the other end to complete the transatlantic link.

NO MATCH FOUND TO DNA SEQUENCE 41280.

"*That's impossible!*" Prescott stared at the computer screen in shocked disbelief. His anger was twofold. He knew the results were accurate, because Mandela never erred, and he knew the samples were pure because he had collected them himself.

His thoughts raced back to his dinner with Vanessa.

Her glass, the lipstick.

He compared the DNA sample he took from the glass while dining with Vanessa, and ordered Mandela to compare her DNA, to the DNA from the second swab taken, when Baron James agreed to have his genetic roots traced, as part of Vai-Genes experiment. All evidence pointed to a perfect match. He knew Mandela would provide the concrete proof. Baron James was the father of Vanessa Sullivan. They even looked like they could be related, and there was also the issue of the money. After his meeting with Mercer, he obtained copies of Baron's bank records from the same man who provided the photos. Why would Baron James pay so much to hide a secret he didn't need to hide? Why would he risk so much for a child who wasn't his daughter? It didn't make sense. Something must be wrong. He knew it in his heart.

"He has to be her father...he just has too...nothing else makes sense..." Marshall stared at the incoming data, for what seemed to be a lifetime, before deciding that if the information was accurate, he had only two courses of action. He could inform Mercer James of his mistake and release Baron from any sense of responsibility and for that matter, political risk, or he could do nothing. He could allow things to remain just as they were. That strategy, however, had one fatal flaw.

"The girl." Marshall knew the girl was the only thing that could derail his plans to control the James campaign and the man who would be the next president. *"The truth lies within her,"* he said softly under his breath.

"And, it must be allowed to die with her."

CHAPTER THIRTY-THREE

"SULLIVAN, git your shit and get the hell out of here." Dirk Adams was no stranger to the man huddled in corner of the Wake County, North Carolina jail cell. His past had more than one close encounter with the face of Gary Wayne Sullivan, and vice a versa. It had been that way since high school.

Every county has one, and Gary Wayne Sullivan belonged to Wake County, North Carolina. No one is born a bigot, but Gary Wayne Sullivan, would die one. He hated everything and everyone hated him. Crouched in the corner of the tiny jail cell, Sullivan was a pathetic wretch of a soul. Yellowed fingertips reflected years of chain smoking, and a lifetime of grease sat beneath each soiled fingernail. Filthy hands stroked a chin that showed three days stubble. He wore a stained wife beater tee shirt that showed arms with little or no muscle tone. On his right shoulder, a tattoo that read, 3/11. Three eleven's was the symbol for the KKK...K being the eleventh letter of the alphabet.

"Your tickets' been punched, you worthless bastard, only this time it wasn't that whore of a sister of yours. She ain't here and ain't gonna be no more. While you were rotten in here, someone out there gutted the bitch! Ripped her up something good!"

The words tore through Gary Wayne, like *he* was the one who had been assaulted. He wanted to rip the man's throat open, but knew that would only produce an "ass kickin'," and more time in the slammer. He knew they were baiting him, and that he would learn the truth, soon enough. For now, it was time leave.

As he made his way past the deputies, Gary Wayne mumbled under his breath.

"*I'll kill you all, each and every one of ya...if I ever get the chance.*"

"You got somethin' to say, say it loud enough for all of us to hear," Dirk Adams shouted, tightly clutching his long black nightstick, just in case. His knuckles turned white as he squeezed harder and harder. Gary Wayne was walking away with his back to Adams.

"Just gettin' my things and gettin' out," was the response. Gary Wayne's protests stopped when he saw the last person he wanted to see standing in the doorway. Her expression spoke volumes.

"Uncle Gary?"

He hadn't seen the girl in years, but in that brief moment, he felt as it he were standing face to face with his late sister. Her presence caused his heart to swell, only to sink again, when he realized that if she was there, something *was terribly wrong!*

"Vanessa..." he stumbled trying to find the right words, and clumsily continued when none could be found. "What are you doing here?"

Vanessa tried hard to fight back the tears and failed. Even though the world hated Gary Wayne Sullivan, the truth was, he was the only thing in the way of a father she ever knew. He raised her, in between trials for murder. It wasn't much of a legacy, and in fact, it sucked, but it was all she had, and she had to deliver the terrible news *his sister, her mother*, had been brutally murdered.

"You haven't heard have you..."

Gary knew what was about to come. He tried hard to deny the reality, at the same time bracing himself for the words that were about to come from her mouth.

"Momma's dead...somebody killed her."

Gary Wayne's mouth grew parched; he wanted a drink to quench his thirst; he was angry. His face turned a dark red, a drunken red, on a face flush with no other color. "When?"

"Last night, someone broke in and...and..." As much as Vanessa wanted, she couldn't hold back the tears. In that single moment, she was standing face to face with the reality of her own existence. She was the daughter of a mother who died a prostitute, an uncle who spent most of his life behind bars, or burning crosses. Sadly, through it all *she loved them dearly.*

Suddenly the tears began to flow.

Not even Dirk Adams had it in him to throw salt on a wound. Especially when the wound involved such a beautiful young woman. Adams remembered Vanessa Sullivan as the scrawny little girl, with dirt on her face. Now, the little girl had grown up; grown up to be a beautiful woman. This time the words that flowed from his mouth had softer tones. "This ain't official but seems like your sister had some enemies. Someone torched her trailer with her in it. Coroner ain't done with the autopsy yet, but it looks like she was hurt real bad, before she died."

"Let's go," Sullivan said, placing his arm around his young niece, and his back still to Dirk Adams, as if he were invisible. Truth was, *she* was the only thing that mattered in his life, and he had a pretty good idea what happened, long before he would ever let on. "You got some sort of car?"

"A rental."

"That'll work; give me the keys."

Vanessa was still crying. "….Where…where are we going?"

"To your mama's trailer. There's some things we need to find, before the sheriff's boys get to 'em first."

"If this is about money, I don't care," Vanessa said, still sobbing softly.

"This is more important than money," Sullivan said as he opened the door to the car. "This is about enemies and gettin' even."

As sad as it seemed, Vanessa also found herself once again wearing the shackles of poverty. Death for the poor wasn't like it was for the rich. Someone had died, and the poor knew, if a murder had been committed, *they had to solve it!* It wasn't like on TV. "Sounds like you have an idea who might have done this."

Gary Wayne started the engine to the car, and listened as Vanessa filled him in on the details she had already been told. He quickly sized up the situation, and knew what they had to do next.

"Your momma had a lot of enemies, but this don't add up. She'd been roughed up a lot in the past, but she knew how to handle herself. Truth is, most men who went there, wound up on the short end of the stick. A *"Louisville Slugger"* she kept in the corner of her bedroom, to be exact. If someone got the drop on your momma, they had to be good."

Vanessa knew the ugly truth, but didn't like hearing it put so bluntly. "You make it sound like momma was some sort of..."

"She was what she was and she wasn't proud of it. But she used the money to pay your way to school ,and them some."

"What about the money *you sent?*"

"*That's* what *this* is about. There's some things you need to know, but for now, it looks like you been up all night. How 'bout some breakfast?"

"You get you some. I'll just rest my eyes, here in the car."

Gary Wayne glanced at his niece as he continued down the road. She was drifting off to sleep. It seemed as if his young niece closed her eyes right after finishing her last sentence. She was beautiful sitting there, with flawless skin, just like Susan's. He could see the resemblance now that she was all grown up. He also could see the face of *her father*. The father she never knew, and the man he vowed, never to tell her about.

The drive to the trailer, took less than thirty minutes. Sullivan stopped once, at a *"Quick and Go,"* for some coffee, but Vanessa never stirred. He wasn't about to disturb her. She already had been through enough. He knew the road ahead, would only get worse.

A yellow piece of crime scene tape marked the spot where the trailer once was. Some of the sturdier pieces of furniture could still be seen smoldering; a *Lazy Boy Recliner*, and what, once, was her sofa. Black footprints marked the spots, where crime scene technicians worked through the night, collecting evidence. From the looks of things, the fire burned quickly. He knew from experience, the only water used to fight it, came *with* the firefighters. There were no hydrants this far out, and unless crews just happened upon the scene, everything was always, a total loss.

Gary Wayne walked through the crime scene as if it didn't exist. He reached out, and tore away the piece that guarded the stoop, and continued. It appeared as if he knew exactly where he was going, and truth be known, he did. The smell of the fire's remains caused Vanessa to cover her mouth with a scarf she kept in her purse. Gary Wayne walked through the only puddle the firefighting efforts left behind, and lifted what appeared to be the remains of a floor board.

"I'll be damned, it's still here."

"What?'

This," he said, digging through the pile of ashes that had formed near the floor, with his bare hands. Two pieces of charred lumber had to be removed, but Sullivan thrust his hands into the still hot recess in the floor, and held up what appeared to be one of those fireproof boxes you buy in a hardware store, just in case the unthinkable happens, or your trailer goes up in flames. "This is the closest thing you'll ever see to her *last will and testament.*"

Vanessa moved closer to inspect the find. "What's inside?"

"Like I said, your momma had *a lot* of enemies. *One*, in particular. The man she believed to be your father."

"My father?"

"You heard me right, your father."

"So she knew..."

"So why didn't she tell you? Ain't that what you want to know? 'Cause she didn't want you to know, that's why. Said it was for your own safety."

"You make it sound like he was somebody..."

"Important? Dangerous? I'll let you decide that. Your momma's dead, someone musta hated her pretty bad to do this. Let's just say, he wasn't really thrilled to learn you'd been born."

"Is it because he was black?" Vanessa asked the question she wanted to ask her entire life. She knew from her own features, her father was not white, unless genetics skipped a generation. She also knew why her mother kept her father a secret so long. Race in the south was different than race up north. Some things, she found, never really changed, and neither did Gary Wayne.

"He's a nigger! There I said it. Don't like it, but that's the way it is here. Worse back when you was born. He was uppity as hell too. Came here, one day, threatening your momma. Talkin' about how, if she had you, *he* would make her life *miserable*. That's when your momma decided she needed *some insurance*." He then held up the box for Vanessa to get a closer look.

In that instance, Vanessa knew this day had been planned long in advance. Her premonitions came true, when she saw her uncle reach deep into his pocket and produce a tiny key, small enough to unlock the mechanism that kept the box closed. Turning it to the right, the box popped open without any hesitation. There were only two keys. She assumed the other died along with her mother.

"Take a look," Gary Wayne, placed the open box on the hood of the car, paused briefly, and declared, "this should answer all your questions."

The box contained papers, that, at first, appeared to be the typical papers someone would leave in such a box...Canceled checks and some photographs of Susan Sullivan in better times. She was young and beautiful in the photos, and happy. They showed signs of wear, an indication her mother had taken them out of the box frequently. A series of newspaper clipping were stacked neatly under the checks, arranged in a manner that seemed to suggest that the man in the articles might have been special in some way. The checks were bound together with one of those red rubber bands that come with the morning paper.

The checks. The name! Baron James!

"Uncle Gary....why would mamma have canceled checks from Baron James?"

"Like I said, your mama knew a lot of people. Some of them pretty important, or so they thought."

"Do you think he is my father..."

"Don't know but seems he was *real interested* in making sure *you never knew*. Made your mama swear to keep his secret, and forked out a shit load of money to pay her off."

"But why?"

"Look Vanessa, you're all grown up now. Look at it…Baron wasn't no stranger to these parts. You probably read it in the papers. Grew up on tobacco road..hell where do you think this is? I knew Baron James when he was just the son of a dirt farmer like me; so did your mama. We grew up together, played together, hell I used to think he was my best friend. That was until all that *affirmative action* crap!" Gary Wayne's voice was starting to show signs of anger, and truth be known, jealousy. "*He* went off to a fancy school and learned to *play football*, while I had to *get a job* pumping gas to take care of your mother. You didn't know it, but your granddad was a no good son-of-a-bitch. Beat your grandma each and every time he got liquored up. She died early, leavin' me and your momma to fend for ourselves. Then one day Baron comes back, like he's the big nigger on campus."

You make it sound like you hate him," Vanessa said, carefully sifting through the other articles and making mental tabulations of the numerous canceled checks the box contained.

"I do, I hate him for what he became. Baron came home, acting like the cocks crow, like he owned the joint. He pulled in the station one day, in a long Cadillac, askin' me to pump his gas. He acted like *I wasn't even there*. Had some girls in the car with him, makin' fun of where he was from. Disrespectin', that's it, just disrespectin' everything and everybody." Gary Wayne searched Vanessa's eyes, as if he were looking for permission to continue. "Went into Raleigh, throwin' money around like it was goin' out of style and got good and drunk. That's when he came lookin' for your mother. She still liked him from childhood. He was actin' smooth."

"What do you mean?"

"She always had a thing for Baron, and he always had a thing for her. Your mama was the prettiest thing around these parts, and he was popular. Growin' up next door, they found out a lot about each other, when they was young. You know...innocent stuff. That night, however, things was a lot different. It's like all of a sudden, he was embarrassed by your mama. She told me she said somethin'...somethin' bad…and that's when...when...he hit her. Knocked her around somethin' good."

"And the checks?"

"Let's just say your momma *wasn't stupid.* When she found out *you* were on the way, she made sure her baby was taken care of. Sure it was a deal with the devil, but down here, that's all you got."

"So you mean the money *wasn't* from any legal settlement you received?"

"No, that was just a lie me and your mother made up. The money come from Baron James and a few other souls that your momma convinced they had what we called '*southern responsibilities*'.

For the first time in her life, Vanessa had been '*schooled*' about her own past. It wasn't easy learning you came into the world following a one night stand with a man who beat your mother, and paid her to *keep it secret.* It was even worse hearing the graphic details of that *one night.* She wanted to crawl into a whole and die, but there she was, surrounded by the burned out remains of a rotten childhood. There was no place to run.

Gary Wayne sensed her pain. "Look around you girl....there ain't no fancy schools for people like us. Hell, I been in and out of jail ever since you been born, shot at and shot up a few times. Life ain't been easy. All we ever had was you, and we both vowed to make things right. Bein' poor ain't no blessin'...it's a curse and money's the only cure. It ain't like we robbed a bank. He got what he wanted...and we…*we got paid.* Plain and simple."

"There's about fifty thousand dollars in canceled checks here."

"That sounds about right. He would send a check for five hundred fifty dollars to your momma every month. Your momma would sign it over to you and deposit in your checking account."

"There's only one problem?"

Gary Wayne looked puzzled. "What's that?"

"That would only cover a fraction of the money you sent me. Last time I checked, my account has close to three hundred thousand dollars in it."

Vanessa could see from Gary Wayne's expression, he too, had no idea where the rest of the money had come from. But in his mind, the countin' would come later. He had a score to settle first, a score to settle with *Baron James.* His sister was dead, and all signs pointed to the one man who had the most to lose. He knew men who knew how to settle scores, and would settle this one himself, *his way!"*

"Baron James," he said softly so as not to be heard. "*I don't care if you are about to be the next President. As far as I'm concerned, you ain't nothin' but a nigger....and a dead one, at that."*

As he looked back toward what remained of his sister's burned out trailer, he saw Vanessa clutching the metal box in her arms as if it were one of those jewelry boxes a mother handed down to her daughter. In his heart he knew she deserved better. He just didn't know how to give it to her.

" *Goodbye mama."*

Once again, the tears were starting to flow.

CHAPTER THIRTY-FOUR

"GIRL, come inside, you look like you've been through a war!"

Vanessa Sullivan arrived home shortly before nine o'clock, the morning after her mother's death. The trip to and from Raleigh had been grueling, twelve hours on the road in a twenty four hour span. She had not yet been able to grieve, and would have to put any thoughts of grief on hold. There standing in the doorway, as she turned the key, was a grimed face Mrs. Avery.

The events of the last twenty four hours took their toll. Any conversation would have to wait. Overcome with emotion, Vanessa made her way through the door, brushing past Mrs. Avery, collapsing on a sofa in the living room. Sebastian appeared to offer the only comfort she would accept. With her cat curled comfortably on her lap, she began to cry.

"She's dead, Mrs. Avery."

"Who child?" Mrs. Avery questioned.

"My mother. That's why I left in such a hurry yesterday, without telling you. They called me and told me to hurry, and I could tell from their voices, something was wrong."

"How?"

"She was murdered!"

"Murdered! But who, who would do something so horrible?" Mrs. Avery was visibly shaken as well. She knew little about Vanessa's mother, but enough to know, there was a long list of those who might have been responsible. She was not prepared for what Vanessa had to say next.

"I believe her death may have something to do with what's inside *this box*."

"Where did you get that?"

"She hid it Mrs. Avery. It was in the burned out ruins of her trailer." Vanessa proceeded to tell Mrs. Avery the sordid details of her mother's life. She had shared much with her in the past, but this time the truth brought with it the horrible realization that Vanessa Sullivan was a child who suffered greatly.

Mrs. Avery walked over to the sofa and sat down next to the young woman, she believed to be her own in many ways, and provided a shoulder to cry on.

"Tell me about the box."

"The box was momma's secret, one she never wanted anyone to know about, unless *something happened.* We'll something happened, she's dead and I think I have a pretty good idea who would have wanted her out of the way."

"What do you mean?"

"Look at these," Vanessa said, pulling the canceled checks from the box. "They're 'motive for murder canceled checks', but that's just the beginning. Wait until you see who from. Let's just say he had *a motive to murder!*"

Vanessa turned the key and opened the box for Mrs. Avery to examine the contents. Mrs. Avery was stunned when she saw the name on the checks. "Am I to assume the name on these checks is..."

"One in the same, *Baron James.*"

"But why would *Baron James* be sending money to your mother?"

"It seems pretty clear, she was blackmailing him. My mother, as you know, was not the most pleasant of women. I know what she did, how she made her living, and have a better understanding than you as to *why* she did it. Growing up poor in the South wasn't easy. Southern women, with money, do the same thing; they just limit the number of partners they entertain, but in the end, it's still prostitution."

Mrs. Avery wanted to express her opinions on the subject, but she knew now was not the time. Vanessa was not only mourning, she was venting, and *Baron James* became the object of her obsession.

"Some of these checks were written recently," Mrs. Avery said, carefully examining each canceled check.

"That's just the half of it. I checked the dates on the checks, and they correspond with the money that's been deposited in my account since I was a little girl. It's almost as if..."

"He's *your father.*"

The gravity of their words struck both women at almost the exact same time, but neither was prepared for what followed.

"Baron James is perfect for America, Baron James is America."

The television set, located opposite the sofa, was as always, left on. Mrs. Avery, like most women her age, used it to keep her company on the nights when Vanessa was away. It was always tuned to the news as Mrs. Avery liked. This time, when the commercial played, they both saw it at the same time. The man in the commercials, the man about to be the next President of the United States, bore a striking resemblance to the woman seated on Mrs. Avery's sofa. It was clear to both women; Baron James could actually be *Vanessa's father*.

Both women put any sense of grief on hold and quickly tried to get a handle on started to grasp the seriousness of the situation. Perhaps

Baron James didn't want to acknowledge a controversial past. What if he was as out of control?, as Gary Wayne described. Would those who pulled *his strings* welcome such a development or try to *silence it*? Was her mother's murder as it appeared a cover-up?

Vanessa's mind was now swirling, sensing she was indeed in danger. She knew enough about Washington to know change was never welcomed. She had studied enough of history to know those in power would do what ever was necessary, to protect their power. For the first time in her life, she was stifled by her fear, and it showed no signs of letting go.

"Do you think *he did it?'* Vanessa asked Mrs. Avery?

"Perhaps, but what if he didn't?"

The sound of the phone ringing on the coffee table put an early end to a conversation that would be continued. The expression on Mrs. Avery's face, and the stern nature of her voice, made it clear, a day of surprises, had at least one more to offer. Handing the phone to Vanessa, she simply said, "Its for you; it's a man who says he's Matt Walker."

"Matt Walker, the TV reporter?"

"That's what he says."

"Hello," Vanessa said with a puzzled sound in her voice. She knew who the man was on the other end of the phone. She remembered calling his office and getting only a voice recorder. Why would he be calling now?

As her mouth dried and her pulse quickened, her first thought was to hang up. Fear trumped logic. Had this man somehow learned of the link between her father, and the death of her mother? Was she caught up in, what would soon become a national scandal?" Her mind continued to race through the conversation pleasantries, and she saw her life play out on the tabloid entertainment shows.

"On the next, *Entertainment Nightly, the President and the Prostitute*."

"Vanessa...Vanessa Sullivan?" For a moment, Matt wondered whether the woman on the other end of the line was listening. He had just dropped a bombshell, and she heard nothing.

"Yes sir," Vanessa responded.

"We need to talk...and we need to talk soon," Matt Walker began. "I have a lot to tell you, but I don't want to tell you on the phone, but it's important," he continued. "I have reason to believe your life may be in danger."

"Where in the hell have *you* been for the last forty eighty hours," Vanessa added sarcastically.

It was not the reaction Matt Walker was expecting. The conversation almost seemed as if she already knew.

"I would be glad to meet you," Vanessa shot back, "but no cameras."

"Actually I was going to say the same thing," Matt responded. "I'm not calling for your story. I'm calling because it seems we have a mutual friend."

"And that would be..."

"I'm not at liberty to say, suffice it to say, he is a very important man. One who says is he very concerned for your safety. Is there someplace we can meet."

Mrs. Avery was following the conversation by piecing together the parts of a one sided conversation she could hear. Looking at her face, Vanessa knew her closest friend in the world aged a decade in just a few moments, but Mrs. Avery was shaking her head up and a down as if to say yes.

"He may be the one man who can make sense of all of this," she offered up.

"Meet me at the Bolivian in an hour," Vanessa said, "do you know where it is?"

"Georgetown, I stop in sometimes when I'm meeting sources."

"Then let's just call me *a source*."

The call on the other end of the phone went dead, leaving Vanessa and Mrs. Avery to be left alone with each other. It was clear, the life of Vanessa Sullivan was spinning out of control, and there was one more person she was concerned about. She remembered the look on the face of her uncle. She knew he would do what ever it took to avenge his sister's death, even if that meant killing the man he believed to be responsible…Even if it meant killing the man history was ready to coronate, as the first black President of the United States and the man Vanessa now believed to be her father.

Placing her head inside her hands, she began to shake, and then, to cry. The events of the last few days were too much for anyone to handle. Vanessa Sullivan was no exception.

Walking away from the living room, so as not to disturb her, Mrs. Avery stood in the doorway and looked back as Vanessa began to mourn. There was nothing she could do, except to wait. The answers she prayed for would come in an hour if Vanessa was up to hearing the truth.

CHAPTER THIRTY-FIVE

IF Matt Walker was anything, he was prompt. Glancing down at his watch, it read 11:55, five minutes before Vanessa was scheduled to arrive. He took a seat at a table facing both the window and the door. It was pure instinct. Reporters, were usually unfamiliar, with whom they were about to meet. Matt Walker had never seen Vanessa Sullivan, but he knew she had seen him. He would scan the incoming customers for the one face that seemed to be looking for someone, the person, who seemed to be *looking for him*. She did not keep him waiting for long.

Vanessa Sullivan walked into the Bolivian at exactly twelve o'clock, and she did not disappoint anyone who watched her make her entrance. Her long dark hair, as always, was combed neatly so that it fell onto her shoulders. It was clear she had been crying, and still, her beauty was undeniable. She possessed the beauty of youth, and beyond.

"Mr. Walker," she said extending her right hand to meet his.

"Yes, and you must be..."

"Vanessa...Vanessa Sullivan...and if you don't mind I prefer we sit here." Vanessa motioned toward a table in the middle of the room. It was a table where any conversation would be noticeable with just the slightest increase in volume. It was the safest table in the room, for the conversation they were about to have.

Matt stood, walked toward the center of the room, and instinctually moved to pull her chair out for her.

"Thank you," she said softly. "Thank you for being so polite."

"With what you've been through, it's the least I can do."

"So you know...about my mother?"

"I do...but I must admit, I wasn't prepared for what I read. I was hoping you could provide some clues."

"And *I* was hoping you could do the same. To begin with, why don't you tell me *who* sent you here?"

"As I said, he doesn't want his identity disclosed."

"So you are his gopher?"

"I wouldn't put it like that. Let's just say there is a story here, but not the one you're thinking about." Matt answered, this time with the slightest hint of defensiveness in his voice. Vanessa noticed she wasn't the only one in the room with visible signs of scarring. "Who did that to you?" She inquired.

"Let's just say it's been an interesting seventy two hours for me too." Matt said by way of breaking the ice, and managing to let a little of his personality escape at the same time.

Vanessa could already see it. She could see how he persuaded so many to tell their stories in the years she had been watching him, in Washington. She still couldn't figure out why her name wasn't already plastered on the evening news. Surely, it was *Baron James* who sent him. After all, *he* was the man behind the messages, and the man, she believed, was her father. Vanessa was never one for mystery, or shyness.

"*Baron James* sent you, didn't he?" she asked, looking Matt Walker directly in the eyes.

"Actually no, but I'm curious, why would you think he sent me here?"

"Because..." Vanessa began, before hesitating once more. Matt wasn't acting like she thought he would act, when she introduced Baron's name. If Baron was his source, Matt was quite the poker player.

"Why?" Matt continued, believing there may be an opening to this mystery. Vanessa realized she had nothing to hide and no one to protect but herself. If she was in danger, she was sitting across from the one man who might be able to help her. She also knew, she needed, and would demand, guarantees. She needed to know that the information she was about to divulge would not wind up on the evening news.

"You must promise me, what I am about to tell you, will not wind up in some story either by you or one of your colleagues."

Matt knew, the door to the truth had opened, but experience told him to tread softly. He knew, that to look too eager, would make him look out of control and inexperienced. He had witnessed it too many times before. He watched young reporters, eager for their first scoop, act like schoolboys, on their first date. He had also watched their potential interviews walk away, fearing the reporter was too inexperienced to handle the truth, or for that matter, confront those who needed to be confronted.

"I can give you some guarantees, but no reporter can give a blanket cloak of protection."

"I assure you *I haven't killed anybody* if that's what you're asking," Vanessa countered.

"No, what I mean is, even reporters, or should I say those of us who still believe in ethics, need to obey the law."

"He's my father." she said in a tone just loud enough to be heard, but lacking the volume it needed to produce the reaction such a declaration deserved.

"Who? Who's your father?"

"Baron James!"

Matt had heard all of the stories before. He heard murderers confess and the priests beg for mercy. He heard the politicians try to explain graft, and adulterers argue they were blinded by beauty, but what he was hearing now, was news, even to him. *Baron James had a child, apparently out of wedlock, and that child was sitting across from him in a coffee shop in Georgetown.*

"*Baron James is your father?* How do you know? Surely you must have proof."

"He is...I just learned about it yesterday… everything I just told you I can prove, and since none of it is against the law, I trust I will not see this on tonight's news." Vanessa knew she was in complete control. She knew it, and so did Matt. She worked him like a seasoned fisherman, who reeled in a prize catch. She didn't do it on purpose, it was instinct. She knew it and Matt Walker was a quick student.

"Your game, your rules. I don't suppose you brought the proof with you...or did you?" Matt said in a whispered tone so as not to call attention to a conversation that everyone in the room would die to be privy to.

"I may look naive, but I assure you I have *grown* a lot in the last few days. If you don't mind, I would like to leave."

Matt Walker rose to his feet once more, walking around to the other side of the table to pull Vanessa's chair out so she could do the same.

"My place?"

"I'm married."

"And I'm only in the market for answers, don't flatter yourself."

Matt Walker liked what he saw in this woman. He knew she could be his daughter, and never entertained the possibility of anything beyond reporter and source. He only wished his own daughter would conduct herself in the same manner, but then again, no parent would wish upon a child the nightmare Vanessa Sullivan had lived through. A nightmare, he knew, that was only beginning.

"I'll drive."

CHAPTER THIRTY-SIX

THE Heritage Motor Hotel on Old Richmond Highway looked just like its name suggested. It was old and sported paintings of the founding fathers, throughout. There was a musty smell, as you entered the lobby, that suggested it might have been flooded at one point in its history, although it was located far away from any flood plains. The carpet underneath the floor was as sticky to walk on. It was consistent with what one might find inside a frat house, where more beer made it to the floor than to the mouths of those who were supposed to be drinking it. The woman behind the counter looked as if she applied her makeup at night with a paintbrush. It was clear she was trying to conceal more than just the lines in her face, but the lines from her past as well.

"Can I help you?" she said looking back from behind a pair of glasses that were already three prescriptions too old. Her voice had a raspy sound, that when combined with her breath, left no doubt she was a smoker. The roots of her platinum hair betrayed that dark brown hair on top. She may have been beautiful at one time, but then again, the same could be said for the Heritage.

"Doctor William Weaver," the man answered, reaching for a pen to fill out the registration cards that were scattered across the top of the counter.

"We don't get many *doctors* in here," she said, winking at the same time. "Will you be spending the whole night?"

"Yes ma'am," the man added.

"If you don't mind me asking, what type of doctor are you anyway. I mean, I wouldn't want you operating on me, with those filthy fingers."

"Do you insult all of your guests?" The man said offering up only a hint of righteous indignation.

"Only the ones who lie about who they are, and I guess that would be just about everyone who checks in. We get people who are running from the law, running from their wives, hell running from just about everything, but we never get no legitimate doctors. So, unless you are planning to perform abortions in that room you're about to rent..."

The man cut the woman off in mid sentence. "Do you accept cash?" he asked, extending a wad of twenties her way.

"They spend just like plastic here. Hell, it's plastic we don't accept Doctor...I didn't catch your last name."

"Sullivan...I mean Weaver. You'll have to excuse me. I have had the problems of a patient on my mind for quite some time."

"No explanations needed," the woman responded, pointing to a sign just over the reception desk that read, "NO QUESTIONS ASKED."

As the man made his way across the lobby toward the elevator that would take him to his room on the third floor of the seedy hotel, the woman at the desk waited for the elevators to close before picking up the phone. Within moments the police were outside, waiting in the parking lot, cash in hand. They also paid cash, money for tips about unusual guests, and this man was as unusual as they came.

"He claims to be a doctor," she said, adding embellishment in hopes of getting more money.

"And what makes you think he ain't?" the officer seated closest to the window asked, moving backwards as she moved closer, to avoid the onslaught of her breath.

"No doctor I know has a tattoo on his forearm, and certainly not the one I just seen."

"Was it a tattoo of his mother?"

"Not unless his mother taught math," the woman responded. "It was some numbers, 3/11."

"So maybe he forgets his address?"

"Sometimes you guys can be *so...thick*, " she said sarcastically. "Where I come from, that's code for the KKK. And if all them headlines are correct, there's a Presidential debate about to happen, and that man running for President...*that Baron guy*...ain't he black?"

The woman was right. The information was good enough for another twenty, which the officers knew would go toward another carton of cigarettes and a bottle of *Irish Rose*.

"You get back inside, before you catch the death of..."

With that the woman started to laugh, which produced a hacking cough that brought with it the day's phlegm. "Hell," she said with a baritone that betrayed her sex. *"Death don't want to have a damn thing to do with this place."*

Back inside his room, Dr. Weaver placed the only bag he carried on the twin bed beside him, removed his shoes and picked up the remote. Surfing through the channels he settled in on a repeat of "*The Andy Griffin Show*." It reminded him of home. It reminded him of simpler times. Within moments he was sound asleep.

CHAPTER THIRTY-SEVEN

ISAIAH Banaku motored up U.S. 1 from the University of Maryland, where he spent most of his days as a graduate student studying U.S. History. The shinny black sedan left little doubt that the Banaku's were "*well off.*" Banaku, chose not to brag, but instead kept a low profile.

The car was a gift from his father, for his eighteenth birthday. Back home in Africa the Banakus were considered royalty. A long line of descendants made their way back and forth between the home of his ancestors, and the home of his birth. Banaku felt equally at home in both places.

As Banaku headed north, the man on the radio reiterated the importance of the upcoming Presidential elections. He spoke of how history was about to be made. The shallowness of the conversations that followed angered Banaku. He longed for the days when politicians stood for something, and believed *his ancestors* would find both candidates *offensive*.

"How can they call this history?'" He questioned, "When so many around the world are dying." Banaku spoke from the perspective of a man who had seen death and dying on two continents. He had been warned over and over again, the areas, in and around the University, were not as safe as they could be, and yet he lived in Prince George's

County, Maryland. Prince George's County was home to the wealthiest black Americans in U.S. history. It also had a staggering crime rate. It reminded him of home.

Nigeria, the land of his birth, was a land of contrasts. The oil that bubbled beneath the country, was some of the purest *crude* ever produced. It needed little in the way of refinement, and that left the wealthy and the powerful, lining up to stake their claim. His two homes had much in common. Both bragged of their wealth, and yet ignored an education system that was in shambles. Students in both places lagged behind in test scores. Banaku believed it was up to African Americans and America's Africans to change all of that.

"Tell me about *education!*" Banaku banged his fists on the steering wheel, and was shouting at the man on the radio, as he continued to babble on about *Baron James*. "What does *he* plan to do to fix the schools of the nation? What are his positions on Africa? Does he consider himself to be African, or white? Someone, *please*, ask him the questions?"

Had he been paying attention, Banaku would have noticed that his car had ventured too far from the beltway, and with each passing mile, further and further away from what some considered the "safe zone." Drive-by shootings were common in this part of the county and beatings from police had been making headlines for years. Scandal after scandal kept the Prince George's County Police Department in the headlines. The Justice Department investigated as did, just about, every journalist who set their sights on TV in the nation's capitol.

Banaku was screaming so loud at his invisible demons, he failed to notice the sound of an approaching car. The flashing lights in his rearview mirror caused his knees to grow weak. He knew he had done nothing wrong, but looked down to check the speed on his speedometer, just in case.

"Fifty five," he said with a horrified sound in his voice. Glancing toward his left, he saw the posted speed limit for the area. "Forty-five!"

Banaku knew better than to reach for his license, until told to do so, and then making sure he did so, slowly. He could see the approaching officer in his rear view mirror, and could see the cop had already drawn his gun.

"No sudden moves," he said softly under his breath. The officer was now less than five feet away.

"License and registration!"

"Was I speeding?"

There was no response from the officer, just a repeat of the same command. "No lip, just license and registration."

Banaku's heart quickened as he reached down, making sure he kept eye contact with the officer, all the while. Slowly reaching down, he then methodically pulled his wallet from his left hip pocket, handing it over to the officer, who still was holding the gun down, almost out of view.

"Isaiah Banaku?" The officer said in an almost accusatory tone.

"Yes sir." Banaku responded. He knew from newspaper articles, to remain calm and stay polite. He had heard the stories of officers who opened fire without provocation. He also knew he was speeding. The ticket would be steep, but it was the embarrassment of being stopped that caused him the most anxiety. His world was moving in slow-mo. He could see the face of every motorist who slowed down because of the brightly colored flashing lights.

"Sir..."

"Shut up…" the officer shouted. "If I need you to speak, I'll ask you."

Banaku could tell from the sound of the man's voice he was Caucasian. It was difficult to tell his race, because the spotlight from the cruiser was positioned to shine directly in his face. All he could see was the outline of a cop, who still was wearing his hat, nothing more.

The officer fumbled with the card for a few moments, snapped it across his wrists as if it were a playing card, and glanced over his shoulder as if he were waiting for the traffic to clear. Where there were no cars in sight, he placed the driver's license on a clipboard he was holding in the other hand. The gun was still clearly out of its holster and lodged just beneath the clipboard.

"Please, place both of your hands on the steering wheel," the officer said barking out another command.

Banaku did as he was told.

The first bullet stuck Banaku in the temple, sending a fine mist of brains, blood, and gray matter across the dashboard of the car. The bullet left his left temple and exited just over the shoulder of the officer holding the clipboard. The second shot entered Banaku's chest, and exited in the back seat of the automobile. Ballistics would later determine the gun was stolen two weeks earlier from a gun store in rural Virginia. Six other shots would enter and exit Banaku's body, before the carnage would stop, and even then it was far from over.

The officer, still holding the clipboard with Banaku's license attached to it, walked calmly over to a man who had stopped shooting, and was now sitting in the front seat of his cruiser. The man was an African American, who said nothing. When the officer left the car once more, to return to Banaku's vehicle, the African man exited the front seat, and opened the car's trunk. There he pulled out a container filled with gasoline.

Walking to the passenger side of Banaku's car, the African man opened the door, wearing rubber gloves, and opened a vial containing two Q-tip swabs. He used the swabs to dab some of the blood that had already started to coagulate on the dashboard of Banaku's car. Banaku was slumped over the steering wheel, lifeless. Once the swabs were safely placed inside the vial, he finished the task.

The gasoline made a splashing sound that caused the officer in the cruiser to vomit once he realized the true nature of the assignment he had just completed. After all, he was a man who had taken an oath to combat crime, but instead had just committed the gravest crime of all. He had taken a man's life, and he did so for money, lots of it. He knew he was being well paid, and had replayed the scene in his mind, as to how he would spend the money. He wanted to get even with his ex-wife, who left him for another man. Then he would move out of the hell hole he called home. As far as he was concerned, the place was full of blacks, who were always killing each other. Being asked to kill one more seemed to make sense. He knew *the money men* controlled everyone, and believed this day was his payday. His deal with the dark side had already been made. It was time to collect.

The sound of a lit match made a swooshing sound that soon increased to a roar as the contents of the car began to catch fire. The smell of rubber, gas, and a human body filled the air. It was a terrible odor that caused the officer to vomit once more. The nights sky was now filled with thick black smoke and crackling embers that rose from the wreckage like lightening bugs in a summer's sky. Both men knew it would be only a matter of time before the others would arrive. Soon it would be time to go...very soon.

"Hurry it up, damn it," the officer screamed out of the front window, or I'll have to bust you just to make things look right once the others get here."

The African man was already making his way toward the passenger side of the officer's car. As the door opened, the officer looked sideways, "Bout time asshole....."

The shot from the man's revolver struck the officer in much the same place as the shot that killed Isaiah Banaku. The African man emptied the revolver, filling the officer with the same number of bullets, he spent on Banaku. Once the pistol was empty, he threw it in the front seat of the cruiser, and emptied what remained of the gasoline, splashing it wildly about the hood and trunk of the car.

It took one more match to complete the task. The African man then walked less than fifty yard down the road. There, hidden in the bushes, was the car he left behind less than a day earlier. The keys were exactly where he left them. The officer was right. It didn't take long for reports to be phoned in, of not *one*, but *two* cars on fire. When reporters got copies of the 9-1-1 tapes, there was glee on the voices of some of the callers, that one of the cars that had been set ablaze was *a police cruiser*.

No one noticed the car making its way back down U.S.-1 in the opposite lane. The man inside made sure he obeyed all speed limits, because he too was black, and he had seen just what could happen to innocent people, who broke what were considered to be simple laws. He had seen first hand, that in some parts of America, things were almost as savage as they were in his African homeland. He hated killing one of his own, but by now it no longer mattered. The cop was a different story. Had anyone been paying attention, they would have noticed the man in the late model BMW was traveling the speed limit… and smiling.

CHAPTER THIRTY-EIGHT

THE sound of the phone startled Matt Walker. He glanced down and looked at Vanessa. She was still sleeping, and in fact Mrs. Avery had placed a blanket on the two of them so as not to disturb them. He checked his watch and immediately panicked when he realized the hour. He had spent the night, and while nothing happened, he knew Cecilia would not be listening to reason. He also knew she had reason to suspect the worse, and only fatigue saved them both from something they would have regretted for quite some time. This situation was salvageable, but the dog house was being warmed up at home.

"Matt Walker!"

"Mr. Walker, this is Max Webb."

"So, I don't believe I ordered any of your product."

"Product?"

"Yes sir…whatever it is that you are selling..." Matt checked to see if Vanessa had stirred, before continuing. He had given his word, to keep Max's identity secret, and if Matt Walker was known for anything, it was protecting his sources.

"By now, Matt, you've probably come to the conclusion *you are* on to something."

"Yes, I must admit, your product has piqued my interest."

"And yet like all of the best reporters, you don't have *all of the answers* and are prepared to *wait*, until you have all of the facts, before pressing forward. Am I correct?"

"Your product does have some holes that need to be filled in before I make a larger order."

"As my grandfather might say… in due time… in due time."

"And how much '*due time*' are we talking about?" "Soon, but now is not the time. I have taken the liberty, however, of sending you some information that should have been transmitted directly to your Palm Pilot. Are you seeing it?"

Matt glanced down at the Palm Pilot on the table and saw that he had three messages. He was certain, at least one of the messages, was from Cecilia, the other two would remain a mystery for the short while.

"I see that what you are saying," Matt answered.

"Good! I have sent you some information on a gentleman I believe you might know something about. His name is Prescott Marshall."

"I am more than familiar with that product as well, but isn't that outside your scope of expertise?"

"Come now Matt, I won't insult your intelligence, if you don't insult mine. I know for a fact the woman I sent you to take care of, dined with him the other night at "The Palm Coast." In fact, if you like, I can tell you what they had for dinner."

"That won't be necessary. What is the nature of the information you sent?"

"When going to war, one must always know *who* their enemies are. I have sent you some background information on Prescott Marshall. Let's just say it will come in handy for you as you piece the pieces of this puzzle together. How much do you really know about *The*

Consortium?" Max Webb could sense he was in control. He knew it was time for this conversation to end as well.

"Oh, and Matt?"

"Yes sir?"

"I assume I'll be seeing you at the debates? This one will be one for the books as they say." Max allowed the line to go dead before hanging up. He knew this would be the most important performance of his life. He knew the upcoming debates would be anything but that.

"Who was that?" a groggy Vanessa Sullivan inquired, as she began to awake, repeating the same process and reacting in much the same manner Matt Walker had just moments ago.

"Just a friend, trying to sell me something," Matt said, gazing back at her. Even in the morning she was beautiful. "Just, a friend?"

"Did we spend the night together?"

"We did, but nothing happened. We have Mrs. Avery to thank for that."

"And Sebastian," Vanessa added, pointing to Sebastian who, as always, was curled up in between her feet and the back of the sofa.

They both laughed an uneasy laugh, knowing a single night had changed their lives forever. They both wondered whether it was the pressure of the last few days, or something more.

"Cecilia's gonna kill me." Matt said jumping up from the sofa, as he realized only one fire had been put out.

"If at all possible, could you pick a more appropriate phrase? Let's just say you have a lot of explaining to do."

"No need to, everything is fine at home," Mrs. Avery said, entering the room with a tray containing two mugs of hot coffee, and some pastries. "I took the liberty of strolling through your phone list last night when you fell asleep. I remember what it was like to lay awake wondering where my loved one was, back when I had one. I spoke to

Cecilia and told her you were in no condition to drive, because of your medication. I told her you took a pill that knocked you out, and that you would be spending the night here. I guess because of my age she believed me, or should I say Matt, perhaps it is because *she trusts you.*"

At that point, Matt didn't know whether to hug Mrs. Avery, or strangle her. He was glad she called, and knew Cecilia understood, because she had received calls just like it before, but her words cut through like a knife. He also knew there still would be hell to pay when he went home. Still what troubled him the most was what he felt last night. He knew, deep down in his heart, Cecilia had reason to worry. *In his heart, he had betrayed her.* As his eyes met those of Mrs. Avery, he could see, she knew it, as well.

"Come now," she said, placing a cup in front of both of them. "It has been a long couple of days, drink up while the coffee's still hot."

The sound of the doorbell was unexpected and caused Matt to almost spill the cup of coffee that Mrs. Avery had just poured.

"Let me get that," Matt said, as he started toward the door.

Matt, breathed a sign of relief, as he glanced through the curtains that lined the panels on both sides of the door. "It just a messenger," he said.

Vanessa on the other hand, wanted nothing to do with messengers any more. She had seen too many in recent days, to feel any degree of comfort. This time, Matt, was there. This time, she believed, she was protected.

Matt returned to the room, holding an envelope that appeared identical to the other one Vanessa had received. Again, there were no markings on the outside, just her name. The letters, as always, were uniform in height, and perfect in their placement on the envelope.

"Open it!" Mrs. Avery said, with an enthusiasm in her voice that startled everyone, including Sebastian.

"Mrs. Avery, I do believe you are enjoying all this." Vanessa chimed in.

"I must admit, nothing like a mystery to get the old girl's juices going."

Matt opened the envelope. Vanessa was the first to see the bewildered expression on is face.

"What is it Matt?"

Matt, reached inside the envelope to show the others what he had already seen. Inside, two tickets to the upcoming Presidential debate, scheduled to take place at Georgetown University the next day.

"I assume these are for the two of you, since I already have my credentials." Matt said.

"What to wear?" Mrs. Avery added.

Vanessa, however, was more perplexed. She already knew students were automatically admitted. She also knew these tickets were different. They were embossed, the type wealthy contributors usually received. These tickets placed her, where she could see, and be seen, *at a time she only wanted to be invisible.*

CHAPTER THIRTY-NINE

MAURICE Lacroix found a comfortable perch at a park located just off I-66 between 66 and the GW Parkway. The park sat high on the hill, and was often used by onlookers, wishing to catch a glimpse of the 4th of July fireworks. This time, the perch was needed for a different vantage point. The spot gave Maurice Lacroix an unobstructed view, through the plate glass window, into the living room of the townhouse belonging to Vanessa Sullivan.

Lacroix reached down to retrieve an object from a leather pouch marked **Diplomatic Immunity.** The pouch had made the journey from Liberia intact, and come nightfall, would be needed once more. Inside the pouch, he found the scope, belonging to the Heckler and Koch sniper rifle that made the journey from Liberia with him. He admired the rifles light weight and the fact, that when broken down, it appeared to be nothing more than a businessman's briefcase. He was the businessman, and his business was death.

"There she is," he said taking in a slow breath as if he were about to make a kill. Even though he was only looking to the rifle's scope, he knew in just a few hours, he would return to the sight and complete his assignment. If all went well, he would receive the call from his contact giving him the green light, and the woman would be eliminated. The woman, however, was not alone. He could see she was now in the company of a man, which complicated matters, but only slightly. "He will have to be dealt with, too."

His preliminary mission complete, he once again placed the scope back inside the leather diplomatic pouch, and assumed his role as just another tourist taking in the sights of the nation's capital. He then focused his attention to the small paper bag sitting next to the leather pouch.

"Lunch" He looked forward to this moment more than any other. Fast food, in Liberia, disappeared with the bloody coups that toppled the governments that welcomed the establishments. Like most Americans, he had become addicted to the taste of fast food. He knew one day it would kill him, but he had escaped death so many times before, it no longer mattered. Even assassins had appetites.

CHAPTER FORTY

A PRESIDENTIAL Debate in Washington, had all of the trappings of a sporting event, and served to highlight the hypocrisy of the world of politics. A row, of some twenty tractor trailers, lined the streets, leading up to the debate venue. McConnell Auditorium, on the Campus of Georgetown University, had been sealed to all outsiders, a full forty eight hours before the debate would begin. Inside, the seats showcased the segregation of American society, along lines of both race, and class. The seats, closest to the stage, were reserved for the high rollers and lobbyists, Balcony seats, went to students, and the seats towards the rear of the auditorium were set aside for those who came to be seen, but would ultimately leave, invisible.

The network anchors were among the first to arrive, complete with their entourages. Each carried with him or her, an air of importance, as if they and they alone, would define history. In tow, a personal assistant, hair dresser, and producer, all of whom demanded the anchor's attention, as if they were more important than the debate itself. The newspaper heavy weights walked around with tissue around their collars, so that anyone who doubted their veracity, could see they were about to be welcomed on the network news shows, to give gravitas to the anchors. Local reporters, like Matt Walker, had their own following, mostly among the invisible spectators in the back. The Matt Walkers of the world broke the stories the networks would later take credit for. They were local celebrities, but seldom had a following outside their region of influence. Washington, however, was different. In Washington, the local audience included the movers and shakers that so carefully crafted their images for the rest of the world to see. A single misstep in Washington could derail an entire political career, or in the case of Watergate, a political party itself. That was where Matt Walker assumed his power.

"Good evening," the doorman said, as Matt Walker made his entrance. He was carrying the standard reportorial equipment, a laptop computer, cell phone and Palm Pilot, to receive and send emails. Each had been placed on vibrate, under orders from the Secret Service, so as not to interrupt the proceedings. Walker chose to wear a simple pair of gray slacks, white shirt, red tie and the traditional navy blazer. It was the uniform of the Washington press corps, and a quick glance, to either side of him, revealed everyone knew it.

"Ma'am, let me show you to your seat." The usher was eyeing Vanessa and she liked the attention. She chose to wear a flattering gray pants suit that showcased her every curve. She knew, as she made her way toward the front of the room, all eyes were upon her, and she was soaking it in, all the while trying to hide her newly discovered fears.

"How far in front, am I?" she asked innocently, noticing the usher didn't stop anywhere near the rear of the room and was almost to the stage itself.

"Seems, from the looks of this ticket, you have the best seat in the house, and if you don't mind me being so forward, you'll look a sight better than those stodgy people who'll be askin' the questions."

"No offense taken," Vanessa replied. "The day a girl turns down a compliment, is the day she dies."

Vanessa, however, found it hard to hide her amazement at her placement in the auditorium. The usher was right. She was being directed to the best seat in the house, and all of the attention, that came with it. She had worked as an usher in this very same auditorium, and overheard the conversations where those who were among the elite questioned how a beautiful young woman like her, got to the top, or as they put it, *on top*!

"She *must* be sleeping with someone," was the usual response, it was as if, beauty and brains could not possibly go, hand in hand. The statements were usually offered up from women who were neither attractive, nor desired. Even in Washington, beauty was a potent weapon that led to the destruction of more than one politician. Amazingly, few ever questioned where the information that brings down the mighty comes from. It is always the Senator or Congressman that is led to the slaughter, while supportive wives stand by their man. Sadly, those wives usually reap the benefits, from the same calamity they created.

Just before ten, central time, the lights went down on cue. Each network anchor was given a minute to introduce their perspective shows, toss to the obligatory reporter, and complete the *round robin,* in time for the debate moderator to begin. The introductions were always without fanfare. Tonight would be no different.

"Ladies and gentleman, I would like to welcome you to tonight's debate," the moderator began. He then pointed to the distinguished panel of journalists, who, in reality, were nothing more than puppets of the process. Nothing was unscripted. Each campaign made sure the questions were screened well in advance, so there would be no missteps. The only drama of the evening had more to do with whether the networks took the wrong camera.

"The rules of the debate are simple. Each candidate will be asked a question. He has one minute to answer it, and his opponent has thirty seconds to rebut the answer. Neither candidate will direct questions at the other." The moderator turned, on cue, to address the members of the audience, which in this case, meant staring directly into the camera. "I would also ask the members of the audience to keep their applause strictly nonpartisan."

The resulting laughter was as scripted as the questions, but at least served to ease the tension that had already begun to build.

"Our first candidate is Senator Max Webb," the moderator said, by way of introduction.

The pool feed director told the cameraman to get a close up of the Senator, as he entered the auditorium, stage right. Webb raised his right hand and waved to the members of the audience, pausing to spot someone in the crowd who seemed more important than anyone else. The truth is, he saw no one special but consultants told him to do it, to add warmth.

All eyes, then, turned toward the left side of the stage, expecting to watch the entrance of Baron James. The moderator paused to add to the drama of the moment, and then began his introduction. The Democratic candidate, in this year's Presidential Election, is Senator Baron James. Again there was a pause, and the perfunctory applause, but no sign of James. A slight hush fell over the crowd as they sensed something had gone terribly wrong. In the scripted world, the unscripted seemed so out of place.

One by one, the heads in the rear of the room snapped to attention first causing a rippling effect, and then filtering down to the front rows. Within moments, all eyes were focused toward the rear of the room, where Baron James was about to make his entrance. James had decided to break from the traditional, and enter the auditorium from the rear. Had the camera been focused on the face of Max Webb, the audience would have seen the anger of a man who realized the moment had been stolen from him, even before it began. James appeared the conquering hero, on his way to a coronation, as opposed to a debate. Members of the audience, who had expected to barely see the debates, instead, were being embraced by the man, who had all but assumed the Presidency. Standing, directly behind Baron James, was his father, Mercer, who, by now, was grinning ear to ear.

The Secret Service hated anything out of the ordinary, but they were getting used to Baron James hogging the spotlight. They realized, Mercer was a master of hype, and would seize any opportunity, that presented itself. This was another of those nightmares in the making.

"*You got my vote man!*" An African American man, who was seated in the last row, chose the opportunity to make sure he said the words that would land him on the evening news. As flash bulbs erupted, another woman rose, and left her seat to give Baron James a hug. She was, at first, restrained by the Secret Service, but James waved them off, embracing her, as the cameramen struggled for a better angle. *It was all scripted. What happened next was not.*

"Remember me?" said a disheveled man, who was now standing directly in James path.

James froze for a moment, creating a sense of awkwardness, that left no doubt the two men knew each other. The problem was, the man standing in front of James didn't fit the occasion. He was every bit as unpolished, as Baron James was polished. A wrinkled blazer covered much of the filth, his blue jeans accumulated. He wore a shirt, but no tie. He had definitely violated the uniform of the evening. The Secret Service stepped in, once more, to break up the unexpected, when Baron James once again waved them off.

"Of course I remember you, we grew up together," James blurted out, embracing the man and whispering a set of instructions in his ear.

"*These men will kill you if you try anything stupid,*" he said glancing back, and seeing the horrified expression, on the face of Mercer James.

"You killed my sister you son-of-a-bitch, and I intend to make you suffer, just like you done her," the man in the dirty blue jeans whispered back.

"I assure you right now, every sniper in this building has been given the green light to take you out should you even consider making a wrong move. I didn't have a damn thing to do with your sister's death. In fact, I just learned about it yesterday. *Besides, I've been sending your..*"

"We'll continue this discussion someplace else, but not here. Just remember the name, *Doc Weaver.* When he calls, you make sure to answer. *Have I made myself clear?*

The two men broke their embrace, smiling back at each other, as if they were long lost friends. With the cameras rolling, Baron continued his pilgrimage toward the front of the auditorium, where a seething Max Webb, awaited. Matt Walker was the only person in the auditorium who knew what had transpired, and his eyes were focused squarely on those belonging to Vanessa Sullivan. The man, who almost made history, was a man he had seen before, in her photos.

Mercer James, sitting in the friend's box, was the next to figure out what had happened. For the first time in years, he was proud of how his son turned adversity into triumph. He marveled at the way Baron embraced a man, who appeared to be homeless, turning what could have been an awkward moment, into a political windfall. He knew the headlines in the next days' papers would read, "Baron James reaches out *to embrace the other side.*" It was a veiled reference, at bridging the racial divide in the country, and while it was clear, one incident couldn't accomplish what years of slavery and discrimination had produced, reporters were rarely factual when it came to issues of race. Mercer was scanning the room to see how the incident was playing with the rest of those gathered, when he spotted *her*. He knew it was all about to come crashing down.

"Would *everyone* please return to their seats," the monotone moderator commented, leaning closer to the microphone, to magnify his voice. He felt the need to portray an image of being in control. He had no idea, how, out of control, the events, were about to come.

In a microwave world, the first wave of positive headlines went to Baron James. Wire reporters had already filed their reports and the first photos of Baron's exchange with a down and out *white man.*

"***The racial divide is bridged,***" roared the headlines of the up-to-the-minute wire report. The reporter, then, went onto describe how Baron James seemed to embrace a man, saving him, from a Secret Service onslaught. The report went on to quote the latest polls, showing the James campaign with a double digit lead. One photographer even managed to capture a photo of a horrified Max Webb, while quoting a political pundit as saying, his campaign had just seen *the last nail placed in its coffin!* Those headlines, however, would soon disappear.

"*Please* take your seats," the moderator insisted again, only this time leaning over the microphone and standing, motioning with his arms, to get the audience to sit down.

One by one, the members of the audience began to take their seats. Then *'she' stood out.* There standing in the middle of the room, in a seat that was meant to attract attention, was the one woman, who would soon send every reporter in the room, scrambling to find out who she was. There, standing in the middle of the room, about to take her seat with the others was Vanessa Sullivan, and Vanessa was less than twenty feet from the man she now believed, to be her father.

Sullivan soaked up the spotlights that came up when Baron entered the room, like a model on the runway of a fashion show. At that precise moment in time, it appeared as if all eyes were on her, and in fact, that wasn't far from the truth. She was beautiful beyond words, in the gray suit that seemed to cover every curve. The reporters, who gathered, knew she was one of *those women*. They knew she had been given her tickets by one of Washington's movers and shakers, and they knew it would soon be their job to figure out who that mover and shaker was. Vanessa tossed her head toward the left, sending with it a seemingly endless flow of her dark brown hair. She spotted Matt in the reporter's area of the room and acknowledged his presence, causing the other reporters to gather around him, looking for any tidbit of information as to who the mystery woman, might be.

"*Just a source,*" Matt told the assembled press, trying to squelch any gossip before it began.

"Source my ass," a reporter for the rival TV station said, loud enough to generate laughter from the rest of the press corps. He added, "If I had a source like that, my old lady would divorce me in a heartbeat." That comment, produced even more laughter, and an angry glance from the moderator, who was still trying to regain control of the audience.

Not to be lost in the moment, a frantic network producer, with a clipboard, was trying to maintain control of the moderator, the crowd, the press, and any semblance of ending the debates in time for the network's prime time line up. "My bosses will have my ass," she said, in to a headset, somehow believing the director on the other end could make a difference.

"Your bosses are loving every minute of this," the director answered back. "There hasn't been this much excitement at a debate since Nixon sweated it out against Kennedy."

That brought a smile to the producer, who realized he was right, and immediately sought ways to keep the calamity going. Order was soon restored, much to the chagrin of the producer, the networks, and the assembled press. It wouldn't take long for the next day's headlines to take shape.

Baron James took his place behind the podium that had been the subject of much consternation, the day before. Mercer made sure his son *measured up*. Neither campaign wanted their candidate to appear shorter than their opponent. Baron wanted to shake the hand of his opponent, highlighting the fact that *he had the height advantage*. Max wanted nothing to do with any such exchange. James glanced over toward Webb, nodded his approval, and reached down to take a drink of water from a glass that was placed just out of sight, when he sighted *her.*

At first, he was struck by her beauty, but then, the sheer horror of the evening set in. He felt his knees suddenly start to buckle, and an awful sickness filling his stomach. He wanted to run, just like a little boy would when confronted with some horrible bully, but *the whole world was watching!* He turned and spotted his father. He could see Mercer knew the potential disaster that was about to unfold, as well.

"Mr. James, you won the coin toss, so the first question goes to you," the moderator began, but Baron acted as if he hadn't heard a word the man said. "Mr. James...."

"Excuse me," Baron responded, trying to make it appear as if he was still caught up in the momentum of his entrance. "I guess, even I was thrown off balance by what has just transpired." He turned again, looking directly into the audience, and the camera, flashing the smile that had been broadcast over and over again in his campaign commercials. He could hear them in his mind, "**Baron James is America**." Only he knew, at this moment in time, Baron James was against the ropes and trying to make it through the round.

He stumbled through the first question which had to do with rebuilding New Orleans. Max seized the opportunity and provided an answer to the question Baron James had somehow managed to duck. James rebutted, "What happened in New Orleans was a tragedy no President should have to overcome," and then suddenly *said nothing.* Webb said, "It is time for America to fix what was broken, once and for all." He then unveiled a massive plan to rebuild New Orleans, block by block, leading to thunderous applause, from those seated in the rear of the auditorium.

The next three questions, from the various panel members, produced the same results. Baron James, fumbling for words, while Max seemed to hold all the answers. The reporters, who just moments ago, were ready to hand the Presidency to the James campaign, suddenly began *to question his qualifications. The man, who was perfectly gray, had finally shown his true colors.*

"Mr. James, the threat of terrorism has been described as....." It was a question that will go down on debate history, as the last question to be asked, before Baron James collapsed. All six foot three inches of history, suddenly collapsed into a heap behind podium, but not before James struck his head on the side, creating a terrible "*thud*" and an even worse gash, just over his eye.

The Secret Service quickly moved in to surround James, but by then the damage had already been done. A chorus of photographers snapped every frame of his fall, and the network cameras broadcast it all live, including the footage of James being carried off on a stretcher, while a horrified Mercer tried to coach him to his feet.

"Get up, damn it!" Mercer said, leaning close to his son. "The whole world is watching." Mercer was slapping his son's wrists as he had done so many times before. He wanted to slap him across his face, but he knew each frame was being broadcast live. When Mercer realized his son would not come to, he turned to address the cameras and began the damage control.

"This campaign has been terribly stressful on my son," Mercer began, before being interrupted by one of the local reporters.

"Has he been sick?" The reporter inquired.

"No, in fact, he has been the picture of health." Mercer responded, before once again being interrupted.

"Then, how do you explain what happened?" the next reporter questioned.

Mercer realized things were not going their way. He knew whatever momentum Baron gained by way of his entrance, had been lost with his exit. He knew, as far as this debate was concerned, all was lost. "I don't know what happened," he snapped at the reporters. "No further questions," he said, pushing the assembled cameras and microphones out of his way, in what would become the last image, to be played over and over again on the evening news.

Few noticed the man on the other side of the stage. Max Webb was standing there motionless. He knew why Baron James collapsed, and why their campaign had begun to unravel. The campaign of Baron James had been thrown off the tracks, although not derailed. The rest was up to him and he quickly seized the moment.

"*Senator, what do you have to say about everything that has just happened?"* The reporters had now surrounded him; in much the same manner vultures surrounded fresh meat when the existing supply had been exhausted.

"This is not the time for politics," Webb began. "This is a time to pray for the health of my esteemed opponent..."

"*Clearly, there must be something wrong with his health?* This time the man asking the questions was a network reporter, and Max knew it was all being broadcast live. He had been given a national stage with which to shape his image, and he knew from experience, exactly what to do.

"I am not a doctor, so I don't feel comfortable talking about a man's health. The office of the Presidency places a tremendous strain on an individual. As you know, we all have been under tremendous pressure..." he continued before being cut off once more.

"Do you think Baron James is fit for office?" The local reporter asked the question that Webb knew would lead to the next day's headlines.

Max paused, as if to weigh the gravity of the question. He knew that if he were to appear arrogant, all sympathies would go to his opponent. No, this was the time to be Presidential. Max turned, making sure he had captured the best angle of all who had assembled, and placed the next nail in the coffin of the James campaign. "Fitness is not for the doctors or the politicians to determine. We have had Presidents who had been handicapped and they persevered. Fitness is for the American people to determine at the polls. I think we owe it to the James campaign to give him the time and space he needs to heal himself, from whatever ails him..." He then paused once more, as if for added effect, and said the words that would create the speculation for the days to come...."*No matter how serious his illness might be. Thank you...no further questions.*"

"Senator...it seems as if you know something we don't," a newspaper reporter inferred, before being drowned out in a sea of similar inquires.

Max Webb, simply smiled and walked away, raising his arms and facing *his* sea of supporters, who still were too stunned to leave the auditorium. The last image of Max Webb would be smiling, victorious. The last image of Baron James was being carried out of the room on a stretcher. He couldn't have planned it better.

He prayed that this would be the final nail in the coffin of the James Campaign. He prayed that *The Consortium* would no longer consider his candidacy a threat.

He failed to take into account, the one man he had confided in, and how he would react. Had he looked to his left, he would have seen it. *Matt Walker was fuming.*

CHAPTER FORTY-ONE

"I BELIEVE the Senator is busy," Betty said, to the angry caller on the other end of the phone line.

"Then make him un-busy," Matt Walker demanded. "And you might want to let him know, there is one pissed off reporter on the other end."

"Hello Matt, what can I do for you?" Max Webb said answering the phone.

"Don't give me that bull shit," Matt said angrily. "You set me up."

"Calm down, no one was set up." The Senator said, trying to diffuse the tension, but to no avail.

"That's a load of crap. You sent those tickets to Vanessa, knowing full well Baron James was walking into a trap."

Even though he knew Matt was right, the truth is Max Webb was relishing every minute of the conversation. He had set Baron James up, but Baron deserved it. In one evening, he had succeeded in stripping away the veneer of a candidate who stood for nothing, and he couldn't have felt better. Matt Walker, however, was a different matter.

"I'm going public with everything I know," Walker continued. "I'll tell them about you, the girl, and her relationship to Baron James."

"You'll do nothing of the sort," Max added, "Unless of course you want to see her dead."

There was a moment of silence on the phone…A moment long enough to let Max, know he struck a nerve, but not long enough to cause Matt Walker to stop his tirade.

"What about going public will get the girl killed?" He inquired.

"Think about it Matt. You're getting ready to derail the campaign of the Democratic candidate for the President of the United States. A lot of people have invested in Baron James, and your story will leave a lot of people looking for someplace to direct their anger. It would be safe to assume they'd take it out on Vanessa." Max knew he was lying, but dared not tell Matt the truth, for fear, his life would be in danger as well.

"When you brought me into this, you made no mention of the fact that Baron James was her father, nor did you tell me her mother was blackmailing Baron James for years; or that she was murdered recently." Matt said upping the ante.

"Blackmail, murder, what type of mystery novels have you been reading?"

That question, prompted an even angrier response from Matt. "You knew about the money he had been sending to her over the years, which is why you put me on to this story in the first place. Well, let me explain something to you, no one will be safer than Vanessa Sullivan, once this story goes public. The James campaign wouldn't dare try to harm her, once the story breaks. Every talk show in the country will be trying to get her interview and I'll already have it. I sat on the Klan photos, but that's the last time I sit on any story for you."

"Correct me if I am wrong, Matt, but you've grown quite attached to Vanessa. I saw you look at her last night. I watched you from back stage as you watched her enter the auditorium. That aside, she has enemies, much larger than the James campaign. As I indicated, people in powerful places would not hesitate to see her dead, if it meant furthering their political agenda. I came to you because *you are her insurance chip*, and because as I promised there is a *much larger story here."*

"I'm not buying it," Matt countered. "I think you'll string everyone along, until the time is right. Then you'll expose Vanessa for all the world to see. The James campaign will be ruined, and you will be President."

Max listened intently before asking the question that caused Matt to freeze almost in mid sentence. "*Then why haven't I done so already? And perhaps even more importantly, why would I need you?* You have to trust me that there is a story here, much deeper than what you think you already know. If you want the truth, then you will have to be patient. I have promised you the full story; you and you only. Once this has played out, I will tell you everything. It will, then, be up to you to decide which parts to tell, and which parts to keep secret forever, but understand this… *The fate of the girl is in your hands. Make no mistake about it."*

Matt waited before responding to the latest challenge from Max Webb. He had been in Washington too long to break a story prematurely. He knew men like Max Webb always had an ace, a card they would play only when there was no other option. He would wait, until he knew what that ace was, before doing anything. He also knew Max Webb struck a nerve, when he talked about his feelings for the girl. He did care about her, and would do nothing to jeopardize her safety. He only hoped it wouldn't cost him his marriage *and* his career in the process.

"I don't like this...not forone minute," he said warning the Senator. "For now, I'll hold off on any story."

"You are wise man," the Senator said by way of response, "A very wise man, indeed."

"Or a damn fool," Matt uttered to himself as he hung up the phone and walked to the other side of the room. "*A damn fool!*"

###

The phone call, from Mercer James to Prescott Marshall, was no less pleasant. The debate debacle left Mercer James feeling betrayed, as well. Mercer suspected Prescott was behind the tickets and the fact the girl was there for all the world to see.

"Prescott, if you had anything to do with that girl being there I'll..."

"You'll what?" Prescott responded to Mercer who was still talking when he interrupted.

"I'll kill you, myself," Mercer added.

"I assure you I had nothing to do with the woman being there, and in fact was as surprised as you were to see her. Nor did I have anything to do with the fact that your son lacks the intestinal fortitude for this kind of stuff. The woman is a distraction, but ***all*** women are. She will be dealt with when the time is right," he continued.

Mercer wasn't in any mood to calm down or cut any deals. "The time is right now. If we wait any longer, there won't be a President James for you to take advantage of. The girl has to go and she has to go now."

"I agree, but that won't solve our immediate problem," Prescott countered.

"And that would be?" Mercer inquired.

"It seems the girl has a rather powerful ally. She was seen last night in the company of one Matt Walker, a journalist with a reputation of getting to the bottom of messy situations like the one you find yourself in." Prescott knew that by introducing Matt Walker into the equation, Mercer would have no choice but to play along. He knew campaigns depended on people like him to do their dirty work which was how they acquired their power. "You asked me to deal with the situation and I assure you I will, when the time is right. I repeat, when the time is right."

Mercer, however, was in no mood to wait. He had already grown tired of this game. Pictures or no pictures he wanted to control his own destiny. As he saw it he had two problems, the photos and the girl. Matt Walker would have to be dealt with separately, but for now the girl had to go, and if Prescott wasn't going to take care of her, he would!

"We'll play it your way, for now," Mercer said.

"I thought you'd see things my way once you calmed down," Prescott added.

"I won't wait for long," Mercer added.

"You won't have to," Prescott offered up, as a guarantee. "I already have a plan."

Prescott waited for Mercer to hang up, before walking calmly to his desk and punching in the number he called on frequently to solve such matters.

"Liberty," he said into the tiny speaker. Within seconds the phone began to ring.

"Is it time?" The man on the other end inquired.

"Yes, but we have a slight change of plans," Prescott responded. "Go to the hotel and wait. I have a package I want to send you. You'll find the instructions to your liking."

CHAPTER FORTY-TWO

THE phone inside the townhouse was ringing off the hook, much to the dismay of Vanessa and Mrs. Avery. Intrepid reporters wanted to know the identity of the person described in the local papers only as "*the mystery woman*."

"Don't they ever quit?" Vanessa said slamming the receiver down. "It's like there is nothing else happening in town."

"You don't have to answer it," Mrs. Avery replied. "Sooner or later they will go away, preferably sooner."

"I need to get some fresh air." Vanessa was already dressed in a jogging suit, replete with baseball cap and dark sunglasses.

"Don't you look like the starlet?"

Vanessa, however, was in no mood for humor. She turned abruptly away from Mrs. Avery, before realizing what she had done. "I'm sorry, Mrs. Avery it's certainly not your fault."

Mrs. Avery knew there was no need for apologies. She, better than most, realized the tremendous pressure Vanessa was under. "We're okay, Vanessa. You need not worry about our relationship. But, I want you to take care of yourself." Mrs. Avery, reached out and tugged downward on the bill of Vanessa's cap, causing her to smile, albeit briefly. The warmth, in the old woman's hands, was always welcomed. She was like a mother, dressing a child, just before sledding. There was always too much attention, but it was the attention that mattered.

"Thanks, Mrs. Avery. I felt I needed to apologize anyway. I never want to take you for granted. Seems lately, people I love have had a tendency to disappear. I can't afford to lose you too."

The frankness of Vanessa's comments caused Mrs. Avery to reflect upon the fact that *she* would not live forever. She realized that sooner or later, she would exit this planet. She was ready, but she feared Vanessa was not. *Life is funny that way. The closer we get to death, the more comfortable we become.* The door slammed, leaving Mrs. Avery alone with her thoughts.

Once outside, Vanessa quickly discovered the phone wasn't the only thing ringing off the hook. The postman seemed to have been working overtime, as well. There were clever one line notes, from *"bookers,"* who wanted the *next exclusive interview.* All, resembled the junk mail that flooded her mailbox on a daily basis. Letters were made to look like something else, until she opened them. One letter, however, *was* different.

The plain manila envelope, as always, bore no other markings. There was no return address, and nothing to indicate it even belonged to her. There was nothing to indicate who sent it, or who was to receive it. Only that it sat on her doorstep. She opened it, and quickly learned, the sender was no stranger.

THAT WHICH IS BOUND BY BLOOD
WILL NEVER BE SHATTERED BY THE SWORD

Father Chiniquy

CHAPTER FORTY-THREE

"VANESSA? This is Father Haynes, if you are there please pick up, it's important." Father Haynes waited for a moment, certain the recording would kick in, and he would be forced to leave a message.

"This is Vanessa; it's good to hear your voice."

"Have you been okay?"

"Now that you ask, no."

"I was afraid you would say that."

Vanessa didn't like the tone of Father Haynes's voice. She sensed something was wrong, and knew, deep down, she couldn't take any more surprises. "Father Haynes you sound troubled. Is something wrong?'

"Yes, but I am not at liberty to speak freely…and I certainly don't want to do so over the phone."

"Father Haynes, you're...you're scaring me!"

"I can only tell you this…You have reason to be concerned. If you get time, I want you to do some homework for me."

"If this has something to do with class..."

Father Haynes, uncharacteristically snapped at Vanessa, "Just do what I tell you!"

Vanessa could hear the anger in his voice. She could tell from the tone that this time he was in no mood for debate. She knew it was *her turn to listen.*

"Vanessa, I met a man last night who says he is close to you."

"You met my father."

"As I said, I am not at liberty to discuss our conversation, suffice to say that I met the man you know, as Chiniquy?"

"Then it *is* my father who is trying to warn me."

"Listen carefully to what I say Vanessa. The man,who identified himself as Chiniquy, seemed quite concerned about his future, and yours."

"Mine?"

"Yes, he seemed very concerned about both of you. He is concerned that history is about to repeat itself."

"Did he explain why he chose the name Chiniquy? Or for that matter, why he refuses to admit he is my father?"

"I'm sorry, Vanessa, I am not at liberty to say anything further. Trust me when I say, history, may be about to repeat itself."

"Father, what does his becoming President, have to do with me?"

"Think, Vanessa, if you are indeed his daughter, what history does he fear? The answer my dear, is in which identity he has chosen to communicate with you. I would argue, you need to examine more closely the life and death of the man Chiniquy was trying to save. President Abraham Lincoln. The man who ultimately freed the slaves!"

CHAPTER FORTY-FOUR

GARY Wayne Sullivan was at home once again, at the end of a bar, where others like him drank to drown away their sorrows. His fifteen minutes of fame were over, and the debates were yesterday's news, but his anger was far from fading.

"He don't give a damn about her," he said, asking the bartender to refill his glass.

The bartender had heard it all before. He heard the stories of the cheating spouses, the broken hearts, and the plots to get even, and had learned to block it all out between beers. Had he been listening, he would have heard something new. The man, sitting at the end of the bar, was plotting to kill the man who would be president.

"I promised you Susan, I would watch out for her," he said. "I went there and met him. She even looks like him, but you should have seen the look on his face when he saw her. It was like...like he had seen a ghost. She was his flesh and blood." Gary Wayne was in a zone that had become familiar over the years. He was drunk. So drunk, he paid little attention to who might hear his outbursts, and because no names were mentioned, he attracted little attention, save one person.

Special Agent Nick Peterson had been assigned to, what was frequently called, the 'redneck patrol'. As a member of the Secret

Service, Peterson acted on all tips that there might be trouble for the President, or in this case Presidential candidate. The woman, at the local hotel, told police she feared the man who had checked in days earlier. She told them, she feared he was not who he seemed.

"Buy the next one?" Peterson said, sliding into the first available seat adjacent to Gary Wayne.

"Sure," Gary Wayne said warily. He had grown accustomed to cops in his life time, and could smell one a mile away. He knew, long before Haynes sat down, he was a cop, and from the looks and smell of things, a Fed.

The sight of a federal agent was sobering enough to bring Sullivan to attention, and yet, he knew why the man was there.

"Damn," he said staring into the glass of beer that arrived just in time for his next tirade. "He don't give a damn 'bout her," he continued.

"Who?" The agent inquired, by way of striking up an innocent conversation.

"It don't matter. It don't matter, to no one, but me and him." Gary Wayne, added.

Peterson had years of training and even more practical experience in bars like this one. He knew the key to information was to keep the stream of conversation going, and the beer flowing. He had been taught to sympathize with, '*the mark*'.

"Always keep, '*the mark*' engaged," his instructor, at the Quantico Marine Base told them, as they were trained to track terrorists, domestic and otherwise.

Gary Wayne, also, had training. He was a graduate of the school of hard knocks; usually upside his head with a nightstick. "He just looked at her and said nothing. He acted as if she weren't his own flesh and blood."

"I had a friend not to long ago, who went through the same thing," Peterson offered up.

"Don't say?"

"Damn straight," Peterson added, pausing, waiting for Gary Wayne to fill in the blanks, so he could continue his story.

"Did he have a kid?"

"Yep."

"So what did he do?"

Sensing, he had an opening, Peterson tried to *redirect the conversation*. That was the topic of the lectures in the second week. Once '*the mark*' was engaged, get him or her to open up. He knew from past experiences, most *marks* would spill their guts, given the opportunity to tell someone they never knew about their problems. He knew Gary Wayne was about to do that.

"Let me tell you how it all went down," Gary Wayne began looking at how closely the man sitting next to him was, watching his every move. He knew real drunks rarely commanded such attention. He knew most blathered away in their beer, and stumbled home anonymously. He knew his instincts were right. This man was a cop, but he was not prepared to leave, without putting on a show. Pausing, once more for effect, he looked the man squarely in the eyes, before launching what would be his last strategy. It was the one that he was sure, that would produce the desired effect.

"I'm gone kill 'em," he began. "I'm gone shoot 'em till he drops dead, because of what he did to her."

"Pretty strong words," Peterson added smiling.

Gary Wayne knew the cop was hooked, and he suspected, wired, as well. It was just like fishing, give'em a little line, and then hook'em. This man had a hook all the way through his jaw. All that was needed was to reel him in.

"Son of a bitch deserves it..." and then he stopped as if he were about to pass out. "Gotta take a leak, be right back." Gary Wayne, abruptly tore away from the bar stool, as if three days laxatives were about to let loose. As he left, he saw Peterson talking into his sleeve. He was right, the man was a *Fed,* and if the past were any barometer, there was little time to plan his next move.

Once inside the rest room, Gary Wayne scanned the room and spotted what he was looking for. It was the oldest trick in the book, but it always worked. Seedy bars rarely had ventilation fans that worked. Instead, they relied on small windows to allow fresh air in, and in this case, to allow him to escape. He knew the man sitting at the bar stool would be waiting for him to return, and say the words that would lead to his arrest, and he knew he wouldn't wait long. Agent Peterson glanced at his watch, as if there were a time limit on a person taking a shit. They hadn't taught him that at Quantico. A minute passed, and then five, before he glanced at his watch, once more. Looking around the room to make sure no one saw him, he once again, lifted the cuff of his right hand to speak into the microphone hidden within.

"Anyone see anything unusual?" he asked the men waiting in the van outside.

"Nothing here, *everything status quo,*" the man in the van answered, preferring to speak *cop talk.*

Peterson waited a minute more before deciding something was wrong. "I'm going in to check."

"Better you than us," the cop in the van answered, sarcastically. "I heard some of them redneck Johns can be *pretty ripe!"* Laughter could be heard in the background, but Peterson was in no mood for humor.

He walked across the bar, making sure no one sensed he was anything more than another drunk making his way toward the head.

Pushing open the door, his nose provided the first clue, all was not well. Anyone, who had been in the rest room that long, would leave an offensive trail to follow. This time, the scene smelled of trouble, because it had no smell at all. He glanced down at the stalls, walking along the row of graffiti scarred doors, looking for anything that resembled a man's legs.

"Damn it," he said screaming into his sleeve. "He's gone! Are you sure you didn't see him leave!"

"Nothing out here has moved," the man in the van answered back.

"Then he either pissed himself away or flushed himself down the toilet," Peterson fired back, slamming the door of a stall in anger, and watching it rebound upon the impact. He tore out of the rest room and abandoned any impression that he was anything but a cop.

Peterson burst back through the rest room door, gun in hand, waving it all around, and looking into the faces of everyone assembled as if he somehow missed Gary Wayne, as he left.

"Anyone here seen anything unusual?" He said, peering into the eyes of about a hundred drunks.

"Just you," one of the men sitting at a table opposite the bar answered. The truth was, they all had had run-ins with the law over the years, and silently cheered for anyone who escaped. They wanted nothing to do with Federal Agent Nicholas Peterson, or any investigation he was conducting, but they also wanted nothing to do with the man Peterson was looking for.

The bartender continued wiping his bar of any spilled beer. Like the others, he had other matters to attend to, although they escaped him at the moment. "Hey!" he shouted, looking angry enough for the veins on his face to explode. "Who's gone pay for them beers?"

"The government," Peterson said, as he was leaving the room. "Put it on Uncle Sam's tab."

The van, with the other two agents inside, was waiting outside the bar with the passenger side door open when Agent Peterson burst through the front doors of the bar, still waiving his gun madly about.

"He couldn't have gotten far," Peterson told the others, as the door slammed shut, the tires squealed and the van lurched forward.

Special Agent Nicholas Peterson couldn't have known how right he was. Gary Wayne Sullivan waited a few minutes before leaving the closet behind the last stall that wasn't a stall at all. Had Agent Peterson taken the time to look closer, he would have noticed that the last stall had no toilet. The owner of the bar was too cheap to pay to have one put in. Instead, he allowed the contractor to continue the row of stall doors, as if there were five toilets, instead of four. The smell of urine on the floor, near the entrance to the closet, made it clear that *Agent Peterson, wasn't the only one to make this mistake.*

Gary Wayne Sullivan, reached down, opening the faucet to wash his hands, filling the room with a sound that probably wouldn't be heard for the rest of the evening. Others would enter, but few would wash. Gary Wayne Sullivan was smiling as he scrubbed away the germs of *"The Feds."* He hated cops, but loved every opportunity to make them look like fools.

Leaving the rest room, he walked to the end of the bar, where his stool was still open, and his drink undisturbed. *He had plans to make, and this time he would make sure no one knew what those plans were.*

CHAPTER FORTY-FIVE

THE sound of a ringing phone was enough to cause the pain to return to Prescott's body.

"Who in the hell is calling now." Pain tore through his fingers as he reached to pick up the receiver. The fact the phone was sitting so close to his bed, made the ring all the more annoying.

"Prescott? You sound as if things are not going well. I called because *notre amis*, our friends, are concerned. We read the papers there, and it seems this campaign, as you call it, is out of control.

"*Your Excellency,* Rest assured, everything here is under control. I anticipate that within the next forty eight hours, my plan will be complete. Then, you will read, in those same papers, there is only one candidate."

"So, you will dispose of our problem?"

"No, nothing quite so messy. If history has taught us anything, it is that your solution does not work, and in fact, sometimes, creates new problems. Your solution will lead to inquires, and commissions and every investigative reporter in the world searching for the clue the last one missed. My solution is much more effective. You have heard it said, the pen is mightier than the sword. *Photos, my dear Cardinal, trump the pen."*

"You should know, Prescott, this problem shows no boundaries. There is talk of similar lawsuits being filed in South America and Africa, should the one in America succeed. We are looking at "*the tip of the spear." We are looking at the end of The Consortium.*

CHAPTER FORTY-SIX

PREPARATIONS for the second debate were well underway. Max Webb was enjoying a sizable bump in the polls, Baron James was licking his wounds, and Washington was abuzz, trying to figure out the identity of the shapely young woman who stopped Baron James in his tracks. As always, the rumor mill spun out of control, and those behind it identified the woman as everything from an illicit affair he was having on the Georgetown University campus, to an unwanted daughter from a past affair. Needless to say, no one knew for sure, and everyone was guessing.

"We have to put this behind us and focus on the future," Mercer said pacing the floor nervously. Mercer was so nervous that he decided to take up smoking again. Baron was a basket case.

Baron hadn't slept in days and it showed. His eyes, now, had sizable dark circles under them. Where white could be seen, lines of red were drifting in. His skin had taken on a paucity reserved for the elderly. He looked like crap, and he knew it, and so did everyone around him. He reminded them every few minutes, as to why.

"Damn it, damn it all to hell, *I knew this would happen. It was her*. I knew she was out there. Someone planted her in the audience. Someone is trying to ruin me." He had repeated the mantra so many times, Mercer had it memorized, and while equally distressed, Mercer wasn't about to surrender. There was still a campaign to manage and an opponent to ruin. He would get even with Max Webb, if it was the last thing he did. The problem was he wasn't sure Max Webb was responsible for the woman sitting in the middle of the auditorium.

"Here's the information you requested Mr. James." The young man speaking was a dwarfish red head, fresh from the ranks of the ivy league elite, spoiled, and ready to take on the world. He had been given a simple task, and performed it admirably. He was told to find out who had purchased the tickets and given them to Vanessa. Not surprisingly, he failed. Mercer James was the first to be told.

Making his way across the room, never once breaking stride, he reached for the papers the young man was holding, barely getting them before Baron arrived at the same destination. "Let me see those," Mercer demanded. Baron could tell from the look on his father's face, the new information was not new at all. The seat belonged to a lobbying firm that had donated handsomely to both campaigns. The firm was quoted in the morning's newspapers as saying, that it had no control over the seating arrangements and knew nothing about the mysterious woman. Whoever sent her to the debate, wanted her to be seen that night, and then disappear.

"Enough of this nonsense, we have another debate to focus on," Mercer announced.

"I know...I know...but..." It was clear Baron remained distracted and absent a quick slap in the face, he would stay that way.

The force of a father's hand coming across the face of his son, caused all, within earshot, to stop what they were doing and take notice. Mercer James, had just slapped his only son, with a force so hard, Baron almost fell backward. There was an awkward moment of silence, before Baron knew that his father had done for him what no one else had the guts to do. He knew his father had slapped some sense into him, and the shit out.

"Focus son...focus. We lost the last debate, not because of some two bit hooker, or cheap college coed, but because you have no clue of the issues. Once *the veneer* of the great Baron James had been peeled back, you became what you are, a sniveling spoiled brat, who has been spoon-fed from birth. If we are to win this next debate, you're going to have to do something you have never done before. You're going to have to study and learn what makes great men great. You're going to have to *study the issues*!" Mercer ended his sermon with a stare that left no doubt in his son's mind, his father meant business. Baron, however, still had to try once more.

Recovering, somewhat, from the assault he had just taken, Baron offered up one more excuse. "There is still the matter of the woman," he said adding to his pathetic existence.

"I will deal with the woman," Mercer added. "I will deal with the girl."

Max Webb, on the other hand, had no such problems. Across town, his staff gleefully diagnosed the latest set of polls, and saw softening in Baron's core support. It seemed black America liked a black candidate, but not if he got his ass whipped on national TV.

Sadly, there were still those who failed to budge, and wouldn't budge, even if Baron had fathered an army of illegitimate kids. They were the type who believed everything was linked to a grand conspiracy. They argued on the nation's black radio stations, that perhaps, Baron had been drugged. They pointed to all the past foibles involving black politicians. All of it, they argued, was part of a conspiracy to keep black men down.

Max liked the rough and tumble of politics. It made his blood boil, in a good sense. It recharged his batteries and while it added years to the face of Baron James, it took years off the face of his Republican opponent. For the first time in months, Max Webb was acting and talking as if he might win. He liked the way he sounded and his staff liked it even better.

"Should we increase our buys in some of the *soft states?*" his campaign manager inquired, entering the room with a handful of updated consultant reports. Max knew the reports would state the obvious, and hated the fact he paid so much for such worthless information. "I think we can make some solid gains in those areas where, just last week, it looked like we should fold up tent," the aid continued.

"No, I think we should keep our cards close to our vest. The next move is up to Baron. We should anticipate he will come to the next debate more prepared. If we are to develop a strategy, we have to attack the James campaign where they least expect it."

"I don't suppose you know of *another woman?"* The young campaign aid inquired.

Webb cracked a smile, acting as if he had planned the evening's events, when, in fact, he was spinning out of control, moments earlier. "You're suggesting *I had something to do with the first*?" Webb then offered the slightest of winks, portraying an image that he had everything under control. "I think our cocky opponent has another Achilles heel. I think it is time we attack Baron James for what he is, or should I say for what he is not!"

A funny thing happens when the ordinary in Washington becomes anything but that. Reporters, who days earlier, dreaded the thought of another boring Presidential debate, were now lining up for their credentials. Members of the media, who flocked to the latest war zone to cover the continuing war on terror, now begged their editors to return to Washington.

"We need tough reporters who will ask tough questions," they sent by way of fax and what ever messenger they could use. "I think there's something here that needs to be sniffed out." Everyone was an investigative reporter now. There was blood in the water, and as far as the Washington press club was concerned, political blood.

When the day of the second debate arrived, every Presidential pundit in the country had weighed in on what they thought would happen. As always, the debate followed the pocket books of the network owners. Networks owned by conservatives, favored Max Webb; liberal owners talked up a comeback on the part of Baron James. Like color commentators at a heavyweight prize fight, both sides were prepared for a showdown. No one was ready for what happened the morning of the second debate.

CHAPTER FORTY SEVEN

PAIN shot through every pore of Prescott Marshall's body. His joints ached so much it felt as if the very cartilage inside had been *set aflame*. He had suffered through the episodes in the past, but this was the worse. This time he wondered whether he would survive.

"This is the price I pay for being a patriot!"

Because of the illness, Prescott barricaded himself inside the confines of his Potomac mansion. None of the staff were allowed to enter. His medicines were left outside the door each morning, and each morning, when no one was looking, he would struggle to the doorway, painfully reach up to turn the knob, open it, and pull the tray with his medicines and breakfast back inside.

Marshall's hands shook violently as he tried to control the contents of a hot cup of coffee, to no avail. Most of the coffee wound up spilling down his robe, and that, like everything else, had the initials, 'P.M.," stitched across the cuff.

"So today's the day. Today's the day."

It was clear that, even with the pain, Prescott was a man in charge. In fact those who knew him over the years remarked he seemed more ruthless when the episodes arrived. It was as if his body was attacking him and he was fighting right back. Prescott knew of only one way to fight, and even if the enemy were his own body, he would cheat.

Not a single panel of drapery was open, and in fact, the room was so dark, it was almost impossible to locate the phone. Somehow, however, he did. With out-of-control fingers, he dialed the number to the one man capable of placing the final nail in the coffin of the campaign of Baron James.

"Mercer, old friend," he began speaking in slow deliberate; "I think it is time we meet about putting this photo issue to bed."

Judging from the silence on the other end of the phone, it was clear Mercer James was stunned. He didn't know whether Prescott was calling to announce he was about to leak the photos, or whether he would announce they had been destroyed.

"It seems, our friend Max Webb, is cleverer than I thought. I didn't like the way things went down at the last debate. Messy...very messy!" Prescott began.

Mercer seemed pleased with the way the conversation was going, but still had little in the way of trust for the man on the other end of the line. "I agree. *It was very messy*, but I assure you..."

"No need for assurances," Prescott said interrupting Mercer in mid sentence. "I just think that if this is to be a fair fight, then the playing field *needs to be leveled.* No one can operate under the pressure Baron has been under. The truth is, I find Max Webb hard to trust. Anyone, who would do what he did to your son, would do the same thing to even his closet of friends. You know what they say...know your enemies, but know your friends even better. Let's just say, I plan on getting to know Max Webb, quite well, over the duration of the campaign."

Mercer sensed progress. It made sense. He knew what Prescott wanted and knew it would be only a matter of time before the real reason behind the phone call was raised. For now, he would play along. The truth was, he knew he had no choice.

On the other end of the line, Mercer was standing and clinging to Prescott's every word. "I think we are seeing things eye to eye. Max Webb didn't get the name "**Lion of the Legislature,"** for nothing, but I must admit, I'm curious about why you are really having this sudden change of heart?"

"Let's just say, the people I represent, are upset, very upset. For them, politics is nothing more than another business deal. They want to make sure that their man in the White House can be controlled. Max Webb...shall I say, is out of control. We have offered suggestions as to how he might tone down the campaign, and take the high road, but he seems to ignore our every suggestion. I doubt I need to remind you about the last set of photos we discussed. You know, the ones that almost laid the Presidency in the lap of your son." Had Mercer been able to see the man on the other end of the phone, he would have noticed that the grimace on the face of Prescott Marshall was starting to fade. Perhaps it was the medicines that were kicking in, but in truth, power was a much more potent pain killer. Prescott Marshall breathed power, and the trap was about to be set.

"I'm not ready to just hand my son over to your people...." Mercer said somewhat defensively.

"No...no...They don't want someone they can control completely, just someone, who will listen a little more to reason. Max is acting as if he already has won the Presidency, when we both know, in politics, a day can change everything. The photos could wind up in the wrong hands, and should that happen, we would be stuck with the unpleasant consequences of our own actions and you would be...."

"Dead," Mercer said finishing the sentence Prescott started. "You need not remind anyone the power of those photos. Hell, I'm uncomfortable even talking about them over the phone. I would like nothing more than to see them go away, and I assure you, my son feels the same way. Of course we know you want something in return, and we would be more than willing to accommodate your associates, but we are talking about the Presidency."

"We are indeed, Mercer. Which is why I am proposing, a sort of truce. Let's take the pictures off the table and let the chip fall where they may. I will have a messenger meet you at Connecticut and K Streets at noon tomorrow. I won't be there, as I have taken ill, but I will make sure my messenger will be, believing he is only delivering *position papers*. You however..."

"I agree...*I will accept them on the other end.* As long as these are the only ones, and there will be no more surprises with the girl." Mercer James was no dummy. He smelled a rat and knew he had no choice but to go along with Prescott's demands. He would have liked Prescott to be there in person, but could hear from his voice, he was ill. "Noon tomorrow…Connecticut and K."

"My messenger will be instructed to make the delivery to you, and you only, and Mercer one other thing…" Prescott had hooked his fish and was about to reel him in.

"Yes Prescott?"

"Perhaps in the future, you will be a little more *trusting* of me."

"I think we can work on that. I know you and I can and I think I speak for my son."

Prescott placed the phone back on the receiver and smiled for the first time in what seemed to be an eternity. Picking up the phone once more, he spoke his command into the receiver, and the phone auto dialed a familiar sequence once more.

"*Le Vashti….*"

As always, the man on the other end of the phone waited for it to ring three times before answering, and then only after the caller had spoken first. The exchange of words between the two men was simple and yet the conversation said all that needed to be said.

"The girl first...and then the father!" Marshall told Barclay that a package would be on the way to his hotel with more specific instructions.

"I understand."

CHAPTER FORTY-EIGHT

A COLD wind rolled into town on the eve of the second Presidential debate. Late October in Washington was full of surprises. Sometimes, the weather seemed downright balmy. On other occasions, it seemed as if winter was still at its peak. It was on days like this that Grebo Barclay missed the warm nights of Africa. He was growing bored of the hotels. The only thoughts that kept him going were the thoughts of the old woman. He knew she needed the money, and he knew he had sent enough to rebuild her school.

"They never gave a damn when it burned; I don't give a damn now," he said as he fumbled with the remote searching for something else worthless to watch on TV. The sound of a knock on the door provided a welcome relief.

Barclay reached under the pillow of his bed and retrieved the nine millimeter glock he kept just within reach. He removed the safety and placed the gun in the back of his belt, measuring each step, as he made his way toward the door. Looking through the peephole, he noticed the man was alone. Still, the occasion called for caution. It always did.

"What do you want?" he asked through the door to the man waiting on the other side.

The man, accustomed to that very question, began to answer even before the question had ended, "Package for Mr. Barclay."

Barclay relaxed, knowing that the man was legit. He had been told a package was on its way and opened the door, making sure the man never caught a glimpse of the glock he was hiding.

"Sign here," the delivery boy asked.

"I don't sign anything," Barclay said tersely.

"Just doing my job, man," the messenger said, indicating he would sign for him if necessary.

"Just set the package on the table and leave," Barclay told the man, noticing he had stopped to collect a tip. Barclay wanted to empty the glock into the boy. He knew the man would make more in a day than his father once made in a month, but he also knew the man was just doing his job. He knew in a matter of hours, he would be doing the same thing. Using his free hand, he reached inside the pocket of his blue jeans and retrieved a twenty dollar bill that he had stuffed inside.

"Thanks man," the messenger fired back. "What name do you want me to sign?"

"Lacroix," Barclay answered. "Maurice Lacroix."

CHAPTER FORTY-NINE

BARCLAY waited until nightfall to complete the first assignment. He welcomed the package, as it had given him something to do. He toyed with the night scope, just as the instructions told him. He would walk the distance from object to object, and use the scope to see if the distances were correct. He marveled at its clarity.

The cab ride from the hotel took less than twenty minutes. Washington, DC, at night, was nothing like it was during the day. The cabbies were more pleasant, and more talkative.

"New to town?" the cabbie inquired.

Barclay looked up and saw that the face of the man did not match the face on the license posted on his visor. Still, he played along with the gag. It broke the boredom. "Louie?" he asked.

The cabbie pointed to the picture on the license, as if no one could have noticed it wasn't him and continued the lame conversation. "That's me," he said, placing his finger on the face, as if that gesture would erase the lie.

Barclay made sure to sit on the side of the cab, opposite of the mirror, so as to avoid being identified. "Well, no Louie, I have been to Washington several times."

"That so...what type of work you do?" Louie had now repeated the second most asked question he had heard.

Barclay noticed there seemed to be an obsession in Washington with what one's occupation was. The truth was, he could have told the man anything, and Louie would have believed him. He chose the truth, knowing full well it would go in one of Louie's ears, and out the other. "I'm an assassin. I kill people for a living."

"That so, and I'm Michael Jackson." Louie let out a laugh that let Barclay know he had succeeded in his rouse.

"And because you know what I do, I'll have to kill you too," Barclay said, joining Louie in the laughter.

"If I had a dime every time somebody said that…"

Barclay continued to laugh as well, thinking to himself, "Yeah, but how many times is it the truth?"

"Here you go," Louie said, as the cab pulled up at the intersection of Nash and the George Washington Parkway. "Should I drop you off at the Lobby?"

"Yeah, that'll be fine," Barclay answered. He knew once the cab left, he would walk across the lobby, and out the side door. From there, he would walk the block or so, to the park, where he had scoped out Vanessa's townhouse days earlier. There, he would wait for the opportune time and complete the first part of his assignment.

At approximately 7:45pm, the opportunity arose. The lights inside Vanessa's townhouse came on, signaling that someone was inside. Barclay picked up the scope for a better look. It was Mrs. Avery, tending to Sebastian. He settled down once more, so as not to draw attention to himself.

A cop, passing by, created the evening's only tension.

"Got some reason to be here?" the cop asked.

"Just waitin' to meet somebody," Barclay responded.

The officer gave him a troubled look. "We don't condone *that type* of activity here in Arlington," he said.

Barclay realized the cop believed he was a homosexual. He found himself almost overcome with laughter, but kept it all inside, so as not to draw more attention to his situation than had already occurred. "Not *that type* of person," Barclay informed the cop.

"Fine, but when I get back, I want you gone."

Barclay knew, *he'd probably be gone*, and realized even if the cop returned, he could handle the situation. He prayed, on the cop's behalf, that he would walk a long beat. That's when he caught the reflection of the door opening, at Vanessa Sullivan's townhouse, out of the corner of his eye.

Looking through the scope he saw the greenish outlines of Vanessa Sullivan and a man who appeared to be the other person, he was told would be there, Matt Walker. Taking a deep breath he did exactly as he had been taught so long ago.

"Point, breathe, shoot."

"Le Vashti," was long gone by the time the officer returned.

12:00 PM

The bells on St. Matthew's church could be heard in the background. Twelve bells, signaling it was twelve noon. Barclay chose to sit across from the park where the homeless men sat feeding the pigeons. To a bystander, he was just another one of the homeless. Few people looked his way, because they knew from experience, to do so, meant they would have to part with some of their hard earned money.

Mercer James arrived first. He had the look of a man who had been living on the edge, pacing nervously back and forth, as if his life depended on the package that was about to be delivered. Prescott's

Messenger arrived less than a minute earlier. Barclay could see from his vantage point that Mercer was pointing to his watch, as if to signal that the messenger was late. Barclay knew his window of opportunity would be short, so he wasted little time assembling the necessary equipment. He was to complete his task and avoid detection. The shopping cart he stole on the way home from Vanessa Sullivan's townhouse provided the perfect mount for his equipment.

"Wait until you see the package being delivered, the package must be in his hands," he said to himself as he breathed in slowly, as the instructions dictated.

The messenger reached inside a pouch and retrieved the envelope he had been carrying. In that brief moment, Mercer stopped his pacing, and seemed to be both relieved and anxious. He was anxious to examine the contents of the envelope, and was relieved that this entire nightmare might be over.

"Look in the envelope," Barclay mouthed.

The expression on the face of Mercer James said it all. Barclay knew whatever was inside the envelope carried with it grave consequences. It was now time for him to act.

"Point, breathe, shoot."

The pigeons in the park left the only impression that anything out of the ordinary had happened. Barclay knew it would only be a matter of time before the whole world learned what had just what had transpired.

CHAPTER FIFTY

SOMETIMES, the ringing of a phone signals much more that someone being on the other end of the line. It is the ring of a child who has been arrested, or a loved one in an automobile accident. Sometimes the ring brought death, rarely life.

Cecilia froze as the phone next to the night stand began to ring. Glancing at the clock to the right, she saw that the hour was late...Too late for any of their friends to be calling. This call was trouble, she could feel it.

"Cecilia," the man on the other end began. It was Matt's editor at the station. Larry Lindsay only called when something had happened. She knew now, *"the earlies"* had come in. "*The earlies,*" were the newspapers printed early for the next day's delivery. Newsrooms, would sometimes dispatch a messenger, to pick them up directly from the Newspaper, if they had been tipped that something big was getting ready to happen.

"Larry?" Cecilia answered.

Larry, as was his custom, spoke in deliberate tones. "I take it you haven't been watching the TV?"

Cecilia wanted to tell him what she really thought about their business, but could sense now was not the time. "Cut to the chase, Larry."

"All right, all right. It's everywhere. The James Campaign is dead. Dead I tell you. Dead in the water and listing."

Cecilia reached down, picked up the remote, and turned on the TV to see what it was that Larry was talking about. It took less than three seconds for the TV to warm up and broadcast its image, and even less time for Cecilia to realize why Larry Lindsay was so panicked. "Oh, my God!"

There, for the entire world to see, were photographs of Baron James, in bed with a woman other than his wife. The man in the photos was obviously younger, but it was clearly Baron James. The announcer, a rookie who had been filling in on vacation, used his deep voice to set up what had transpired over the last few hours, repeating the phrase, "We've also been told," over and over again. The second set of photos showed Mercer James accepting, what appeared to be, the first photos. A second sequence of images showed him handing a messenger cash, in exchange for the photographs.

The commotion was enough to wake Matt, who had taken a sedative and was lying in the bed next to Cecilia.

"Sweetheart," Cecilia began cautiously, "You'd better get dressed."

Within seconds, Matt processed why the tone in his wife's voice seemed so concerned. The images on the TV needed little in the way of explanation. He jumped from the bed in a fit of anger and betrayal, the likes of which Cecilia had never seen. "*That son of a bitch*!" he shouted. "*That son of a bitch!*"

"Who?" Cecilia demanded.

"Max Webb, that's who," Matt answered, putting on his trousers and reaching for a wrinkled shirt that had been lying in the corner. "He knew this all along and he set me up."

Cecilia had never seen her husband so angry. It was as if his entire career was flashing before his eyes. The clues, the murders, and the woman. It was all becoming much clearer. There *was* a story that would reshape history and *he was being used* to make it all happen. The real story was right there before his eyes. If there was a Watergate for his generation, this was it, and he missed it."

"That son of a bitch!"

Matt rushed out of the room, leaving a bewildered Cecilia to follow the rest of the story on the evening news. She knew her husband had blown it, and she knew he had blown it big. There were thirty other reporters in the newsroom, but he was Matt Walker. There would be hell to pay for missing the scoop of the century, and Matt Walker was about to feel the heat.

CHAPTER FIFTY-ONE

IT was late. The rest of the world had gone to sleep, but Baron James was still wide awake. He had barricaded himself inside a restroom, in seclusion. His face had turned so red; the veins across the top of his head were bulging outwards. His shirt tail was out, and the cuffs had traces of vomit on them. Mercer was beside him, trying desperately to salvage that which could not be saved. He was also bearing the brunt of the blame.

"How could this happen?" Baron screamed at his father. "You were supposed to handle this!"

For his part, Mercer was in no mood to be criticized. "Me? Where do you get off, trying to pin this on me? This wouldn't have happened if you would have kept your penis in your pants! I told you that woman was trouble long ago, but you didn't listen. Instead, you did your talking with your dick, and that's why we're here today."

Baron was like a little child, curled up in the fetal position on the restroom floor. He hated it when his father screamed at him. He hated the fact that his father hated him, and he hated the fact that he knew, deep down his father never really loved *him*, but instead, the son being groomed to become the nation's first black president. He never knew why, but he was about to learn the awful truth. He was about to learn his father's secret.

"You're just like your mother...."

Baron stopped cowering long enough to realize their conversation had taken a serious twist. "Leave mother out this, what's she got to do this?"

Mercer angrily moved toward his only child, grabbing him by the collar, and forcing him to look in the mirror. Once Baron's eyes were focused, he placed his head beside that of his son. "Look closely and tell *me* what you see."

"What are you trying to say...." Baron paused, for the first time realizing exactly what his father was trying to say. As he looked closer at the features on his fathers face, and those of his own, his thoughts raced backwards. He knew his father seemed distant, but never knew why. He always attributed the callousness his father displayed to the fact that he was obsessed with the presidency.

"Do you see any of me, in you?" Mercer shouted loud enough for the others posted outside the door to hear. "Have you ever? Every time I look at your face, I see every man who laughed silently at me behind my back, while your mother kept her tawdry little secret. She knew she was pregnant, and made it seem as if *the baby was mine."*

Baron was now hurt and puzzled. His life had just changed forever, and for the first time in his life, he had no one to turn to. The man he once believed to be his father, was a stranger, looking back at him in the mirror. In the span of just a few short hours, he had lost the presidency *and* his father. It was all too much to bear.

Mercer continued, "She treated *sex* like it was *an addiction*, and look where it got *her*, *knocked up and pregnant*! Worst still, *everyone* knew it before *me."*

Baron summed up the courage to ask the question, the answer to which he knew in advance, he didn't want to know. "*So if you're not my father...then...who...*"

Mercer laughed sarcastically, in a tone that cut through Baron like a knife. "That's the beauty of it all, your mother never knew, she had no idea who knocked her up. *A dirty little secret she took to her grave*. She left you with me...*her bastard son*...while everyone around us laughed!"

Baron was searching for anything from his past to hold onto, any sign that there once was something between the woman he called his mother, and the man he once believed to be his father. "Was there ever?"

"Once," Mercer said lowering the tone of his voice. He could see the hurt on the face of his son. In anger, he uttered the words he swore never to say. There was no turning back, and for the first time, Mercer realized, the child before him, *possessed all that he hated and loved about his late wife*. "I was very much in love with your mother. She was the most beautiful woman I had ever seen. Like the woman who betrayed you, I learned beauty, sometimes, is only skin deep. Behavior, on the other hand, is genetic…it is who we are. She could not escape her past, and neither can you."

For the first time in his life, Baron knew why his father was so distant. He also knew why the episode, with the woman, seemed to destroy whatever relationship they once had. Placing his face inside his hands, he began to sob softly, at first, and then uncontrollably. The only comfort came from the hand he felt on his shoulder…the hand of the man who truly *was* his father. They were betrayed by biology, but bound by emotion.

The commotion, that proceeded the moment, prompted the two Secret Service Agents who had been assigned to the James campaign, to burst through the rest room doors. One Agent was talking into his sleeve, while the other, stood in the doorway, stunned at the sight of a collapsed relationship and campaign. Both had been listening outside the door and knew everything that had just transpired. It was a sad fact of political life. They were there to guard the candidate, even if it meant protecting him from his father. *Even if the candidate had no conceivable chance of winning!*

CHAPTER FIFTY-TWO

THE newsroom was buzzing with activity when Matt walked in.

Sighting the eleven PM producer, Matt glanced at his watch to see how much time he had to get ready. "I can be ready in about five."

"Don't bother," the producer said abruptly.

Matt already knew there would be hell to pay, and the producer's demeanor was the first step into the dark abyss of nothingness. The world of journalism is about today's story. There is no such thing as yesterday's story, and Matt knew it. As far as the producers were concerned, he was yesterday's news, and today's news was breaking all around him.

"They're gonna give the kid a shot," the producer shouted as he passed Matt, headed toward make-up, which lead straight to the control room. He added, as if he sensed further explanation would make things better, "They say he's got sources on this one."

Matt hated reporters like him. Their sources were in the newspapers of America, or online chat rooms, where gossip became fact. The news cycle was spinning so rapidly, guys like him were becoming obsolete. No one had time to check facts, or for that matter, apologize when they got it wrong. "The kid" in this case was good looking, cheap, and dumb enough to believe this story would last forever. Matt also knew his bosses were in no mood to listen to anything he had to say. He got beat on *"the big one,"* and he was the guy who was supposed to be breaking *"the big ones."*

Oddly, a strange smile crossed his face as he walked through the newsroom. The friends, who were so concerned just a few days earlier, were now mentally measuring his office, to see if their belongings would fit. He knew what the future held. There would be meetings without him, and meetings with him. It was the latter he dreaded. They would say he was slipping, when in fact, they were only concerned with saving his salary. Then, he would be fired. He had seen it before. The station actually hired a guard to stand over one anchor as he cleaned out his desk. The man had been there for decades. If he were going to steal something, he would have stolen it already. It was the most humiliating day of the man's life.

He was back in his office now, back where it was safe. All three televisions played endless versions of the same story. ***Baron James was dead in the water***. It *was* the biggest story of the century. Matt knew the century was young and there would be others, but for now he was *persona non gratis.*

"**Can Baron James recover**?" the talking head on channel 4 asked.

"Asshole," Matt said, as he continued to turn up the volume on the various sets. "Let me see if I have this right, your ass is featured prominently in every newspaper and TV set across America, with a woman under it, there are only two days to before the president election, and oh yeah, there's one more thing…YOU'RE THE CANDIDATE!"

Matt turned up the volume on his station. "The kid" was using his anchor voice full time. He sounded like a cheap impersonation of those anchormen you see in the bad movies, only this was real. Matt was looking at his replacement and no one seemed to care that his replacement stunk.

"IN OTHER NEWS TONIGHT," The kid reported, **"HOLLYWOOD HAS BEEN SHAKEN BY THE DEATH OF ONE OF IT'S MOST BELOVED ACTORS,"** Matt turned up the volume, even louder, and almost stumbled trying to clear his desk to get closer to the monitor. He couldn't believe the face on the graphic over the left shoulder of "the kid."

Fumbling through his desk, he located it; the copy he made of *"The list."* There, three names down, was *the name of Dickie Hankins, the Hollywood actor*, who had just been found, dead, inside the burned out remains of his car. According to the fact bar at the bottom of the screen, the car careened out of control and crashed in a canyon. It then, suddenly, burst into flames.

Matt started to run into the newsroom, and then stopped dead in his tracks. No one would believe him or *"The list."* There was also the issue of the girl. He had promised to protect her. He knew it wouldn't be long before they would go back over the footage from the debates and place her in the cross hairs of every anchor and talk show host in the nation. They would identify the woman in the photos, and discover that the woman at the debates was her daughter. She would be forced to tell her story and her life would be ruined forever.

Standing there in the middle of the newsroom, in the middle of the chaos, Matt knew his career was over. It ended as suddenly as it began, with neither a whimper nor a bang. The only thing that was missing was the guard over his shoulder.

The sound of his cell phone startled him. He looked down and immediately recognized the number. It was her, it had already begun.

"Matt?"

Matt paused before answering, because he had little to say. He wanted to tell her that he sat on the story because of her, and that because of her, his career was ruined. He wanted to demand she come to the station, sit down, and tell everyone about her mother, the threatening letter, and the canceled checks.

"Vanessa, I…"

"Matt…Mrs. Avery says it's no longer safe here. She says I should go somewhere, but I have no place else to go."

Matt could tell by the sound of her voice that she was crying on the other end. He knew no matter how bad things were for him, her world was even worse. And he knew, no matter how much he tried to deny it, he had feelings for her.

"Vanessa..."

"Yes…"

"I can pick you up in about ten minutes; can you meet me out front?"

Vanessa wasted little time responding. "I'm already outside."

Matt closed the door to his office wondering whether he would ever open it again. The producer was, once again, in frantic mode. "The kid" was starting to run out of steam and then needed someone to "vamp."

Matt had seen it all before. "Don't bother," he said brushing past the producer with the list in hand. "You two deserve each other!"

As he made his way across the Key Bridge toward Vanessa's townhouse, he looked back at the city as if he could hear each and every conversation taking place. It was a strange feeling. Washington, on nights like this, was one city focused on one thought. Tonight, everyone was talking about Baron James, and everyone was looking for one woman. The woman he was about to pick up.

"Cecilia," he said speaking into the receiver of his cell phone.

The sound of Cecilia's voice let him know that she knew, too, that things were not going well. "Where are you? I've been watching the news all night and they've been broadcasting around the clock, but you haven't been on."

Matt wanted to lie, but he knew doing so would be wasting his time and hers. "It's not good, Cecilia. I'm the last person they wanted to see tonight. I got beat, and I got beat pretty badly."

Cecilia knew there was more at stake than just a story. She knew her husband had been fighting a battle for years, to get back what he had lost. She knew how much this story meant, and knew she was talking to a man who had everything to gain and nothing to lose.

"So what are you going to do now?"

"I'm on my way to pick up Vanessa; she's expecting me." Matt could hear the silence on the other end of the line. He knew Cecilia, too well, and she knew him. He knew, she knew, that the girl was danger. He knew she hated the fact that they would be together.

"Are you coming here?" she said, but before she could finish her question the announcer on the television station answered it for her. There in a picture located below the photo of Baron James, the woman, Mercer James and the money, was a freeze frame taken from the debates. The announcer identified the woman as Vanessa Sullivan and quoted sources as saying the FBI was interested in talking to her about the photographs and where they may have come from. The announcer then went on to speculate that they were concerned about the timing of her appearance in Washington, and the mysterious photos of her mother in a compromising position with a man who was about to be elected President.

The silence on the other end of the phone had gone from uncomfortable to curious. "Cecilia?"

"Matt, you *can't* come here. *Everyone's* going to be looking for the girl, and I suspect before long, you, as well." Cecilia hated the words that were coming from her mouth, but she had been with Matt too long to lie.

For the first time all night, something had gone Matt's way. He knew before she called that reporters would be looking for her and he knew he couldn't take her home without bringing all that trouble with him. He had a plan in mind, and it wouldn't take long to execute. Vanessa was where she said she would be. She was there, in the rain, standing on the landing of her townhouse, and from the puffiness in her eyes, she had been crying for quite some time.

CHAPTER FIFTY-THREE

THE ride to Breezewood from Washington, DC took less than four hours. I-270 became I-70, once the confines of Washington had been escaped. It was where the urban decay ended and the country began. Real estate prices, attitudes and even the political tilt changed when the two roads merged and disappeared and went their separate ways. The best thing about the ride was that it would take them far away from the city, and the hordes of reporters, who would soon be on their trail. Matt also knew there was a side benefit to this particular route, the closer they got to Cumberland, Maryland, the sooner the chatter on the radio would disappear. The mountains swallowed everything that was Washington. Vanessa broke the silence and reached toward the radio, "Can't we find anything else?"

"I'm afraid not. Every station is talking about the James campaign, *and everyone is talking about you.*"

"They act as if I broke some law or committed a crime," Vanessa said defensively.

"The truth is, in Washington, you did. As far as the public is concerned, your mother is the woman who destroyed a dream. You can rest assured, Baron will pay for his sins, but most of the time, society will blame the woman. Remember, *"The bitch set me up*?" Think of a campaign that's gone up in smoke, and there's a woman to blame." Matt could see he was not scoring any points with Vanessa, and settled in for what was going to be a long ride.

"You make it sound as if *you* blame my mother," Vanessa snapped back.

"That's not what I'm saying at all. What I'm trying to say is, that no matter what happens, *history always blames the woman*, that's all."

"And who writes the history? Men!" Vanessa crossed her arms defensively and slumped further down in the seat. Matt chose to focus on the road ahead. He found an ally in the gas gauge. The car's gas tank was on empty and the signs said the next service station was less than six miles up the road. They were the longest six miles of the journey.

"Would you like some coffee?" Matt said, hoping to renew any spirit of friendship, as he prepared to exit the car.

Vanessa answered tersely, "No thanks."

The door slammed and Vanessa found herself angry at both Matt and herself. He had placed his entire life and his career on the line for her, and she treated him like he was a common stranger. She felt terrible for how she reacted, but knew he would understand. The radio was a different story. As she fumbled through the stations, she glanced down at Matt's notes scattered across the seat. That's when she saw it... *the list*...and even more incredibly...her name was on it. Any anger that had gone away was back. Vanessa could feel the blood rising to the surface. She wanted answers, and the man she wanted answers from was about to open the door and feel her wrath, once more.

Matt realized something had changed the minute he opened the door. He could see it on her face, and from her body language. That's when he knew he had carelessly left his notes on the seat. In his haste to get out of town, he had collected his belongings from his office and sped out of the parking garage. *The list*...was on the seat, and it was out of his briefcase.

"I can explain!"

Vanessa, reached for the door, as if she was going to run, and then realized she had no place left to go. With one hand on her hip, and the other on the door, reflecting an attitude that said, *no bullshit*, she looked at Matt and said, "Then explain."

"I got the list from Senator Max Webb," Matt began. The deal was, I would get the list, but I had to keep it a secret. When you called that day, I thought your story was one of the most outlandish stories I had ever heard. Then I saw your name on the list. Max said he was sending me the story of the century. I'd certainly heard that before, but there was something in his voice. Even still, I didn't pay much attention to it, until your name surfaced. I knew there was too much in the way of coincidence, so I decided to investigate. I never knew any of this was going to happen..."

Then why didn't you..."

"Why didn't I tell you?" Matt was now finishing Vanessa's' sentences. "Because, as a reporter, I swore I would keep the list a secret. Max was a source, just like *you* asked to be. Max knows nothing of our conversations, and you know nothing of his. That's how it works. Do you honestly believe I wanted any of *this?*"

Vanessa relaxed her arms and took her other hand off the handle of the door. She was now both angry and curious. "One question and no more *source bullshit*...it's just you and me now, and the last time I looked, the world is chasing us. How closely have you looked at this list?"

"Your name was the first to catch my attention, and then tonight, the strangest thing happened," he added before Vanessa cut him off again.

"And that was?"

"I was watching the news in my office before I came to pick you up. Truth is, I didn't have anything else to do. I'd been relegated to the bench," he added, searching Vanessa's eyes for any sign of sympathy.

He was right, and Vanessa reacted as if on cue, "I'm sorry, I was so focused on *my problems* I forgot about *yours.* I guess your bosses are pretty upset with you for not getting the story."

Matt was happy to see they were speaking civilly again. "*You have no idea.* Wait until they find out I'm headed west, with the one woman everyone is looking for, and wait until they find out about the canceled..."

"Wait a minute buster," Vanessa interrupted once more. "No one can know about the checks. That is how my mother would have wanted it. The pictures are hideous enough, but the checks reduce her to a common...., Vanessa paused, as if she realized the gravity of her next word...*whore.*"

Matt knew there would be a time and a place to discuss the list and the checks, and now was not that time. He knew he had to place as much distance between Vanessa and an angry mob of reporters, as possible. Vanessa, however, was not finished. She was still examining the list and he could tell from the expression on her face, she spotted something he had not seen.

"What are you looking at?" Matt inquired.

"Have you looked closely for any connections to the names on this list?"

"Other than yours, no. The truth is, ever since I met you, my life has been moving a little faster than even I'm used to." Matt found himself smiling, as he said those last words. The truth was, he never felt more alive than when he had met her. He could see she was smiling too.

"What I am saying is that some of the names on the list seem familiar. Enloe, for instance, is the name some historians believe was the real name of Abraham Lincoln's father. And this is the name of a well known Hollywood actor."

"*Former Hollywood actor*," Matt chimed in. "*Dickie Hankins died tonight!*" According to the idiot who was reading the news, authorities in Hollywood found his car at the bottom of a canyon. They had to identify the poor bastard by his dental records. That didn't take long, since just about everyone in Hollywood can be identified by either their dentist, or their plastic surgeon."

Vanessa laughed, before continuing her line of questioning once more. "Do you think everyone on the list is dead?"

"The truth is," Matt began, "I never got chance to check. Things were unfolding so quickly, I've spent most of my time trying to figure out why someone would want you killed. Once the connection was made to the James campaign, it kinda became clear."

"An illegitimate daughter is always kinda messy, and a *half breed* one at that." Vanessa was once again defensive.

Matt sought to calm her concerns. "No, that's not it at all. I think, *"The Consortium,"* is behind all of that..."

Vanessa thought about the phone call from Father Haynes. *"History repeats itself. Chiniquy."*

Matt could tell, Vanessa knew more than she was letting on. "Now who's keeping secrets?"

"Matt, I never got the chance to tell you about a phone call I got from Father Haynes. He called late in the night, and we haven't had a chance to talk since then. He said he was concerned for my safety, and indicated he may have talked to my Father."

"Your father contacted Father Haynes?"

"I couldn't get it out of him, seems he has to protect his confidences as well…something about the men in my life. He said something else, though, that has been ringing in my head ever since. *History repeats itself.*"

The next day, I went to the campus library and pulled all of the books I could, about *Chiniquy*, and Abraham Lincoln. *Chiniquy* wasn't a conspiracy buff. He had real concerns that the life of the President was in danger, but that's not all."

"You mean there's more?"

"Yes, another book raised even more questions…questions that really hit home. They were questions about who Lincoln's real father was. It was written by a man named Cathey, back in 1899. Cathey, it seems, believed Lincoln's real father was a man named Enloe. Correct me if I'm wrong, but wasn't that one of the names on your list?"

"Okay, but what does ancient histories have to do with our present dilemma?"

"Think about it Matt, Baron James was about to be the first black president in the nation's history. If Lincoln was assassinated, as Chiniquy maintained, for freeing the slaves, and angering Europe, imagine what damage Baron James might have been able to do."

"And you are his daughter."

"At first, I too, thought it all boiled down to my being his blood relative. Then I thought about something else. I also represent his DNA. What if the others on the list represent the DNA of Lincoln?"

"And your point is? Now who sounds like the conspiracy theorist?"

"Think about it Matt, remember Thomas Jefferson and Sally Hemings? Their love story was *gossip* until the descendants of Sally Hemings sent their DNA off to be tested. Lawyers are lining up on both sides."

"So this is about proving Lincoln was black? That book's been written and shot down"

"No," Vanessa answered quickly. "That's the problem. Everyone wants everything wrapped up in a black and white bow, when the truth is just about everything being a shade of gray. Take Baron James; does anyone really believe James is black? He's got more ingredients in his DNA tree than the recipe on the back of a bottle of *Heinz 57 steak sauce.*"

Inwardly, Matt laughed. Outwardly, his expression stayed the same. For the first time, he saw the passion that drove Vanessa. They had been so obsessed with keeping her alive, he knew little about why *she* lived. "Tell me about this double major of yours."

"I have a *dual* major…American history and the Human Genome."

"That's pretty weighty stuff don't you think?"

"It's the next logical step for all historians. Think about it. So many of the mysteries of our country can be answered with DNA…did Lincoln have Marfan's disease? Was he black? Dig up Lincoln, Jefferson, and all the others."

"But what would that prove?" Matt asked.

"To begin with, we might define *our founding fathers*, as just that. Fathers. There is every bit of evidence to suggest America *truly became the melting pot*. Baron James was not the first politician to dip his wick, and he won't be the last. That's the hypocrisy. A lot of those people who want his head on a platter are upset because the woman in those photos was white."

Matt studied Vanessa's face closely. He knew she was on to something…something big. Race in America has often been referred to as the *third rail*. A topic so electrifying that few, if any, candidates would even talk about it. It was true what she said about Baron James.

Clearly his past was not what it seemed, but no one seemed to care. He said he was black and the public believed him. Matt also knew Baron James wouldn't be the last politician with an army of public relations reps, lining up to clean up his dirty laundry.

"Okay I'll bite. But I doubt even that rises to the level of murder."

"Matt, DNA is the short technical name for the 1.3billion gene that comprises what you know as, the double helix. Some say it looks like a ladder, but critics say it is more like a sword that cuts both ways. Let me take you to my world for a moment."

Matt was listening intently. The road ahead seemed to go much smoother, now that they were talking.

Vanessa, on the other hand, seized on any opportunity to talk about a subject other than politics. "In the world of DNA, Matt, you belong to *M89.* Your genes originated in Africa."

"Tell me something I don't know."

"Here's where it gets sticky. Caucasians, or whites, belong to a *Haplogroup,* called *Haplogroup R.*

"Haplo…what?"

"Stick with me Matt, *Haplogroup, R.* Every person in *Haplogroup, R* is identified by a chromosome mutation known as *M173.* We're talking about seventy percent of the people that emigrated from England have the mutation, ninety-five percent of all Irish, and the same goes for Spanish. Everyone, who belongs to that group, can trace their lineage back to the marker known as *M168."*

"You're not saying that genetically every white person can trace their lineage to..."

"Africa! That's exactly what I' m saying, and because almost every white person has *M168*, that means, in the world of DNA, race no longer matters."

"But Murder?" The reporter in Matt kicked in again. Always the skeptic.

"Think about it Matt, what would America be without race? No census according to race, just DNA. Immigration policies would be based on a fairer system of percentages, as opposed to the way it is now, where certain European countries, can immigrate to the United States, without risk of rejection."

"It also explains something else," Matt offered up.

"What?"

"It also explains why one of the most powerful men in Washington would suddenly appear out of nowhere, to woo the heart of a beautiful young coed. Perhaps Mr. Marshall was interested in more than your looks. Perhaps he had his sights set on your DNA as well."

"Why, thank you Matt," Vanessa responded somewhat sheepishly. "I think."

Matt smiled allowing the slightest crack in his stoic expression.

"What?" Vanessa asked.

"I was just thinking of something else."

"What is it this time?"

"Can you imagine the membership of the NAACP?"

"Funny, Mr. Walker, funny."

Vanessa was in her element now, and Matt's mind was moving even faster. She was on to something, but nothing that would rise to the level of murder.

Good enough for a conspiracy theory, but not yet good enough to print.

The sign ahead indicated that the tiny town of Breezewood, PA was less than six miles ahead. Matt knew no one would ever find her where they were about to go.

CHAPTER FIFTY-FOUR

BARON James managed to do something no other candidate in U.S. history could accomplish. Every pundit, black, white and other, had solidly lined up predicting his defeat. The history maker was now Washington's latest scandal, and there was to be no recovery at the polls. "Dead," James Christopher proclaimed on his cable show. "Even Christians wouldn't put their money on the resurrection of the James campaign."

Another pundit, much older remarked, "America is not ready for a president whose background is more *mongrel* than *pedigree.* Baron James is *trailer trash."* He added with a distinct southern drawl, "Where I come from, we call that, *trying to put a dress on a pig!"*

Even the black radio stations had their say. "Hell," one of the most outrageous talk show hosts said, "He wasn't *really black.* I mean look at him. That's when his darker skinned co-host picked up the banter. "I told you so! I told you that from the get-go. The *white side* of Baron James is getting whipped. *The black side knew better.*" That produced enough laughter to get them to the commercial break.

Max Webb chose to keep it low key. The overnights showed he had a commanding lead over his opponent. The only way he could lose was if he were to be assassinated, and even then he'd probably win the write-in vote. There was another factor. The truth was, Max felt sorry for Baron. He wanted to win, but not this way. He hated what politics had become, and knew it was only going to get worse. He also realized that he probably destroyed the broadcast career of Matt Walker. He had dinner with Walker's bosses the night before, and they so much as placed the anchor crown on "*the kid*." As much as Max hated politics, he hated what had happened to broadcasting even more.

Prescott Marshall may have been the only one in Washington smiling. He had single handily obliterated the campaign of Baron James, and reduced Mercer James to a sniveling pile of humanity. Better still, everything was going according to plan, and those plans were playing out to perfection. The members of "*The Consortium*" were happy, and so was he. *That smug Boucher even called to kiss my ring.*

"We are joined today by Mercer James," the radio host began, almost sounding apologetic. Years earlier, he himself, had been removed from the airwaves, for his racist remarks. Now, he was the only radio host willing to give Mercer James an honest interview. "Mr. James, in your own words, what happened?"

Mercer no longer cared about the presidency. He knew it was over even before the votes were cast. His concerns were with rehabilitating the image of the man he had finally accepted, warts and all, as his son. "I think this is about making mistakes," Mercer began, "None of us is without sin, and my son is no exception." Mercer seemed to be right. The station's switchboard lit up. The problem was, most people still wanted to know more about Baron's sins, and he was certain several of the callers were reporters, still seeking his son's blood.

Mrs. Avery watched the day's developments with Sebastian by her side. She had not heard from Vanessa since she left with Matt Walker, and because of that, she assumed she was safe. She had heard from Prescott Marshall, who said he, too, was concerned about Vanessa's safety, although she now believed *that* to be anything but the case. Claire Shannon called again with more information about Prescott, *The Vai* and *The Consortium*, and none of it was good.

"Matt, do you think he stands a chance?" Vanessa asked, watching the TV coverage from the hotel room they now shared.

Matt knew, deep down, Vanessa believed, in some strange sense, she was to blame for the collapse of the James campaign, and he had spent days trying to soothe her fears. "No Vanessa, one thing Baron James has got to learn, is that he is responsible for his own sins. I think Baron's political life is over." Matt knew the same could be said for him. Perhaps Baron James wasn't the only casualty of this campaign.

Mr. and Mrs. Bannaker had been staying at the Fort Dix Motor Inn for two days, and so far, no one expected anything shy of a September/December romance. They rarely left the room during the daylight hours, and sneaked out at night for food. The rest of the time, the room was lit by the light of the TV set that was on constantly. *"The Fort Dix*'" was a 'don't ask, don't tell' facility, and the *Bannakers* were paying cash.

"Good evening ladies and gentlemen," *'the kid'* was back in his announcer voice, broadcasting the results of an election that surprised no one. Unlike the suspense of the 2000 campaign, where America went to sleep with one President and awoke with another, this campaign offered no surprises. "Our exit polls predict Max Webb will win by a landslide," *the kid* proclaimed. "The same report was being broadcast on TV monitors in the studio, as one by one, the race to see who would proclaim the death of Baron James was on. The pundits worked, well into the night, offering up their version of what went wrong. Only Baron James knew the truth, and one other person, who was no where to be found.

CHAPTER FIFTY-FIVE

GARY Wayne Sullivan watched it all unfold on television. He witnessed the national humiliation of his sister, and the witch hunt for his niece. He knew there was only one man to blame, and only one solution to his problem. He had been drinking heavily for days, and reeked of alcohol.

"You did this," he said, as he watched the 'slow mo' images of Baron James walk across the television. "I knew you was no good then and you ain't changed a bit." Gary Wayne continued his venomous spew. He prepared to leave the wretched hotel he had been living in, ever since being forced out of the hotel on old Richmond Highway. This time, everyone was threatening to kill Baron James, black and white, and the Secret Service was flooded with phone calls pointing out nut cases.

Sullivan brought only two bags. One contained his personal belongings, the other, a long suitcase he never opened once during his stay. Today, he would open it for the first time, and he suspected, the last time ever.

"Mr. James?" the maid, at the hotel where had secluded himself, was knocking on his door. "It's time to service the room."

The secret service detail that guarded Baron James so closely prior to the election, was now sitting in the hotel coffee shop, waiting for their assignment to shake off his latest hangover. The truth was, Baron never felt more liberated. The whole world knew the horrible secret he'd hidden for so long, and he knew the truth about his father, even though he had no idea who his real father was. That secret broke the ice between him and the only man he ever knew to be a father. *He actually liked Mercer James.*

"Morning fellows," Baron exclaimed, as he made his way across the hotel lobby. A group of guests spotted him, immediately, and closed in for an autograph. They were stopped by the Secret Service Agents, who still did their jobs, even though they hated the man they were assigned to guard.

"Everybody back," the larger of the two agents shouted, as if Baron James were Moses about to part the Red Sea." Please back up and give him some air," he continued.

It didn't take long for those guests who were not close to the action, to realize they were in the presence of a celebrity. Everyone wanted to get a glimpse of the man who almost became president. In a strange sense, infamy carried with it its own fame.

"Can I get an autograph, Mr. James?' a woman in a bright blue dress asked, with her child in tow. Her voice was whiny, as if she came from a state where everyone spoke through their noses. "I *actually* voted for you," she said sheepishly before realizing how foolish she sounded.

For the first time in his life, Baron acted Presidential. There was no need for pretense, and Baron accepted *any* compliment that came his way. He had heard so few in recent days. "Here ma'am," he said reaching for the woman's napkin that still had traces of bacon grease on it.

After he signed his name, the woman raced away as if she had struck it rich on a lottery ticket. "I can sell this on *EBAY!*" she shouted! One of the agents actually found the entire episode amusing. Baron James turned a bright shade of crimson.

Because of the incident, no one noticed the street bum who approached the contingent from the rear of the room. In a distinctly Southern drawl, he reached out to Baron, "Excuse me sir....," he said... taking long pauses in between until he had finally locked eyes with Baron James, "I, too, would like your autograph."

Baron froze for the moment, recognizing who was standing before him. He had known Gary Wayne Sullivan since childhood. At one time, they were even best friends. He knew this day would come, from the minute he slept with his sister. As children, he had been warned that she was *too good* for him, and now the tables had been turned.

The larger of the two agents spotted Gary Wayne immediately, and spun around with both arms in a sweeping motion as if to knock away anything that was headed toward the one time candidate. The other agent, slowly turned around, still oblivious as to what was about to happen. There was only one man in the room who seemed to be prepared for what was coming, and that man was Baron James.

"Gary...I...."

"Time for talkin' is over."

Those were the last words Baron James would utter or hear. Gary Wayne Sullivan opened his trench coat, reached inside with his right hand, and pulled out a sawed-off shotgun.

"When we was kids, I told you, she was off limits. It's payback time, *nigger.*"

The first shell struck Baron in the chest, sending him backwards across the room. Fragments from that shot, also struck the Secret Service agent, closest to Baron, in the hand that held his gun, leaving behind a bloodied stump. As the second officer reached for his weapon, Gary Wayne emptied the second chamber of the rifle, at point blank range. The shell landed right inside the man's chest, produced little in the way of blood at first, and then became an open cesspool of the man's internal organs. The man fell to the ground in a heap of blood, flesh, and bone fragments near the woman who had just secured the last autograph Baron James would ever sign. Sullivan then reached with his left hand inside his coat pocket, to retrieve two more shells. In a single motion, he jerked the gun upwards causing it to snap in half. The sound sent shock waves through the room, much like a bomb exploding. He then placed the two shells inside the chamber, and repeated the motion, causing the gun to close.

Baron was on the floor, face up, with a slight trace of blood gurgling out of his mouth. Because the shell shattered his spine, he could not move, or offer anything in the way of defense. He was even unable to shield his face from the onslaught that was about to continue.

"I told you to stay away from her, but you wouldn't listen. Who's high and mighty now? You had it all, but had to have just one, more thing!" Gary Wayne said, as he calmly walked toward Baron. "To you, she was just another score, just another piece of ass."

Even though there were several people in the room who could have stopped him, no one intervened. Instead, they watched the drama unfold, as if it were a show playing on TV. For his part, Gary Wayne Sullivan never took his eyes off his intended target…walking, ever so slowly, one step after the other, until he was hovering directly over the bloodied body of Baron James.

Then there was nothing, just silence. No shots, no words, nothing. Just the sound of a man dying and another man enjoying every minute. A lifetime of hatred had just been unleashed in the form of two shotgun shells. It was the hatred of a man who believed his best friend, since childhood, had betrayed him, and a brother who mourned for his sister. It was also the anger of white supremacist that grew up believing he had been betrayed by affirmative action. It was America's racism unleashed and for all the world inside that room to see, it was ugly.

"*Good-bye Baron,"* Gary Wayne said quietly as he pointed the barrel of the shotgun directly in Baron's face. The muzzle of the barrel was less than six inches away. There was no possibility Baron would survive the attack, and even if he could, he would have been disfigured for life. Sullivan squeezed the trigger slowly, causing the muscles in his arm to spasm from the tension, and then, it was over.

The ferocity of the blast erased any facial features that once belonged to a man whose face was known to everyone. Several of the patrons ducked for cover as Sullivan swung around and prepared to make his exit. Few noticed the Secret Service Agent who had now managed to get a grip on his service revolver, by placing it in his left hand, and was pointing it at Gary Wayne Sullivan. Gary Wayne turned toward the man and prepared to fire the second shell, but then, for some reason he stopped. Both men locked eyes, and for reasons unexplained, the agent also never fired his gun.

Gary Wayne Sullivan, with the sawed-off shotgun inside his coat, walked slowly out the door.

Baron James was dead.

CHAPTER FIFTY SIX

"WE interrupt this broadcast to bring you breaking news!"

Vanessa had just returned from the shower when the announcer broke into regular programming. He appeared out of breath, and she could tell from his demeanor, whatever happened, was serious.

"Baron James, the disgraced one time presidential Candidate, **has been assassinated!"** the announcer continued. "Details are sketchy, but it appears that a man wearing a trench coat and speaking with a Southern accent walked into a downtown hotel and opened fire, killing James and a Secret Service Agent, and leaving another agent fighting for his life."

Vanessa dropped the hair dryer and frantically reached for the remote to turn up the volume. The announcer said authorities were on the lookout for the man believed to be responsible for the killing.

"Oh my God, " Vanessa said, now dropping her towel and the remote.

The announcer tossed to a reporter, who seemed to be even more out of breath than he was. The reporter, wearing the customary tan trench coat and speaking in an even deeper voice than the announcer, said "Authorities are looking for this man. He has been identified as Gary Wayne Sullivan, a native of Cliffside, North Carolina."

Vanessa stared in horror. The picture shown was from the debates. The reporter continued.

"We have learned that a nationwide manhunt has been launched for the man Baron James embraced, during the first presidential debates." He went on to say that the FBI was asking the media for any raw footage they had of the exchange, so that it could be studied more closely. Trained lip readers were also said to be studying the footage. The reporter said they had no idea where Gary Wayne Sullivan might have been hiding out, but that he might be seeking to rendezvous with his niece, a coed from Georgetown University.

Matt entered the room with a tray holding two hot cups of coffee. At first his eyes locked on the naked body of Vanessa standing there. When she turned, he could see from the look on her face that the world had changed since he snuck out for coffee.

"Authorities believe, the coed identified as Vanessa Sullivan, may be in the company of a local TV reporter identified from this photograph as Matt Walker."

Matt stood motionless as the picture on the screen seemed to linger longer than any other image. It was not his staff photo, but appeared to have been taken outside Vanessa's townhouse. It had been taken the night he picked her up and fled town. The night the photos of Baron James and Susan Sullivan first surfaced. The pictures showed him and Vanessa, in an embrace. *The photo made it appear... as if they were lovers.*

"Oh Matt," Vanessa said, stooping to pick up the towel out of embarrassment. "Tell me when this nightmare will end?"

Matt wanted to speak, but he was still frozen in place. For the first time ever, he felt it was all finally spinning out of control. He knew, not that authorities believed that, he was somehow connected to the assassination of a one time presidential candidate, and so was

Vanessa. He also knew, from the cell phone vibrating feeling on his hip that things were about to get worse, if that were possible. The *caller id* displayed the caller's number, well before he clicked the phone on. Panic, worse than what he had just felt, had set in.

"Cecilia...I can..." Matt searched for words, but he knew this time no words could heal the wound he had opened. Cecilia was on the other end of the line, sobbing uncontrollably. She said nothing, and had it not been for the caller id, he wouldn't have had any inkling that it was her.

"Matt?" Instinct told her, and Matt's face confirmed, the caller on the other end of the phone was Cecilia. Vanessa next did what she believed to be the right thing. Walking across the room, she once again put on her towel, and reached over to seize the phone that was frozen in the Matt's grip.

"Cecilia...this is Vanessa..."

The silence continued on the other end.

"I know you don't believe me, but your husband has done nothing wrong. I can make this right...I swear it on all I believe."

Again there was silence, and a few seconds later, the display on the phone indicated the call was over. Cecilia had hung up.

The announcer was now describing Baron James as if he were a moral pillar of the community. The photos of he and Susan Sullivan would be buried forever in history. *There was a new story to tell, and this one had just gotten better.*

CHAPTER FIFTY SEVEN

"BETTY, track down Matt Walker!"

"Senator, do you honestly believe he wants to hear from *you!*" Betty was never the type to hide her anger from her boss, and today was no different. She knew how dirty politics could be, and she had watched his political career unfold. Some of the things that happened, she agreed with, but this was different. She, along with the rest of the world, watched as an innocent man's life was being ruined. It had happened before, but this time she knew the man, and his wife.

"Senator, you've got to do something to help..." She started to say before the Senator cut her off in mid sentence.

"What do you think I'm trying to do," he said emphatically. "Now get me Matt Walker on the line and get him now!"

"Yes sir," Betty answered. She had never seen her boss like this, especially now. They had just been celebrating his resounding victory at the polls and were in the process of putting together a transition team. Donors were lining up, pledging their allegiance to the Webb presidency. She knew something was wrong. Something was terribly wrong.

The phone at the Walker residence continued to ring, and would not have been answered, had it not been for Cecilia's instincts. She knew this call was different. This call, she felt, *needed* to be answered.

"Hello," she answered, although she momentarily thought about hanging up.

"Cecilia, this is Betty..."

Cecilia's finger moved toward the disconnect button, but the sound in Betty's voice caused her to pause.

" I know you want to hang up, but the Senator says he needs to find your husband and he needs to find him quickly," Betty said.

"The Senator and everyone else, or should I say the President Elect," Cecilia fired back.

Betty wanted to defend her boss, but knew this was not the time. "Cecilia, Matt's in trouble, you know it, I know it, and the Senator knows it. The Senator, err President, may be the only person who *can* fix this." She then paused and said, "He may be the last friend Matt has."

Cecilia wasn't taking the bait, and wanted more before giving up the man that she wondered if still loved her. "Why should he, Max, of all people, want to help? Correct me if I'm wrong Betty, but things were going well here, before the Senator called the last time. Now, my husband is gone, you boss's opponent is dead, and there's a beautiful woman in the middle, who says, for some stupid ass reason, that *I should trust...her.* Pardon me Betty, but I may have been born at night, but I wasn't born last night."

"Cecilia, I don't think it's Matt he's trying to save, I think it's the girl," Betty shot back.

"Oh and that makes me feel *one helluva of a lot better!.*" Cecilia said sarcastically.

"What I'm trying to say, Cecilia, is that I know the Senator. He's a mean son of a bitch, but not this mean. This whole thing is spinning out of control, and I suspect the Senator may be the only one who can fix it, and I think, it all has something to do with the girl."

"Put him on," Cecilia said, "*But make it clear, I am in no mood for any of his Bullshit.*"

CHAPTER FIFTY-EIGHT

THE funeral of Baron James was one for the civil rights record books. It was as if he died and had risen. There was talk of the fact that he was poised to become the nation's first black president before a white supremacist took him out. There was no mention of Susan Sullivan, Max Webb, the pictures, or for that matter, his legislative record.

"He will go down in history among the greats, beside the kings and the queens of the movement," the preacher shouted from the pulpit. He was the first in a long string of speakers, each one elevating Baron James higher and higher. By the time the four hours of speeches had ended, Baron James, once again, was eligible for sainthood. No one seemed happier than Mercer James, who received each of the dignitaries individually, as if he were the head of an organized crime syndicate.

President Elect Max Webb stunned the civil rights community when he petitioned the Senate to allow Baron James body, to lie in state, inside Statuary Hall of the Capitol Rotunda. James became the first African American to do so since Rosa Parks, years earlier. Webb also announced his plans for his first one hundred days in office. He called for sweeping changes in the nation's civil rights laws, and health care systems that brought him praise from his critics, and blanket condemnation from his own party.

Not to be outdone, Vai-Gene, announced that it was launching a scholarship fund in Baron's name. "No black child who wants to go to college will be denied that chance," Prescott Marshall proclaimed as the cameras of the Washington press corps clicked away. Marshall relished the attention that Baron's death placed on all things African. It was good for business. "This type of hatred must be vanquished in our generation," he added. "Baron would expect no less."

The funeral procession carrying the caisson of Baron James, twisted through the Nation's capitol, beginning in the poorest of neighborhoods and retracing the route of the caisson that carried the bodies of Presidents John F. Kennedy and Ronald Reagan. This time, as little boys raced to catch a glimpse of history, history could be seen. Mercer James walked the length of the procession on foot.

All three major broadcast networks carried the funeral live, as did the cable networks. The black radio talk show hosts that ridiculed James days earlier, praised him today. One by one callers phoned in to say that they believed his death, was a racist conspiracy. Internet activity soared, and before days end, pictures were being circulated, that claimed to reveal the real face of the man in the photos. A man who *was not* Baron James. Washington had returned to normal, but all was still not well.

Most of the dignitaries, on hand for the funeral, assembled at the house of Mercer James. Soul food was served in its various forms. Mercer thanked each guest and calmly walked past the well wishers who had gathered, and excused himself for the evening.

"It has been a trying time for him," an icon in the civil rights movement remarked, as he made his exit. She then helped herself to a heaping portion of sweet potato pie, and promptly continued to stuff her face.

"Baron's death must be avenged," Mercer said as he tucked the butt of the nine millimeter glock pistol in his waistband. As he buttoned the jacket, he checked his face in the mirror to see if he showed any tell tale signs of strain. *"I believe we know who the guilty party is,"* he muttered and slowly walked toward the bedroom window, opened it and crawled onto the roof, lowering him onto the street below. He then crossed the alley to a car that had been parked there prior to the arrival of the guests.

Mercer knew exactly where he was headed and sped north along the GW Parkway, past the location where the Park Police usually waited for speeders. He paid little attention to the pundits on the radio, who continued to eulogize his son, well past the hours where anyone cared. *"Someone has to pay, and someone will."*

Once he reached the divide in the highway, separating the roads that lead towards Virginia and Maryland, he took the Parkway into Maryland, and onto River Road. From there, he had less than six miles to go, before reaching his destination. He continued to check the gun, which rested on the seat next to him, making sure everything was okay. He got the gun from a street thug, with a guarantee that it had been stolen, rendering it untraceable.

The journey was quick. As he turned into the driveway of the house at the end of the road, he turned off his headlights and shut down the engine, allowing the car to coast to a stop. He wanted his entrance to be a surprise. He knew he would not be welcome. *"Hello Prescott, remember me?"* He had rehearsed the lines over and over in his head. *"I'm the father of the man whose life you destroyed."*

Prescott was inside the residence tending to the business of *The Consortium*. It had been a good month. Stock holdings across the board were up, and he decided to celebrate with his only friend, Beethoven. He uncorked a bottle of his finest wine to allow it *to breathe*. As far as Prescott was concerned, all was right in the world.

Mercer was surprised to see that Prescott's home did not appear to have an elaborate alarm system. *"You're getting sloppy Prescott. Surely a man like you knows he has enemies."* He didn't see the security camera that spun around, following his every move. The camera was activated by motion sensors, and relayed pictures of any intruders to an off-sight security firm.

"Mr. Marshall, excuse me for interrupting, but it seems you have a visitor," the security guard on the other end of the phone announced. "Should we dispatch a unit?"

"No, I believe I know who this particular visitor is," Marshall responded. "He'll be fine."

The cameras continued to follow Mercer's every move. He parked the car in the front of the house, and walked slowly towards the front door. He was surprised to find the door was left wide open as he reached for the doorbell.

The security cameras inside now whirled into action. One by one, they followed his path of progress. Mercer James was a rat in a maze that was designed for people just like him.

"Come closer, Mercer," Marshall said looking at the monitors in front of him.

Mercer's heart was racing. He knew he was getting close, and grew concerned he was getting too close, too quickly, but it was too late to turn back. He didn't care if he got caught; he just wanted to settle a score. He, like Prescott Marshall, couldn't walk away. He knew, sooner or later, the two would meet.

Marshall sat back in the armchair behind his desk, watching the monitors, until Mercer came into view. He was standing outside the door of his office, alone. Marshall knew why he was there, and Mercer made no attempt to keep his business a secret.

"I suppose we both knew this day was coming." Mercer added.

Prescott rose slowly from behind his desk. He started to make his way across the room, as if to extend a welcome to Mercer, when Mercer ordered him to stop.

"That's far enough," Mercer ordered.

Prescott was locked in on Mercer's eyes as they darted wildly black and forth. He knew Mercer was armed, and at any moment *he could be dead*. He could see Mercer's hand, inching closer to the gun that was tucked inside his belt.

"Perhaps, before you die, you would like to tell me the truth," Mercer said inching closer with each word. "I just want to know why? What was wrong with my son? I thought we had a deal. He would have been a good president..."

Prescott interrupted, stopping his unwelcome guest from uttering any more stupidity. "He would have been a complete disaster! He wasn't running for president, you were. Let me put it this way, Mercer, your son had no balls."

Mercer James could feel the anger welling up in his stomach. His hands were beginning to sweat and he could feel the perspiration under his arms as well. He knew in his heart that what Prescott was saying was right, but hearing it, was like rubbing salt in a decade old wound. He wasn't there for his son, he was there for himself. He hated men like Prescott Marshall, because they were rich, and powerful, and white.

"No Prescott, the problem lies with men like you. You control everything. This isn't about whether or not Baron would have been a good president; you, so much as said it. This is about control. Look back on history. *Are you saying that those men were all qualified for the office*? The bar got lowered well before this election. My son was just a casualty in a racist war, where no black man will ever be good enough for the presidency."

For the first time in his life, Prescott Marshall was speechless. He knew Mercer James was right. It *wasn't* about whether or not his son was qualified. The truth was, for people like him, no black would be good enough to sit inside the oval office. Baron James was just the latest in a long line of causalities. He knew people like him didn't want America to be a melting pot. They wanted America's version of European royalty. Blacks were meant to be workers, along with Hispanics and other ethnic groups. That was the natural order of things. It had always been that way.

Mercer reached inside his coat and removed the revolver. Slowly and deliberately, he took aim at the head of Prescott Marshall. Marshall never moved a muscle. It was as if he was prepared to die. If he had a weapon, he would've never reached it in time. Prescott knew it, and so did Mercer.

It is time for you to die, Prescott. This is for my son.

The single shot shattered any solitude Beethoven had produced. In a security station, miles away, the security guard witnessed it all, and was powerless to act. It took a few seconds to sort it all out. A shot had been fired inside the residence of one of the most powerful men in Washington, and it was too late to stop it from occurring.

Suddenly, Mercer James's knees buckled, his eyes still locked on those of Prescott Marshall. The gun he was holding so firmly, just seconds earlier, fell from his hands, striking the floor and coming to rest, a few inches from Prescott. Mercer collapsed to his knees, before his body slumped, and in a single movement, he fell forward, face down, at Prescott's feet. .

The man in the security station frantically dialed 911 to summon police, before placing the phone back in its cradle. The cameras captured the image of a police officer entering from the rear of the room, with his gun still drawn, smoke coming from the barrel. .

"Saw it all unfold Mr. Marshall. Thought you were a goner," the cop said, still trying to catch his breath.

Prescott tried to act surprised. "I would be dead had you not arrived on time." He looked down at the phone that was ringing loudly on his desk. "Prescott Marshall," he said into the receiver.

The frantic security guard on the other end of the phone said, "Are you all right, Mr. Marshall? We watched it all from here. If that cop hadn't shown up..."

"Yes, but he did, " Marshall said, "I would appreciate it if you would collect those tapes. I believe this man," he said motioning to the cop, as the cameras still rolled, "will need them for evidence."

"How did you know?" The cop asked, while at the same time, pulling out a little white notebook to start taking notes.

"Let's just say it was deja vu," Prescott added wryly. "It was deja vu."

"Whatever it was, you are one lucky son of a bitch," the cop added. "How do ya' spell *deja vu?*"

CHAPTER FIFTY-NINE

WHEELING, West Virginia was a perfect place to hide…a city that had long since died housing two people who wished they were dead. Wedged between the foothills of the Appalachian Mountains and the Ohio River, it was also a city trapped between better days, and worst times ahead. The death of the coal mines and steel industry made cash king and questions unnecessary.

Matt opened the sliding glass doors to the phone booth and marveled at how much progress had passed by the working class town. The light that came on when the doors closed behind him brought with it an even more unpleasant surprise. The face in the reflection on the opposite side of the phone booth bore little resemblance to the broadcaster Washingtonians had come to love and identify with. His beard was now full and only served to highlight the massive bags that had formed under his eyes due to the stress. The working class shirt betrayed the fine wines and lavish dinners that were all part of the Washington social scene. He had gone under before, on assignments, but never before, this deep. This time, he was living the life of a man on the run. The face staring back at him left little doubt.

Matt placed two quarters in the tiny slot of the phone, and carefully punched in the numbers. He knew the pay phone was safe and would be difficult to trace. Ever since the drug wars of the nineties, pay phones were unable to accept incoming calls, and the outgoing number was blocked. Cops could get the number, but it would take time.

"Captain Hinton speaking…"

"Shaun, it's me, Matt."

"Where in the hell have you been man? Everyone is looking for you, MPD, the FBI; hell I even heard the CIA wants to talk to you about some international conspiracy to assassinate Baron James."

"Let's just say hell is a good way to put it Shaun. I called because I need to cash in that chit. Those names I gave you, did you find anything?"

"I need to talk to you about those names, Matt." Hinton's voice trailed off enough to suggest there was more to what he was about to say, but then he thought better.

"So they led nowhere."

"No, those names are enough to put you behind bars for the rest of your life...Matt,. they're all dead."

There was a pregnant pause on the other end of the line.

"But then again, I suspect you knew that before you gave them to me. How many other names do you know about Matt?"

"Let's just say, there are enough to put both of us behind bars. You didn't tell anyone about the names did you?"

"No, but I gotta tell you, this shit makes me uncomfortable."

"Me too Shaun, me too. So what did you find?"

"Matt, you got one sick ass serial killer on your hands. He is the most twisted son-of-a-bitch I've ever seen. When I put the names into the NCIC computer like you asked, they all came back positive hits…five seemingly random murders, except for you. Somehow, you knew these five people were all connected."

"Did you find anything else?"

"At first no, then the autopsy photos and reports suggested, like all serial killers, this one was leaving behind his own personal signature…a gruesome one at that."

The words coming out of Hinton's mouth took Matt by surprise. He expected to hear that the people on the list were all dead, but a signature was a different story. That suggested that the man who was doing the killings, was actually enjoying the deed. Contract killers rarely enjoyed their work. They simply killed, cleaned up the scene, collected their bounty and left. Serial killers on the other hand, took great pride in taunting police and investigators. Sometimes, years would go by before all of the clues added up. "What type of signature are we talking about?"

"Matt, this sick bastard kills the victims first, and then, once they're dead, he distorts the bodies to leave behind some type of sick clue. In the case of one of the victims, he actually broke the hand of the body, after rigor mortis had set in, to open the clenched fists he had before he died."

"Anything else?"

"Yeah, there is something else I missed at first, because the locals did such a sloppy job."

"What's that?"

"The lady, Susan Sullivan, the broad who got whacked in North Carolina? After he killed her, he used her finger to write something on a mirror. The mirror almost got destroyed by the fire, but when I saw it in the autopsy photos, I had the medical examiner, down there, run a sample on what was used to write the message. It was written with her own blood!"

The thought of knowing the gruesome details of the final moments of Susan Sullivan's life sent shivers down Matt's spine. He was used to the gory details of death, but as a reporter, he kept a distance from his subjects. This time, the victim's daughter was living with him and he was protecting her. If there was a line to cross, he crossed it long ago. He was on the other side this time, and he didn't like it. "Shaun, what did the message say?"

"It wasn't really a message Matt, it was a word. One that still doesn't make any sense, backwards or forwards…'ERUTNE'."

The word left Matt feeling puzzled as well. First the fact, he might be dealing with a serial killer, as opposed to a contract killer, as he had long suspected. Then a clue that made no sense.

"And Matt?"

"Yeah Shaun?"

"It ain't like I'm telling you something you don't know, but watch your back on this one. This guy, or whoever you're tracking, you know the one who gave you these names, is dangerous. You wouldn't want to give him up would you?"

"I can't Shaun, he's a source." Matt thought about Max Webb and the phone call. His mind was racing back at a hundred miles and hour and slammed into a brick wall called murder. Was there something he was missing? Was Max Webb using him to cover his tracks? Was he the man behind the murders and not some grand conspiracy as he suspected? Then he thought of the money and the fact that Max was always there, but never publicly. Was he being set up?

"Matt?"

"Yeah, Shaun?"

"This source of yours…," Shaun paused long enough for the weight of his words to sink in. He had been Matt's friend for years, and his source even longer. They had been through battles before, but never one so dark, so desperate. "Matt, this source you're protecting…he either knows who's whacking all these people, or he's killing them himself. If I weren't your friend, I'd be hot on your tracks and his too!"

"But you are my friend, aren't you?"

"Yeah, Matt, I'm still your friend, and lucky for you, Cecilia's as well."

Matt listened for the dial tone on the other end, before placing the phone back in its receiver. Through the glass window of the phone booth, he looked up the street. There were no signs of life, just the cold gray skies of winter in West Virginia. He missed Cecilia and their life together. He missed Washington, and for the first time in a long time, he felt afraid.

CHAPTER SIXTY

"WHO could that be calling now?" Mrs. Avery said, pushing Sebastian aside to answer the phone,

"Mrs. Avery?"

"Yes, this is she."

"This is Cecilia. I was wondering..."

"Yes?"

"I was wondering whether or not you've heard from my husband. The last time we spoke, he was headed your way, and that was so long ago..."

Mrs. Avery could hear Cecilia crying on the other end of the line. She wanted to talk, to tell Cecilia all she knew, but now was not the time, and this was not the place. "Cecilia, we need to talk, but this place has eyes and ears, if you know what I mean."

Cecilia had been warned by Captain Hinton that Vanessa's townhouse was being watched. She remembered the stories Matt told her about the lengths the government would go to, to obtain information. Wiretapping, electronic eaves dropping, none of it surprised her anymore.

"There is something I need to give you. Is there someplace we can meet?'

"Do you like coffee?" Mrs. Avery asked.

"Tea."

"Then I know the perfect place. Have you ever been to The Bolivian.?"

Cecilia eyed the envelope sitting next to her. "Isn't that in Georgetown?"

"Please come alone."

CHAPTER SIXTY-ONE

Two Months Later

THE pride of Wheeling was Wheeling Jesuit College. Founded by Jesuit priests, the College bragged of its ties to the Nation's space programs and other federal programs. Powerful friends in Washington opened the financial floodgates, and the money flowed north to Wheeling Jesuit College. It was that money that allowed the University to attract some of the most prolific speakers in the country.

"I find it difficult to believe that so many of you are suddenly interested in the sex lives of our nation's past presidents," the speaker began, much to the delight of the coeds who had gathered. Father Michael Haynes was well known as an expert on the subject, and the Baron James Scandal had second semester students lining up to quench their appetites on the nation's latest scandal. "Are there any questions?" he asked finishing up his speech.

"Yes sir, I have one." The woman speaking was an attractive girl with short blond hair.

"And you might be...?" Father Haynes inquired.

"Lucinda sir… Lucinda Hanks." the woman answered.

"And what might your question be Mrs. ..?"

"That's Ms. Hanks, and my question has to do with historians like yourself. Why do they refuse to correct history they obviously know is wrong?" As the woman spoke, one by one the students in the auditorium turned to see who this woman was, who dared challenge the great Father Haynes.

"I am assuming you are a graduate student?" he said smiling politely. Glancing at a seating chart, he continued. "Ah yes...Ms. Hanks. A curious name indeed, but let me answer your question. The truth is... money. Quite simply, rich men have made millions painting portraits of great men as they were not. You've probably have heard the phrase, "To the victors go the spoils". It is much the same way with history. No one wants to hear that their leaders were drunken philanderers. Jefferson's letters to Virginia leave little doubt that he was a racist, and yet history simply glosses over that chapter in his life. It is not that these facts are not known. It is that we simply choose to ignore them, and so many students are lazy". Father Haynes glanced at his watch, announced that that was the last question, and prepared to leave. "Ms. Hanks," he asked, "Is it possible for you to hang around after class?"

The young woman responded proudly, "It is not only possible, I wouldn't have it any other way."

Vanessa Sullivan, AKA Lucinda Hanks, ran down the auditorium steps taking them two at a time. When she reached Father Haynes, she greeted him with a warm embrace that caused several of the other students to question just what was going on.

A sheepish Father Haynes looked up and declared, *"We share a passion for history."*

Vanessa laughed and proceeded to catch up on old times.

"I heard you were in town, and I wouldn't have missed this for the world," she said barely able to hide the enthusiasm in her voice. She had been on the road for two months and had not heard from anyone she once considered to be her friend. Father Haynes, she knew, was more than a friend. He was her mentor, as well.

"Mrs. Avery wants me to tell you hi," he said reaching into his brief case.

"How is she...and Sebastian?" Vanessa asked.

"They're both fine. They miss you dearly. I talk to her every other day. She is quite the mystery woman. It seems she knows a lot more than she lets on. She knew where you were and swore me to secrecy." Father Haynes handed Vanessa a copy of a book he had been keeping inside his satchel. "I thought you might like to have this," he said, handing her the book.

Vanessa eyed the copy. It was in mint condition. The faded leather cover left little doubt that it was an antique, but few outside of historical circles knew just how precious of a gift it was. *The Genesis of Lincoln,* by James Cathey, 1899, she said examining the book closely. "You do know the way to a girl's heart."

"I thought it might help with your current field of study."

"It will indeed. Hungry?"

"Starved," Father Haynes answered.

"Good," Vanessa responded. "I know just the place."

It took less than fifteen minutes to reach the house. Vine Street was a gravel road off the beaten path, and yet conveniently located less than five minutes from the center of town. The original owners sold the house and moved to Texas some five years earlier. It had fallen into disrepair, the roof leaked, the hot water frequently ran cold, but for the last two months, it was home. The crock pot on the stove sent forth an aroma that signaled dinner was ready. Inside the door, Vanessa officially welcomed Father Haynes to what had become "their humble abode."

The two spent hours catching up on old times, and savoring Vanessa's concoction she had cooked up in the crock pot. Father

Haynes told her of how Washington had moved onto new issues. "The microwave attention span," he called it. The twenty four hour news cycle created an appetite for the latest disaster, and sadly the controversy surrounding the life and death of Baron James had taken its course. The conversation abruptly ended with the unexpected opening of the front door.

Vanessa turned quickly, her heart beginning to race out of control. Her eyes first focused on the front door. *The door was unlocked.* Matt had warned her not to get sloppy, but in her excitement to see Father Haynes, she had done just that. The sound of tires on the dirt road usually signaled someone was approaching, but she was so engrossed in their discussion she heard no such sounds. Slowly the knob to the front door began to turn. *There was nothing they could do.*

CHAPTER SIXTY-TWO

THE door opened slowly as if the person, on the other end, had been warned to expect trouble. Vanessa was clutching the grip of the Louisville Slugger so tightly, her knuckles were white. She took a deep breath and reared back, raising the bat above her head, just like her mother had taught her. *Let gravity do the rest.*

"Anyone home?"

The door opened with a slow creaking sound that left little doubt; if she survived, it would be among the first things she would oil. Because the lights were low, it caused dark shadows to creep across the ceiling, eclipsing all light. Suddenly a man appeared.

"Oh shit Matt!...I almost launched you into the outfield." Slowly Vanessa lowered the bat, just in time to stop from lowering the boom on Matt.

Matt smiled and allowed the bat to descend slowly into his outstretched hand. "Here, I'll take that. The door was left open. I was afraid someone had arrived here before me, and things were so quiet." That's when he noticed Father Haynes. Matt was stunned to see someone other than Vanessa sitting at the kitchen table. They had been so careful keeping their location secret, paying for everything in cash, and assuming new identities. A task made somewhat easier by, of all people, Max Webb. At first Matt was skeptical of the newly elected president, but a sizable amount of cash and a promise that the FBI would be kept otherwise occupied, caused him to reconsider the offer, although he still was unclear why Max Webb was so interested in pursuing the names on the list, now that Baron James was dead. Suddenly, the words of Captain Hinton gripped him with fear. Hinton was right, the man who gave him the names, either knew the killer, or was the killer himself. The sight of Father Haynes rekindled fears that they had been discovered. Fears, Vanessa moved quickly to ease.

"This is Father Haynes," she said. "You've heard me talk about him."

Matt studied the man briefly. He could see the man standing before him was at ease, and the fact he was wearing a collar, went a long way as well. Trust however, was another story.

"She talks about you all the time. The truth is, Father, she practically worships you." He could tell from the smile on Father Haynes face, the man truly was taken aback. The smile eased some of the tension causing Matt to believe, at least for the moment, they were still safe. He then noticed the copy of the book sitting on the table. *The Genesis of Lincoln?*

"It's a story I thought Vanessa, or should I say *Lucy* might like."

"I don't understand what genetics has to do with our current situation." Matt shot back, once again bringing the gravity of their situation into the conversation.

"I understand, Matt. But you see, *The Genesis of Lincoln* is the story of the real Lucy Hanks. The real Lucy Hanks and Vanessa have a lot in common."

Matt picked up the book, examining its cover.

Vanessa next tried to explain it. "Lincoln, it seems, as I mentioned briefly back on the road, comes from *questionable* lineage. It was always one of my favorite chapters that history chose to forget. Lucy Hanks, his grandmother was quite the woman for her times."

"That would be an understatement. It seems she was *promiscuous*!" Father Haynes added.

"Are you saying that the grandmother of one of the most famous presidents in history, was a..?" Matt began.

"That's one way of looking at it," Father Haynes said. The truth is, she was actually *charged with fornication* in 1789."

"Imagine," Vanessa said sarcastically, "the grandmother of one of the greatest presidents of all time...*a fornicator*."

Vanessa's sarcasm broke the tension in the room. Father Haynes began to laugh and Matt realized the man behind the collar was indeed harmless. It felt good to laugh, and while he first feared Father Haynes's visit, he knew they had been in hiding for too long. He knew something had to give. "Father, if you'll forgive me for being so blunt, but..."

"Why am I here? The truth is, I have known your whereabouts ever since you left, as has Mrs. Avery." Father Haynes answered. "And so has your friend, Captain Hinton."

"How do you know Captain Hinton?"

"That, Matt, is a story for another day. By the way, he sent *you* this."

Father Haynes handed Matt a manila envelope, stamped **CONFIDENTIAL** on the front. Matt took it, tore open the seal, and almost instantly knew what he was looking at. Father Haynes could see Matt was encouraged by the contents of the envelope, even if he was less than enthused to be receiving any company.

"Were you followed?"

"I don't think so. Trust me no one knows I am here. I don't even know where *here is.* I have not betrayed your trust, and neither did Mrs. Avery. As for the envelope, she got it from Cecilia."

Hearing Cecilia's name took Matt by surprise. He tried to keep busy to keep from thinking about her, but she was never far from his thoughts. "Then you have been in contact with her?"

"I haven't, but Mrs. Avery has, and she is fine, although very concerned about your safety."

"Why are you doing this? Why are you here?"

Father Haynes smiled a comforting smile. "Matt, the truth is, we *Jesuits* are used to keeping secrets. Throughout history we have been referred to as a ruthless band of assassins and believe it or not, far worse. I prefer to think of us more as an order that has a history of *hiding* people we believe to be innocent. Not once did anyone really *believe* Vanessa was somehow associated with Baron's death. Ms. Sullivan, perhaps you can enlighten Mr. Walker, on the history of a certain Father Healy, the first President of Georgetown University."

Vanessa continued the story. "Matt, the *Jesuits knew* all along he was hiding his *real* racial identify. It was his fellow priests who choose to hide him all those years. His secret was safe, until he started to raise money for what you know as, Healy Hall. Father Healy's health started to fade once the donors started to question his ethnicity. When they found out he was black, they had already committed a fortune. It was too late to turn back. So the school's history was written to reflect what the times were willing to accept. Father Healy became white, and for decades stayed that way. Now few students even notice the plaque in the entrance, that tells the true story of Georgetown's first *black president.*"

Slowly Matt was beginning to feel more at ease. He could tell Vanessa liked having company, and felt at ease with Father Haynes. He had learned to trust her feelings as well as his own. Perhaps hers, more so. Instinct told him to walk over to the window and look to see if any headlights could be spotted. "I would feel more comfortable if we got rid of some of these lights."

"So Matt," Vanessa continued, "What Father Haynes is saying, is that he can be trusted with our secret."

Matt was in no mood to argue. Ever since his conversation with Captain Hinton, he was eager to try and figure out what the killer was up to. If his cursory examination was correct, Captain Hinton, somehow managed to get his hands on the autopsy photos of the people on the list who were killed. "Vanessa, if I could borrow the good Father for a second, there is something I would like him to see."

Matt took Father Haynes by the arm and led him from the kitchen into what once was the dining room of the house. Matt had converted it into to a makeshift war room. Charts lined the walls with newspaper and Internet articles that had been downloaded. Red yarn connected sights on a map with articles highlighted in yellow. Matt acted as if he were some type of military general tracing the movements of a war. In fact, he believed, he was. Sitting in the middle of the table, were the last two things he would ever receive from his precious Cecilia, a laptop computer and a petition for divorce, which he refused to sign. It was good to hear she was still concerned for his safety. Perhaps there *was* still hope.

Matt refocused his attention on Father Haynes, "Father, we have been hard at work researching the names on a list I was given by a person I swore to keep anonymous. I have been staring at this wall for hours trying to make sense of it all. I was hoping you might be able to help. "

Father Haynes was already one step ahead of Matt. "So I can see. It appears as if you have been very busy indeed." Father Haynes ran his finger across the top of the yarn to the various sights. He stopped at a pin stuck in the mountains of North Carolina and the newspaper article pinned beneath it. The article described the crash of a van with a family of five inside. The van burst into flames upon impact, killing all inside. There were no survivors, but it was the family's name that sparked his curiosity. *"Enloe."*

"Yes father, Vanessa told me about the connection between Lincoln and Enloe, that much I already know." Matt was following the yarn, just as Father Haynes did, stopping at another article, this one about the murder of *Dickie Hankins* in Hollywood. There were several stories attached to the pin underneath, and Father Haynes recognized their contents, immediately, from the various news accounts that had blanketed the airwaves. *Dickie Hankins*, a well known Hollywood actor, who was beloved by his peers and respected in the industry, died in a fiery crash. He was also known as being among one of the most cautious of the Hollywood elite. Reports surfaced, there were drugs and alcohol in his bloodstream, even though he was said to attend church regularly, and never touched a drop of liquor.

"Do you know the connection, Matt?"

"Yes, Vanessa explained that as well. *Dickie Hankins*, the actor, is a distant relative of Nancy Hanks, Lincoln's mother. So once again we have Lincoln as a common denominator."

Father Haynes focused on another spot in Tennessee, where vandals had broken into a grave. It was, however, not any grave. It was the burial plot of a former President and his wife.

"Like I said, I have been looking at this wall for hours, trying to figure out, why these people were killed, and some of the deaths don't add up."

"I must say, this is an impressive body of research," he said stroking his chin as he studied each site on the map. "It appears that the obvious answer is they are all directly related to past presidents."

"I agree, but that does little to explain why they were all killed. Murder is a harsh way to prove one's point. Not to mention the fact the actor is the only one who had any money. The others were middle income or poor." Matt added, "Then there's Chiniquy."

"So it sounds as if Vanessa brought you up to speed on our friend Father Chiniquy," Father Haynes said removing the glasses from his forehead as if he were teaching a class.

"She did," Matt continued," but none of these murders rise to the level of anything more than one sick bastard and an unusual set of circumstances."

Matt sensed Father Haynes knew more than he was letting on. He played along hoping to see if the priest would forget his vows and slip. "There is nothing to point to a global conspiracy…or is there?"

"I believe what you are looking for has to do more with *why* our friend chose the name Chiniquy, than *what* is on this board. Chiniquy was Lincoln's confidant. We know for a fact, Lincoln knew he was about to be assassinated. I suspect *our* friend, Chiniquy, knew history was about to repeat itself. You two were chosen for a reason, as was the work of our mysterious Chiniquy."

Vanessa's mind was racing far ahead of the others. "You're speaking in the past tense. Then that means you believe *Baron James was Chiniquy?"*

"For your sake, I wish I could answer that question, Vanessa. Mrs. Avery told me about the canceled checks." Father Haynes studied Vanessa's face for any signs of betrayal. "Don't worry, she told me in confidence, and because I am a priest your secret is safe with me. She was simply trying to help, as we are both concerned for your safety." Father Haynes then turned and faced Matt. "As for our friend Chiniquy, I don't know who the man was who called or visited me. He disguised his voice when he called *and* during his grotto confession. I never got a good look at him before or after he arrived. I'm afraid, our friend Chiniquy is, and always will be, a phantom."

Sensing he was hearing nothing new, Matt refocused his attention on his maps.

Father Haynes could tell he was at an impasse. "Matt, what do you *really* see?"

"Like I said, I see one sick bastard, forgive *my French,* Father."

"Don't worry; I feel your frustration, and have ever since my visit from our mysterious Mr. Chiniquy." Father Haynes studied the map and articles one more time. It was not in his nature to prejudge things. It was part of his academic training. He knew the obvious sometimes lied, and he wanted to make sure his next words were carefully measured. "Let's go over what we have. Sometimes it works better, to hear ourselves walk through a set of problems. Vanessa taught me that in my own classroom. Let me walk you through your findings. The family in North Carolina, "he began, *The Enloes,* have been fighting in recent years to have the body of Abraham Lincoln exhumed and reexamined. It is their contention that Lincoln's blood is *their blood.* They also contend he was born, not in a log cabin in Illinois, but in the hollows of North Carolina. I would say it is also curious that the *Dickie Hankins*, slain here, is a distant relative of Lincoln's mother, Nancy."

"Father Haynes," Matt began, his face even more serious now. "There is something you don't know about. Something I just learned of yesterday. It seems our killer fancies himself as a historian, as well, unless Chiniquy is the man behind the murders!"

"I don't understand." Father Haynes said moving in for a closer look.

"These are the autopsy photos of all involved." Matt moved quickly to make sure the photo at the top could not be seen. "Here, look at this one. He *broke the bones* in the hands of this victim, intentionally leaving one palm open, and the other fist closed, clenched; does that mean anything to you?"

"Strength and compassion," Vanessa said softly, in a tone barely audible to the others.

"What did you say?"

"Strength and compassion," she continued. "Lincoln's statue in the memorial has one fist closed and the other open. At first, scholars thought the sculpture Daniel Chester French left behind was a sign for his daughter, Alice, because of the way the hands are positioned." "I don't get it," Matt said.

"In sign language, Lincoln's hands look like he is signing the letters A and L."

As always Matt was impressed with how quickly Vanessa could recall the most intimate details of history, so matter of factly. "A second body," Matt continued, "was found, minus a molar. He was a dentist and the killer used an extraction tool he found in the office. Made quite a mess of it, according to police."

This time Vanessa was stumped. "That one doesn't ring a bell. Were there others?"

"Yes, but we can talk about those later." Matt moved quickly to close the envelope, but it was too late.

"Matt, *my name* was on that list as well, as was *my mother's*."

"Yes Vanessa, we've been over this before, and as far as I can tell, despite your alias, you weren't related to any past president."

"No, but I *would have been* related to a sitting President, had *my father not been killed."*

"And your point is?"

Vanessa hated that tone in Matt's voice. She noticed in recent weeks he had become distant, a fact she chalked up to the arrival of the divorce papers. He *had* stopped drinking, but the wall was becoming an obsession. "My *point* is, Matt, are my mother's photos in there? If they are, I would like to see them."

Before Matt could stop her, Vanessa had located the photo of her mother. She froze instantly when she recognized what once was the trailer her mother called home. The photos looked so cold and made things look so sterile. The photos revealed Susan Sullivan died in an agonizing manner. The right arm of the burned out corpse, was extended, as if she were pleading in the last minutes of her life. Her face, once a thing of beauty, had been burned beyond recognition. "These are horrible!"

"I didn't want you to see those."

Vanessa fought back tears. It was clear she was not prepared for what she had seen. "If you don't mind, I think I've had enough history for tonight...recent and otherwise." Vanessa turned, but paused as she was about to leave the room. "Matt?"

"Yes, Vanessa?"

"Did it ever dawn on you that the person, who gave you the list of names, is the person doing all that killing? Maybe that person had a lot to gain. Maybe that person is Chiniquy or, should I say, Max Webb."

Vanessa's words cut through Matt like a knife. It was the second time in less than twenty four hours that someone close to him had questioned his judgment. He wanted to come clean about Max, but knew he could not reveal a source. Matt's sudden silence said it all.

"I didn't think so," Vanessa stated in a matter-of-fact manner that cut like a knife. "My point, Matt, is perhaps you need to focus more on the *obvious*, than what you *choose to see*. Perhaps the reason my father is dead isn't that complex at all. Perhaps it's because Max Webb just wanted to be president. That sick bastard you refer to, is just that, and he's creating a trail for you to follow, *at the same time creating his alibi.*"

CHAPTER SIXTY-THREE

PRESCOTT Marshall pressed the gas of his Mercedes Roadster and floored it, causing the auto to lurch forward, and the speedometer to soar well past eighty miles an hour. The speed was addictive, as was the risk of getting caught. He was, once again, on the GW Parkway and approaching the Park Police station. He could see the outline of the cruiser up ahead, and decided to back off, just as the officer was locking in on his radar.

The lights of the police cruiser would have caused most motorists to panic, but not Prescott. Instead, he mashed on the accelerator until there was no room between it and the floor. The officer pursued the auto until he reached the outer loop of the beltway, on the Maryland side. Zipping in and out of traffic, he then made a quick turn onto River Road, as if he were headed to Potomac, and made a sharp right onto Democracy Blvd, and killed his headlights. The officer sped by, believing the Mercedes was well out of sight. Prescott reached down, with his left hand, and turned the knob to the right, once again, illuminating the headlights. He lived for moments like this, no matter how brief, as did the Park Police. He would do it again, and they would be waiting.

The adrenaline provided the clarity Prescott needed when mysteries arose, and the one facing him seemed utterly impossible to solve. He was certain there was a connection between Max and the girl, but he couldn't put his finger on it.

"What are you hiding from me old friend?" he pondered, as the Mercedes once again headed west on River Road. The speeding police car was now headed in the opposite direction, once again lights flashing. "Is it possible that you are not who you say you are?"

He was thinking back to the origins of the Vai, and the first round of DNA tests. "Max was there, I saw him swab his mouth. I watched him turn his sample in with the others. It had to be his!"

Of course old friend. It was there all along.

The Mercedes sped into the driveway and screeched to a halt. The front door was open and he rushed in, and went straight to his study. The study was an exact duplicate of the one he had in Liberia, all the way down to the wood paneling. He placed his coat on the back of a wing back chair in the corner of the room and hurriedly took a seat behind the massive wooden desk in the center of the room. Opening the drawer in the middle, he once again produced the computer terminal that had served him so well in the past. His fingers quickly went to work.

A half a world away, the government's stolen super computer quietly came to life, and connected to the even more super secret ECHELON program. The panel of red and green lights offered the only clue that there was activity in a room that few, if any, knew existed. The computer lights cast a soft glow to an otherwise empty chamber, just the way Prescott would have liked it.

The tests.

Senator Corris Cullen was one of the most conservative members of Congress. He represented one of the most backward regions in the country and won solely because he appealed to the NASCAR vote. Like the drivers behind the wheel, his legislation went round and round, and in the end, got nowhere. On the day of the test, Cullen, who was also the oldest member of the Senate was fast asleep during most of the festivities, save one. A quick jolt from Max Webb brought the aging senator to life just before the cameras could record his slumber. The older reporters, in the room, chuckled at how he had been spared the embarrassment of being videotaped, asleep, at the switch once more, while the newer members of the press corps bemoaned the fact they were doomed to have to cover the DNA press conference itself.

In the end however, the joke was on Cullen. He was shocked to learn *his DNA* had African origins. The embarrassment cost him dearly at the polls. Cullen, the results said, originated in the Mediterranean region of Africa, but that was only the beginning of the embarrassment. The test also confirmed the presence of Indian blood. No one could figure it out, but with a one in three billion chance of being wrong, no one was willing to blame science either.

"*Mandela,*" Prescott said as he typed the instructions, "*run a sample of Swab 291,* against the sample I just provided."

Prescott then turned his attention to the TV monitors that lined his office. He quickly learned the evening's news would provide little in the way of comfort.

"We've just learned that the FBI has launched an investigation into one of the most secretive agencies in Washington," the anchor began. The anchor, then, talked over footage of agents with bold yellow FBI letters on their jackets carrying boxes out of *The Consortium's headquarters*. "According to our sources *The Consortium* is being investigated for money laundering, gun running," and then the anchor paused for added effect, "Murder!"

"*Whatever,*" Prescott said as he turned down the volume. He had heard the allegations before. Charges in Washington came and went with each passing administration. "*Let them indict their President!*" Prescott knew investigations in Washington were designed more to embarrass than to jail. It was also a way to keep high priced lawyers in their yachts.

The sound of the printer coming to life caused him to turn away from the monitors and focus his attention on the incoming printout. *Mandela is unusually quick tonight,*" he said in a barely audible whisper. Walking slowly toward the printer, he retrieved the printout, ripping it off with one quick jerking motion. Glancing down, he first saw the words, "**COMPUTATIONS COMPLETE**." The words that followed needed no further explanation.

He dropped the print out on his desk and once again headed toward the door. It was early. He had time to celebrate and much to savor.

Mandela had come through again.

CHAPTER SIXTY-FOUR

Prescott hated the call he was about to make. The arrogance of The Cardinal was sometimes too much to tolerate. Tonight, he knew, would be another one of those nights. Despite his misgivings, he searched his rolodex for the number Boucher had given him in case of emergencies. If this didn't count as an emergency, nothing did. As always, the phone rang several times before Boucher picked up.

"Bon jour Monsieur Marshall, c'va bien?"

"Hello Boucher, and I guess by way of cutting to the quick, all is not well." There was chewing in the background. Prescott pictured, a bulbous Frenchman, eating an entire turkey leg as he talked with food spilling out of his mouth.

"I do not understand. We have been following the events from this side of the ocean, and it appears all has been going well. Are you calling me to say it is not?'

"That's exactly why I am calling. It appears we have a problem."

"Why type of problem. I have been reading about the tragedy that struck our dear friend Baron James. The other members of The Consortium inform me that all of the items we sought have been collected. Prescott, you worry too much. This is a glorious time in our organization. It is only a a matter of time, before we control The White

House, and the power that goes along with it. Rome will be very happy indeed."

"Not so fast, Boucher. It seems we have been betrayed!"

"Betrayed? By whom? Who would be so foolish as to cross us? Quite simply, we control everything."

Prescott could hear the chewing as Boucher continued consuming whatever it was that he was eating. "We control everyone, but the man who will be President, barring any unforeseen tragedies. Max Webb."

"It sounds to me as if you are saying the wrong man is dead."

"That's exactly what I am saying. Baron was not the girl's father. DNA proves it. It seems our friend Max pulled a switch on us."

"But Baron was dead anyway, was he not? "

"Yes, our plan was to eliminate him, because we all agreed he could not be controlled. Even though his father promised otherwise, once Baron took office, all bets were off."

"So then, what is this problem, to which you refer?"

"I have *intel* that Max Webb tipped off a reporter, and that reporter is hiding the girl. Seems, our associate has a soft spot for beautiful women. If we cannot control him now, we will not be able to control him, once he becomes President. I suggest, we take care of this situation before it grows any worse."

"Surely you are not suggesting we eliminate another of your Presidents?" The pomposity in the voice of Cardinal Boucher could be heard loud and clear. "Who would that leave?"

Prescott waited before answering to give the appearance he had given his next answer considerable thought. "Max is not well liked among all circles here. Truth is, a lot of people can't stand him, and believe he became President in an unseemly way. His Vice President however, is far more manageable."

"You mean stupid, don't you?"

"Perhaps, but I suspect he will not question the turn of events, if things can be properly arranged."

Boucher stopped his eating long enough to hear Prescott's plan. "It sounds as if you have thought this whole thing out."

"I have. We will use the reporter. He must be eliminated. An impeachment is out of the question. Too many possibilities. And there is one other thing."

"And that would be?"

"You need to invite our newest friend to the Vatican." Marshall waited for the response. Never before had things gone so wrong as to involve the Vatican itself. "Can that be arranged?"

"All things are possible, when it comes to *The Consortium*. You should know that by now. Sounds like you are bringing the snake to the nest."

Again there was more chewing.

"Is there a problem?"

I assure you we will clean up your mess. We always have. "Give me the dates and I will arrange an audience with the Holy See."

Prescott placed his finger on the receiver, disabling the phone before slamming it into the wall.

CHAPTER SIXTY-FIVE

THE fire at the National Museum of Health and History quickly grew to five alarms.

"We're going to have to let it burn," Captain Mark Garrett told the reporters who gathered around him. Garrett was wearing the white helmet and the white coat that signified that he was in charge. He also was wearing the expression of a man who was fighting a losing battle.

"We have breaking news at this hour," the kid said, using an even deeper anchor voice than before. This time he had been coached by the finest talent coaches in the nation. Focus groups determined that he needed more graying along the hairline, darker suits and a *"more professional look."* The end result was an anchor clone that resembled each and every anchor in town and across the nation, for that matter. He had risen to the top of the broadcast heap on the story of the death of Baron James, and he was now on the downhill side. **"There has been a major fire at the National Museum of Health and History; we go live, now, to our reporter on the scene, Vernon Smith."**

Vernon Smith was everything that the kid was not. He was cocky and confident, and spent years studying under the tutelage of Matt Walker. He toiled for years, working in smaller markets, honing his craft, and it showed during his coverage of the museum fire. "This fire, not only, has claimed a building, it has claimed a part of our history," he said authoritatively. "The building housed some of the most important medical exhibits in the nation's history, including the surgical tools, bones and bullet fragments collected, when doctors tried to save the life of..." He paused for effect, as if to understand the importance of what he was about to say**... "President Abraham Lincoln."**

Smith tossed back to the studio where the kid tried to act as if he knew the significance of the fire. The truth was, he knew little about Lincoln, other than the fact his face was on the five dollar bills he handed out like candy as tips. Had he been watching, he would have noticed the meeting taking place in the News Director's office just down the hall. They liked what they saw in Vernon Smith and the kid was about to be replaced.

The last fire company left the scene at four o'clock in the morning. Captain Garrett, an experienced fire investigator, immediately told reporters that the fire spread too quickly. He suspected that there was some type of accelerant used. "All signs," he said, "pointed to arson."

Vernon Smith smelled a story, and immediately returned to the newsroom to check the city's database to see who owned the building. It was federal property, but many of the exhibits inside were there on loan. A computer check caused Smith to stop in his tracks. *Lincoln, it seemed, was having a bad year. There was another burglary he needed to investigate as well.*

CHAPTER SIXTY-SIX

"IF I remember correctly, you like your eggs done over easy," Vanessa asked.

Father Haynes decided to spend the night, and she was happy he decided to stay. That night, when Matt and Father Haynes went to bed, Vanessa vowed to put her past behind her and focus on any future she had left. She lived her entire life not knowing who her father might be. Now she suspected he was dead, and died trying to save her life. She also had come to believe, if her theory was correct, the man who killed him could not be stopped, and if there was a consortium, neither could it. Everyone she knew was dead. She was alone, truly alone for the first time in her life, save an uncle who was wanted for murder, Matt, Mrs. Avery, and an impatient priest waiting for his eggs.

"Vanessa, have you forgotten about my eggs so soon?"

"Father Haynes, last night we were talking about the patience of the Jesuits. This morning, it appears you are ready to *kill* just for a plate of eggs."

"If that's what it takes to be fed around here, then so be it."

The trip back to Washington by car was at least five hours. She hated the fact Father Haynes would have to navigate the mountains of both West Virginia and Pennsylvania on his way home. She feared for his safety, but the larger truth was, she missed the close company of someone other than Matt. "They'll be ready in a jiffy."

Matt walked into the kitchen, from the war room. Vanessa could see, he hadn't slept a wink. "Mornin'."

"Good morning Matt, eggs?"

"Thank you Vanessa, and some coffee." Matt looked directly into Vanessa's eyes. "I think you'll want to join me."

"Why?"

"Because I think I have some information that might lead us to the man who really killed your father."

"Matt...I think it's time we moved on..."

"One day Vanessa, but not now. There are a lot of things you know about me, but I never quit. We can quit when we are on top, but not right now. A killer is on the loose and he's claimed too many lives already, not to mention my reputation and yours."

It was difficult for Vanessa to keep the tears from falling. Never before had anyone other than Father Haynes fought for her. No one had fought as hard. "If that's what you say."

"I insist."

Vanessa placed a fresh cup of coffee in front of Matt and began to fix his eggs. She knew how he liked him, and welcomed any news he might have. She felt she had been too harsh, and wanted things to be right between them.

"I first need to thank you Vanessa, for forcing me to take a closer look at the obvious."

"So you agree Max Webb is our killer."

"No, in fact, I think that's what Chiniquy is trying to tell us... that and the evidence."

"What evidence?"

"It was there all along. We all focused on the photos, but the autopsy reports that were attached held the answers."

"I don't get it." Vanessa placed Matt's eggs in front of him and took a seat to his right. *"If I were a younger man..."*

Matt quickly noticed she had gone to bed wearing his shirt. Her legs were tone and tan, part of what most men would consider to be the *entire package*. If he were not attached, he would have made his move long ago, but the truth was he was still hooked. He was still in love with a woman back home, whom he prayed was still waiting for her 'knight in shining armor'. He hoped somewhere out there Cecilia was still waiting for him. It was time to focus on getting back home...back into her arms. "The autopsy reports all had one thing in common."

"And what might that be?" Father Haynes inquired.

"*Cassava leaves* and *Palm Ashe*. It seems our assassin is taunting us."

"I don't understand."

"Vanessa, *Cassava leaves* were used by child soldiers in Africa. They would rub the leaves in their eyes, turning them fiery red. People in the West African nation of Liberia burned *Palm Trees* to cook. The soldiers would take *Palm Ashe*, and rub it on their skin, giving them the appearance of a ghost."

Vanessa's mind raced back to their first conversation about Prescott Marshall. She remembered Mrs. Avery telling them Marshall was once was stationed in Liberia, West Africa. She then recalled their mysterious date, and how he surfaced seemingly out of nowhere, and then disappeared. She remembered his arrogance. Suddenly it all added up. "So you think our killer is.."

"Prescott Marshall!" Matt answered.

"Prescott Marshall?! Why would he....what did I ever do to deserve..?"

"I think Chiniquy was the clue, Vanessa. I think he's been taunting authorities all along, almost daring them to find him. Men like Prescott, never believe they will be caught. I think that's why our source used the name Chiniquy. Chiniquy warned Lincoln that powerful men were plotting to overthrow the United States. John Wilkes Booth hanged for his crime, but the conspiracy was never really solved. John Surratt was the mastermind and he walked away scott free! Chiniquy had the answers but, in the end, was declared a fool." The gravity of Matt's last statement could be seen on the faces of all present. "We are being played for fools."

Father Haynes interrupted, "You're right Matt, no one ever believed Chiniquy, or his conspiracy theories, not even when he surfaced at the Vatican, wearing the uniform of a Papal Zouave!"

"Exactly! The real bad guys got away. They always do."

Matt couldn't help but notice his copy of *The Wheeling Post* that was sitting on the kitchen table. "When did that come?"

"I took the liberty of walking out front this morning and collecting it. I hope you're not offended."

"No Father Haynes, but have you read it?"

"Cover to cover, and I should point out, it didn't take long."

"Not the inside, just the front page."

PRESIDENT TO VISIT SNEEDVILLE, TENNESSEE.

"I read the article, Matt. Seems like the networks are up in arms because our dear President will be delivering his speech at *6:05 central time,* not at the top of the hour as the networks prefer. They want him to push it back, making it 7:00 prime time, east coast time, but he steadfastly refuses."

"Father Haynes, when is he scheduled to deliver that speech?"

"Two days from now, on January 30th.'" Father Haynes couldn't help but notice the change on the expression of Matt's face. He seemed pleased. "Why did you ask?"

"Let's just say, we have an invitation to go to Sneedville, from the President of the United States!"

Matt continued to scan the headlines. What he was looking at seemed too convenient to be believable and too believable to ignore. He immediately spotted the article about the fire in Washington, and the connection to Lincoln. It was all starting to add up. He was not prepared for what he saw next. "Vanessa, Father Haynes, we need to leave first thing tomorrow morning."

"Why the rush, Matt? Tennessee isn't that far from here." Father Haynes could tell by the urgency in Matt's voice, whatever he discovered was important.

"Because, Father Haynes, if my instincts are right, then Prescott Marshall is not Chiniquy, someone else is, and he's trying to tell us *history is about to repeat itself!* I believe the President's life, is in danger!"

CHAPTER SIXTY-SEVEN

MATT looked through the rear view mirror at the man sitting directly behind him. He had been in similar vehicles, making his way through the mountains of Kosovo while on assignment. Always, he knew what was up ahead. Those trips had been well planned by his producers so he knew what to expect. This time, however, was different. Never before had there been so much on his shoulders. He looked at Vanessa sitting to his right. For the first time that he could remember, there was calmness in her face, as if soon, it would all be over. The black turtleneck sweater she wore for warmth only added to her beauty. He thought about Cecilia.

"So Matt, why Sneedville?"

"Call it a hunch, and *Google*, Vanessa."

"*Google?*"

"Precisely. I *Googled* Sneedville last night. Needless to say, I was surprised at what I found?"

"Nothing?"

"Quite the contrary Vanessa. It seems Sneedville has quite the history. Both of you would be impressed. Are you familiar with the story of *"The Lost Colony?"*

"That one escapes me Matt but perhaps you would like to enlighten us."

"The Lost Colony" was a group of settlers who disappeared long before Captain John Smith landed and established Jamestown, in Virginia. For years, it was believed they simply vanished into thin air. Plays have been written, and archeological digs have found nothing. It's as if they never even existed. Now historians believe it's because they never died. One by one their descendants are coming forward to tell their true story."

"So are they, *The Lost Colony?"* Vanessa asked.

"I don't know, Vanessa," Matt continued. "It's hard to tell from what I read online last night. It seems, historians now believe they came here from Morocco, Angola, or the Mediterranean area. They came here as indentured servants, and worked to gain their freedom. Once freed, they settled along the Appalachian Mountains."

Father Haynes had been sleeping, but the mere mention of history caused him to sit up and take notice. "In fact," he began, "if my limited research is true, many of the names we have credited with being Indian, have roots in the Turkish language."

Vanessa turned her body, to be able to focus on every word offered up by Matt and Father Haynes. "For example?"

"For example, Vanessa," Father Haynes began, "I read in a magazine article that names we assumed were Indian, like *Alabama, Kentucky, Tennessee, and Appalachia*, were not Indian words at all."

"Then what was their origin?"

"Most of those names have Turkish and Arabic origins," Father Haynes continued. " For instance, Allegheny closely resembles the Portuguese word, *All genis*. Other words like Arkansas also have similar sounding words in the Appalachian mountains. Arkansas sounds like

Ar Kan Sah, Kentucky, *Kan Tok*. There are so many words that sound similar that historians now believe the group deserves further study."

"According to the Internet," Matt continued, "these people call themselves, *Melungeon*, which is Turkish for *cursed people.* Many of those who believe they may be *Melungeon* have had their DNA tested. That DNA matches the DNA of people from those regions, as well as the regions in and around Iraq, Libya, even Syria. Put simply, *they are* the descendants of Turkish slaves, who settled in Southern Virginia, married and migrated to the mountains. Some married Indians, others married blacks."

"So why did they call themselves cursed?" Vanessa asked.

"Because Vanessa," Father Haynes added, " they believed *they were cursed*. All they wanted was to be left alone. They were born free and for years, lived as such. The census identified them as *freed blacks*. Some were former slaves, others owned slaves. Then, skin color came into play. Virginia and the rest of the South identified people of color as anyone who had just *one drop* of black blood. That made it open season on the Melungeons. Their children were stolen and sold as slaves and their wives were raped. Faced with extinction, they moved further and further into the mountains."

"I can see why they considered themselves cursed now...so are you saying those people we think of as mountain people are..." Matt began before being cut off by Father Haynes continued excitement over talking about something other than murder.

"America's true melting pot…as ethnically diverse as they come Matt. Some are dark skinned; others have blond hair and blue eyes. They seem to be comfortable in their skin, which is more than I can say for the rest of the world."

Vanessa enjoyed her brief history lesson, but she was still concerned about what might lie ahead. "Okay Matt, that answers the

Google part of your reasons for heading to Sneedville, but what's the hunch?"

"The hunch, Vanessa, is that Max Webb picked Sneedville, for a reason."

"Do you think he's..."

"I don't know what to think anymore. All I know is he is scheduled to give a speech in the most God forsaken place on earth, for reasons only he knows. I also know, he wants the world to be there and he wants them there at a time he determined long before being elected. "

"What makes you think that?"

"This list I was given had some numbers on the back that didn't make sense until now." "What were the numbers?"

"1-31-60/5. Max Webb will be delivering his speech, on January 31st, at exactly 6:05, Eastern time."

"And he wouldn't budge on the time."

"Exactly, Father Haynes. It seems our assassin isn't the only one capable of sending signals."

"Then why the urgency, Matt? After all it's just a speech. Wouldn't we be safer in Wheeling?"

Matt took his eyes off the road long enough to establish eye contact with Vanessa. "Call it a hunch Father, or just a bad feeling, but I don't think any of us will be safe, after tomorrow."

CHAPTER SIXTY-EIGHT

THE next thirty miles were nothing but scenery. The jeep struggled against the magnificence of the mountains, and they had a different story to tell. For his part, Matt saw for the first time, a side of civilization he had ignored during his previous trips through those same mountains. This time, he focused on their names. Offensive names like *Big Negro*, or *Kaisers Ridge*; another was named *Big Pollack*. All had been there for years. The more he drove, the more he was starting to hate his country. How could such blatant racism be allowed to exist on a major interstate?

"Father Haynes?"

"Yes Matt."

"Why does history conveniently forget the flaws? I'm looking at the names on these mountains, and it reminds me of the stories you and Vanessa tell about our founding fathers. Each one had problems, and yet those problems are glossed over by historians."

"The Presidents, the men we have talked about, all had one thing in common. They all loved their country. They were flawed, but most tried to do the right thing."

'You speak as if you've had some experience in this area," Matt said.

Father Haynes leaned forward placing his arms on the back of Matt's seat, "I do," he said, "I do, at my own school."

'"Matt," Vanessa began, "it was not so long ago that Georgetown had to confront its painful past. The stories first emerged in the campus newspapers, and then the historical journals, that the University, like so many other institutions in and around Washington, had been built on the backs of slaves. Some, within the institution itself, say *that* alone is reason for reparations from the Catholic Church."

"I was among them," Father Haynes chimed in. "If there is to be healing in this country, it must begin at home. What better home can there be, than the church."

"Why are these history lessons so hard to learn?" Matt questioned. "Forgive me for being so callous, but it seems as if we are moving backwards"

"The truth can be painful, Matt," Father Haynes continued. "It took two centuries for an American President to even apologize for slavery. Now you want textbooks written that detail the sex lives of the founding fathers? Some of those women *were raped* Matt. The names on these mountains may be offensive, but they are the least offensive things in a long list of things that need to be corrected. These things take time. Too much time, some would argue, but they take time. The truth is slowly making its way to the surface."

Vanessa also wanted the truth. "Matt, when we left Wheeling, you acted as if this were a matter of life and death."

"I believe it is Vanessa."

"Why? What was it you saw in that newspaper that caused you to be so concerned?"

Matt spoke, never taking his eyes off the road, for fear he might slow down. "The Vice President won't be in Sneedville.'

"So?"

"He'll be in Rome. The other article in the newspaper reported he agreed to go to Rome to meet with The Pope."

"Isn't it unusual for a Pope to meet with the Vice President, before meeting with The President?'

"History repeats itself," Father Haynes mumbled. "Matt you have done your homework."

"I also *Googled* Lincoln's assassination out of curiosity," Matt began. "At Fords Theater, Vanessa, the night Lincoln was assassinated, the Vice President wasn't there. He was supposed to be, but took ill at the last minute. Booth shot Lincoln, and the rest was history. They suspected the Vice President at first, but later settled on Booth and the other conspirators."

"You think our friend Chiniquy not only knows he is going to die, but the date and time as well?"

"All I know, Vanessa, is there are too many coincidences to ignore, and too many bodies to bury. I'm also tired of running."

"If that's the case," Vanessa added, "how much time do we have left?"

Matt looked toward his eager young investigative apprentice. "Enough time for you to close your eyes and get some sleep. I'll wake you when we get close."

"Matt?"

"Yes Father."

"Correct me if I'm wrong, and I rarely am, but the people you were talking about, *The Melungeons; o*ne of the reasons they received so much publicity, when their story first broke, were the famous people they claimed to have been from Melungeon descent."

"And who might that be?"

"Daniel Boone, who blazed a trail through these mountains, and Abraham Lincoln, the man our friend Chiniquy seems to be so interested in."

Matt pressed the accelerator on the jeep, causing it to suddenly lurch forward and conquer the next mountain with relative ease. Father Haynes could see his words struck a nerve. He knew Matt was closer, now, to the truth than ever. So did Matt.

"Father Haynes?"

"Yes Matt, what is it?"

"One last question."

"Yes?"

"The Holy Alliance, do you believe they were ultimately responsible for Lincoln's death?"

"I believe historians oversimplified his assassination, yes."

"That doesn't answer my question."

"Do I believe there are far too many coincidences, as you would say, to ignore? Yes. And I believe all signs point back to Rome. That being said, bad blood between nations and presidents does not an assassination make. Why do you ask?"

"I was curious. If The Holy Alliance, assassinated Lincoln, perhaps Chiniquy is convinced, history is about to repeat itself...*only this time as The Consortium!*"

CHAPTER SIXTY-NINE

GARY Wayne Sullivan reached the tiny community of Sneedville first, and quickly discovered he fit right in. The city had little in the way of civilization and that was just the way he liked it. There were a few stores lining the Main Street, and little else. A stop sign controlled the only flow of traffic, in and out of town, and there was little traffic to control.

As he made his way through the town, he thought about the phone call from Vanessa. She knew not to call him on his cell phone unless it was an emergency. "*This is an emergency*," she said, and she was right. He knew nothing of a man named Prescott Marshall. The newspaper article indicating he would be in Sneedville was perfect. *It was all he needed to make good on a promise, to Susan.*

"Good morning, ma'am," he said, making his way through the door of the town's combination gas station and eatery. He grabbed a soda from the 1950s cooler sitting on the wooden floor of the room, picked up a tin of tuna, and asked the woman behind the counter, to make him a BLT.

"You're not from here," the woman said smiling from behind the counter as she made the sandwich. Her hair was pinned up in a beehive style, and blue eye shadow accented her eyes. The dress was plaid with a stitched on apron. "I guess you're here for the same reason everyone else is, although I got to admit, you don't look like the Washington type."

Gary quickly surmised that the town was getting ready for the first and only visit from a sitting or soon dead President. He wasn't good at small talk and could tell from the expression on the woman's face she had exhausted her entire vocabulary. "No ma'am", he answered politely, "just passin' through."

"Too bad," she said eyeing Gary's butt as he left the room. "Too bad."

Gary left the filling station and headed west to the outskirts of town. Parking his car in the foothills of the Appalachian Mountains, he took off, on foot, into the hills. He knew to look for the trails that the power crews left behind. Every five or six years, they would clear a path to service the towers in an effort to prevent the massive outages that plagued the region. It was an ongoing battle against nature, and nature frequently won.

The mountains would provide the perfect backdrop for what he had in mind. As he made his way upwards, it reminded him of his past. In the past, he made the trip when he served his country. He was a sniper in Vietnam, mainly because, unlike the kids who made their way to war from the cities, he found that the hillsides reminded him of home.

"Find the highest spot," talking to himself and repeating the words of the instructors who taught him his trade. He then set the short suitcase down, on the hillside beside him. The "Kochler and Heck Assault Rifle" was the only thing he kept from that cursed war. It served him well then, and he knew he would need it again someday. Looking through the scope at the town he had just left moments ago, he focused in on the square that would soon be the center of all activity.

"Point, breathe, kill!"

CHAPTER SEVENTY

"YOU don't look like you're from these parts," the woman behind the counter of the filling station said, as Maurice Lacroix entered from the road. For his part, Lacroix made sure the woman had little to remember, walking quietly over to the freezer in the rear of the room and taking a supply of drinking water and chips. He placed five dollars on the counter and walked out the door without saying a word. "Don't you want your change?" the woman asked as she heard the screen door slam. She then peered out from over the counter, and watched as Lacroix sped off into the distance. "Takes all kinds," she said sliding the two quarters in her pocket and resuming her spot behind the counter. She continued to read a magazine that detailed the break up of yet another famous Hollywood couple, and described the death of Dickie Hankins, a man the magazine called "The greatest actor of his generation."

Lacroix took the only road headed west out of town, and like Gary Sullivan, headed toward the hills. As a soldier in Liberia, Lacroix was also tailor-made for the task he had been assigned. He got the call just a day earlier, and had grown tired of sitting in his hotel room watching an endless series of crime dramas that all seemed to be "ripped from the pages of magazines."

As he made his way up the mountain, he thought of the old woman. The money he sent would make her happy. She would be sad if she learned how he earned it. He thought about the school where she once taught. He thought about his tiny desk in the small dirt floored room and remembered what it was like to be young. He remembered the sun, and how it bathed his face in a warm light that reminded him of better days. He remembered her smell and how he left her sleeping in her room. It seemed eons ago.

Sadly, he also remembered the old priest. He sent many marionettes marching off to sea, but he believed only one would send *him straight to hell. The priest had done nothing wrong. The school was his life. Both were snuffed out in an instance.*

"Find the highest spot," he muttered as he made his way through the thick brush. He too had been trained by America's finest. He, too, had been taught to kill for his country. He had been taught to kill by those who trained the 'Kwi-ir-ru,' and he had been taught by soldiers wearing the uniform of the United States Government.

"This will be perfect," he said, with traces of his African accent slipping through. "This is where I will take my stand."

Lacroix had been warned, in advance, that this time he would not be going home. His only request was granted. There would be something extra for the woman. She would be told he died a noble death, fighting for his country. He didn't want her to know the truth. She was the only one whoever believed in him.

Using the scope from his rifle, from the diplomatic pouch he carried with him, he eyed the village below. First, he used it to scan the front of the small store he had just left behind. He playfully followed the woman behind the counter, as she leaned into a car that was parked out front. Through the scope he could see the outlines of her panties and a garter belt that held a pair of black fishnet stockings in place. Her hips were swaying back and forth. "A boyfriend," he said smiling. "So you are not alone. It is I who will die in solitude. This place will be my grave."

CHAPTER SEVENTY-ONE

"SNEEDVILLE?! Where in the hell is Sneedville?!" Prescott demanded of an aide who was copiously taking notes, as if somehow the answer would leap from his clipboard. "Why couldn't the bastard pick a more suitable site, like hmm….let's see...New York?"

"Because Mr. Marshall..." the aid began to answer before realizing it wasn't a question aimed at him at all. Prescott Marshall was talking to himself and when he did, he wasn't expecting an answer from any of the minions who worked for him.

Things were not going well for *The Consortium*. The FBI had launched investigations on several levels. *Interpol, the French Directorate of Territorial Surveillance* (DST) and *MI5* had launched similar probes. It was as if the organization was being betrayed from within. Working with an unidentified source, they were looking into allegations ranging from gun running to money laundering to murder. As the American face of *The Consortium*, Prescott was also showing the signs of strain. To compound matters, the disease that had plagued him throughout his adult life, had returned with a vengeance. The man making the trip to Sneedville was no longer the robust picture of health, but instead a hobbled old man, who appeared to be in the advance stages of *rheumatoid arthritis*.

Prescott was going over the latest batch of legal briefs, mumbling beneath his breath the entire time, "I know the old bastard's behind all this, it has to be him. No one else has access to the details, and yet he knows the consequences. If he is betraying us, he will pay…Even if he is the President."

CHAPTER SEVENTY-TWO

"POTUS is in play, I repeat, POTUS is in play." Bart Jabloski, or Ski for short, was the Special Agent in Charge of preparing for the President's arrival in Sneedville. He had been in town for two weeks prior to the President's arrival, and would depart soon after for the next location to be secured. He conducted interviews with each and every person who would be on the podium with the President, including the town's Mayor and Fire chief. He also met with the town's only member of the press, who fortunately was also the Mayor. POTUS stood for President of the United States, and Ski quickly found others in the city picking up on the Agency's terminology.

The code word for Max Webb was Lion. Max liked it, as it reminded him of simpler times in the Senate. He hated the fuss that the Secret Service made each and every time he traveled. To them, the entire nation was the enemy; sadly history had proven them right. Terrorism had changed the landscape forever, but not the uniforms of the Secret Service. Ski was wearing his standard issue, blue suit, white shirt, red tie, and black shoes. The shoes were actually a pair of cowboy boots he had picked up on assignment in Texas. Because of the boots, some of his fellow agents called him Tex. He liked "Tex" much better than the name "Ski…Ski stuck."

One of the greatest engineering feats in history took place each and every time POTUS traveled. The massive black Presidential Cadillac Limousine arrived hours before each flight, on a C-130 transport plane, also known as a Super Hercules. Along with the limousine, the plane transported the SUVs that Ski and his fellow agents would ride in, plus a separate SUV that was used by the traveling press corps.

The local media was locked down hours before the President's arrival. Loosely translated, the Mayor appeared to be the loneliest man in town, sitting on the small platform that he soon would share with the most powerful man in the world. There he sat, in a brown polyester suit, white shirt and traditional red tie. His wife brought the tie at the local "Thrift Mart," just for this occasion. Around his neck, he sported an arsenal of cameras to take the pictures the local newspaper would need. It wasn't that he needed the cameras, he just wanted to make sure one actually worked.

'Penny for your thoughts?" Betty asked Max Webb, as the presidential motorcade snaked its way through the mountainous terrain.

"I was just thinking about how much this reminded me of home," he said.

Betty learned forward, in the seat opposite him, gazing deep into his eyes. "You never talk about home. Of all of your secrets, you seem to guard that one the most." She could see the mist forming in his eyes. She had struck a nerve she never knew existed. One that was very raw.

"In Washington, Betty, information is used as a weapon against the weak," Max responded. "Seemingly innocent tidbits of information become cannon fodder for the constant news cycle that needs its daily feeding. It is never the politicians who get hurt," he added, " but instead, it is the innocent people who just want a small piece of fame."

"You make it sound as if you don't like being President," she said in a moment of raw honesty.

"Not being President," he replied. "Perhaps, it's that I don't like what the Presidency has become. This nation was built by flawed men, who wanted to escape Royalty, and yet we have become a nation of vultures who can't wait for men to fail. The end result is candidates like Baron James. In years past, he never would have even been considered for such an office. Now the decision as to who runs and who sits, is left up to consultants and lobbyists; the money men who believe the office can be bought and sold. Think about it Betty," he said returning her gaze, "name one other job where people raise hundreds of millions of dollars for an office that pays less than $400,000 a year."

Betty, sensing Max was about to lose his composure, added a brief moment of levity to the conversation, "I'll trade you paychecks any day of the week, boss. "

Max laughed briefly and then returned to the window where he could see the tiny town of Sneedville, now in sight.

The local marching band struck up a tune, when it had been given the cue that the Presidential Motorcade was in sight, and then stopped abruptly when they learned it was only a delivery truck bound for Kentucky. They wore bright red and white uniforms that had been purchased for the special occasion. Balloons were tied to the town's three street lights, and red and white ribbons were added as a finishing touch.

The Mayor was still sitting on the podium.

The woman, at the town's only store, placed a "*closed*" sign in the window, and hid her uniform underneath a brown coat with a fake fur collar. She was joined by the man who had stopped by earlier to see her.

Matt, Vanessa, and Father Haynes were less than three miles away from the Presidential Motorcade, which had finally arrived. The marching band missed their cue but picked up the music just in time for the President, who was now stepping out of the limo, along with the usual staple of Secret Service Agents.

The members of the traveling press, reluctantly, took their positions, stretching as they walked, awakening for the first time from the long journey.

"Where in the hell are we?" Wallace Howard asked. Wallace became Wally when he lost his anchor seat and replaced by Vernon Smith. Smith was waiting back at the station, in the anchor seat he had just inherited. "What is a Sneedville anyway?" Wally asked.

"Sneedville, for your information, is the County Seat of Hancock County, Tennessee, which is named for the former signer of the Constitution, John Hancock." The girl doing the speaking was one of the brightest new reporters on the beat. She started in a small town, like Sneedville, and worked her way up to the prized spot of traveling with the President. "The problem with people like you, Wally, is you have no appreciation for what this country is all about!"

"Yea whatever," Wally replied, taking his place on the podium.

In the mountains above town, Gary Wayne Sullivan waited patiently for his moment to strike. He picked a place less than twenty yards from the spot chosen by Maurice Lacroix. Neither detected the other's presence.

The first car to arrive on the scene, following the Presidential Motorcade, belonged to Prescott Marshall, who had been invited as a special guest of the President. Marshall emerged from his car, looking like he had arrived in a foreign country. The truth was, it wasn't even another time zone.

Marshall flew by helicopter to nearby Smythville, Virginia and made the rest of the journey by car. "*Funny,*" he said sarcastically. "*This is exactly the type of place I expected Max Webb to come from!*"

Matt parked the jeep two blocks north of Main Street and walked the rest of the way toward the podium where the President would speak. He was amazed at the number of people who lined the road the last two miles. This was a part of America, he too, had never seen. Still, he wore a ball cap that touted the virtues of a smokeless tobacco, on top of his head, just in case he was spotted. Vanessa, on the other hand, was attracting all kinds of attention. In a town where the gene pool was limited, she represented fresh new DNA. No one was paying any attention to Father Haynes.

The Mayor fumbled with his cameras and speeches as he prepared to introduce the President. He learned, at the last minute, that he was not the person to do so, and had nothing meaningful to say. Max smiled as he had watched this scene unfold before. Instead, the duties of introducing the President were left up to Prescott Marshall, who took his seat right next to Max.

Marshall strode slowly to the podium that had been put into place hours before the President's arrival. The podium was bright blue and bore the seal of *The President of the United States*. There was a single microphone perched on top. Reporters, a little less than a hundred yards away, plugged into a "*feed box," to* get their audio. The tractor trailer, that days earlier, had been carrying hay, was converted to serve as their platform.

Prescott was told to keep his remarks short. He quickly obliged. Few noticed his eyes scanning the hillside, wondering where Maurice Lacroix was hiding. As he scanned the pool of reporters, whose boredom was more than apparent, he knew this would be a day they, and Sneedville, would never forget.

Matt stood behind a little boy sitting atop his father's shoulders, and contemplated his next move. He knew from experience that to approach the President quickly was suicide, something that only happened in the movies. He would have to wait and hope to make eye contact. Only then would it be safe to make his entrance.

The marching band played another number, just as off key as the first. The trombone player's hat was obviously too big, causing him to lose his place in the formation. There was little room to march but they had practiced, and this *was The President*. Each member of the band focused on the assembled press, and they obliged by making it look like they were videotaping their every move, when in fact no tapes were rolling. It was well rehearsed choreography that had played out in cities like Sneedville, for decades.

"*Ladies and gentlemen, the President of the United States, and former Senator from your great state of Tennessee, Max Webb...*" Prescott finished his introduction, turned and prepared to take his seat.

The roar of the crowd seemed unusually loud for such a small town, but they had been instructed by the President's advance team to act as if they were ....well cheering for *The President of the United States.*

The first shot was inaudible. Only Matt Walker realized something was wrong! Something was terribly wrong! The rest of the events unfolded in slow-motion, as one by one, the members of the audience realized someone had been shot.

The startled look on the faces of the Secret Service Agents caused everyone to panic. The Mayor abandoned his cameras and the President, and dove off the right side of the podium. The assembled dignitaries, who included the Governor and several other local Mayors, fled the scene, as well. Each security detail, in tow, attended to their respective responsibilities. Folding chairs and balloons flew everywhere. Chaos had come to Sneedville.

In a sweeping motion, Max pushed the little boy, his father, and Vanessa out of the way and headed straight toward The President. "Ski" was caught between a woman and her young child and fell forwards over a stroller. ***The President was exposed.***

"***Point, breathe kill,*** "Lacroix said to himself, pulling the trigger and launching the second shot. The high caliber projectile struck Matt in the right shoulder, just below the collar bone, causing him to lurch forward and appear to have tackled President Webb, who had already started to fall.

"On the hillside!," Ski screamed into his wrist, looking back toward the mountains after seeing the muzzle flash from Lacroix's rifle. Snipers posted along the roof tops had already spotted their target and opened fire. Their precision left little doubt as to the difference between amateur and professional.

Maurice Lacroix rose from his position and faced the hail of gunfire as if he were some type of matador welcoming an oncoming bull. It was his last moment of defiance in a world that had shown him nothing but killing. The first round struck him in the center of his skull, as did the second and the third. The autopsy would later show all three snipers struck their target dead center. Four shots, in all, were fired.

The fourth shot, struck the mound of dirt that now contained the lifeless body of Gary Wayne Sullivan. He had stripped down to his waist, and was surrounded by the wrapper of the sandwich the lady at the filling station prepared for him, and an empty bottle of water. The ferocity of the round that entered the left side of his skull, and exited the right, left little, of what once was his head, to identify. Authorities quickly determined who the second sniper was, by the tattoo on his arm that read, *311*.

Matt Walker *groaned* in agony, as Secret Service Agents pushed his near lifeless body to the side in a valiant attempt to get to President Webb, who was now almost covered with blood.. As they rolled him over on his side, his eyes focused on the vacant gaze of Prescott Marshall. Marshall, it appeared, had been felled by a single shot to the head. The shot was clean, and produced little in the way of blood from the front. The back of his head had been blown completely off. Ballistics would show he was felled by the first shot that came from the position occupied by Gary Wayne Sullivan.

"*Mr. President! Mr. President*!, Ski shouted, trying to determine the extent of his injures and remove him from the chaotic scene at the same time.

A host of Secret Service Agents appeared, seemingly as if out of nowhere, pinning Matt to the ground, despite his agonizing cries that he had been shot. One slapped a pair of handcuffs to his wrists, while another quickly jerked him to his feet, causing the blood from the wound to spurt out.

Another cadre of Agents seized Vanessa by the wrists. "Come with me…it'll be better if you don't struggle." Vanessa looked back over her shoulder, and could see a third group of Agents surrounding Father Haynes, who by now, had already made it clear, he didn't want any trouble.

The President had long since been removed from the scene and bodily thrown into the Armored Cadillac, with the fleet of Surburbans racing down the roadway behind it. The Helicopter was preparing to lift off. Matt was not fairing well.

"He needs help," the Agent yelled out, at the same time realizing Matt posed no real threat and was too close to death to mount a challenge. He reached down and removed the cuffs, while a team of paramedics tried to stem the flow of blood.

"*Cecilia....*" Matt muttered, hoping someone might hear his desperate cries for help. *"Cecilia."* Matt knew the wound was severe, and feared it might be fatal. He felt his arm grow numb, almost immediately after hearing the sound of the first gunshot. He wasn't certain whether he had managed to save the President's life, but he knew his was no longer guaranteed, either from the wound or the Secret Service. He thought about the last few months, and wondered whether any story was worth it. He worried about Cecilia.

"Matt!..Matt!.." Vanessa cried out, as she was being led away by the Secret Service Agents. "Can somebody help him?" With tears flowing freely, she pleaded with anyone who might help, grabbing arms as most were still fleeing. "*Pleeaasse!..*" she cried!

"Ma'am, where's he's headed he's gonna need all the help he can get....if he lives." The Agent answered, sneering as he looked at the almost lifeless body of a man being loaded onto a helicopter to be airlifted to the nearest hospital.

In the middle of Sneedville, folding chairs, broken plates, and abandoned cups of coffee, could now be seen mixed in with the empty syringes, papers, and bloody compresses. Sneedville looked like a war zone. The truth was, some war zones actually looked better.

CHAPTER SEVENTY-THREE

George Washington University Medical Center

THE operation to remove the bullet from Matt's shoulder lasted six hours. The high velocity round shattered much of what once was his right clavicle, barely missed his aorta, and exited, doing a great deal of damage to his third and fourth vertebrae, close to the sternum.

"He's lost a lot of blood." The doctor performing the surgery warned the others. In a strange sense, Matt was lucky he had been airlifted to such a first class trauma center. It was a strange twist of fate. The closest helicopter was part of the Presidential fleet of three. One transported The President, while the other two served as decoys. A decision was made in flight, to stabilize Matt long enough to get him to Washington. There, the doctors would be better prepared to handle *"such a crisis."* It was an odd fact of life in Washington. The nightly dose of drive-by shootings and other violence, made the "*Murder Capital*" one of the best places to be, if you were shot.

Matt had done stories on the Hospital's trauma center, and was no stranger to the staff. They knew him well also.

"Lost him," the head trauma surgeon cried out. "Get the cart!"

"Can't!" the other surgeon responded. "He's not stable enough!"

"Won't matter if we don't get his heart started, he's gonna die anyway. CLEAR!"

"NOTHING! Come on damn it Matt. Don't quit on us."

"CHARGING!"

"CLEAR!'

"NOTHING." The doctors were used to close calls, but this one was worse than any they had experienced. The velocity of the bullet, combined with its caliber, created a hole in Matt's shoulder large enough to place a normal sized man's fist into it.

"CLEAR."

The shock waves, caused Matt's body to lift off the gurney, and fall lifelessly back on to the bloodied sheets below. The doctors turned their attention away from Matt and onto the heart monitor to the right. Nothing. The thin green line that started on the left and ended all the way to the right, indicated that Matt's heart had given up. Too much damage had been done.

"Time of death..."

"Doctor, look!"

The thin green line rose slowly at first, showing no apparent pattern, then resumed it's normal path, indicating the heart had returned to sinus rhythm.

"Matt, you are one stubborn son of a bitch."

Not all of the doctors were celebrating. They had seen the reports on the news. They knew the life they had just saved, may have been responsible for an assassination attempt on the President.

"Should have let the bastard die!" The youngest trauma surgeon said.

"That'll be up to the courts to decide. We don't decide who to save, we just save'em," the senior surgeon said, snapping off a pair of rubber gloves, jerking off his mask and then storming through the door, by way of protest. "*Hang in there old buddy. I never believed a word.*"

CHAPTER SEVENTY-FOUR

"YOU'RE one lucky young lady," the jailer said, sliding the massive door to the cell to the side. "You're free to go."

Vanessa looked up and saw the smiling and concerned face of Father Haynes and Mrs. Avery.

"It doesn't make sense," Mrs. Avery said.

"What," Vanessa asked.

"The President," Mrs. Avery said, "he posted your bail."

"But why?"

Father Haynes shrugged his shoulders. "That's the part that seems so hard to understand. It's almost as if he knew we went there to save his life."

"Time to collect your things, and get out of here," the jailer added. It was clear from the expression on his face, he didn't care who sprung for their release. He knew what was waiting outside, and so did Mrs. Avery.

"We don't want to go out through the front," she said.

"Why?"

"Because every member of the press, in the city, is waiting for you to walk through those doors."

"Do we have a choice?"

"Actually, yes. A limousine provided by....the President."

"Father..?"

"Yes, Vanessa."

"How is Matt? Did he survive?"

"The good news is, he survived. Let's just leave it at that. He survived."

CHAPTER SEVENTY-FIVE

"CECILIA?" Matt said, as he opened his eyes for the first time. "Where am I?"

"You're in the hospital," Cecilia said quietly. "You almost didn't...." her voice trailed off, followed by the tears that had been flowing almost nonstop.

Matt struggled to lift his hand to comfort her, but found it was handcuffed to the railing of his hospital bed. "What the fu..."

"You're a prisoner, Matt; they think you had something to do with trying to kill President Webb."

"We didn't go there to kill him; we went there to warn him. Prescott?"

"Dead. The second bullet that was intended for President Webb, struck you."

"Who was doing the shooting?"

"There were two gunmen. A professional hit man, and Gary Wayne Sullivan, Vanessa's.."

"Uncle? What the hell was he doing there? Do they know who shot who?"

Cecilia leaned in, positioning her body between Matt and a surveillance camera that had been installed in the room for moments just like this. She whispered, "No, ballistics aren't back yet, but it looks pretty bad. One of the cable networks is reporting that Gary Wayne and Vanessa went there to avenge her mother's death. They think you..."

"Fell in love with Vanessa?"

"That's exactly what they think." Cecilia turned away, not wanting to hear what Matt was about to say next.

"Is that what you think, Cecilia?"

"I don't know what to think, Matt. This whole thing has been spinning out of control ever since you left. I've had to explain those photos to everyone. I can't go to church, the kids have been staying home from school, and even our relatives have raised questions. I hope I haven't been lying."

"You, better than most, should know photos can lie. I went there the night the first set of photos hit the airwaves, because everybody and their brother would be looking for Vanessa. This whole thing has been like a vortex, sucking everybody in. It doesn't matter who's innocent, and who's not. People are making the pieces fit the puzzle. She's a story Cecilia. Nothing more, nothing less."

"But you've been acting so unusual. So distant."

"Cecilia, this is the biggest story of my career, and it's not over yet. There's so much to tell you. I wanted to talk to you when we stopped in Breezewood, but I knew from the tone of your voice, you were in no mood to talk. Then the papers came."

"I didn't want to, but the lawyers told me to, to protect myself. They said..." Cecilia's voice trailed off enough to let Matt know he wasn't the only one hurting. The only difference was her wounds were on the inside and would take much longer to heal. He was lucky to have lived, but deep down, for the first time, he wanted to die. Matt struggled to sit up, to raise himself up enough to look Cecilia in her eyes. If he couldn't touch her, at least he could try and explain the last few months. He wanted to hold her, but his shackles made that impossible. He wanted to tell her, that nothing mattered more at that moment, than the fact that she was at his side.

"I know…I know."

Suddenly, the door to the hospital room burst open, and Secret Service Agents fanned out, searching every corner. The first to enter the room took a spot nearest the window, while another stood sentry close to the entrance to the room. Neither said a word. Within seconds, President Max Webb entered the room.

"Clear the room boys...clear the room."

Cecilia stood in defiance. She was angry, even though the man who had just entered her husbands hospital room was the President, she didn't care. "I'm not going anywhere! I don't give a damn who you are. Truth is, I didn't vote for your sorry ass in the first place."

At first, Max seemed startled. Then he realized, the woman opposite him was more than his match, and mad as a hornet, to boot. "No...I guess you're not going anywhere. If anyone has earned the right to be in this room...it is you."

Matt was now sitting up looking defiant as well. "Max, you've got some sort of nerve."

"Might I remind you both, you are addressing the President of the United States."

"I'm speaking to a coward who would sell his soul to keep his office."

Cecilia was equally incredulous. She had never seen her husband like this. She was familiar with how he played hard ball with politicians, *but this was the President.* Even though she was angry, for some reason she wanted to apologize for her outburst. Matt put any such foolishness to rest.

"I saved your life back there, you son of a bitch! That bullet had your name on it. If I hadn't pushed Prescott out of the way, you'd be playing *bid whist* with Baron James!" Matt jerked his arm upward to show how he was cuffed to the rail.

"You did indeed Matt, but that was then, and believe me, I am grateful. But those men standing outside that door believe you tried to have me killed. They think you, the girl, and her crazy Klan uncle, were there to avenge her mother's death. The press is having a field day. That crazy ass prosecutor in the District is talking about seeking the death penalty. Because of the priest, some are alleging a much broader conspiracy. They're comparing the whole damn thing to the Lincoln assassination."

"But you can set the record straight. Tell them everything. Tell them the truth, or I'll tell them what I know."

President Webb moved to within earshot of Matt, and whispered. "What is it about me that you *think* you know?"

"I know everything, and when I get out of here..."

"You mean, if you get out jail. This thing has more ballistics than the Kennedy assassination. Hell, you might have been the only person in Sneedville without a gun."

Matt failed to appreciate, the humor. "Let's talk about *my world* for a moment. At this very moment, every booker from every show in the universe is trying to line me up for tomorrow morning's news shows. This town loves a scandal, and the last time I checked, I'm sitting on one of the biggest scandals in our history."

"So was Hinckley, Matt...so was Hinckley. The last time I checked, he was on your short list of people you wanted to interview. Everyone else gave up on Hinckley, and they'll give up on your sooner or later. There aren't many reporters left like you, Matt. Most want quick interviews and instant results. Know this Matt Walker, one day they will give up on you, as well."

Cecilia could see the anger rising in her husband. She had heard enough, and now she wanted her own answers. "Matt, what exactly is it that *you know?* And would someone please let me in on this little story?"

Matt knew he was speaking to an audience of one…the one person he cared enough about to want to tell. He vowed, at that moment, not to pull any punches, even if the man sitting across from him was the most powerful man in the world. "The President is a sell out, Uncle Tom, you name it. The truth is he sent me *The list,* because he knew I was the only reporter in town stupid enough to believe he was interested in saving someone else's ass, other than his own."

"And that is where you are wrong. I was interested in saving someone else's ass, as you put it...and now I'm here to save yours!" Max, walked to the foot of the bed, where he could be seen by both Matt and Cecilia. He wanted to argue his case, but knew time was of the essence. He knew time, for Matt Walker, was running out. "If you're done with your pity party..."

Matt stopped his struggling. His anger was taking a toll on him physically. The wound to his shoulder was starting to bleed again. A tiny spot of blood formed on the bandage, small at first, then growing larger. Cecilia could see it too. This round would go to the President; he had no choice but to listen.

"Let me simplify this for you, Matt. The world believes you went to Sneedville to try and kill me. I happen to be the one person alive, that anyone would believe, *who knows* otherwise. My word alone could get you out of here. But *your* comments, no matter how far fetched, could cause *me* problems, as well. I would think we are looking at a stalemate."

Cecilia touched her husband's arm. "What is it you have on Max?"

Matt answered, but never took his eyes off the President. "No more secrets, Max."

"Cecilia deserves the truth Matt. You are released from our agreement."

"Max came to me asking for my help. *The list* that led to this nightmare came from his office. *The list* contained the names of seemingly random people, who somehow kept cropping up dead. Why, I don't know, but I have my suspicions. "

"*The list*, as you call it, was part of a much larger study put together by Prescott Marshall and *The Consortium*. I was in the meeting when he handed it out to the members. Copies were sent overseas. It sent shock waves through the group on both sides of the ocean. It was attached to a lawsuit that was about to be filed."

"When did *The Consortium* learn of the lawsuit?"

"Let's just say Max, I have sources other than you...and..."

Cecilia interrupted. "A lawsuit? This is about some damn lawsuit? Settle the damn thing Max, and let us get on with our lives."

Matt looked at his wife with the look of a man who needed to explain two hundred years of history in less than two minutes. "I'm afraid it's not that simple. This wasn't any lawsuit. Correct me if I'm wrong Max, but it has something to do with reparations for slavery, doesn't it, and the DNA of dead Presidents?"

"It is true what the others say about you. Your tenacity, and nose for the facts. The lawsuit was about slavery. The men who worked on it spent decades, putting in countless hours of painstaking research. They realized reparations would go nowhere unless two things were to happen. The first was a black president. There were candidates in the past, but none showed any promise until Baron James. Baron, you see, was their savior."

"So you had him killed? You and the other members of *The Consortium*, rather than go to court!," Cecilia shouted loud enough to be heard, but not enough to cause the guards posted outside the door to enter the room.

"He was dead long before the campaign began," The President added, at the same time asking Cecilia to lower her voice. "*The Consortium*, was never about to let a black president get elected, or any other ethnic for that matter. America was, and is, white Anglo Saxon Protestant. You see Cecilia, there was too much at stake. The lawsuit sought damages of 1.4 trillion dollars, but that wasn't their concern. One of the largest landholders in the U.S. is the Catholic Church. The men, who filed the lawsuit, had a wicked sense of humor. They sought the symbolic relief of land. A small plat, for the descendent of each slave…"

"Forty acres and a mule, minus the mule." Matt chimed in.

"Precisely Matt, except, at the time that promise was made, no one could predict any land in the U.S. would be beyond value. The framers of the lawsuit took their quest one step further. They targeted the land holdings of the Vatican…their land, the mineral rights, and authority over that land. Look at how much money the Indians have made from casinos, alone."

"So Baron James was never going to be elected, was he?"

"No, Matt, they toyed with him, much like a cat would a mouse. Prescott Marshall, pulled the stings and paid the man who pulled the trigger. He was a mercenary from a West African nation Prescott was once stationed in. Make no mistake about it, however, *The Consortium* killed Baron James, and set up your husband. I suspect, once he walks out that door, you husband is as good as dead, as well."

"But you're the President," Cecilia said incredulously.

"This nation has had a history of dead Presidents, Cecilia, and conspiracy theories. Some believe Castro killed JFK in retaliation for The Bay of Pigs fiasco; others say the CIA conspired with the mob. Some historians believe Lincoln was assassinated by the Vatican because he was seeking other creditors to rebuild the South. Back then they were called *The Holy Alliance.*"

"And they are now *The Consortium*." For Matt, all of the pieces were coming together, and they were coming together quickly.

"I see you have done your homework, Matt."

"Let's just say I have a new appreciation for history."

Cecilia was not interested in history; she was more concerned about what was going to happen to her husband once he walked out that door. "The last time I checked, you are a member of *The Consortium* and they deposited a tidy sum in *your* campaign coffers, as well. If any deals with the devil were made, seems like you made them, already. Why not just pick the phone and call your friends".

"Believe me, Cecilia, I already know my sins. I have spent a lifetime trying to atone for them."

"Then fix this. Let's see, The Consortium, The Klan, what's next, the Hitler Youth Corps?"

"You will find Cecilia, not everything is as it appears. One day I will tell you the true story of what happened, but not today. Your husband needs to realize that it is only a matter of time before the people who came for Baron, come for him...and for me."

Unsatisfied, Cecilia stood, staring at Max Webb, hands firmly planted on her hips. Her eyes were locked on The President and she refused to blink. She didn't care about conspiracy theories, or *The Consortium*, for that matter. She only cared about the man she almost lost and the danger he still faced. There would be time to sort out her feelings later, but right now she was a lioness trying to protect what remained of her pride.

"Are you saying, you can't order the CIA or FBI to track down these guys and lock'em up?"

"It's not that simple, Cecilia. In some cases, the people we're talking about, *are the people* you would go to for help. I trusted your husband with a secret that I have never shared with anyone, but I had to be sure he was the one."

Matt began to speak, his voice cracking to hold back his anger. "You wanted me to know. The numbers at the bottom of the list, 1.31/60/5. It was a code. It took awhile, but Vanessa is a font of information on DNA. She said it one night, over coffee. The chances of DNA being wrong are one in 1.31billion. Sixty percent of all blacks have some type of white blood in them. Five percent of all whites have black blood. Once I had solved that part of the mystery, the rest fell into place. You choose to deliver the most important speech of your life in a town no one had ever heard of; Sneedville. Sneedville, Tennessee has only one identity. It is the home of a group of people who call themselves, *Melungeons.*"

. "Coincidence, Matt, coincidence, but you had concrete evidence of one of the greatest stories in history." The President was about to reveal the details of his darkest secret, but there was still one test. One more hurdle he would place in front of Matt. Crossing that hurdle would remove any doubt he had chosen the right person. "You had evidence that Baron James had an illegitimate child. It was the story of a lifetime, and you had it long before any of your competitors. You could have broken the story, but that would have involved breaking the girl's heart, something the great Matt Walker would never do, even though we both know those wounds would eventually heal. So why didn't you?"

Cecilia slowly removed her hands from her hips, refocusing her attention on Matt. She, too, wanted to know, why he was willing to walk away from his marriage, and the biggest story of his career, for a woman he barely knew.

"Tell me this isn't about the girl."

"No Cecilia, it never was, and never will be. It was always about the story. Max chose me, because he knew, believe it or not, I still took pride in being right. It was *too easy*, just like all of the other stories history leaves behind for us to clean up. At first, I, too, thought Vanessa was Baron's child, especially when I saw the canceled checks."

"Canceled checks, what canceled checks?" Cecilia asked.

"Baron had been sending Vanessa's mother, money, believing *she was* his illegitimate daughter."

Cecilia's hands were back on her hips. "Matt, that story was air tight. You had the girl, and the checks. Clearly, Baron was being blackmailed. Why not go with the story? Unless, Max is right, unless you *did* have feelings for the girl."

"Cecilia you know me better than that. I have feelings for Vanessa, but not those feelings. I was ready to go with the story, until it hit me, something was wrong. Something just didn't add up. You see there was one problem with the whole story. The man, who *is* Vanessa's father, *is the man standing on the other side of this room."*

Cecilia carefully studied the President's face. She watched as Matt spoke, and saw how The President's gaze never left Matt's eyes. His face never cracked. She knew she was looking at the face of a man who was hearing the truth for the first time in his life. She sensed he wanted to hear it, and could tell he had been preparing for that moment, for as long as he could remember. For some reason, she believed it was cathartic.

"You wanted me to know, didn't you Max."

"Not at first Matt. When I called you that night, I guess I was looking for a way out. I had been drinking..."

"You were drunk!"

"Okay, I was drunk! Despite that, I didn't think I said anything that night that would've given me away."

"Actually you did. I never will forget it. You kept repeating yourself. I was about to hang up, when I began to realize, it wasn't *what* you were saying, but *how* you said it that revealed the truth."

The President seemed perplexed. He was going over the conversation in his mind, and even though he was drunk, he could recall no words that would have betrayed his inner most secrets.

"You rambled for a while, about the people on the list being innocent, and how too many people would die. That's when it dawned on me. You kept saying, "*We* need to protect the people on the list. Our legacy is in danger. It was almost as if you were talking in what we once called *code."*

"*Code!?"* Cecilia said.

"That's what I thought at first, too, Cecilia," Matt answered. "He started to sound like those old civil rights people who talked of *the movement* as if it were a member of the family. Broadcasters refer to, *we*, or first person plural, as the language of the oppressed. The most famous three words in American history begin with '*We the people*'. Lincoln used first person plural, numerous times in the Gettysburg Address. Non minorities phrase things differently. It is as easy to spot for minorities as a *Southern accent* is for a *Yankee.* Non minorities frequently refer to minorities as *'those people*'. 'Something', they would say, 'something must be done to protect '*those*' people on the list'. *Only minorities* speak as if the civil rights struggle is *personal*."

Cecilia started to walk toward the President. "Matt's right. *Code* has always been a way blacks talked without saying a word. It's strange, but it's a way of phrasing things, only another minority would recognize." The gravity of her words forced Cecilia to realize what it was she was saying. "*Oh shit.* Are you telling me that Max Webb is...."

"That is exactly what he is saying," The President stated matter-of-factly. "Cecilia, *that is my secret*, one that I am not proud of, and have hidden from everyone for years, until now."

"*So* why not just come out and say it, and what does this have to do with why my husband being accused of trying to kill you?" Even though she could tell by the sudden change in the expression on his face, Cecilia still had questions. Questions only she would be brave enough to ask, and only he could answer. "Why, the big charade?"

"As I was saying, it's not that simple. People were dying. These people are cold blooded killers."

"Then why not go to the cops?" Cecilia asked, once again restating the obvious.

"Again, Cecilia, in some instances these people are the cops. This was about money and power, the two great evils of our time." The President was standing. It was clear as he spoke a burden was being lifted from his very soul. "We have to go back to the lawsuits. You see, there was not one lawsuit, but seven. Six of the messengers were intercepted and *disposed of*, by Prescott's' henchmen. For awhile, it looked as if *The Consortium* had nothing to worry about. Then they received word that one of the lawsuits made it to the courts. A young man, it seems, slipped in just in time. He had help from the inside."

Matt was no longer struggling, and spoke in more curious tones. "I still don't understand what the lawsuit had to do with *the list?*"

"You need to know *how* the lawsuit was structured, Matt. It was filed in the names of former Presidents, all of whom are believed to have been, of mixed descent, like myself. There were supporting documents from African Americans who believed they were *their direct descendants.*

It is no secret, hundreds of African American families believe they are related to various U.S. Presidents. Those African Americans were more than happy to provide samples of their DNA, as well as supporting documents and photographs. In one of the lawsuits, a man located a lock of Lincoln's hair. It's hard to argue with the legitimate heirs of the greatest men in history, our dead Presidents! That's why *The Consortium* pulled out all the stops to make sure the lawsuits never saw the light of day."

Cecilia still had questions, "What were they going to do with the DNA?"

"They filed writs of Habeas Corpus, or surrender the bodies in the court, seeking matching DNA samples from the Presidents in question. It was a far fetched plan that hinged on one thing." "Baron James!"

"Exactly. Cecilia, those who filed the lawsuits, believed a Baron James administration offered the best chance for *success in the courts!"*

"Max, one thing, I don't understand, who are the members of *The Consortium*?"

"They, Matt, represent what you call, *"old money,"* and some of the oldest companies in the world. They are the people who profit from all things evil. The original members owned the ships that transported the slaves, or for that matter, financed The Civil War. *Consortium families* supplied both sides with the guns we used to kill each other. They were the European royalty, and the Vatican elite, who wanted the South to win the war. The "*old money*" died off but the families continued their legacy. These people have been financing wars, almost since, the beginning of recorded history. Few realize how profitable war really is. The problem is "they got greedy."

"Served their asses right!" Cecilia looked at the President. "The bottom line seems to be that you still put my husband through this shit to save a few companies?"

Max chose not to answer Cecilia's question directly, but left no doubt there was more at stake than just a few companies. "As I mentioned, Cecilia, throughout history, Presidents have simply disappeared. Their careers, unexplainably ruined, because they tried to do the right thing. Sometimes, it was an unexplained collapse of the economy. Sometimes it was scandal. Those who couldn't be seduced with women, power, or money were killed. The constant has been *The Consortium* for these people; Baron James was just the cost of doing business. I knew I would have been..."

"Next!" Matt interjected. "You knew they were close didn't you? I figured it out, so why couldn't they? I was the so called, "*canary in the coal mine."* You knew it was only a matter of time, before they figured it out as well."

"That's not entirely so. I kept my secret well hidden, very well hidden. I really wasn't concerned about my own safety. *I was only* trying to protect the people on that list. I couldn't go to the police. Hell, the head of the Secret Service and Marshall's Service answered directly to Prescott Marshall. He has a list of every cop he has bought and sold. It is quite impressive. One of those cops found out about the pictures of Baron and Susan, much to my dismay."

"And," Matt began. "Baron James wasn't the only person *who knew* Susan Sullivan. You *knew* her, as well."

"*Well obviously I knew her, but I also loved her.*" Max paused, momentarily, his lips moving but making no sound. He struggled to end the sentence. "When I saw her name on the list, my whole life ended. I knew she was good as dead, and I could do nothing to stop it. I knew how Prescott worked. I knew Susan would be followed by..."

"Vanessa....." Matt said.

Tears began to well in Max Webb's eyes. "Exactly, Vanessa was next, and I had to do something. I knew if Prescott ever discovered the truth about Vanessa it was all over for both of us. So I watched as he toyed with Vanessa and Baron and you, waiting for the opportunity to strike. When Prescott invited Vanessa to the debate, it was all I could do to take my eyes off of her. She was beautiful."

"That's when I first sensed that there was more here. I saw it in your eyes," Matt added. "While the rest of the press corps focused on the spectacle Baron James created with his entrance, I was looking at you. That's when I saw it, that look on your face. Baron's face was filled with panic when he first saw Vanessa in that room, but your face was filled with love, the type of love a father shows for his daughter."

Cecilia couldn't contain her emotions any longer. "Damn, first the white President is black, AND he's got an illegitimate daughter. This is better than the soaps!"

"So why didn't *you* go public Matt? The story of my illegitimate daughter was just as juicy."

"Proof, Max. I would have needed your DNA for any story, of that magnitude, to get past the lawyers, but from that night on, I couldn't get close enough to collect a sample. Contrary to what you see on those crime shows, people don't just drop DNA everywhere. Imagine how stupid I'd look, saying you were not only black, but also the father of Vanessa, without DNA evidence? I would have been the laughing stock of Washington."

Cecilia was starting to see the resemblance. "Other men have tried to allege some of our Presidents engaged in hanky panky, but no one cared."

" Books, volumes have been written," Matt continued, "making the same allegations, and no one cares. I also needed to convince myself, as well. After the debate, I went back to the station and played back a piece of tape that had been sitting on my desk for the longest. It was the tape of that first news conference involving *Vai-Gene.*"

Max smiled. He knew Matt had truly discovered *his secret.* He knew it was always hidden in plain sight. People just needed to take a closer look at the tape.

"The *Vai Gene* press conference was a stroke of marketing genius. Vai Gene, with Prescott Marshall at the helm, announced it wanted to trace the DNA of every African American member of Congress back to their perspective homelands. You may recall there was one snafu."

"Corrice Cullen," The President offered up.

"Exactly every station played the tape of Corrice Cullen, waking up just in time for the samples to be collected. He looked like a deer stuck in the headlights. Cullen was one of two white Congressmen who supported Vai Gene, out of sense of racial solidarity. No one doubted their ethnicity. No one ever does when it comes to white people. That's why you almost got away with it."

"So you saw my little slight of hand?" The President added.

"Not at first. Like I said, I reviewed the tape, back at the station, the night the photos were leaked. I knew too much was happening too quickly. My back was against the wall that night. I was being put out to pasture, and yet, I was sitting on the biggest story in history, if I could've proven it. So I studied the tape over and over again, and then I spotted it." Matt rose from the bed as far as he could. "*You,* Mr. President, *swabbed Cullen's mouth*! Then you placed *his* swab on the table, and swabbed *your* mouth. At first I missed it, but then, there it was."

"What?" Cecilia asked. "What?"

"He switched them...he switched the swabs. Cullen got his DNA, and he walked away with the DNA of a white man."

Cecilia smiled. She caught herself thinking back to the embarrassing headlines proclaiming one of the most racist Senators in U.S. history, was in all likelihood, black. "So that's why that old codger wound up *being black!* I knew it was a mistake!"

"It wasn't a mistake on my part, but it was the closest call of my career. I hated what I did to poor Corrice, but he was old, and the truth be known, he *deserved* the embarrassment. No amount of humiliation was ill deserved. His voting record was deplorable when it came to blacks, and yet every member of Congress knew he loved his black women, and couldn't keep his hands of anything black that walked through the doors of his office."

"I knew the night you called, you were protecting something big. I had no idea, until that night, how big it was." Matt paused for a moment, taking solace in knowing he had just cracked the biggest story of his career. He also knew that it was a story that would never be told. He, too, had just become a victim of history.

Cecilia was stunned, and for the first time in as long as Matt could remember, speechless. Her head was spinning. In less than forty eight hours, she had learned her husband was wanted for questioning in connection with the murder of a Presidential candidate. She then learned that her husband had been shot, and now he sat in a hospital bed, handcuffed and charged with trying to kill the man whose life he saved. A man who was now admitting his accomplice was his daughter. *That man* just happened to be, The President.

"Does *she* know?"

The President replied. "No Cecilia, she, like the rest of the world, *she still believes* Baron was her father. I suppose it is better that way."

Matt turned toward Cecilia to look for the license to say the words that were about to follow. "Max...Mr. President, it's never better to live a lie. She wants to know who her father is. She deserves that. No country has the right to stand in the way of a father and daughter!"

"I suppose not, but that will not solve the immediate problem of your situation and mine. What has been said in this room tonight *will alter the course of history.* In my brief time as President, I have learned that this country exacts a terrible price from the men who take the oath. I was prepared to sacrifice my own life, but not the life of my daughter. Should the members of *The Consortium* learn my secret, none of us will be safe. Which is why, Matt Walker, I need your help."

"I will help you, *but you will have to tell Vanessa the truth."*

"I agree, but for now, you have to believe it must be done in the right way at the right time."

"As long as it gets done. I'm tired of lies, and if you don't mind, I'm especially tired of getting shot!"

CHAPTER SEVENTY-SIX

"LADIES and gentlemen, The President of the United States."

The United States Navy Band played the traditional "Hail to the Chief" as Max Webb made his way toward the podium. The members of the Washington Press corps had been told to assemble. The news conference would take place in prime time. No one knew why, or what to expect, save the man who entered the room with The President.

Jaws dropped as Matt Walker, his arm in a sling, was wheeled in, by none other than the President's Press Secretary. To make matters worse, for the assembled members of the media, Matt was smiling, and so was his wife Cecilia.

"Members of the media, I have summoned you here this evening on such short notice, to bring you up to date on what has been one of the biggest threats to our democracy since the terrorist attacks of September 11th, 2001. By now, you know of the attempt on my life. What you do not know is who was responsible for saving it. *That man is Matt Walker!*"

The sound of countless motorized shutters filled the room, as the photographers turned their cameras away from The President, and toward Matt Walker. The numerous flashes created a strobe effect, making each of Matt's moves appear more pronounced.

The President continued, "As you know, I was once a member of an organization most of you know as, *The Consortium*. One of the leaders was the man who was killed, in the attempt on my life, Prescott Marshall, but that is only part of the story."

The President went on to describe the lawsuits that had been filed, and how *The Consortium*, feared it, more than anything else on earth. For good measure, he made it seem as if Baron James was in on the story, as well, and died in service of his country. The President described Baron, as, *"a hero."* "Matt Walker, he told reporters, was the *only* person in Washington he could trust. It was Walker who put the pieces of the conspiracy together, The President said, "at great sacrifice to his reputation and family. We, our nation, owe him a tremendous debt of gratitude."

The press corps burst into spontaneous applause which was more than unusual for the normally staid crowd and a shock to Matt. Questions that normally would have been directed to the President were, instead, directed at him. Only one person was missing. Vanessa Sullivan sat alone in her townhouse watching the entire drama play out on the nation's TVs.

"I don't understand Mrs. Avery. Somehow, something doesn't add up. Why wouldn't my father just tell me my life was in danger? Why all the Chiniquy notes? Why did he have to die?"

"There's something sleazy about that Max Webb," Mrs. Avery added. "Something very sleazy." She then placed her hand gently on top of Vanessa's. "I can't put my finger on it, but not to worry Vanessa. It is time we put our lives back together. It is time that we move on."

The pundits were analyzing the evening's events when Vanessa reached for the remote. She was startled to hear the phone ring at precisely the same moment as when she switched off the TV. It was Matt.

"Vanessa? I know it's late, but I know of a great place where a girl can get a cup of coffee."

CHAPTER SEVENTY-SEVEN

THE long stretch limo pulled up to the North Entrance of the White House. Two white gloved Marines reached for separate doors…one for Matt, the other for Cecilia. The strobe effect was on once again. The fact that it took Matt longer to enter only caused the photographers to intensify their efforts to capture *the shot.*

Matt was struggling. He knew the wound had reopened during the news conference but vowed not to let on.

"Where to, Mr. Walker?" The driver asked politely. He was a third generation driver for the Executive Branch of the government, and like most jobs of prestige in Washington, his was passed on from generation to generation. The pay was small, but the perks were great. He had driven the rich and powerful, and Hollywood elite, to and from, and today his guest was Matt Walker, the nation's newest hero. "Never doubted you for a minute. The Mrs., on the other hand, she saw those pictures of Vanessa and...well lets just say she doesn't have much faith in the male species. Nothin' personal, Mrs. Walker."

"I need you to take me to the Bolivian Coffee Shop in Georgetown." Matt answered between grimaces.

"Sweetheart, don't you think this can wait?"

"No Cecilia, like the rest of us, I think she has waited long enough. Too long."

As the Limo made its way through the gates of the White House and onto the Ellipse, Matt reached forward and tapped the driver on the shoulder through the opening in the glass window.

"Once around the mall if you don't mind?"

"Sure thing Mr. Walker. Whatever you say."

Washington, at night, was a completely different city. Massive floodlights bathed each of the Monuments in a glow that made those they were supposed to memorialize, look at peace. Tonight, Matt knew that was anything but the case. For the first time in his life, he could feel the pain and frustration each of the Presidents must have felt. Lincoln, he knew, couldn't have acknowledged any past he may have had. The nation barely survived the Civil War. It was in no mood for a President who wanted to explore his *ethnicity.* Washington, Lincoln, Jefferson, all of these men were trapped, not only inside the skin that made them human, but inside the times that made the truth more difficult to tell; and so, generation after generation, that truth was pushed beneath the surface, until the story that suited history emerged, but not necessarily the facts.

"M Street, Mr. Walker?' The driver asked. "Do you want me to take you through Georgetown?'

Georgetown! Home to Washington's first working class. Maids, drivers, and staff members of Georgetown lived in the brownstones first. Then, when it became fashionable they were moved out, to make way for wealthier families who claimed the neighborhood as if it had been theirs all along. The only reminder of days gone by, were the cemeteries whose bodies were black.

"You can drop us off, but you'd better wait around the corner," Matt told the driver. He realized the press corps would respect his privacy, but the limo made it seem more like he was involved in some clandestine meeting. In a sense he was.

"Should I wait here?" Cecilia asked still wondering to herself whether the woman they were about to meet held a portion of Matt's heart.

"No Cecilia, I never want you to leave my side again."

Matt reached for the door and quickly withdrew his arm from the pain. As always Cecilia was there. When the door opened, it quietly framed the coffee shop's lone occupant. Vanessa was sitting at the same table where she and Matt first talked.

"Hello Mrs. Walker."

"Cecilia."

"Cecilia, I feel like I know you already."

Cecilia was not so warm. Her gaze was icy...guarded.

"Matt, you shouldn't be here..."

"No, this can't wait. You need to know the truth. You deserve it."

"I watched the news conference. You were excellent."

Cecilia felt the hair rise on the back of her neck. She was usually the one sharing in Matt's excitement. She knew their relationship had been strained. She wondered whether it had been broken beyond repair.

Instinctively, both Cecilia and Vanessa reached for Matt's chair. The clumsiness provided the evening's only levity and a clumsy attempt at laughter. The rest was strictly business.

"I heard about the lawsuit," Vanessa began trying to ease the tension. "It's a pity those poor people will never have their day in court."

"Perhaps," Matt answered. "Perhaps, but that is for another day. Tonight we need to talk about you."

"What about me?"

"There are some things that were not said at the press conference... some of which I'm sure you have already figured out. To begin with Max Webb is not the man you think he is."

"You mean a sell out? A politician? I guarantee you, Matt, he's all of that and more. He acted as if he wasn't *The President.* That lawsuit could be settled today, but like all of the other Presidents, he chose to pass the buck onto future generations."

"It's not quite that simple for Max." Vanessa stopped, and measured some degree of surprise, that the one man she thought would be agreeing with her, was instead taking the side of a man she now despised. "Did you ever wonder who sent me that list?"

"I always assumed it was one of your sources."

"It was, but in this case the source was *Max Webb!"*

Vanessa listened intently as Matt told her the story of *The Consortium* and how they planned to derail the lawsuits by assassinating anyone whose DNA even closely matched that of a former president. He outlined the deaths, one by one, leaving no stone unturned.

When Matt finished his story, Vanessa seemed less than impressed. "So why would the great Max Webb care about the people on the list? Surely a man who once belonged to the Klan wouldn't care if a bunch of black people suddenly started dying."

Cecilia reached over, across the top of the table, and placed Vanessa's hands in hers. They were so young and smooth. They were so innocent and naive. "He would have cared, if he were *black.'*

Matt had never seen Vanessa speechless. She sat at the table, trying to take it all in, finally placing her hand in Cecilia's. For months, they had been chasing the ghosts of dead presidents who were believed to have been black, when all along the real McCoy was running for the white house. "All the more reason he should sign off on the lawsuit."

"And risk being killed?" Matt asked.

"Goes with the job," Vanessa answered. "You think any of those slaves got a chance to assess *their risks?* How about the people on the *Underground Railroad*, or *Rosa Parks?"*

"How about Martin or Malcolm or Stokely, and just about every other person who opened their mouth on the issue of race? Emmett Till might have *whistled at a white woman* . What about Nat Turner, Jim Brown? History has made those who dare to speak out pay a high price."

"Including my *real father*, Baron James."

Matt wanted to shout the truth to the world. He wanted to tell Vanessa Baron was *not* her father, but he had given his word. He hated the fact that in a world where deals were broken day in and day out, he still believed *a man's word was his bond.* "You must understand, Vanessa, groups like *The Consortium* have been here throughout our history. They have been behind the scenes pulling strings and manipulating the powerful. Max found himself right in the middle of one of the worst conspiracies our nation ever faced. He could have called the cops. They were sitting right across the table from him. He knows the horrible price that he will pay for keeping his silence, and knows that this is a burden that he will take to his grave. He sent me to apologize to you."

"Perhaps, he should do so in person." Vanessa pulled her hands away from Cecilia's. "I'm not buyin' this bullshit. It's time for someone to stand up and take a stand. Presidents take nations to war. This time it's *his* turn to take the risks. What about the lawsuit? How much longer do they have to wait? It took two hundred years for a president to apologize for slavery. Someone needs to at least apologize for stealing a people from a continent and bringing them across the ocean in shackles. They were beaten, raped...castrated, both physically and emotionally. The end result is a nation of people like *me. Look at me Matt. I'm not like you.* I'm not like any of those lines on the census. What line says 'bastard child of a black presidential prostitute and a white whore'?"

Who will apologize for making my life a pure hell?

Cecilia looked at the pained face of her husband. For the first time, in her life, she realized how painful it was to keep secrets. She had seen the side of a man who told the truth, for all the world to hear. He told her about his *sources* in the past, but she never knew the terrible burden they exacted. Now she wanted to reach out to Vanessa. To tell her about the meeting in the hospital. To tell her about *her real father...* but now was not the time. She prayed that the time would come soon, for her sake, and for Matt's.

"You will be hearing from him soon," Matt said, pushing back the chair as he prepared to leave. "Keep an open mind. Just keep an open mind. Truth is like DNA. It cuts both ways, and sometimes there are many possible truths hiding beneath the surface."

Vanessa watched the two walk through the doors. The driver pulled up in front, as if on cue. She was angry, and curious. She knew Matt too well. *She knew he was keeping a secret.*

CHAPTER SEVENTY-EIGHT

MATT Walker bypassed his old TV station completely, although not before signing the termination notice that arrived at his house with a tidy severance packet. He then signed an exclusive, five year, no-cut contract, with the largest of the three broadcast networks. He also signed Vernon Smith, on, to act as his producer.

Matt wrote a five page Article in the *Washington Gazette,* outlining the activities of *The Consortium* and *The-Vai,* and their combined web of murder and gun running in Africa. Matt pointed out in his articles that there were twenty seven names on the list, all of them dead. The dentist who died, kept a piece of Lincoln's jawbone; the Enloes were descendants of those who were believed to have been Lincoln's true relatives; and Dickie Hankins, the Hollywood actor, was the last remaining biological link to Nancy Hanks, Lincoln's mother. A similar scientific trail could be traced to each and every name on the list, which was broken down in columns for the newspaper. Not to be outdone, the TV Network Matt was now working for, dedicated three hours of programming to the topic. It was the highest rated show in decades.

Matt chose to make no mention of Max Webb or Vanessa, except to say both were instrumental in breaking the vice of *The Consortium.* The President, he argued, knew the members of *The Consortium* who permeated all ranks of Washington. Vanessa, most concluded, was genetically linked to Baron James. Baron James, as a result, became a martyr. All of Washington was abuzz as to whether the descendants of the former Presidents indeed had black DNA. That secret would be hidden from history forever.

The U.S. Attorney's office handed down sweeping indictments against the members of *The Vai,* in the United States and overseas. *Interpol* and *MI5* did the same with *The Consortium.* The arrest of Cardinal Boucher made headlines in Europe, and the War Crimes Tribunal in Belgium announced it would conduct the trial. Two members of *The Consortium* committed suicide, rather than face trial. The others stood, defiantly, behind lawyers proclaiming their innocence. Matt knew in the end, it was the lawyers who would win out. They would collect fees from both sides.

Congress passed sweeping laws making it a crime to steal or covet anyone's DNA. They were called *"The Lucy Laws,"* after the odd coincidence of the names of Lincoln's grandmother, and the fact that scientists long concluded that all mankind came from a single woman in Africa they called "Lucy."

Cecilia was icy at first, but soon warmed to the fact her husband was now working at home. He assured her that he had done nothing improper with Vanessa during their months on the road, and even said he wanted to hire her as a researcher when she graduated in the spring.

Cecilia said words to the effect of, "Over my dead body," and the matter was closed forever.

There was still one problem. The Consortium had succeeded in destroying all the DNA that would link the African Americans, who believed they were descendants of Presidents, with the actual Presidents themselves. No one had the guts to exhume any of the bodies. It seemed, on that count, *The Consortium had won!*

CHAPTER SEVENTY-NINE

VANESSA toiled over whether she should even open the package. It arrived days after her meeting with Matt. Matt's last words lingered long after the meeting. She called for clarification but was surprised when his secretary said, *he was out of the office.* Cecilia was different. She was always there to talk to. Vanessa could see what Matt saw in her. She was, indeed, a rock. After her conversations with Cecilia, she had vowed *to move on,* but as Cecilia put it, she deserved to know the truth first.

Sitting on the deck of her townhouse, she soaked in the sunlight, realizing that soon spring would come, and Washington would once again wake from its slumber, as if it ever slept. The day seemed perfect, so she decided if she were to ever open the envelope and examine its contents, now was the time.

The outside of the package left no doubt as to who sent it. The address in the upper left hand corner read simply, THE WHITE HOUSE, OFFICE OF THE PRESIDENT OF THE UNITED STATES. Taking a deep breath Vanessa opened the package and saw a letter and another smaller package. First the letter, the other contents of the package would wait. She almost dropped it when she realized the formal heading had been crossed out. The words "The President of the

United States, had been crossed out with a single stoke of a pen. Above the line, someone scribbled the word, *"Dad."* It read:

My dearest Vanessa,

You have your father's eyes and your mother's tenacity. I wish I had more of the latter. You need to know where it all began, and this is my best attempt to tell you.

It all began with a train ride.

It was a journey south, but it was my journey to escape the racism that plagued the times in which I lived. Plecker's law forced thousands to abandon their race. I wasn't seeking to escape my ethnicity, but instead to find a job. The depression hit Tennessee hard, and the battle between food and family forced all young men to seek their fortunes in the big city. One day, my father, your grandfather, returned home from work, clutching a single train ticket in his hand. He gave it to me and told me to go and seek my fortune.

At the train station, I saw the signs that defined my generation. I knew where I was to go. Just like I knew which restrooms to use and theaters to sit in. Times were different back then. I hope America never returns to those days. I was angry and on my way to my place until I walked down the aisle. That is when *I saw her.*

She was sitting there, alone. At the time I thought she was the most beautiful woman in the world. Her long blond hair flowed freely, draping her shoulders perfectly. Her blue eyes pierced my very soul. I not only could see her, but I could smell her as well. She smelled *"clean"* in a world that had grown so cold and dirty. She was motioning for *me to sit.*

To you, it probably seemed to be a simple decision, but for me, it was the single act that would begin a life filled with compromise. Every fiber of my being told me to keep walking...to stay in my place, but I couldn't. I was young and stupid, and for that moment in time, I believed, in love. So *I sat* where her hand patted the seat.

The train ride to Nashville was like the helicopter ride back to Washington, when I realized it was you I was betraying. It opened doors, and my eyes, in ways I never knew existed. I wasn't in love with her race; I was intoxicated with the freedom she represented. She could say things I could not. She was white. I knew I was not.

I was almost discovered by the conductor and had to excuse myself to go to the restroom. The one marked, *"Negroes only."* In that brief moment, I returned to my world. It was the last time. The *eyes* that were fixed on me as I made my way toward, what was known as "*the steerage*" section, reminded me of the world I longed to escape. I was not angry at them. Instead, I found pity in their faces. Many would have done the same thing I did. Those who were much stronger...did not.

Much has been written about Rosa Parks and the other pioneers of the Civil Rights Movement. Their courage has been etched in stone...how they took a stand against the injustices of the time. History, however, forgets the cowards, and I knew in an instant I, too, would be forgotten, but it was too late.

I returned to my seat to take my place next to the woman I would later marry. In that instance, the little boy, the coward who boarded the train named *David Reid,* disappeared from history forever *and the lie that became the life of Max Webb was born.*

Our early life together was filled with bliss. She introduced me to her father, who was one of the most influential men in Tennessee. His business connections and my desire to escape all that I had become, made for powerful allies. All the while, I knew I was *living a lie.*

One day, out of the blue, her father asked me to take a trip. He said I should pack some clothes, saying it would be a long journey. I feared I had been *discovered.* As we made our way out of town, he talked of *business* and how *business* in the South worked. He talked of friendships and bonds that went beyond those boundaries. He was pouring his heart out to me. Strangely, it was the first time in my life I felt *accepted.*

The journey took four hours to complete. We arrived in the mountains of Tennessee, in an isolated patch of ground that looked like it belonged to a local farmer. Night had started to fall.

That's when I saw it. The hillside was illuminated in hate. The burning cross towered above all else. I knew I had either been accepted or betrayed. The *fea*r I experienced that night was like none other.

Her father introduced me to men I had worked with, and they introduced me to another side of hate. This time they were wearing *sheets and hoods.* Their bigotry was without limits. They hated everything that wasn't white. They hated everything black. I knew, deep down, they hated me and on that night, *I began to hate myself!*

I could have confessed, but I would have been killed. In many ways I feel as if I would have been better off dangling from the end of a rope than a lifetime of close calls. Death would have been kinder than the life I had come to know.

We said little on the way back. There was little to say. He had exposed his entire world to me, and I hated him for it. For the second time in my brief life, my world had changed. I knew it and his daughter knew it, as well.

She died two years later. We never bore any children, so you have no other relatives from that dreadful chapter in my life to speak of. Upon her death, I decided I would dedicate the rest of my life to changing the hatred I experienced that night, but as I quickly learned, fate is an awful taskmaster. The people I wanted to help saw me as something I was not. I had nothing in common with the people who now accepted me. *I made a deal with the devil and the devil had come to collect.*

It was my *enemies* who elected me to my many years in Congress. The ones I met that night who wore the *sheets and hoods.* The more I tried to escape, the more they were determined to make me one of their own.

I met *your mother* during the depths of my depression. On a fundraising trip to North Carolina, I sought comfort in her arms. Suffice to say, ours was a business relationship at first. One trip became many. *You should know you were conceived out of love.* I soon learned, I was not the only one *living a lie*. For your mother, survival depended on beauty and her wits. There were *other men*, one of whom was *Baron James.* I later learned, your Uncle Gary, Baron James and Susan were friends, growing up. Integration changed all of that. Baron went on to star in sports, receiving scholarships, and endorsements. Gary was forced to fend for, and feed the family. Susan turned to prostitution.

Baron, I later learned, *brutally attacked* your mother, upon realizing the gravity of his potential mistake. *He believed he was your father*! He led a guarded life, and feared the possibility someone, perhaps his father, would learn he had taken comfort with a prostitute. It seems he tried to do to your mother what he feared doing to his father. We thought we would lose her, but she recovered. She was never the same.

The decision to seek money from Baron was based on her hatred for him, and her love for me. She knew that a child out of wedlock would ruin my reputation in Congress. There were also fears, real or unreal, that the child would come out *black*. Your mother was the only other person with whom I shared my terrible secret. Pinning the pregnancy on Baron made good political sense. She took my secret to her grave. We both vowed to raise a better child than we had been, as adults. *That child was you!*

I am the one responsible for the extra money you found in your account. I wanted you to have everything that I did not, but I wanted you to be hungry enough to fight for everything you had. In that sense, I believe your mother and I succeeded. My journey, however, was far from over.

Traveling overseas on one of my many trips to Africa, I met another man grappling with many of the same issue as I. His name was Prescott Marshall. One day he suddenly fell sick, and on that day, I knew his world had changed forever. The cramps and abdominal pain…I knew them well. *Familiar Mediterranean Disease* is common to our people. It is almost like it is God's curse on our people. Some say *Melungeon* means, "*Cursed people*." I believe that to be true. Oddly, it is genetic.

Perhaps out of stupidity, or some desperate longing to right my many wrongs, I bought into the dream that Prescott expressed in his vision of *Vai-gene*. Like you, I believed DNA could erase the stain of racism and link the continents of Africa and America. I was so naive.

Prescott introduced me to *The Consortium* and it wound up being more racist than the Klan could ever be, but these men were *far more deadly*. They had the money and resources to carry out their racist agendas. For once in my life, I decided to make a stand in the only way I knew how. I would change *The Consortium* from the inside out. I also knew that any plans to the contrary, would mean certain death.

The' list' changed all of that, because of you. I was suddenly forced to make a decision, and I decided your safety was more important than any aspirations I may have had. I trusted only one person with your fate. I trusted the man who chose not to betray me, when he held my fate in his hands. He paid an awful price. I knew, from the meetings of *The Consortium,* who had leaked the photos, and how his bosses reveled in the fact that he was a broken man. I wanted to do something, but could not. This was my way of setting the record straight.

Baron James was a different story. He was *never* going to be President. *The Consortium* would have made certain of that and indeed they did. America has never, knowingly, elected a black President, and history has never really asked why. The history books are littered with the prices those men paid, but that is a story for another day.

That brings us to each other. I hope you can forgive an old fool for a life of lies. I hope you find solace in knowing I will spend the rest of my days trying to restore, to you, and this nation, that which was lost. When I walked down the aisle of that train, I was but a boy. Today I am a man, ready to face my fate, whatever it may be.

Always,
Your father
Max Webb, The President of the United States.

Vanessa placed the letter beside her and examined the package for the rest of its contents.

Turning it upside down, she placed her hand at the bottom, and allowed the contents to fall into her palm. The first item to fall from the package was a single glass vial, containing, what appeared to be, two cotton swabs. She knew what it was almost instantaneously. Proof, if she ever needed it, as to who her true father was. She already knew.

The second object was much heavier, and was very carefully wrapped, as if it contained something old and valuable. As she carefully unwrapped it, she smiled.

A book...Fifty Years in the Catholic Church, by Father Charles P.T. Chiniquy

> *P.S.* The book was given to me by an old Priest I met at a mission in Liberia, West Africa. He said I looked like a man who needed it. *I guess he figured out my secret long before anyone else.* At any rate, like Lincoln, I confessed my sins to a priest and he took them to his grave. *Now my secret lies in your hands.*

The book was leather bound and bore the date of its publishing on the inside cover of the first page. It was a first edition of the book that had become so important in recent days, but there was something else.

It's a signed first edition:

To Father Grebo Barclay

May God follow you on your journeys overseas. Remember the truth is what we make it.

Father Charles P.T. Chiniquy

As always: Isaiah 51:1

That's when it struck her. She had reached the end of what had been the journey of a lifetime and had nothing to show for it but two dead relatives, a father who would never publicly acknowledge her and a book. *A damned book!* As she rose to walk away, she spotted a trash can. Ready to cast the book right over the rim, she debated whether to dispose of it there, or in the nearby Tidal Basin.

You're not worth my anger. Not anymore. The book is valuable, but not to me. Father Haynes would love another copy of his precious Chiniquy. As for you father, you can rot in hell.

CHAPTER EIGHTY

Arlington National Cemetery

"READY...AIM...FIRE...READY...AIM...FIRE...READY...AIM... FIRE.."

A steady rain fell over Arlington National Cemetery, drenching the soldiers who stood sentry, the barrels of their rifles still smoking. Burials had become as routine as the twenty one gun salute, and because of that, few noticed that this one was different. Never, before, had a solider been laid to rest, under such a shroud of secrecy. No family members were present, or members of the press, for that matter, although the event was more than newsworthy.

"Here lies the body of an unknown hero, whose heroism, the world will never know," the soldier began. "Ashes to ashes, dust to dust, his body is hereby laid to rest at Arlington National Cemetery, with the gratitude of his Nation for saving the life of President Max Webb."

It was a compromise of sorts, between Matt, Vanessa, and The President. Ballistics test results revealed that the shot that felled Prescott Marshall was fired from the gun of Gary Wayne Sullivan, which came as no surprise. Vanessa told Matt that she called Gary Wayne, on his cell phone, once Matt had presented overwhelming evidence that Prescott was the man pulling all the strings. Matt, then, told The President about Prescott's plan to assassinate *him.* The President needed little in the way of convincing.

The surprise came when the same ballistics tests revealed that a second shot was fired from Gary Wayne's rifle. The second shot felled Maurice Lacroix, whose bullet struck Matt Walker in the shoulder. That bullet was intended for the President. Lacroix had another shot loaded in his chamber that he never fired. No one would ever be able to explain why Gary Wayne decided to fire on Lacroix. Both men died before they could be questioned. The Secret Service killed Gary Wayne, but by the time their bullets struck Lacroix, he was already dead.

Vanessa argued that her uncle deserved to be buried as a solider because he saved the President's life. Her impassioned pleas, that he killed Baron James because he was a pawn in a much larger conspiracy, found fertile ground with the President who knew the real reason behind James's assassination. Max Webb knew that men like Gary Wayne Sullivan, were always nothing more than pawns. He agreed to a Presidential Pardon, permitting the burial, but only if the pardon remained sealed forever, and Gary Wayne be buried anonymously, along with Susan's Ashes. The inscription on Gary Wayne's tomb was ordered to read.

"CHINIQUY"

CHAPTER EIGHTY-ONE

THE young woman standing inside his doorway was a shadow of the once proud student that commandeered his classroom. Her illusion of a simple life had been shattered by single pen stroke and the word "Dad." Standing there, rain soaked and clutching the letter in her hand, Vanessa needed a shoulder to lean on and a sympathetic ear.

"Come inside Vanessa," Father Haynes said as he opened the door wider for her to enter. "You're soaking wet!"

"He's my father," Vanessa answered revealing for the first time the fact the rain had masked her emotions. "It was there in front of us all along. I have searched for my father my entire life; only to find out he's been watching me from afar the whole time."

"Who...has been watching Vanessa? I don't understand."

"The President. Max Webb is my father." Vanessa then handed the letter to Father Haynes. "Read this and you'll understand it all. He sent me a letter...a stinking letter!"

Father Haynes studied the letter and could feel the pain that must have accompanied each word written. He had come to know them both and felt as if they were family. Now that family was being torn apart, not by the truth but by the lies that hid it for so long. When he had finished reading the letter he stretched it out on a table so that it would dry without being ruined. He knew Vanessa would read it again, and again. He knew it was history and her's

"Vanessa," Father Haynes began, "you have learned lessons no classroom can ever teach. Your life is one of those chapters historians will one day study looking for a much larger truth."

"I don't care, Father Haynes. I don't care. I just want my life back. The one before all of the killing and all of the clues…I want..."

"Normal? Is that what you are asking for? I knew, from the first day you walked into my classroom, you were special. Normal has never been in your vocabulary. This, Vanessa, is the hand you have been dealt. You must play it through!"

The words coming from Father Haynes were not the words Vanessa wanted to hear. She wanted sympathy, not cold and calculating logic. She wanted a father. Someone who would understand his daughter was hurting. Now she had a father and realized the answers she sought could be found in one place and once place only.

"Father Haynes?"

"Yes my child?"

"Do you think he loves me?"

Father Haynes knew the answer to this question would be the difference between a lifetime of healing and a life filled with future hate. He had seen it before and heard it in the confession of the man who feared only for his daughter's safety. The man who had confessed his sins as Chiniquy. "I believe he loves you as no father has ever loved a daughter. He loves you enough to sacrifice himself for your safety."

"You mean the White House! That's all he cares about. That's all he ever cared about."

"You don't understand," Father Haynes interrupted.

"Then make me understand. Prove to me that for once, something matters to Max Webb more than his precious politics!" Vanessa eyed the letter sitting on the table and felt the anger rise up. "And you Father Haynes. Your precious history is nothing more than a collection of lies. Just like the lies in that letter."

"Vanessa...there is something you need to know. History sometimes involves more that that which we can see. Sometimes it is colored by that which is never supposed to be known."

"I don't understand."

"Vanessa, words rarely convey emotion. There is pain in that letter. A lifetime of lies spelled out in black and white. When men come to confess their sins, the Bible tells us that we are not to judge them, but to listen."

"I'm tired of listening, Father Haynes. I'm tired of all the lies and the half truths. I'm tired of Chiniquy."

"Then it is up to you, Vanessa." There was a sternness in Father Haynes' voice Vanessa had never heard. "You are looking for pity. You didn't come here to cry. You came here to vent. You know what must be done. History is for those who seize it. This is your moment and that is your father. What happens next will not be up to him. It will be up to you."

Vanessa was frozen with fear. The next step would be the most important of her life.

Somehow she had to find the courage to do what she knew in her heart needed to be done. She had to confront the past, her father and The President of the United States. She had to do it alone. As she turned to make her way out of the room, Father Haynes grabbed her arm squeezing it softly, but firm enough to let her know what was about to be said caused him great pain.

"Vanessa?"

"What is it Father?'

"Just remember, sometimes the truth is not what we want it to be, but what we make it. Don't ask me how I know, but I can tell you that he loves you more than life itself and yes, even more than the presidency!"

CHAPTER EIGHTY-TWO

"MR. PRESIDENT, your nine o'clock appointment is here."

"Thanks, Betty, I've been expecting her for quite some time. *Longer than she'll ever know.* Please send her in."

"The President will see you now." Betty then showed Vanessa to the door and added, "and give'em hell. He can take it."

"Thank you. Thank you very much for all that you have done." Vanessa entered The Oval Office, and was immediately struck by the fact that a room could exude such shear power. She had seen the dark blue carpet, with the Presidential Seal, emblazoned in the middle, in countless movies, but never expected to see the real thing. Even though America was a government of the people and by the people, the real people had no way of appreciating the power of the United States. Most people saw the President on TV. Few, if any, witnessed the long motorcades that were common in Washington. Fewer still had ever stood where Vanessa was now standing. "Mr. President.."

"You can call me Dad…"

"I don't think so. As far as I'm concerned a letter and a book do not a father make. You got a lot of talking to do and I'm here to listen. So as I was saying...Mr. President?"

"Okay, I guess I deserve the formality."

"I'm puzzled...okay pissed." Vanessa was about to shed any pretense of formality. She was prepared for a lot of things. She was not prepared for the anger she now could no longer suppress. "Where in the hell have you been? Why didn't you contact me sooner? I have spent my entire life, wondering who my father was, and to learn that you were just around the corner, the entire time I was in college...how could you?"

"Vanessa, you saw what happened to Baron James. The same thing would have happened to you, had Prescott had his way. All my life, I've watched the powerful destroy men, and use their families as bait. I know it doesn't sound like much but I did my best...."

"You're right! It really sounds pretty shitty when you look at it from my perspective. Forgive me for denying you a Kodak moment, but I would have gladly given up the trust fund for a father. Real fathers are there for birthdays, and weddings, and everything else. You, Mr. President, missed it all."

"I promise to walk you down the aisle Vanessa...."

"How, when no one even knows you have a daughter? Face it Mr. President, you're ashamed of me just like you're ashamed of your past and your race!"

"I guess you're right...but you need to know your mother and I always said we would present you to the world when the time was right..."

"Don't you ever mention her name again!" Vanessa had heard enough and the mention of her mother's name sent her over the edge. "She deserved better. I don't care who you are, or were."

The President stood motionless. Inside The Oval Office, he was the most powerful man in the world, but the young woman standing before him possessed an authority over him he had never known. She was his daughter and he was her father. The most painful part of it all, she was right.

"Vanessa, I know this may be difficult for you to handle, but I am asking, no, begging your forgiveness. I tried to explain..." The President reached out only to watch Vanessa withdraw.

"You wrote a letter, a lousy stinking letter. Touching, yes, but enough to erase a lifetime of anger? Not so fast buddy, I respect the office, but I could give a damn about the man. I really don't know *who* he is?"

Again the President reached out, this time walking toward Vanessa, with open arms, as if he wanted her to move closer. He was pleading.

"I'm not ready for that."

"Then I'll wait...as long as it takes," he answered pulling his arms inward along with his damaged pride. "This time, I'm not going anywhere...without you." Then came the words she never thought she would ever hear. "If it will end this...this anger...then perhaps it is time we let the world know…the truth."

The President's frankness caught Vanessa by surprise. She expected him to continue the charade, but she never expected to hear him prepared to confess his sins publicly. Her father was not only acknowledging paternity, but seemed prepared to do so, to the world.

"Paternity, Vanessa, is easy. Race is the other issue we have to confront. They may be ready to accept the fact I had a daughter out of wedlock. I'm not sure the world *is really ready* for a black president."

Again Vanessa saw the walls going up. The walls to the truth both she and history deserved.

"If not now, then when? When will the time be right?" The anger was still present in Vanessa's voice but nothing like it was just moments before. "This country is over two hundred years old...two hundred years old...and when I walked into this building, this tomb, I noticed a long string of white men lining the halls, but not one person of color, or at least no one willing to admit the truth."

"Touché, young lady, touché. As I said, Father Haynes warned me to be ready. I guess I should have listened more closely."

"And while we're on the subject of true confessions, why all of this bullshit about *Chiniquy* and Lincoln? This time I want...no check that, I demand the truth. I deserve that...and so does she!"

Bringing up the ghost of her mother was more than the President could handle. He had dreamed of this day for years. In his dreams it was difficult, but reality proved much more challenging. There was so much he wanted to say, but the words wouldn't come. Chiniquy was much easier to hide behind.

"Vanessa, by way of background, you should know why I spent so much of my life trying to learn about Lincoln. As strange as it seems, betraying ones race, is like walking away from who we are. I knew, first hand, what it felt like to be trapped inside my own skin. Like most people, I sought others, who might have walked the walk."

"And you think that was Lincoln?"

"Yes I do. Lincoln's opponents thought he was black, as did others, who lived during that same time. Remember the times. Back then, all it took was *one drop*. One drop, to start a rumor, steal a slave, and ruin a reputation! His tomb was a rumor that science would not allow him to disprove."

"And you died from self-inflicted wounds!" Vanessa wasn't about to let her father off so easy, even if he was the President. "Lincoln didn't walk away from history...or for that matter his daughter."

"Ethnicity had nothing to do with my fascination with Lincoln. It was a fact about the man few know about to this day. Something that made him perfect for his times, and ours."

"And that would be..."

"The truth is, Vanessa, Lincoln, was not black. Nor was he white. He was neither. What I found was that unlike most of us, he was *colorblind!* God blessed him with eyes that could not distinguish color, forcing him to search for the true beauty of black and white." He paused and looked at a picture of the former President he kept on his desk. "That is why I admired the man. That was the genesis for my fascination! As for us...your anger...there is nothing about Lincoln or Chiniquy, for that matter, to heal the wounds I have caused. I hoped this day would be different. I can see now, too much has passed for there to ever be an 'us'. I only ask your forgiveness."

For the first time, Vanessa realized the toll the lie had taken on the man sitting behind the desk of the most powerful nation in the world. She lived a life without a father. He lived the life of a lie and was now trapped inside it. She lost a mother, but he lost someone too. She wondered whether he deserved to lose a daughter. Sadly she realized she was all he had, while at the same time, realizing he was all she had, as well.

"Colorblind?"

"Yes Vanessa, doctors determined he was colorblind, but there was more." He was glad they were talking about something. Even if it was history, at least they were talking.

"I'm all ears," Vanessa added providing an opening for the conversation to continue.

"Sadly, Vanessa, so was he. He was also so unattractive that he used to joke about his own looks. He towered over his opponents, had large ears, warts and described himself in his autobiography as black, with coarse hair. Lincoln was anything but politically correct, which made him the perfect President, black and or white."

"So," Vanessa continued, " you identified with Lincoln."

"Vanessa, not knowing where we came from is a terrible legacy from slavery. Hiding who we are, is even worse. When I came to Washington, as a freshman member of Congress, I was angry at everything and everybody, but mostly I was angry at myself. I was mad at the lie that I was living, but mostly I was mad, because without that lie, I would still be waiting tables in Sneedville. Back then, as a black man, *no* doors were opening. When I became a white man, the world became my playground. Back then, black people weren't being elected to Congress or even dog catcher from small towns like Sneedville. We weren't even allowed to sit in the front of the bus or a movie theater. I identified with Lincoln because he never stopped fighting no matter what hand he was dealt, or how many times he lost."

Vanessa listened closely, but now it was her turn. It was her turn to end this insane obsession with a man long since dead. "What about people like Rosa Parks? She made a difference, by refusing to sit where she was told to sit. You could have made a difference, but instead you chose to run." She knew her words were biting but she was determined not to let this man...this President...her father, off the hook.

"You must remember, Vanessa, Rosa Parks was an adult when she made her decision. I was a boy when I boarded that train." The President then walked across the room and took a seat at the massive oak desk on the other side of the room. "It's not an excuse, but it is the truth. I knew I was a fraud, but admitting your whole life is a lie, takes courage. Courage that I never had. Instead, I vowed, then, to expose the others who were forced to live lies, just like me"

"And what did you find?"

"Like you, I spent hours in the libraries, researching the histories of our Presidents and politicians. I also spent countless hours on the mall, looking closely at the images that I believed betrayed the truth. Like you, I saw the hypocrisy. The illegitimate children history ignored..."

"Like me?"

"Yes...like you. The more I studied the past, the more I realized history kept repeating itself over and over again."

"So why didn't you just come clean?"

"It's difficult for your generation to understand how things were back then."

"So try me."

"The girl on that train represented more than just a woman. She was everything you were told you would never have. She was the forbidden fruit, someone else's property to covet. In a strange sense, I was taking, that, which I never believed, I would be able to earn...."

"You were black and she was white, so what?"

"I was stupid, but not blind. Black men back then were being lynched for whistling at white women. I was *married* to one, in what was still the deep South. That was my first lie."

Vanessa, continued her questioning, never giving the man sitting across from her time to breath, or for that matter, collect his thoughts. She could tell from his body movements, he was uneasy about her line of questioning, but he deserved each and every one of the questions she was about to ask. Because of him, her life had become a nightmare. Her mother died, never knowing the true love of a man who would ultimately become the most powerful man in the world, and she grew up not knowing her father. The least he could do was answer a few more lousy questions.

"So that explains why you didn't admit who you were as a young man, but what about when you got older? Racial barricades have come down, and fallen quickly. If you studied history as closely as you say you did, then you must remember a little speech given by a preacher named Martin Luther King? Surely you're not saying that America wouldn't understand a melting pot President? For God's sake, look at Baron James!'

This time it was the President who found it difficult to keep his anger in check. "Baron James was what America *wanted* a black president to be!" he shot back. "He was black in his commercials, but did nothing for anyone of color. I, on the other hand, had the perfect voting record on issues of color. What did it get me? Black voters couldn't get past my one stupid mistake."

"Did you expect them to?"

"Did you expect me to jump up at that rally and say, 'hey guys, guess what, I'm black'. Be realistic, Vanessa, timing is everything when confessing one's sins, and some sins should remain hidden forever."

Vanessa then stood, signaling the conversation, the games about Chiniquy, and the history lesson about Lincoln were over. "Then perhaps this is where we should leave it," Vanessa answered curtly. "You with your past, and me with my future. I'm comfortable. And you can forget your childish riddles!"

Rising from his desk Max Webb faced the most important decision of his life. He knew allowing Vanessa to walk out that door meant they would never see each other again. He had walked away from a woman once and vowed never to do so again. That woman was her mother. He would not do the same with her daughter. With the force that only a father can exhibit, he grabbed Vanessa by the arm, resisting her attempt to pull away. "Follow me young lady!"

"First tell me where you are taking me!"

"For a long overdue trip, home."

CHAPTER EIGHTY-THREE

"I THOUGHT you might like some coffee."

"Thank you." Matt said. He placed his hands over Cecilia's, waiting for the recoil, as she offered him the first warmth he had felt, or wanted in months. Their lives had returned to normal, although he knew it would never be the same. They had been through a lot, in recent months, but nothing compared to the strain that had been put on the country. Still, it was their relationship, he feared, that would not heal.

"Matt, we need to talk." Cecilia spoke softly. The anger was gone from her voice. Her emotions had run the gamut, from anger, to jealousy, to anger, to fear, that the one man she wanted most, was gone forever. "We can't keep acting as if nothing happened!"

"I know, Cecilia, I know."

"I just need to know one thing and I want an honest answer." Cecilia braced herself for the response to the words that were coming from her mouth. "When you were on the road, did you ever..."

"No."

"But you didn't know what I was going to ask."

Matt placed the cup of coffee on the table and wrapped his massive arms around Cecilia. She struggled against him at first, but he squeezed harder, until she finally surrendered. He reached up and placed the palm of his hand against her head, and pressed her head firmly on his shoulder. He was now speaking almost in a whisper. "The entire time I was gone, I couldn't stop thinking about you. About what we had, and what I left behind. I went off pursuing a story and almost lost you. It wasn't until I realized that what I had gambled would leave me with nothing." "Then why did you go?" Cecilia asked, raising her head and looking directly in his eyes. If he were lying she would know. She had to know.

"I was lost Cecilia. I thought, somehow, a story would help me find myself. I had something to prove, to the world, and to myself."

"But Vanessa...she's so young...so...beautiful."

Matt knew why he was hearing the words coming from her mouth. His journey to find himself involved a story, achieving the impossible. For Cecilia, it was the girl, it was Vanessa.

He reached down, placing his finger across her lips. "Shhhh...I am holding the most beautiful woman in the world. I am holding you."

A tear formed in Cecilia's eye. One she tried to hide at first, and then allowed to flow freely, where it found a home on Matt's shoulder.

He felt its warmth and the chill of Cecilia's demeanor, starting to thaw with it. For the first time in a long time, he sensed they too, would be okay.

"Matt?"

"Yes."

"If it's okay with you, can we skip lunch and dinner and go straight to bed."

Matt's arm then slid downward from her shoulders caressing her buttocks. Cecilia felt a rush of warmth overcome her as her body fell limp. She was powerless now, and Matt's, for the taking. She liked it. So did Matt.

CHAPTER EIGHTY-FOUR

WALKING through the hallways of the White House and out to Marine One, Vanessa wondered whether she was staying for the President or for her father. The twin engine Sikorsky stood at the ready, its rotors coming to life, with Marine guards standing by. Each branch of the military played a role in transporting the President. Marine One was the shinning star of the Corps. A crisp salute and the door closed behind them. Within seconds the helicopter was airborne. They were one their way. They were going home.

The journey south took less than an hour to complete. Normally, a Presidential trip required notifying the press corps and alerting the local authorities. This trip, however, was not planned, although it had been in the making for years. The landing pad was a trailer park parking lot. A second helicopter landed moments earlier and made sure the location was secure. No one would see the President come or go.

"Why did you bring me here?" Vanessa asked.

At first the President was taken back by the yellow "crime scene" tape that still littered what remained of the trailer. He then realized how much had been lost. "I thought we owed it to her," he said as the moisture began to form in his eyes.

"We owe her the truth." Vanessa fired back. The journey south did little to extinguish the anger that decades without a father could produce, even if that father was the President.

"Sadly, Vanessa, I'm not sure America will ever be ready for the truth," he answered, reaching down to pick up a piece of the charred remains of what once was a door.

"Are you saying American will never be ready for a black President?" Vanessa then looked around her. She looked at her humble beginnings and felt the anger rise from within. "Is it because we are from here?!"

"Again, Vanessa, things are not that simple." The President was no longer acting Presidential, but more like a father trying to explain the intricacies of racism to a child, who wanted only to see the world through rose colored glasses. "It has nothing to do with here! Or there! Or any damned place on this planet! When I first contemplated doing so, telling the world who I really was, events quickly took over."

"Or you copped out!"

"Vanessa, you must understand." There was a pleading tone to his voice, once again. "It's not like I haven't tried. The news conference with Senator Cullen, was my *first* chance to set the record straight. *Vai-Gene's* news conference followed the broadcast of *Roots*, the most successful mini-series in TV history. African Americans found new reasons to be proud of their heritage. Bookstores were flooded with people lining up to trace their *"Roots."* America, it seemed, was finally ready for the truth, or so I thought. At the last minute, I decided to switch swabs with Senator Cullen, out of fear, and I'm glad I did. You saw what happened to Senator Cullen. I would have been ruined. When it comes to DNA, the truth is, *it is a sword that cuts both ways."*

"But America has been waiting for a man like you and because you refuse to come forward, most people think, you're a racist."

"And that is my cross to bear. I knew that no matter what, I would never be forgiven for belonging to one of the most racist organizations in history. If the truth be told, however, I did more damage to the Klan, from the inside, than any one civil rights organization could ever have done.

Vanessa's mind wandered back to all the history lessons she so painfully learned. She remembered Father Healy, a priest, who was forced to hide his true ethnic origins. She remembered, Bannaker, and Booker T., even the great Frederick Douglass, all, came from mixed blood. That's when it dawned on her, her own search had also been for something, she too, would never find. She had been so fixated on proving to the world she was black, she failed to notice the true color of her own skin. Like Jefferson, and the others, she had seen only what she wanted to see. In her case, it was not her black ancestry, but her white genes. "I guess Watson was right!"

"Watson?"

"The man who discovered the human Genome. That is why some scientists refer to DNA as Watson's sword. Because it is complex...and dangerous!" Now, it was Vanessa who was looking at what remained of her childhood. She realized her mother died not because she lived in a trailer, but because of her DNA. The gravity of what faced Vanessa in the life ahead suddenly sunk in. "Perhaps you're right. The truth is we already know how the story ends. We all wind up tracing our DNA back to Africa, but somehow that's not good enough. We're not looking to prove who we are, but instead, who we aren't. That's why, when it comes to race, America sees only what it wants to see."

The President realized Vanessa had finally seen things as he had seen them for years. "All I am saying is, that it is not that simple."

Vanessa was still not willing to surrender completely, "You're saying, America will never get past seeing the world in terms of black and white, or just won't, aren't you?

"Not when it comes to race. I traced my DNA and sought my Roots. It didn't prove I was black...or white…just American, which is as mixed up as it comes. Science only proved I came from many long lines of history. All of my DNA that I had privately tested, traced back to Northern Africa, just like anyone else who want to uncover the truth," the President answered.

"Kinda like Dorothy and the Wizard, all roads lead to Kansas, or in this case Africa. Huh.?."

"There is something you should know about us. About these people who live here Vanessa. My lineage…our lineage…*originated in Northern Africa*, near Tunisia and Angola. We were slaves, but not in the traditional sense, more like indentured servants. The first true Americans landed in Virginia. They sailed from Europe, in a ship called "*The White Lion.*"

"That's why you never objected to the nickname, the *"Lion of the Legislature."* You actually liked the title."

"History knew them as, *The Lost Colony*, and I believe that to be true. They are Indian and African and Irish. Those people were my grandparents, and aunts and uncles. Your true blood relatives."

"Just like these people." Vanessa then turned and pointed to the rest of the trailer park she once called home, "The invisible Americans."

"There is more to their story than what you find in the history books, Vanessa. History takes a human toll on all of us. They were hunted as slaves and fled to the mountains where the discrimination continued. They became hillbillies, and mountain people, so they created their own race. They called themselves something more palatable for a melting pot America, *Black Irish.* They hid for a reason. The same reasons I found myself hiding."

Vanessa interrupted, only briefly. "So like these people, you found it easier to head for the hills than fight for who you were!"

"Are you familiar with the name Prescott Marshall?"

Vanessa was surprised to hear the one name she thought had disappeared from history forever. "Yes...why?"

"Like I said, I took the liberty of having my own DNA tested, privately, under an assumed name. It came back with a strong Mediterranean mix, of African, Irish and American Indian blood. I dove into the books, learning everything I could about, my people. Their traits and triumphs…Even their diseases."

"So what does that have to do with Prescott Marshall?"

"I found, many of my ancestors suffered a debilitating illness that causes terrible swelling of the joints at the most inopportune times. Its symptoms are frequently mistaken for Sickle Cell, but it's actually Mediterranean Familiar Syndrome, the same disease, Prescott suffered from."

"So you're saying...Prescott Marshall had reasons to question *his ethnicity?"*

"Exactly. That is why he fought so hard to eliminate any and all vestiges of his past. The prospect of the truth haunted him to the day he died. The truth was he wasn't any different than the people who live here or for most Americans. That's the real reason I brought you here. You need to understand, Vanessa, this is the *real America*."

Vanessa stopped and picked up a handful of what remained of her home. The burned out ash of the trailer she so desperately tried to escape was somehow different. Suddenly she realized she was home. Suddenly she realized she was American.

"Dad?"

The sound of the word pierced a heart that had become hardened by the reality of race and racism in America. His was not the worst sin committed in the name of racism, but it was the one on the table. He realized, long ago, the terrible toll it had taken on both he and the country he so dearly loved. The simple acknowledgment of paternity convinced him of the terrible toll it had taken on something he never knew, his family.

"Yes Vanessa."

"Thanks for insisting that I come here. It's going to take some time, but I think this was good place to start....but..."

"What is it now?"

"They won!"

"Who?"

"*The Consortium.* The DNA. It's all gone. Those people. My mother. They all died in vain."

CHAPTER EIGHTY-FIVE

Monrovia Liberia, West Africa

"GRANDMA! Grandma!" The little boy said as he tugged at the hem of an old and wrinkled dress. "Come quickly.!"

The woman who had become known as "grandma" first fetched the long walking stick that had become her staff. Taking long strides, she followed the little boy up the trail to Bendu Mission. The mission was once the home of a flourishing school and campus where thousands of Liberia's came to learn. Following the war, it was torched with the books being used to light the bonfires. She had grown weary of the journey, and each and every time she saw the charred remains of what used to be her life, she found it almost impossible to go on. This day, however, seemed different.

As she crested the hill, the anticipation on the face of the little boy seemed to intensify. She could hear activity in the background. It sounded like saws and hammers. For a moment she allowed her mind to wander, but squeezed the staff to return to reality. The lines of her face told the story of a long journey. A journey much longer than the one she was about to complete. A school teacher by training, the last twenty years of her life had seen nothing but war. She was tired, and she was ready to die.

"Look!" The little boy said, with the enthusiasm of a child witnessing his first Christmas.

"Oh my God, my God, there is a God," the old woman said as she saw the beehive of activity that was taking place around the compound. There were men with saws and hammers, and children frantically working paintbrushes, adding whitewash to walls that had been black for decades. A pile of fresh cut lumber arrived overnight as if by a miracle. The crates with the saws and hammers sat nearby. The labor came from the villagers who were eager to lay down their weapons and take up the trades they missed almost as much as she missed teaching.

All of the workers stopped what they were doing as the old woman made her way to the top of the hill. A caravan of trucks was making its way up the hillside behind her with perhaps the most important delivery of all. Six truckloads of books arrived overnight from the United States. Each bore the markings of "The School System of Tennessee." Inside each book there was a letter written by a Tennessee school student to their counterpart in Liberia. Each drew pictures letting the old woman know the students truly understood the two nations were bound by more than blood.

As the last truck approached, a man wearing a white suit and matching hat, walked toward her holding what appeared to be a vase. The vase contained the ashes of Maurice Lacroix. "Grandma" knew exactly what it was, the minute she saw it. She read the letter he left behind the night she last saw him drive off. It read, "I will not return, but I will see to it that you live on, forever. Always, your favorite student."

Then everyone watched as the woman who became known as Grandma, dropped to her knees and began to cry. They knew, like the old priest, she cared more about losing the one than saving the many.

CHAPTER EIGHTY-SIX

THE flight back to Washington was far less contentious than the journey south. The mountains that had seemed so cold and callous,, just days earlier, now seemed to welcome her from below. She had a real home and finally, a father. Vanessa finally understood the man she would, one day, reluctantly call her father. She had questions, but knew they had a life time to figure them out. Save two.

"Did Prescott know about his past?"

"I suspect he did. Like me, Prescott spent his entire life running, only in the opposite direction. He was haunted by the specter of his own ethnicity. I chose to hide; he chose to destroy everything in his past. It was as if he believed he could bleach his blood white, by destroying all things black. "

Then Vanessa remembered their trip through the mountains and Chiniquy. "I know of your fascination with Lincoln, but the killer...he knew too much..."

The President smiled. "Prescott was obsessed with finding out the truth about who he was, as well. Like you and me, he followed the same path to the truth. Read the same history books and like you he was obsessed with the topic. Haunted by it, if you will."

"What about the others? Why did they have to die? They weren't all related to Lincoln were they?"

"Lincoln, Vanessa, came from the same region as I did. As did Daniel Boone; even Elvis and the family of Dickie Hankins, that Hollywood actor who died at the hands of *The Consortium*." The President looked away toward the window. "All of their DNA was part of the foundation for the lawsuit." When he refocused his attention, he noticed, Vanessa was no longer smiling. Something was upsetting her. "What is it, Vanessa?"

"I was just thinking, now all of that DNA, regardless of what it contained, is gone. Destroyed by " *The Consortium.* "Without it, there can be no lawsuit!"

The President started to smile. "Vanessa, I have done some things right! You should know the minute I learned of The Consortium's plans, I hatched a plan of my own. While they did manage to destroy the DNA of the others, they didn't get it all. At least not when it came to Mr. Lincoln. There was one last piece of information that escaped them and there was only one person I could trust with that information."

Vanessa remembered the letter, Chiniquy's book, and the code Father Haynes had unraveled." It was a clue, wasn't it?"

"The book was always meant for your hands."

"Are you saying, the book contains Lincoln's DNA?"

"No, but this does." The President opened his coat, and produced a single envelope, no larger in size than a dollar bill. He reached over and handed it to Vanessa.

Vanessa took the envelope and quickly took note of the word, "EUTURE," that was typed across the front. "EUTURE." That's the misspelling on the monument. I don't understand?"

"Above Lincoln's statue, at the Lincoln Memorial, are Angels painted by Jules Guerin. They are welcoming a freed slave. I thought that was God's way of blessing the monument and my plan. In 2005, the monument was badly in need of repair. I, which should come as no surprise to you, headed up the committee. Committee members wanted to correct the monument's only mistake. I objected at first."

Vanessa's right eye arched upward. "Somehow I get the feeling you changed your mind."

"I did. If you go there today, you will find the word, EUTURE, no longer appears. Instead, it reads as it was supposed to, FUTURE."

"So I'm assuming the FUTURE is…"

"Believe it or not, in your hands, and Lincoln's DNA is right back where it belongs, inside the rock, from whence it came. Isaiah, 51.1," The President said almost boasting.

"I guess that brings us back to the importance of this envelope? I can only assume because you have handed it to me, it contains...."

"The answer to the first clue you were given and Father Haynes unraveled. Examine the envelope closely."

"I almost forgot. The first clue. *That which is bound by blood shall never be shattered by the sword!"* Vanessa was studying the envelope as if she had been given the most valuable object of art in the world... something so precious, it would shatter if dropped. The anticipation of learning its contents, caused the hairs on the back of her neck to stand, and little bumps to appear on her forearms.

"Give up?"

"Uncle! or should I say 'Dad'…"

"Those words were written on the back of an invoice, attorney Lincoln, presented to Chiniquy. That is the invoice you are holding in your hands."

Vanessa continued looking at the envelope's contents. "I don't get it?"

"The bill, as you can see, was for fifty dollars. Chiniquy, it is said, in historical accounts, *wept*, upon receiving it, because he thought it would be much larger. He also believed Lincoln saved him from the Catholic Church."

Vanessa interrupted, "So that is why you used him in your clues to protect us from *The Consortium*."

"Exactly. Chiniquy saved Lincoln, a priest saved you. History did repeat itself. Almost to the letter. You see the Catholic Church was suing Chiniquy, and he believed the lawsuit was their attempt to silence him forever. Because Lincoln pulled him from the clutches of the church, he was expecting a much larger bill…one say, about two thousand dollars, which would have been a fortune back then. Too much for a priest to pay."

"But what does this invoice, have to do with Lincoln's DNA and *The Consortium*."

"Everything Vanessa...it is one of two remaining pieces of Lincoln's DNA in existence"

"Two?"

"Yes..."

"*Bound by blood*? Chiniquy…Lincoln. Are you suggesting..."

"No, they weren't related. What began as a joke took on biblical proportions when I learned of the lawsuit and the plot to kill everyone with Presidential DNA. Look closely at the back of the invoice."

Vanessa looked at the invoice for a second time, not seeing what had excited her father. "There's nothing here but a stain."

"That stain as you put it, is a drop of the blood of the Sixteenth President of the United States, one Abraham Lincoln."

"What was Lincoln's blood doing on the back of an invoice?"

"Vanessa, Chiniquy suggested, like the Pope, they seal the deal, which in this case meant the letter itself. Papal seals were always red.

Lincoln had no red wax. So, you see, he took a small pen knife from his pocket, and after presenting the invoice to Chiniquy, pierced his right index finger. That's the story the antique dealer tells and he made me pay dearly for the invoice, because of the story."

"Are you saying you believe that dark spot contains Lincoln's DNA? His blood?"

"That's exactly what I am saying...they considered themselves...at that moment in time, literally bound by blood."

"Lincoln's DNA, the rock from whence ye are from, Abraham. Isaiah 51:1, it all makes sense now." Vanessa found herself thinking back to Father Haynes's history classes. "You've been inside Healy Hall, haven't you?"

"Once, long ago, as part of a discussion panel. I found the artwork to be extremely hypocritical and jotted down the scripture scrawled across the top of the blackboard. Like everything else in this city, it was there for a reason, and no one bothered to figure it out."

"Father Haynes once told me there was one other who figured out the mystery, but he never said it was you."

"He never knew. Like your clues," the President continued," my solution came to him in the form of an anonymous letter. So I used it to my advantage. I created a trail, for someone to follow, and that someone wound up being you. So now, Vanessa, I believe you know all that that there is to know about me and Father Chiniquy. It seems you and I both share a passion for history. I guess it's in your genes."

"Well, if I learned anything from you and Matt, it is that nothing is real unless it can be proved. This could be anyone's blood, and unless you exhumed Lincoln's body...."

"What I was about to say is that this sample can be compared to a sample stolen from Lincoln's grave, four years ago, by one Prescott Marshall. It seems, The Consortium was hard at work long before I learned of their plans. Marshall hired a two bit con to drill into Lincoln's crypt, in Springfield, Illinois, and steal a sample of Lincoln's tissue; all of which was confirmed by the FBI, so we know that sample is real.. "

"I never read anything about that?"

"Nor will you. The Feds were so embarrassed by the spectacle, and alarmed at the methods, that they covered the whole thing up. It's been classified ever since."

"Why? Why didn't they just arrest Prescott?"

"Because the trail was wiped clean and they had major egg on their faces."

"I don't quite get it."

" The man, the thief, was murdered using the same 44 caliber Derringer Pistol that killed Lincoln. The same pistol that was stolen in the early eighties from Fords Theater."

"Ballistics, " Vanessa spurted out.

"Now you're starting to see the picture. The bullet taken from the man's skull matched the bullet from Lincoln's skull that was still on display at a museum in Washington. The striations matched perfectly, and that left only one conclusion."

For Vanessa all of the pieces of the puzzle were finally in place. "The shot that killed the thief was fired from the real gun that was used to assassinate President Lincoln. That means the gun at Fords Theater, was, and continues to be a fake!"

"Yes, stolen by thieves in the sixties. It was retrieved from The Consortium, during a raid conducted days ago in Europe. Prescott held all the cards. If the FBI fingered him, he would simply say the Fed's had the wrong man, just like they had the wrong gun at Fords Theater."

Vanessa smiled as she realized which sample it was that was stored... "Safe inside the rock!"

"And Matt has a microchip containing Lincoln's DNA code, just in case. You are the two people I trusted with my life. I now trust you with this tiny bit of history to do with as you please."

"Father..?"

"Yes... Vanessa."

"Will you ever tell them?"

"About us?'

"Yes."

"Tell the public? I learned from Lincoln, it is not the color of a man's skin that makes him great, but the decisions he makes while sitting inside this office. Lincoln's ghosts, I learned, haunts us all. Those ghosts leave no DNA as their legacy, only greatness. That will be up to history to decide. As for me, Vanessa, I now have you. You will be my legacy."

The helicopter then banked over the national mall with the monuments to Washington, Lincoln and Jefferson, all in plain sight, as it prepared to land on the front lawn of the White House.

"Who knows what other secrets are buried inside those walls," Vanessa added.

"I don't know," the President answered. "But I suspect if anyone uncovers the truth, it will be you and your friends!"

EPILOGUE

EVEN though it was spring, it was still cold at night. Matt Walker dropped the top on his 2006 Mercedes Benz, and gunned the engine,, as he made his way west on the GW Parkway. Instinctively, he slowed down when approaching the Park Police Station, and opened it up again once past.

"Matt Walker," the man on the radio said, "May go down in history as being greater than Woodward and Bernstein."

Matt reached down to turn off the radio, realizing that greatness is not in the stories that are broken, but the secrets that are kept. He had lived through hell and was looking back on the other side. Sadly he wanted more.

The three black SUVs in front of him all carried agents from the FBI. Their investigation into the working of *The Consortium,* uncovered an organization with tentacles so far reaching, the government had to decide how to proceed along grounds of national security. It was funny how Washington worked. The good worked along side the bad in the name of making the world a better place. It rarely worked.

"President Webb," the pundit on the radio continued, "has his work cut out for him over the next one hundred days. His proposals are ambitious, but democrats are lining up to oppose, many of the same social programs they once touted as among their very own."

Matt laughed, "politics." He then reached down to crank up the heat. Despite the fact it was one of the clearest skies he could remember, the wind whipping past his face chilled any warmth the air might once have possessed. Even with the seat warmers and heater going full blast, the chill broke through his jacket. It also served to irritate the wound that was slow to heal. Matt used the opportunity to constantly remind him that the toughest decisions in life require great sacrifice.

The first suburban arrived, followed by the second, and third, in secession. Matt arrived last. The bulk of the task force was assembled in the courtyard. The agents, representing just about every foreign government imaginable, were asked to stay off to the side, for fear of creating an international spectacle. Each was looking for additional information to prosecute the members of *The Consortium* that operated on their shores.

"Break it down," the Agent in Charge barked, as the officers behind him arrived with a long cylindrical battering ram. It took five blows to break through the doors before it splintered into pieces exposing the long marble hallway that once was Prescott Marshall's foyer. "After you," the Agent said, gesturing for Matt to go inside.

In exchange for saving the President's life, Matt was given the privilege of ten minutes alone in the house before the Agents would take charge. He knew exactly where to head.

Making his way up the steps, Matt marveled at how ornate the house was. He knew Prescott to be a man of great extravagance, but the house exceeded all expectations. Expensive Italian marble statues sat in vestibules that lined the steps as he made his way upwards. A fresco, showing God reaching out to man had been painted on the ceiling.

"How appropriate," Matt said, finally reaching his destination.

Matt walked calmly through the doors of Prescott's impressive study and took a seat behind his massive oak desk. It took less than a moment to spot it. The keyboard to the computer was located where his knees met the desk. Reaching down, he pulled it out and the motion caused the screen on the desk to come to life.

"Hmm.." Matt mused as he saw the lights flash, "ENTER PASS CODE."

There was little hesitation in his next movements. He had spent a great deal of time wondering what type of password a man such as Prescott Marshall would use. He had no loved ones, and was not known to celebrate any birthdays. Nothing seemed precious to Prescott, save one thing.

Using both hands, and showing no signs of second thoughts he typed in M-A-R-S-H-A-L-L

Within seconds, the computer on the other end responded:

INVALID ENTRY

"Okay, let's try this..."

T-H-E V-A-I

Again the computer responded:

INVALID ENTRY

Only this time the response had an unexpected caveat:

FAILURE TO ENTER THE CORRECT PASSWORD IN THREE ATTEMPTS AUTOMATICALLY TRIGGERS ABORT SEQUENCE

Matt paused for a moment. He knew there was a font of information inside the computer, and a third failed attempt would erase it all. He was also watching the clock. Soon the Feds would come bursting through the door. *Ten minutes and that's it*, he had been told over and over again by the agent in charge. *I don't care who you know in high places*. That's when it struck him. A smile came across his face, as he marveled at the simplicity of it all. One by one, his fingers delicately typed the following sequence of numbers and punctuation marks:

1.31.60/5.

Within seconds the computer came to life.

PASSWORD ACCEPTED

The dark screen that moments ago sought information now seemed prepared to offer new information up.

"ANALYSIS COMPLETE."

The message on the screen was flashing as if the mainframe on the other end was expressing some type of pride in what it had uncovered.

Matt used his right index finger and pressed the ENTER key. A millisecond later, the copier on the opposite desk came to life, one by one printing out pages until, in the end, seventy eight pages called for his attention. PRINTING STOPPED, the copier signaled.

Matt looked at the computer. It was hungry for more.

"SEEKING NEXT COMMAND.'

Matt however, chose to see what the computer had offered up first, before moving onto the next task. Picking up the papers, he found himself stumbling backwards into the large leather seat Prescott Marshall so cherished.

Each page contained as many as fifty names. Each name had beside it a detailed DNA analysis. It was the third column that caused Matt's heart to skip a beat. His throat grew dry as he read the information in front of him. Every person on the name had an historical link, because of DNA. Some were descendants of civil rights leaders, others he recognized as related to prominent members of the religious community. Some were white, others he quickly recognized as black.

Scanning the list further, he thought of the one mystery his previous encounter with the Vai had left unsolved. There, on the list, was the name of Calvin Banaku, the young man who died in a fiery accident in Prince Georges County, that left a cop dead and a mystery unsolved. In the third column, the printout revealed Banaku as the original African name of the great African American architect of Washington, Benjamin Bannaker.

Looking further, he saw two names toward the bottom of the sheet that signaled his investigation into the Vai was far from over. On the seventy eighth page of the computer printout were the names Matt Walker and Max Webb…three entries below it.

Matt was startled by the sound of the Agents who had now entered the foyer and were making their way upstairs. Stuffing the computer printouts inside his backpack he reached down, logged off the computer, and quietly typed in three more faulty passwords.

A half a world away, in a darkened room made exclusively for Mandela, a countdown began.

SELF DESTRUCT SEQUENCE NOW UNDERWAY...

ALL PERSONNEL SHOULD VACATE

THE PREMISES FOR THEIR OWN SAFETY

three...two…one...

GOOD-BYE MR. MARSHALL

Printed in the United States
93008LV00003B/1-63/A

9 781434 335937